Spirit King

Return of the
Crown

DASHIEL DOUGLAS

Spirit King
Return of the Crown
Copyright © Dashiel Douglas, 2021

First Print Edition

ISBN: 9798728841791 (paperback)

Cover Design by Jelena Gajic
zelenagajic@gmail.com

For Pamela, my wife.
I am among the lucky souls who is married to
the best human being they have ever met.

Ushindi

Nanjier

Hasira brid

AMANZI MO
(WATE

UPEPO MOUNTAIN
(AIR)

TABERN

JOTO MOU
(MINE

N

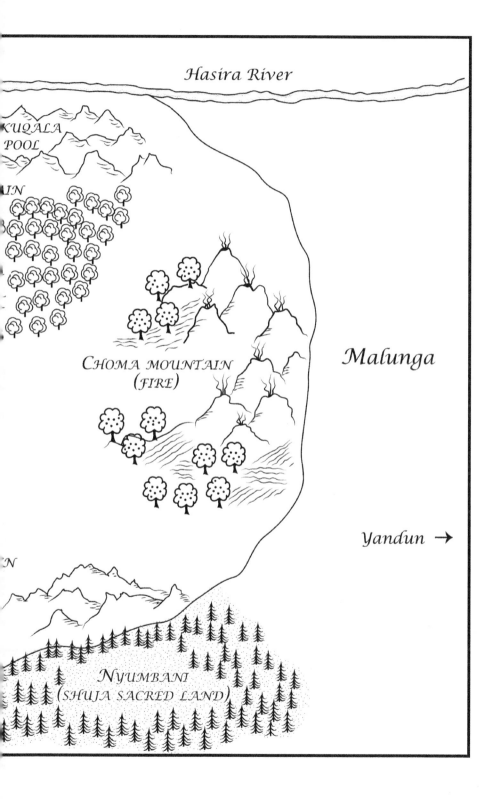

Hasira River

KUQALA
POOL

Malunga

CHOMA MOUNTAIN
(FIRE)

Yandun →

NYUMBANI
(SHUJA SACRED LAND)

Contents

The Legend of the Spirit King

Two millennia ago, barbarism reigned supreme in many areas of the world. Africa was no exception. Bloodthirsty tribes systematically ravaged their vulnerable, less warlike neighbors. Some of these more benevolent but unfortunate peoples were able to flee before being slaughtered or enslaved by their conquerors. They wandered harsh deserts and suffocating jungles, often only to succumb to nature's unforgiving elements.

But legend has it that four tribes survived their journeys and, together, became the guardians of the world's most treasured secret.

From far-flung regions of the continent, each of these fugitive groups found their way to the same mountainous haven in Central Africa. Within days of each other, the four tribes converged in a new land that held the promise of a peaceful future: the Amanzi (Water) tribe from North Africa; the Choma (Fire) tribe from East Africa; the Joto (Mineral) tribe from Southern Africa; and the Upepo (Air) tribe from West Africa. They settled on this mountain range, which offered a peak for each tribe and encircled a central valley, like a most formidable natural rampart. Some say the tribes were chosen, guided there through promptings of the Great Spirit.

But before long, these neighboring tribes devolved back into the very savagery from which they had once fled for their lives. For many ensuing years, they brutalized one another for the right to rule over the lush land they had at first peacefully shared. Tens of thousands of lives were lost in the massacres.

Then, on a stormy summer day, a miraculous event forever changed the fate of the tribes, and, in turn, the world.

It all started with an unassuming Amanzi woman named Leda. On the morning of that fateful day, Leda awoke to the soft gurgle of the brook rippling next to the hut she shared with her husband, Kulani. Like almost every morning on Amanzi Mountain, the sun bloomed above the mountain peak in persimmon-colored glory, its golden petals gracing the rich azure sky. Leda had no idea that these moments of serene normality would be the last she would ever enjoy in this cherished place.

As the first amber rays caressed Kulani's countenance, Leda saw with anguish copper-hued lumps covering much of his face. They had begun to appear weeks before but were small and less conspicuous. Now, nary a spot on his body had been spared the advancing growths. Horrified by Kulani's appearance, their fellow tribespeople surmised that the devil had taken over his spirit and demanded that he be put to death.

Before the villagers could execute their intention, Leda and Kulani stole away, navigating the long climb through untamed forest to the summit of Amanzi Mountain. Reaching the peak just before sundown, they sought shelter for the night. They found a natural cavernous alcove on the north face, tucked under the split in the Mapacha (Twin) Waterfall. The falls reunited in the Ukuqala (Genesis) Pool on the mountainside fifty feet below.

Just then, a storm gathered and darkened the skies outside their refuge. Kulani slouched on the damp floor. "My love," he said soberly. "Fleeing is futile. Death is nipping at my heels. Even if I escape the spear, I will surely soon succumb to this disease ravaging my body." Kulani wiped the tears now dripping down Leda's cheeks. "Please rest assured, my heart is at peace. My only regret is not having left behind children to carry forth our family." Leda and Kulani had tried to conceive a child for years, with no success.

As Kulani slept that night, Leda wept agonizingly through the dark hours. With gnawing desperation bellowing from the innermost recesses of her heart, she implored the Great Spirit for help.

The storm rumbled on, but just before dawn, a delicate gold fringe shined through on the horizon. In that dim glow, the silhouette of a wiry man took shape in the arched entrance of the cave. Oddly, Leda didn't feel threatened. On the contrary, a rush of tranquility cascaded through her. She squeezed the tears from her eyes to make sure this glorious figure wasn't a figment of her imagination. The man lifted an open palm. "Come, my child," he urged gently in a strange tongue. His foreign words bypassed her ears and wafted straight into her heart. "Follow the dawning sun. You will find me there," he directed, then vanished as mysteriously as he had appeared.

By the time Kulani awoke, Leda had gathered at least a few weeks' worth of food, arranging it by his side. She tenderly informed him that she must leave but would return with the cure for his ailment. She chose not to mention the mysterious man, knowing that Kulani didn't share the depth of faith that she had.

Her eyes moist with heartbreak, Leda assured him, "You will be safe here until I return." Her hand reluctantly slipped from his cheek.

"I wish you wouldn't go. But I know there is nothing I can say that will change your mind." Kulani pushed a smile onto his face. "I will see you again, my love. May the strength of your faith bring you back to me."

And then, with dispatch, Leda set out on the journey—to where, she had no idea.

For long days, Leda weathered nature's most extreme expressions and traversed alien lands, some thick with obstacles, some bare of vegetation, always skirting the spears of savage tribes. Desolation of all kinds, it seemed, stretched eastward to the horizon, where she hoped to find her savior "under the dawning sun."

Two months into her grueling trek, exhausted and dehydrated, and under a punishing sun, Leda collapsed upon a dusty hill. "I'm sorry," she muttered hoarsely—to her husband, to her unknown guide, to the universe, she wasn't sure, no more than she knew where she was meant to go. "I'm just not strong enough to make it." She cried a tearless cry, too parched to produce a single drop. Directing her anguish to the mysterious man, she whimpered, "I'm afraid you chose the wrong person. Please, watch over my husband." Leda closed her eyes, hoping it would be for the final time. In that moment of perfect stillness and surrender, a familiar sweet voice again penetrated her heart.

"My choices are infallible," he assured her. "You are stronger than you know. Rise, my child, and embrace your destiny."

Feeling a stirring of her strength, Leda mustered every ounce of vitality remaining in her frail body. She stood up and staggered to the top of the sandy hill. There, her eyes fell upon a most welcome sight: a beautiful deep-running stream. Living on Amanzi Mountain, she had never before known the desperate hardship of having no water. She stumbled to the stream, knelt down, and cupped her quivering hands in the crystal liquid. Her chapped lips stung gratefully as she gulped handful after handful.

"Slowly, my child," she heard the mysterious man say. "The river is not going anywhere; you can partake as often as your heart desires." Leda turned her gaze upward and glimpsed him through squinted eyes. The midday sun shone bright behind his head, rays emanating from his shaded face.

He extended a hospitable hand. "Come. We have been awaiting your arrival." Her legs wobbled as he helped her stand upright. "You are the last of the *Akhtiar*, the chosen handmaidens." He led her along the riverbank, and she tottered wearily behind him. He glided with the omnipotence and grace of a king but, in equal measure, with the meekness and humility of a servant. His tunic, remarkably white for such a dusty region, swung hypnotically with each step.

Seemingly out of nowhere, a shady tree appeared, oddly out of place in the otherwise barren expanse. A group of women, perhaps a dozen or more, with varying hues of skin, were reveling in its leafy shadow. The hair crowning their heads was various, as well—light and dark, long and short, curly, waved, and straight.

The mysterious man addressed the Akhtiar with great power and tenderness. He spoke at length, but for how long, Leda wasn't sure. It was as if time had no purpose there.

He bemoaned the lamentable condition of the world. "The children of the Great Spirit are roaming as a lost tribe in the wilderness of hedonism, falling fast prey to the ravenous predator of self-serving passion. This spiritual disease is leading to ruinous wars, unbounded greed alongside unbearable poverty, and the shredding of the communal fabric that binds humanity. Through the Great Spirit's supreme animating power, you, the Akhtiar, have been summoned here from every region of the globe to heal your ailing brethren and sistren as an initial step toward the rehabilitation of all humankind."

The mysterious man dipped a wooden bowl into the lucid river. He then pricked his finger with a cactus spine, drawing a bead of blood. While chanting, he methodically stirred the scarlet bead into the water, as if lulling it into a trance. He then touched a fingertip to each woman's forehead, applying a droplet of the pinkish solution. Upon being dabbed, Leda's senses were stunned, as if a lightning bolt had surged through her body.

"Now," he said to each, "you are a Milpisi, a healer. Your purified blood has been endowed with extraordinary healing powers."

The mysterious man then bestowed upon each Milpisi a seed to plant in their homelands. "Within this seed lies Haya—the Tree of Life," he said. He instructed them on how to administer the mighty tree's nectar, the elixir of the ills of the world. "Haya will ensure that, long after the sun of your life has set, the healing power of the Great Spirit will continue to grace humanity. And with those final words, he left. A twisting wind kicked up a sand cloud behind him. When it settled, he was gone.

Strengthened with renewed spirit, Leda undertook the long and treacherous journey home. When she finally arrived at Amanzi Mountain, a heavy weight settled in her gut. She was afraid that she would be too late to save her husband. She peered into the alcove. Kulani wasn't there. She searched frantically for him, praying that an empty stomach urged him to the forest to forage for fruits and nuts. Finding no trace of him, she returned to the alcove, sobbing mournfully. Then, the most melodious sound wafted into her cheered ears.

"Why do you cry, my love? Are you not happy to see me?" Leda's tears turned joyful. She rushed over to hug him but stopped short. She was momentarily taken aback by Kulani's deteriorated condition. The sores had overwhelmed his body. One eye was covered completely under a large growth, and the other wasn't more than a slit between lumps. Endowed with her new healing abilities, Leda immediately took to curing him. She retrieved a loose vine from the forest. Then she pierced a finger to draw blood. Kulani's expression turned petrified.

"Trust me," she said. She squeezed a drop of blood onto the vine and lowered it into the Ukuqala Pool. The water vibrated and electric currents sizzled brilliantly like a lightning storm. She chanted, "A iilhi, al'akthar nqa'an," as she raised the vine and gathered a droplet of the blessed water on her finger.

"What are these strange words you speak?"

"These strange words, as you call them, will soon welcome you back to health." She brushed the water across Kulani's forehead. He shuddered, his eyes rolling back in his head. Leda scrutinized him up and down. Nothing. Her heart raced, worried that she was not pure enough to be a Milpisi. Then the mysterious man's voice solaced her heart.

"My child, have you so swiftly lost faith in me? Remember, my choices are infallible."

Leda turned her attention back to Kulani. "Oh, oh!" His deformities were healing before her eyes. The effect of the purified water was as rapid as it was remarkable. She ululated her profound gratitude from the depths of her soul. Her trill reverberated mightily from the alcove like a clarion call announcing to the world that a new day had dawned.

That same night, as if their reunion and Kulani's returned health wasn't bounty enough, they were blessed with an even more magnificent miracle: a pearl formed in her womb.

The next morning at dawn, Leda made haste to fulfill the promise of the Akhtiar. She planted the seed of the Tree of Life at the base of Amanzi Mountain. She and Kulani then warily set out to rejoin their tribe, unsure of what welcome they would receive. But it turned out to be a fortuitous moment in time for someone possessing the gift of healing. The fierce and relentless attacks of the Choma people were taking a deadly toll on the Amanzi. The tribe was teetering on the edge of extermination.

When they entered the village, the Amanzi chief rebuffed them at first, as he attributed Kulani's extraordinary recovery to the handiwork of the Evil One. Unable to convince the chief that her healing abilities had been bestowed upon her by the Great Spirit, Leda realized that action would be her best proof. She sought out the wounded Amanzi warriors and, one by one, healed them, even those presumed mortally injured.

After this miraculous display, the chief no longer concerned himself with where Leda might have received her healing powers. He immediately commanded her to go to the front line of the battle. There she rehabilitated warriors before they succumbed to their wounds.

Needless to say, with warriors that don't die, within months, the tide of the war shifted in favor of the Amanzi. The Choma chief was enraged as well as baffled by the sudden turn. But he would soon discover the secret of how the Amanzi ranks had suddenly become so formidable.

In the midst of a furious battle, Leda stumbled upon a mortally wounded Choma warrior. He looked no older than fifteen years. As she gazed into his childlike frightened eyes, she remembered the counsels of the mysterious man. The power to heal was entrusted to the Akhtiar for the rehabilitation of *all* humankind. Fulfilling her bounden duty, she saved the life of the enemy warrior, not realizing the peril it would put her and her tribe in.

Infinitely power-hungry, the Choma chief, upon hearing about this supernatural act, became obsessed with bringing Leda under his command. With her abilities, he thought, nothing could stop him from conquering all of Central Africa.

With empty promises, he coaxed the Joto tribe into joining forces with him. Soon after, during the worst storm to hit the region for as long as anyone could remember, the two tribes initiated a savage assault on the Amanzi in the middle of the night, catching their warriors off guard. While the storm raged, the Choma slaughtered their way up Amanzi Mountain.

Leda and Kulani fled, battling the deluge to the mountain summit and to their earlier hiding place. Leda's now bulging belly hindered her climb. Every few minutes, she bent over and winced with harrowing pain. She clasped her tremulous hands, wet with rain and sweat, over her mouth to muffle screams of agony, as her labor pains set in. Kulani scooped her in his arms and trudged to their protective alcove.

The Choma warriors clambered in hot pursuit to the summit, but the cavernous alcove was well hidden. Finding no sign of Leda, they assumed she took cover in the underbrush. Just as they were about to scour the forest, a faint cry echoed between the crackle of lightning strikes. A second muted scream steered them to the alcove.

When Kulani realized they had been discovered, he rose with noble fearlessness.

Leda clutched his arm. "There are too many," she cried in a hushed voiced.

"I will not stay here and watch these barbarians slaughter you and our unborn child." He laid a consoling hand on her belly. "I will be honored to offer my life defending my family." Just before exiting the alcove, he turned to Leda and smiled. "Eternity is ours."

Kulani settled strategically on a ledge above the narrowest part of the path along the mountainside. As the warriors approached, he sent the heaviest rocks tumbling down the mountain. A few warriors were caught unaware and plummeted over the precipice to an inglorious death. The other warriors took aim at Kulani. A flurry of spears and arrows cut with deadly intention through the wet air. As Kulani scrambled for safety up the rocky bluff, the burn of a spear penetrated his leg. He wobbled and clutched onto a jutted rock. Before he could reach cover, an arrow sliced into his arm. He lost his grip and hurtled down the mountainside. In a final act of heroism, he snatched two Choma warriors and pulled them over the ledge with him.

The remaining band of warriors continued their murderous march toward the alcove. A tiny cry reverberated, then another, then another. Just before they reached the entrance, Leda emerged with a baby in each arm. The fire of faith burned intensely in her eyes. The warriors swarmed menacingly toward her, their spears readied to deliver razor-sharp death.

"Sorceress," the head Choma croaked, "your death today is not inevitable. If you agree to perform your sorcery for my people, I will spare your life."

Leda replied serenely, "My abilities were granted to me to heal the world. I realize now that saving those who will use their lives to conduct savagery upon their brethren and sistren would be contrary to the will of the Great Spirit." Leda's eyes swept pityingly through the bloodthirsty horde, halting at a particular young warrior whom she recognized. She addressed him directly. "Only days ago, you lay dying on the battlefield. The Great Spirit saw fit to grant you another chance to live a life of worth. Now you stand before me, prepared to do the evil bidding of these savages, to take the life of the one who laid the balm of compassion and mercy upon you."

The child warrior lowered his eyes and tossed his spear aside. "I cannot be a part of this barbarism any longer," he said to the head Choma. Fully aware of the repercussions of his defiance, he opened wide his chest, ready to receive his earthly consequence. The head Choma drove his spear with fury into the warrior's heart. Just before taking his final breath, the child warrior turned his gaze to Leda. Her moist eyes dripped with forgiveness and pride. Redemption was his.

The head Choma then shifted his murderous rage back to Leda, moving within striking distance.

"The spilling of my blood is but a harbinger of the new day," Leda proclaimed. "The souls of the righteous and the very earth itself have been long-suffering, yearning for this day in great anticipation. It would be most inconsiderate of us to delay its arrival for even one more moment. So let us now proceed with your folly and bear witness to the Great Dawn in its full glory."

"As you wish," the head warrior spit.

Leda marched to the edge of the path between the split in the waterfall. "You can kill me," she declared boldly. "But you will not kill my babies." Her immeasurable love for her children would not allow them to die at the end of a spear driven by hate and ignorance.

She gazed down at the perfect bundles in her arms. "Don't worry," she said. "I'll see you again." She then let out a trilling cry and dropped them into the Ukuqala Pool far below. She then stepped with intention toward the alcove but was blocked by a line of warriors. "May the Great Spirit protect you," she said solemnly.

Leda turned away and stretched her arms out at her sides, embracing the brutal death awaiting her. The head warrior clenched his teeth, cocked his spear, and plunged it into her back. The merciless blade pierced Leda's heart and burst through her chest. Crimson pulsed in thick, dark streams into the pool below. Leda collapsed to her knees. She raised faithful arms heavenward and let out a triumphant cry. Then her silent, lifeless body hurtled down toward the pool.

The warriors called out with sinister delight, "The sorceress is dead!" They pranced victoriously to the summit, heedless of the extraordinary forces about to be unleashed.

As Leda's body neared the pool, the water stirred in anticipation of this long-awaited moment. It surged upward to greet her, its depths celebrating with flashes of sparkling luminescence. Brilliant bursts sizzled thunderously in the ominous clouds crowning the mountain. The ground itself rumbled, a reminder that even a mighty mountain stands only at the will of the Great Spirit.

The warriors began to tremble. Then, they gasped a terrified breath. A youthful figure rose from the Ukuqala Pool, floating atop a tower of swirling water and enshrouded in a hooded, golden-fleeced cloak.

After a few spellbound moments, the head Choma gathered his wits. "Kill him," he ordered his warriors. Frozen in awe, they didn't budge.

"I said, KILL HIM!" he roared.

The startled warriors drew back their bowstrings dutifully and released pointed fury. The youthful figure was unfazed by the arrows cutting lethally in his direction. Just before they reached him, he casually raised a hand. The arrows instantly diverted, whizzing harmlessly into the dawning amber sky.

The young man lifted both arms above his head, bent at the elbow. Spheres of water as large as a man's head formed in his palms and churned rapidly into tight coils. He launched them at the head warrior, smashing him violently through the forest. Trees in the path of his mortal flight shattered.

The youthful figure then cried out, "*Viboko kupanda!* (Hippos rise!)" The forest quaked with exhilaration, igniting its creatures into a jubilant chorus. Twelve fearsome hippopotamuses emerged from the Hasira River edging the northern foot of Amanzi Mountain. The warriors threw down their weapons and dropped to their knees.

"*Falme Roho! Falme Roho!* (Spirit King! Spirit King!)" they chanted.

The tower of water bent toward the summit. The youthful figure stepped onto land, strode purposefully to the alcove, and disappeared within. He reemerged with a baby nestled in his majestic arms: his newborn sister. The warriors didn't know that Leda had borne a third child, but realized then that that was why she attempted to return to the alcove.

With his sister in his lap, the Spirit King rode a hippo toward the central valley of the four great mountain ranges. There he addressed the four tribes, marking the birth of a nation.

"Oh, *Wapendwa*—loved ones of the Great Spirit. Rejoice! By the overflowing grace of the Great Spirit Kipaj, all that has occurred prior to this day is forgiven. Let this moment rend asunder the shackles of the old ways and usher in the promise of a new day."

He then proclaimed the four tribes to be one, calling forth a humble and unified homeland. "We are a single tribe with a single consciousness. This blessed soil upon which we stand, from now until the end that hath no end, will be known as Kipaji—home of the servants of Kipaj."

PART I

King of the Court

"All that tyranny needs to gain a foothold is for people of good conscience to remain silent."

—*Thomas Jefferson*

CHAPTER ONE

Sunday Dinner

The wall clock chimed nine times. *Dong, dong, dong....*

"D'Melo," his father called. "It's time for our show."

Every Sunday evening, they performed the same song and dance. D'Melo Bantu's father, Imari, wanted to watch *The World This Week* together, to widen D'Melo's perspective beyond their neighborhood and sports. But D'Melo, a high-school basketball standout, was content in the small, comfortable world he had created for himself.

D'Melo stumped into the living room, his towering, athletic frame slouched. "Baba, why do I have to watch this?" He always referred to his dad by the Kipaji word for father. "There are only horrible things happening out there." His griping about having to watch the news was as regular as the donging of the wall clock.

"Come, son," his father encouraged, patting the sofa cushion next to him. "You need to understand the world you live in."

D'Melo sighed and plopped himself down.

The newscaster opened with a story from Washington, D.C. A woman had been killed in a car accident on Christmas morning.

D'Melo shifted uncomfortably in his seat. A drunk driver had slammed into the woman's car and pushed it into oncoming traffic. A military truck barreled into the car, flipping it several times. D'Melo's heart began thumping heavily against his ribs. He cast a wide-eyed gaze at his father, who seemed to be watching as emotionlessly as he would a program on the history of square dancing. D'Melo's eyes flashed back to the TV. He cringed at the sight of the woman's broken body being dragged out of the mangled metal. Nausea pulsed through him. The paramedics sealed the woman's body in a shiny plastic bag and slid her into an ambulance. D'Melo couldn't bear any more. Just as he reached for the remote to turn off the TV, two shrill pops reverberated sharply in his ear. Warm liquid splatted the side of his face. He spun to his father. He tried to scream, but no words came out. A lump in his throat threatened to choke him. His father's body slumped into the sofa, dark red leaching across his white button-up shirt.

D'Melo became light-headed. His vision was going in and out of focus. He sensed a presence lurking in a shadowy corner of the room. He swiveled toward it in a panic. The outline of a hooded figure slunk back, deeper into the murk. Through the fog of his addled mind, distant cries urged D'Melo to run. He couldn't. His limbs, paralyzed with fear, answered to nothing.

Suddenly, a blanket of darkness descended ominously in the house. Even the faint glow from the streetlights flickered out. D'Melo's chest constricted, his breath ragged. On the edge of consciousness, he attempted to even his breathing. His mind snapped clear when the hardwood floor creaked with footsteps. He shot off the sofa and stretched his arms searchingly in front of him. He tried to latch onto anything that felt familiar, but nothing did. He ran his quivering hands along the wall, hoping desperately not to encounter the presence from the dark corner. Finally, he reached his bedroom, the place where he was most comfortable.

He slipped stealthily into his bed. But then the rusted hinges on the bedroom door squeaked. He yanked a blanket over his head. The chill of the demonic presence loomed over him. His heart hammered in terror.

"D'Melo!"

His body rocked.

"D'Melo!"

He drew in a sharp breath, then jerked up into a sitting position.

"It's okay, son," Baba said comfortingly, as he reached to the nightstand and clicked on the lamp. D'Melo's forehead was beaded with sweat. Baba pulled him into his arms and held him against his chest.

"It's over, son."

D'Melo took a long, shuddering breath.

"Same nightmare?"

D'Melo shook his head, as if to cast out the demon. "Pretty much. But this time it started with the other nightmare—the one where I'm play-fighting with that kid in the wildflower field. I could feel the blood streaming down his face, as if it was my own eye bleeding. I can't believe I did that."

Baba laid a consoling hand on D'Melo's face. "Son, you didn't do anything. It's just a dream."

"But it's not, Baba," D'Melo said, his body rigid. "I see it even when I'm not sleeping."

"Oh, son," Baba sighed sympathetically. "You've had this dream so many times that you're starting to believe it really happened. You were only three when we moved to America. Do you remember anything from Kipaji?" He waited a moment for his question to sink in. "You see, it's not possible, son. You were too young."

Over the years, Baba had become an expert on D'Melo's inner turmoil. Like a skilled psychotherapist, he zeroed in on the root cause. "You have to let your mother go, son. It's been ten years. Holding onto her is gnawing away at you."

"I try, Baba," D'Melo sighed. He squeezed his eyes shut, exasperated, trying to press the horrifying images out of his head. "But this time, it was worse. You were also killed. I was all alone."

"I'm right here, son." Baba rocked him reassuringly. "I'll never leave you."

The death of his mother weighed on D'Melo's heart like the heaviest of anchors, mooring him to an insular, sheltered life. Growing up without his mother was difficult enough, but the circumstances surrounding her death had added another crushing burden; he couldn't reconcile the police's official findings with his own memory of the incident.

D'Melo pulled out of his father's arms. "Baba," he said, leveling his eyes with his father's. "I'm telling you. That guy *tried* to kill us."

"It was a tragic accident, son," Baba said, trying to assuage D'Melo's anger as he did every time he made this assertion. "Please let it go," he pleaded. "As long as you keep telling yourself that the driver intentionally killed your mother, you'll never be at peace. He was drunk. The police found his car a couple blocks away with an empty bottle of vodka in it."

"But they never found the driver!" D'Melo snapped, then paused, catching himself raising his voice. "I saw his eyes, Baba," he said, his words softening into a familiar and respectful tone. "He wasn't drunk. He knew exactly what he was doing."

"D'Melo, I know you believe that's what you saw, but the doctors said you were in shock. You weren't in the best state of mind to make that judgment."

Baba again drew D'Melo into a warm embrace. "Please, please, son," he implored. "Move on with your life."

D'Melo knew Baba was right about his mother's death eating him up inside. But he still wasn't convinced that it was merely an accident. As his father rocked him, D'Melo's breathing settled and his consciousness ebbed. His body sank heavily into his bed. Baba stayed at his side until he drifted back to sleep.

Early the next morning, Baba rapped a rousing wake-up call on D'Melo's door. "Sun's up, and so should you be!" he said. "Time to catch the worms."

There was no such thing as sleeping in at the Bantu house. D'Melo wished he could have a harsh word with the person who had told Baba the saying, "The early bird catches the worm." He flung his covers off, begrudging the people who were able to sleep until their eyes opened naturally. He swung his legs over the side of the bed. A chill radiated down his spine, his feet were planted where the malignant spirit lurked hauntingly in his dream. During his years of coping with the demon, D'Melo had developed a strategy for warding off the evil, at least temporarily; he scrubbed the satanic images from his mind with blissful thoughts. Today, he reminded himself that it was Sunday, the most effective anti-evil day of the week.

Sharing a meal with his friends on Sunday evenings had become a most cherished tradition. Nary a Sunday dinner had been missed since D'Melo and his father moved to the Lincoln Downs neighborhood of Philadelphia ten years ago. Being an only child had never been easy for D'Melo. So eating dinner "like a real family," as he called it, was a weekly treasure.

Communal dinners were one of the few things D'Melo appreciated from his Kipaji heritage. Each week, the preparer of the meal rotated. Because D'Melo's friends were descended from different countries, Baba requested they cook meals from their native cuisines. Kazim's father was from Chad and his mother was from Japan, Marley's grandparents were Sudanese and Ethiopian, and Jeylan's family was from South Carolina— but he claimed his ancestors were taken from Ghana as slaves, so he made Ghanaian dishes. But that night, it was D'Melo's turn.

D'Melo greeted his friends at the door. "I have something special for you guys today," he said excitedly.

"Are you finally gonna make a Kipaji meal?" Jeylan said, already knowing the answer. D'Melo had never much embraced his Kipaji roots. As a child, he was incessantly badgered with ignorant questions. "Do the kids ride zebras to school?" "Were you always hungry?" And on the worst days, kids would accuse him of carrying some exotic, hideous disease, hollering its name and then scattering from D'Melo in the alarm of their own making. Although the rounds of torment were short-lived (often thanks to Jeylan's protective fists), D'Melo began distancing himself more and more from his Africanness, and rarely looked back.

"No," D'Melo replied briskly. "We're making barbecue chicken, fried fish, mashed potatoes, macaroni and cheese, and corn on the cob."

Jeylan pursed his lips, disappointed. "The only way this meal could be any more American is if we have apple pie for dessert while singing 'The Star-Spangled Banner' with the American flag sticking out of our—"

"Eh hem," Baba cleared his throat.

"My bad, Baba," Jeylan said apologetically. D'Melo's friends referred to his father as he did.

"Oh, thanks for reminding me!" D'Melo said. "There's an apple pie in the oven. And Jey," he smirked, "I have a flag in my room if you want to stick it somewhere."

"Hey," Kazim piped. "Please tell me you're gonna throw some bacon bits into the mac and cheese."

"Kaz, what kinda Muslim are you?" Jeylan chided. "You don't pray, you eat swine, and you be chasin' girls all day"—Jeylan paused to set up the jab—"and not catchin' any."

"Man, you just don't know," Kazim countered. "I pray a lot. I pray that someone around here will finally make me some pork chops."

They all shuffled into the kitchen. Baba joined them to supervise, and to make sure the dinner would be edible.

The tantalizing aroma of Southern cooking soon permeated the house. Marley removed a slender electronic device from his tattered sports coat. He stabbed the shiny metallic point through the crispy, golden coating of the fried fish. "Oh, that's interesting," he mused, eyeing his phone screen. "The fish has riboflavin and omega-3 fatty acids."

D'Melo scratched his head. "Marl, what are you doing?"

"It's a Lumalink," he said, as if everyone should know what a Lumalink was. "It tells you the components of things. This way you can always know what you're eating."

Jeylan chimed in. "You spent your hard-earned money, flippin' burgers at Chubby's, to buy something that tells you what you can just read on the package? Dawg, you gotta be the biggest nerd on the East Coast."

"But it does more than that," Marley raved. "Watch this." He raised the Lumalink to Kazim's diamond earring. "You see, this ain't real." He read, "It's zirconium dioxide, otherwise known as 'the poor man's diamond.'"

Kazim slapped the Lumalink from his ear. "Get out of here with that, nerd!" It launched from Marley's hand and landed perfectly in the mashed potatoes.

"Ahhh, man," Marley whined. "Look what you did!" He glanced at his phone and his expression changed from dismay to elation. "Awww." He threw his arm over D'Melo's shoulder. "Thanks, man! You flooded the potatoes with butter. You know I love butter. *And* you used the real stuff this time, not that nasty margarine you usually use."

"So Marley," Baba said, giving D'Melo, Jeylan and Kazim a grinning wink. They frantically gestured for Baba not to get Marley started. He ignored their plea. "How does this thing work?" D'Melo inclined his head and sighed.

Marley explained in glowing detail how the Lumalink gathered information, which allowed it to analyze materials to authenticate objects.

Finally, Kazim asked, "Can it help you tell whether a hottie is into you?"

"Kaz," Jeylan quipped. "You don't need to waste your money on a Luma-whatever to answer that. I can tell you for free." Jeylan leveled his eyes with Kazim. "She's not!"

"You just a hater!" Kazim replied, pushing back a smile.

The brotherly banter cascaded joy warmly through D'Melo's body. He gazed at his surrogate family with tender eyes. For him, absolutely nothing could be better than this.

Baba never failed to open Sunday dinner with a morsel of wisdom for the boys to chew on. He worried that the often self-serving and hostile world of Lincoln Downs left them starving for hope and affirmations of their worthiness. So before diving into the Sunday meal, Baba first nourished their souls.

"As you enter this final year of high school, you are a different person. You're not the same as you were before."

"That's true, Baba," Jeylan said. "But I wish you would tell that to Kaz's head. It still got that same 1980s Jheri curl it had last year." The table burst into raucous laughter. Even Baba murmured a restrained chuckle.

Baba paused until decorum returned to the table. "You're the same person, in a sense," he continued to an occasional giggle. "But you aren't, in another sense. It's like the sun that rises in the morning. You can say it's the same sun as yesterday, but it's also a different sun because it dawns on a new day. In Kipaji we say, 'Macho mapia, fursa mpia.' This means, 'New eyes, new opportunity.'

"So, as you enter this year, it's time to ponder your future using your new eyes. Don't let society dictate your fate. Dream your dream, then set your minds and hearts on achieving it."

"Baba," Jeylan said. "That all sounds nice, but life's hard out there with white folks running everything. They just want to keep us down." Jeylan's face tensed. His brother, Tyreke, was recently accused of stealing drugs from the pharmacy where he worked. His boss warned him to return the drugs or he would be fired.

Jeylan bit his lip, trying to keep his anger at bay. His family had a history with unscrupulous shop owners. His father had been swindled by his white business partner out of tens of thousands of dollars.

"I know Tyreke didn't steal any drugs," Jeylan asserted. "What would he do with them? He doesn't use, and he ain't no pusher. It's just that this white dude hates black people."

"You mean that German guy who owns the store on Cherry Street? That guy isn't racist," D'Melo refuted.

Jeylan fumed. "Why are those Germans even in this neighborhood? They just runnin' their shop and taking money out of the black man's pocket. This is *our* community!"

"Well," Marley interjected sheepishly. "Actually, it was their community first. Lincoln Downs was a German neighborhood before all the African immigrants started to settle here in the seventies."

Baba tried to bring peace back to the table. "Jeylan, I understand how you're feeling. But I want you to realize that this thinking is only hurting you. There are a lot of barriers out there for black people, but none insurmountable. The only barrier that will prevent us from realizing our dreams is the one we erect inside our own minds.

"I'm going to tell you a story to illustrate my point. There was a magician named Harry Houdini who could seemingly escape from the most difficult of confinements. He boasted that he could break out of any jail in the world. One prison took him up on his challenge. As the cell door clanked shut, Houdini slipped a pliable piece of metal out from beneath his belt. He thought he would be free in minutes. But he couldn't open the lock. After some time, he became frustrated and gave up.

"Houdini collapsed against the door, which then slid open." Baba delivered the punchline: "You see, the cell door was never locked. Well, I should say, it was never locked except in Houdini's mind. The barrier he created in his head was the most formidable obstacle he had ever come across. It was so powerful that it broke his spirit, which made it impossible to achieve what he could have easily accomplished."

Baba's eyes panned the table, pausing momentarily on each of them. "I pray that you will not construct barriers in your mind that will prevent you from becoming everything you desire to be in this world."

"So, Baba," Kazim said. "You always wanted to be a biology professor?"

"Sometimes your path is chosen for you by the Great Spirit. And when that happens, it behooves you to follow it."

Baba was a doctor in Kipaji before his life took an unexpected turn. When he moved to America, his medical degree was not accepted. Being in a new country without two pennies to rub together, Baba didn't have the time or resources to get a new medical license.

"D'Melo was little," he explained, his lips stretching sentimentally into a smile. "I didn't want to miss one moment of him growing up. I'm happy with my choice."

Taking his cue from the rumble in D'Melo's stomach, Baba wound up the pep talk. "Go after whatever you're passionate about. And trust that the Great Spirit will assist you in achieving it."

"Truth," they chorused. "Take 'em to church, Baba!"

Baba raised his glass of cranberry juice. "*Kwa uzima,*" he toasted. "To life."

"*Kwa uzima,*" they repeated.

Typically, the dinner conversation was rife with tomfoolery and harmless ribbing. But on this day, somehow the subject of marriage came up and quickly took center stage. Baba stressed the importance of finding a good partner, "It's the biggest blessing in this world." He peered at D'Melo and clarified, "When the time is *right.*"

"Oh, you don't have to worry about me, Baba," D'Melo assured him. "I'm not messing with any girls. It's books and basketball for me; that's it!"

"Man," Kazim said. "I don't know how you do it. You get mad

hotties all over you. And this year, it's gonna be even worse. They gonna be sniffin' that NBA loot."

D'Melo had planned out his life to the finest detail—and the plan didn't include girls right now. He worked hard in high school because he was planning on getting a scholarship to the University of Pennsylvania. After college, he figured he would play in the NBA or become an American history teacher. Either way, settling down anywhere other than Lincoln Downs was out of the question. "If I make the NBA," he said, "I better be drafted by the Sixers, so I can stay right here in Philly with Baba and y'all fools! Then," he avowed, "I'll get married and have four kids."

"Four!" Jeylan exclaimed. "You want four little rug rats running around here!"

"*At least!* I want more, if my wife's willing. You guys have brothers and sisters. You don't know what it's like being an only child. I look at big families and I see the kids playing, laughing, fighting, doing everything together; it's beautiful. If I had a wife and kids and nothing else, I'd be the happiest person in the world. I just want a normal life, like normal people."

D'Melo had always met his high school sports celebrity status and apparent lucrative future with casual sobriety. His detachment was often misperceived as humble. Although D'Melo possessed humility in abundance, if truth be told, his nonchalance had more to do with coping. The very thought of being separated from Baba, his friends, and Lincoln Downs made him nauseous with anxiety.

After the dinner, Sundays had come to host another, less propitious tradition. As soon as the last crumb of dessert had been devoured, the reasons why D'Melo's friends had to leave before clean-up began to fly. Over the years, the excuses, initially irritating, had become a welcome and highly entertaining part of the evening.

"Wow, I'm stuffed," Jeylan muttered, leaning back heavily in his chair. "You hooked it up, D." He then glanced at the mountain of dirty dishes in the sink. "I wish I could help y'all, but I gotta dip. My sister's learning a new violin piece and needs my tutelage." D'Melo and Baba exchanged an amused glance, silently acknowledging Jeylan's creativity in crafting his entry for dodging the dishes.

"But Jey," D'Melo played along. "You don't play the violin."

"I know. It's crazy, ain't it?" he deadpanned. "She must be desperate."

Kazim was next. "I gotta bounce, too. I got homework to do."

"What!" D'Melo blurted. "School doesn't even start until Tuesday!"

"I said I got *homework*, not *schoolwork*. I gotta get crackin' on my honey plan." They all shook their heads at the lameness of Kazim's excuse. "Do you know how much work that is?" Kazim attempted to justify his urgent duty. "There are like a thousand girls in our school. I gotta be prepared."

All eyes turned to Marley, wondering what he had come up with. "I have to run—I have a group call tonight with the Mechanics Club," he declared. "We're deciding on what we're gonna build for the Inventors of Tomorrow competition. All the schools in the region are gunning for us because we won last year."

"You guys are too much." D'Melo indulged them with a warm smile. "Alright, I'll see y'all tomorrow."

After clean-up, Baba settled down on the living room sofa. D'Melo headed to his room. *Dong, dong, dong* . . . the wall clock chimed nine times. Another Sunday night tradition was about to unfold. "D'Melo, it's time for *The World This Week!*" D'Melo hemmed and hawed about how the news was depressing, then dragged himself to the living room and plunked down limply. Truthfully, D'Melo looked forward to spending this time with his father. But he didn't necessarily want Baba to know that; he *was* a teenager, after all.

The news program opened with a report on the country of Malunga in Central Africa. Baba straightened attentively on the sofa.

Geographically, Kipaji was part of Malunga, but was a sovereign region within it. So any news about what was happening in Malunga was of special interest to Baba.

Malunga had been marred by nearly two decades of an on-again, off-again civil war. Rebels from the minority Shuja tribe had been fighting against the discriminatory practices of the Borutu-led Malungan government, but with only sporadic success.

This was the first time that Malunga had been in the news for a year or more, as far as D'Melo could remember. The civil war had grown quiet since the mysterious disappearance of the Shuja rebel leader, Waasi Madaki. Now, Malunga once again found itself in the bright light of international scrutiny, but this time for non-war-related news. Baba and D'Melo listened together as the newscaster unfolded the report.

Newscaster: "While pharmaceutical giant, Pharma, is having one of its best years on record, some are protesting its methods of discovering new medicines. In recent years, Pharma's bioprospecting in Central Africa has resulted in three drugs that their CEO says will make great advancements in the fight against cancer. However, hundreds of protesters have clustered outside Pharma headquarters in San Francisco. They allege that Pharma is exploiting the Shuja tribe and their rainforest. The company extracts medicinal plants from Shuja forests and makes millions of dollars from them, yet it has provided no compensation to the tribespeople.

"While Pharma claims to be saving the lives of tens of thousands with these medicines, it sells them at such high prices that the common Shuja can't afford to buy them. The irony in this is, Shujas are dying every year from some of the very diseases that these medicines, which came from *their* land, are designed to cure.

"There is another allegation brewing among the protesters. In the process of bioprospecting for medicinal plants, Pharma is desecrating the *Nyumbani*, the sacred homeland of the Shuja tribe. They assert that Pharma's president of product development for Africa, Wilem VanLuten, has struck immoral, if not illegal, deals with the Malungan government for unfettered access to the Nyumbani, a land known to be rich in natural resources, particularly medicinal plants.

"To the Shujas, the Nyumbani is much more than merely their homeland. It's where Shujas believe the spirit of their ancestors still live. Now Pharma has turned this sacred land into its own bioprospecting playground. Since Pharma's invasion of the Nyumbani, the Shuja community has become disillusioned and has fallen into despair.

"So the debate rages: Should Pharma be allowed to continue bioprospecting to bring potentially life-saving medicines to the world, when doing so is decimating the culture, traditions, and the way of life of the Shuja people? You be the judge."

"You see, Baba," D'Melo said, feeling validated. "There are always terrible things in the news. And Africa's the worst! You're so lucky you were able to get out of there."

"D'Melo," Baba replied stiffly. "Do you think what you see on TV is Africa? You watch a clip about a continent with a billion people and fifty-four countries, and you think you know Africa? *That's* not Africa," he asserted, pointing to the TV. "Every place has struggles. But for Africa, all that's reported *are* the struggles. There are wonderful and amazing things happening in Africa that will never find their way onto this screen.

"Son, Africa isn't something you will ever be able to understand sitting on a couch in Lincoln Downs. To really know Africa, you have to touch it, you have to breathe it, taste it, smell it." Baba paused as his mind filled with images of the vibrant Kipaji mountains and forests. He shut his eyes and breathed tranquility: he was back home on Amanzi Mountain, lazing in the soft tangerine light of sunrise, absorbing the prattle of a crystal brook, drawing the perfume of lavender, jasmine, and gardenia into his nose and lungs. Cool mist from one of the many waterfalls freshens his face with a caress. "It's a place of spirit, son," Baba said wistfully. "So to understand it, you have to lead with your soul. Once you do, you'll realize that Africa is pure magic."

Baba's attention drifted to the drawing beneath the wall clock and his nostalgia deepened. D'Melo's mother, one of Kipaji's most beloved artists, had sketched it soon after they arrived in America.

"I never stopped being amazed at how your mother could create such beautiful things." Baba's eyes misted. "Do you remember all of her art in our house in D.C.?"

D'Melo shook his head.

"Well, you were still little at the time."

"Why didn't we bring Mama's art when we moved to Philly?"

"After she died, I realized that I wouldn't be able to bear having so much of her around me." Baba's voice wobbled. "But I couldn't leave all of her, so I brought this one." Baba gestured toward the drawing.

"Why this one? I mean, I like it, but it doesn't look like anything."

"It's abstract," Baba said, bemused. "Your mother would get so riled up over injustice in the world. It would tie her up in knots." His jaw tensed. "Creating art helped her work out her turmoil. But this piece in particular was special to her." Baba grimaced, and then his gaze morphed into a bristling glare. He closed the conversation with the same thing he always said after he had been looking at the drawing: "*Haki inakuja kwako!* (Justice will find you!)"

The following evening, Jeylan, Kazim, and Marley were hanging out at Jeylan's house, engaged in their typical high jinks as they waited for

Tyreke. They were going to shoot pool at Wilson's Billiard Hall, one of their main pastimes. It helped keep them out of the trouble, which had an uncanny knack for finding young men in Lincoln Downs.

Then Jeylan's phone rang. It was his brother, Tyreke, calling from the hospital. His girlfriend had overdosed on oxycontin and was fighting for her life. Jeylan told him that he would come immediately, but would stop at the drugstore on the way to inform Tyreke's boss that he wouldn't be able to work in the morning.

"Don't bother," Tyreke said. "He just fired me."

"What!" Jeylan fumed, his vision blurred red. He clicked off the call and brushed tensely past Marley to the garage. He snatched a can of spray paint off the workbench.

Marley grabbed his arm. "Where you goin' with that?"

"That Nazi went too far this time! He fired Tyreke while his girlfriend's dying in the hospital!"

"Now that's just downright cold," Kazim quipped. "Firing someone on Labor Day!"

Marley narrowed his eyes at Kazim, *This ain't time for jokes!*

Jeylan jerked loose of Marley's grip and stormed out.

While his friends were usually off at the billiards hall on Monday nights, D'Melo volunteered with Baba at the Lincoln Downs Health Clinic. Although Baba wasn't allowed to practice medicine, he mentored the younger doctors. D'Melo didn't do much in terms of work. He went mainly to see his father in action. He reveled in Baba's energized spirit. His father was finally in his element, like a fish released into a lucid pond. D'Melo beamed with pride at how much the clinic staff admired and respected his father. He could have stayed there forever soaking it in. But that night, his time was cut short.

His phone buzzed. It was Marley in a tizzy explaining how Jeylan was about to get himself into serious trouble. "D'Melo, you gotta get down to the drugstore and stop him. You're the only person he listens to."

D'Melo bolted out of the clinic. By the time he reached the store, Jeylan had already managed to get inside. Just as D'Melo was about to enter, a light went on in an upstairs window. For a brief moment, he wavered—his life, his future in the balance. If he was arrested, he could lose the scholarship he needed to go to college, and the orderly and ordinary life he desired so deeply. But as usual, his heart bested his wary mind. He could never hang his friend out to dry.

He nudged the door ajar, careful not to chime the shopkeeper's bell dangling behind it. Jeylan was spray-painting his indignation in huge letters on a wall.

"Jey! Let's go!"

D'Melo yanked on his shirt but Jeylan wriggled free.

"Hey! We gotta get out of here!" D'Melo whispered desperately through clenched teeth. "Someone's upstairs!"

"No one's here," Jeylan grumbled, nearly finished with his hateful display. "My brother said the Nazi and his wife are out with friends."

D'Melo snatched the paint can from Jeylan's hand. "I'm telling you, someone's upstairs!" D'Melo exhorted, emphasizing as much urgency as he could in a hushed voice. "A light came on."

He clutched Jeylan's arm and steered him forcefully to the door. The creak of a loose floorboard at the rear of the shop pierced the silent darkness, throwing them into a panic. Jeylan flung the door open, neglectful of the bell. *Ding-ding! Ding-ding!* Usually the soft chime of the bell evoked old-fashioned mirthful images of festive holiday times. But now it sounded more like the locking clank of a prison-cell door. D'Melo spun around. The silhouette of a woman brandishing a baseball bat materialized on the stairway in back.

D'Melo hustled Jeylan out of the store. A police siren wailed in the distance. They ducked into a dark alley and flattened their bodies against a brick wall. A red light whirled over their tense faces as the police car screamed past. They peaked around the corner to make sure the coast was clear, then skulked the few blocks to D'Melo's house, keeping low and in the shadows.

"What were you thinking?" D'Melo shouted at Jeylan, his heart pounding.

Jeylan knew that D'Melo avoided trouble like his ancestors had avoided lions. "I don't know, man," he panted, trying to catch his breath. "I just lost my head." He laid an apologetic hand on D'Melo's shoulder. "I'm sorry I got you into this."

D'Melo's mind was churning. *What if the woman recognized me?* D'Melo was very well known in the community because of his basketball stardom. *I'm screwed.* His heart dropped when he thought of Baba. *What if Baba comes home and he sees me getting arrested?* He massaged his temples, trying to ease the dizziness in his head.

"Jey, on your way home, you gotta stay out of sight," D'Melo cautioned. "If the police see you at this hour on a school night, they'll assume it was you that broke into the store."

"Alright, dawg," Jeylan concurred. They clasped hands into a shoulder bump. Jeylan scanned the length of the street, then vanished into the night.

D'Melo stirred fretfully in bed. *It was too dark in there. I couldn't see her, so I'm sure she couldn't see me either.* While this thought provided him with a sliver of comfort, he was mostly waiting in knots for the police to pound on the door any second.

An hour passed. D'Melo twisted and turned until he finally fell into a restless sleep, marred once again by images of his mother being killed. But this time, he was the one driving the car that thrust her into oncoming traffic. The police arrested him. Baba staggered, feral-eyed and unkempt, into the dank prison visiting room. Reeking of alcohol, he settled himself at the cold gray metal table that separated him from D'Melo.

D'Melo recoiled at Baba's pungent whiskey breath. "Baba, have you been drinking?"

Baba's eyes, glassy from tears of disappointment and drunkenness, rose to meet D'Melo's. "Son, I never expected this from you," he slurred. "I must have done something wrong. I can't live anymore knowing that you're in here because I failed you." He removed a shiny pistol from inside his coat.

"Baba! What are you doing?" D'Melo checked the room frantically to see if any guards were watching.

Baba jabbed the pistol into his own chest.

"No!" D'Melo lunged across the table. He was too late. An ear-splitting gunshot rang out and Baba collapsed to the floor. D'Melo tried to dive down to him but was jolted back by the heavy chains anchoring him to the table. He yanked desperately to free himself of the shackles keeping him from his father. A dark maroon shadow crept along the floor around Baba's lifeless body.

"Baba!" D'Melo screamed. "What did I do!"

D'Melo jerked awake, his heart thumping fiercely. Baba rushed in. He wrapped concerned arms around D'Melo. "It's okay, son. Just another nightmare."

D'Melo squeezed so tight that Baba struggled for air.

"Baba, I'm so sorry," he wailed. D'Melo then stammered through what had happened with Jeylan at the drugstore.

Baba seemed to have let out a small sigh of relief. Things could have been much worse. In Lincoln Downs, hardly a day passed without a tragic story. Senseless killings, police brutality, and drug addiction headlined the array of misfortunes that plagued the lives of the young men in the community.

"All I ever wanted was a quiet and peaceful life," D'Melo groaned, disappointed with himself. "What if the police find out I was there? They'll never believe that I wasn't a part of vandalizing the store."

"Son, you didn't do anything wrong. You must trust that the Great Spirit will work in your favor."

D'Melo's alarm clock shrieked to life. He exhaled a heavy breath.

"Breakfast is already on the table," Baba said. "Your first day of school—new year, new eyes."

D'Melo dragged himself out of bed. The excitement he felt just a day ago had been replaced with the anxious gnawing in his gut that had become all too familiar. Perhaps he subconsciously sensed that before long, the reality of his life would be far more horrifying than his nightmares.

CHAPTER TWO

"I'm Zara. Zara Zanič."

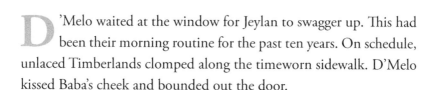

D'Melo waited at the window for Jeylan to swagger up. This had been their morning routine for the past ten years. On schedule, unlaced Timberlands clomped along the timeworn sidewalk. D'Melo kissed Baba's cheek and bounded out the door.

On the way to school, neither mentioned the previous night's foolhardy fiasco. Giving voice to it would only have provoked D'Melo's volatile angst and made Jeylan feel guiltier than he already did.

A block from the school, Marley and Kazim were clowning at the corner, waiting for their friends. The four had been inseparable from the day D'Melo moved into the neighborhood.

Just after Christmas of 2008, ten years ago, Baba and D'Melo had arrived in Lincoln Downs. Their moving van ground to a halt in front of the brick row house Baba had rented. D'Melo's seven-year-old legs wobbled as he lugged boxes nearly as big as he was up the stoop stairs. Then, the moment they were more or less settled into their new house, D'Melo scooped up his basketball and started for the door.

"It's too cold for basketball," Baba cautioned.

But mere frigid air couldn't deter D'Melo from the love of his life. "It's never too cold for basketball," he chirped.

The local court was tattered and neglected—frayed nets clung to the hoops for dear life and there were more weed-filled cracks on the court than visible painted lines. But D'Melo couldn't have cared less. As long as there was a court and a hoop, he was good to go.

He squeaked open the rusted chain-link gate, having no idea he was about to enter hallowed ground. The Citadel, as it is known in Philadelphia, was a celebrated institution at one point in time—"The Pride of the City." Many Philadelphia basketball legends had graced the Citadel with their mastery. Some even went on to memorable careers in the NBA.

Because of the Citadel, during the summers Lincoln Downs was transformed into a basketball mecca, buzzing with life and excitement. The community was treated to a packed schedule of tournaments, slam-dunk contests, and shooting competitions—and, of course, the over-the-top bravado of the competitors, who whipped the crowds into a frenzy.

But over the years, the talent declined and the glorious summer games gradually withered away. Eventually, and tragically, the thrills and athleticism on the court were replaced by gang activity. So the Citadel, once a shining symbol of community harmony and the epicenter of a vibrant Lincoln Downs, lost its allure and fell from grace.

The day D'Melo arrived, he was delighted to see boys his age engaged in a heated three-on-three game against a rival neighborhood. Jeylan, Kazim, and Marley were already losing badly when Marley twisted his ankle and couldn't continue. Jeylan and Kazim, always up for a challenge, were going to finish the game with just the two of them—Marley, being a tad plump and athletically-challenged, was never much help anyway.

But then a mousy voice screeched from the warped wooden bleachers. Unbeknownst to the small group of bystanders braving the cold, this was the seminal moment that would eventually return the Citadel to the height of basketball glory it once enjoyed.

D'Melo was waving his hand at them enthusiastically. "I can play!"

Jeylan scrutinized D'Melo warily, sizing him up like a seasoned scout. "Are you from the LD?" he asked, his breath creating a cloud in the cold air.

"The LD?" D'Melo puzzled.

"Dawg—Lincoln Downs."

"Oh! Yeah, I just moved here."

Jeylan's eyes flashed to Kazim for his approval. Kazim shrugged, blowing into his small kid hands to keep his fingers from becoming icicles.

"Come on then." Jeylan waved D'Melo onto the court.

The smattering of bored onlookers turned their attention to the lanky kid sashaying across the frozen concrete. Jeylan pulled D'Melo aside for a pep talk.

"Listen, dawg. This game ain't no joke. I don't wanna lose to these fools. If we do, we gonna hear it *all* week in school about how we got beat by these Carver Heights jokers. Game's to twenty. Make it, take it. We losin' eighteen, thirteen. You pretty tall, so you guard their big guy."

When the game resumed, D'Melo called for the ball, but Jeylan and Kazim only passed between themselves. Then Jeylan shot and missed. D'Melo leapt, snagged the rebound, and scored a left-handed reverse layup. Jeylan and Kazim gaped. Next possession, they passed to D'Melo. He dribbled hard left, spun back, and scored a floater in the lane. Murmurs of curious delight rose with sporadic puffs of white mist among the handful of now roused spectators.

Jeylan huddled with Kazim and D'Melo. "Hey, if we hit a three, we win." Jeylan turned to D'Melo. "You kinda big. Can you shoot three-pointers?" D'Melo nodded confidently. Jeylan mapped out a play on his shivering hand and then broke the huddle. Kazim drove to the basket. He passed to Jeylan cutting backdoor. D'Melo slipped out to the corner three-point line. Jeylan zipped him a timely pass. D'Melo set his feet and let it fly with all that his seven-year-old body could muster. *Swish!*

The crowd bounced to its collective feet and burst into cheers, as if Lincoln Downs had just won the state championship. Jeylan and Kazim dashed to D'Melo and gave him a running chest bump. Jeylan swaggered over to the Carver Heights team and shot out his hand. They reached into their pockets and cobbled together ten dollars.

"See y'all suckers next week!" Jeylan gloated.

Before Jeylan could even feel the weight of the cash in his hand, Marley hobbled over and seized it. "I'll take that," he interjected. "Nice addition to our grad fund."

D'Melo was befuddled. "You play for money?"

"Yep," Jeylan said happily. "And now with *you* on our team, we gonna be rich!"

From that day on, their friendship evolved into the tightest of brotherly bonds—and gained them much notoriety. The denizens of all the local neighborhoods started respectfully referring to them as "the LD Boyz," or simply, "the Boyz."

As D'Melo entered the school, his emotions were swirling wildly. They ranged from elation about getting his final year underway to mourning that his extraordinary high school experience would end in just nine short months. From the anticipated thrill of stepping back onto the hardwood court to the dread of the bright light of stardom, a double-edged sword that would stalk him incessantly throughout the year. From reveling at the thought of the pride Baba would feel on graduation day to grieving about his mother not being there to see him receive his diploma.

Still, he found himself smiling as he took in familiar and comforting sights. Marley was poking unwitting students with his Lumalink, informing them of what their clothes were made of; Kazim implemented the first stages of his honey plan and was met with sneering rejection; and Jeylan stomped a pace ahead of D'Melo, as if he was his bodyguard. This was just what D'Melo needed to settle the pendulum swing of his emotions. Like Baba at the clinic, D'Melo was back in *his* element.

As he cleared the metal detector and the police pat-down, he was immediately confronted by what he dreaded most: attention. Life-sized banners picturing him in his basketball uniform festooned the length of the gray, institutional hallway.

"Oh, come on," Jeylan muttered. "For real?" Jeylan, knowing D'Melo better than anyone, rolled up the banners one by one. "Don't worry, D," he said. "I'll talk to Mr. Jamison about this." Mr. Jamison, the school principal, meant well but didn't fully grasp the extent to which D'Melo loathed the spotlight.

Other than the banners that pained his privacy, nothing of note happened during the school day. Just the usual exaggerated chatter about what everyone did over the summer and updates on the community—who got arrested, who got killed, and who got the new LeBron sneakers. D'Melo relished its normality.

In addition to his basketball accomplishments, D'Melo was student council president. As such, he occupied an office in the administrative suite after school every day. These office hours were for students to consult with their elected leader for the purpose of expressing their grievances or offering thoughts on how to improve the school.

However, since D'Melo's election last year, only three people had ever shown up to talk to him—Jeylan, Kazim, and Marley—and it never had anything to do with the school. They just came to hang out. Even so, D'Melo hadn't missed a single after-school session as president.

This day in his office was like pretty much all the others. After an uninterrupted session, D'Melo packed up his notebooks and got ready to leave.

Then, just as the office clock was about to tick 3:30, *she* blew in.

D'Melo was certain she was new. Even in a school of over a two thousand students, not noticing her was inconceivable. Not only was she just one of seven white students in the whole school, but she was particularly impossible to miss. The moment she bounded through the door, the energy in the office seemed to spike, like the numbers on a Richter scale during an earthquake. Her dynamism radiated through the chipping cinder-block walls. And if her vivacious aura wasn't enough, she looked like a model. Her shiny, perfectly coiffed red hair with a natural tinge of fiery orange, slightly wavy toward the ends, swung just below her athletic shoulders. Her alluring countenance featured a sculpted jawline, high cheekbones, a perfectly rounded forehead, and minimal makeup—perhaps in recognition that to cover that face would have been nothing less than criminal.

Her well-thought-out ensemble completed her super-stylish presentation. She teamed light blue skinny jeans with a slim fit T-shirt tucked only in the front. A fine scarf made of an African-patterned fabric was looped gently around her elegant neck, its earthy tones floating from over her shoulder to her elbow. Her outfit was pulled together by a rustic beaded necklace, at the end of which hung a Bohemian polymer clay pendant of concentric circles dangling just above her belt line.

D'Melo scurried around his desk. He ducked behind the doorframe and peered stealthily out into the reception area. *Is someone filming a movie in our school?* he wondered. His enraptured gaze tracked her as she marched toward principal Jamison's door. Her brown suede, knee-high boots clacked with purpose on the worn wooden floor until . . . "Ugf!" She rammed into the corner of the receptionist's desk.

"Oooh," D'Melo winced. "That's gonna bruise."

The stranger paused, apparently allowing the stinging throb to subside. She composed herself, then tramped straight past the expectant secretary into Mr. Jamison's office—she didn't even bother to knock.

"Dang," D'Melo thought, riveted. "This girl's got some serious gumption . . . or she's just straight-up whacked."

After a few seconds, she burst out of the principal's office. Her eyes darted around before locking in on D'Melo's door. She made a beeline toward it.

D'Melo's chest tightened. He hurried back to his desk, launching himself into his swivel chair. He overshot and sent himself rolling past the desk. He scooted back, feeling cartoonish. He made it just in time to recline in his chair, trying to look casual.

She entered like a Midwestern tornado. D'Melo's heart thudded against his ribs.

"Are you D'Melo?" she snapped, without the courtesy of any one of society's customary polite greetings.

"Ahhh, yeah," he gulped, his mind unusually flustered.

"I was told you're the person I need to talk to."

D'Melo didn't really hear anything she was saying. Her voice receded to the background, lingering faintly, because, at that moment, everything besides her sparkling emerald green eyes was irrelevant. They held an extraordinary mix of intimidating power and melting tenderness. They were kind of like an army invading a country while eating soft-serve ice cream.

She slid her backpack off her shoulder and rested it on the desk, but it landed precariously and promptly toppled to the floor. D'Melo shot chivalrously from his chair.

"I can do it," she said, asserting her self-sufficiency. When she rose, the strands of hair that had been dangling obediently in front of her left eye now broke ranks and tickled her nose. She blew a sharp upward breath to settle them back home.

"So," she dove right in, "my family pays taxes." Her eyes burned a hole into D'Melo's face. "And those taxes are used to operate this school, right?"

"Ahhh, yeah," he managed, fidgeting nervously with his loosely twisted hair.

"So don't you think I should be able to have a vegan lunch option so that I can eat?" she asked, without really asking. She tucked the wayward strands of hair behind her ear.

D'Melo noticed that her pupils were haloed by a delicate hazel ring that flared out in streaks, like the golden blossom of a dawning sun.

"Ahhh, yeah," he murmured, forcing himself back to the conversation.

She paused, probably baffled by D'Melo's less-than-sane behavior. "But there wasn't a vegan meal today. So I haven't eaten. You can see I'm wasting away here," she said, sliding her hand down the front of her body, which didn't help D'Melo regain his sanity one iota.

"Ahhh, yeah," he mustered again.

She narrowed her eyes. "Are you sure you're the student council president? Because so far you're not really impressing me with all this, 'Ahhh, yeah' stuff."

D'Melo finally snapped out of his stupor. He straightened in his chair. "Well, we probably don't have vegan food because you're the first vegan in the school."

"Is that right?" she said.

He could feel her baiting him like a Venus flytrap coaxing in its prey for the kill.

"That's interesting," she continued. "Because I asked around. And guess what I discovered?"

D'Melo held out his chin, attentively.

"Well, it turns out there are at least six other vegans and even more vegetarians in this school."

"What?" D'Melo said, dismayed. "But no one ever said anything!"

"That's because people don't want to cause trouble. They just accept that they have to bring their own lunch, even though they have a right to a school lunch. I'm sorry, but I won't sit idly by and let this continue."

"You don't need to be sorry. You're right," D'Melo said contritely.

She furrowed her brows and bit her ample bottom lip. She was clearly suspicious, maybe expecting pushback disguised in disingenuous remarks about how she was going to die without protein.

"Okay, let me see what I can do," D'Melo said. "But in the meantime, you may want to bring your lunch. This kind of thing can take time. Last year, we asked for more books. Three months later, we finally had enough for everyone. But don't worry, I got this."

She tilted her head, perplexed. "You got *what?*"

"What do you mean?" D'Melo uttered, just as perplexed.

"You said, 'I got this.' You got *what?*"

"Oh!" he said, surprised. *How could she not know what that means? She must not be from this area . . . or this universe for that matter.* "It just means, I'll take care of it."

She shrugged. "Then why wouldn't you just say that?"

D'Melo's intrigue was growing by the moment.

"Well, thanks," she said, her tone much softer. "I appreciate you trying to help." She hoisted her backpack and turned for the door.

D'Melo couldn't help himself. "Hey, I can show you around if you want," he blurted.

She hesitated. "Sure, thanks."

For a resource-poor school, Lincoln Downs High boasted several interesting clubs. He first brought her by the sports, chess, and math clubs—each of which he was president.

"Is there anything you're *not* the president of?" she quipped, earning a grin from D'Melo.

"Well, actually yeah. The Zen Club."

"Wow. That's really progressive. I've never heard of a school having a Zen Club."

"We needed a safe and peaceful place for students to meditate anytime during the day. Life in this neighborhood can be stressful."

"So who's the president of the Zen Club?"

"Well, technically, there isn't a president. The head of the club is called the Zen Master."

She peered up at him. "That's you, isn't it?"

D'Melo grinned.

"Show off," she said, pursing her lips. "Hey, you haven't shown me the Environment Club."

D'Melo's face blanked.

"What! You don't have an Environment Club?" The fire returned to her eyes. "Do you realize that our environment is under siege?" she asked, but again, without really asking. "Our planet's warming by the minute. Our oceans are dying. Over a million species are at risk of extinction. *And* it will be irreversible by 2030!"

"I hear you. But, to be honest, folks in this neighborhood don't think much about the environment. People focus more on trying not to catch a bullet on their way to the grocery store. Plus, there aren't a whole lot of trees in Lincoln Downs."

Her eyes widened. "I know you didn't just reduce the environment to trees. How do the people in this neighborhood feel about having air to breath, clean water to drink, or uncontaminated food to eat?"

D'Melo shrugged abashedly.

"How do I start a club?" she said.

"I don't want to be a doubting Thomas, but I don't think anyone will join it."

"I don't care," she replied obstinately. "I'll be the whole club then."

"You need at least three people to register for a club to be approved. I'll announce it in morning. Hopefully, some students will show up."

"You do the announcements too! Is there anything you don't do around here?"

D'Melo searched his mind sincerely. Not finding much, he said, "Well, this school and community have been very good to me."

"Well, I'm impressed with your commitment," she said. "Thanks for the tour." She pivoted to leave.

"Hey," D'Melo said. "You didn't tell me your name."

A tint of embarrassed pink rose in her cheeks. "I guess I just kinda tore right into you, didn't I? Sorry."

D'Melo spread a tiny space between his finger and thumb. He put it to his eye. "Maybe just a smidgen."

She pretended to unscrew the top off a container. "Clunk," she said, motioning as if dropping something inside it. D'Melo scratched his head, bewildered. She explained, "That was a good word you just used, 'smidgen'. So I put it in my good word jar." She cupped her hand to show D'Melo an imaginary jar and then abruptly started to leave again.

D'Melo cleared his throat. "But—your name?"

"Oh yeah." She tapped her forehead as if trying to jump-start her brain. She shot out her slender hand. "I'm Zara. Zara Zanič."

D'Melo's ample hand swallowed hers. "It's nice to meet you, Zara."

"You too, Mr. President… of everything!"

Zara exited the school with a stumble. She clutched the metal rail along the steps. Her backpack flung upward, its weight nearly flipping her over the railing. She gathered herself and sauntered off, seemingly without a care about how she must have looked to her new schoolmates.

D'Melo had never met anyone like Zara. He found it difficult to pin her down—she was focused yet aloof, powerful yet fragile, elegant yet goofy. She was a walking dichotomy. He couldn't tear his eyes away, as she bounced across the bustling street.

The next day, after no one showed up to his student council office—surprise, surprise—D'Melo nabbed Marley and Kazim and dashed to the club rooms. He was glad Zara was still there. She was sitting by herself, tapping her fingers exasperatedly on the desk.

D'Melo introduced his friends. "This is Marley, and this is—"

Kazim cut short D'Melo's introduction. He seized Zara's hand and cooed, "Mmm girrrl, I'll hug a tree with you *anytime.*" He lifted her unaccommodating hand to his lips. Zara slipped out of his grasp just before he kissed his own palm.

"I'm Kazim," he murmured, in his best suave voice. "But you can call me Pimp Daddy."

Zara glared at him through the top of her eyes. "Well, as lovely as that name is, I think I'll stick with Kazim . . . if anything at all," she said, a little snarky, a little playful. "And, D'Melo," she said, gathering her papers. "You were right. No one came to sign up."

"What do mean?" D'Melo threw his hands out to his sides. "What do you think we're here to do?"

A hint of a smile gleamed in her eyes. She slid the sign-up sheet across the desk.

"Oh, I almost forgot," he said excitedly. "Principal Jamison assured me that the school will have at least one vegan option for lunch every day."

"Wow!" Zara said. "How'd you get that done so quickly?"

Marley chimed in. "When Jamison wasn't going to do anything—"

D'Melo shook his head vigorously at Marley.

"Please, Marley, continue," Kazim said, smirking. "This sounds like it's gonna be interesting."

"D'Melo went to the head of the school board's house," Marley said, ignoring D'Melo's nonverbal plea. "In exchange for her support, she said D'Melo would have to give her children basketball training. "And he agreed," Marley shot D'Melo a disapproving glare, "even though he knows he's already stretched thin."

Zara's eyes softened. "Aww, that's so sweet. Why would you do all of that?"

"Yeah, D'Melo," Kazim goaded. "Tell us. Why *would* you do all that?"

D'Melo gritted his teeth at Kazim, *Oooh, man. You're really pushin' it!*

"Zara has a right to have meals she can eat," D'Melo contended.

"Ohhh, I see," Kazim said sarcastically. "You're such a righteous fella."

Kazim and Marley trifled home while D'Melo stayed behind to help Zara finish the club paperwork. She thanked him for his support, which he shrugged off humbly.

"Well, I better get home," she said.

"Where's home?" D'Melo asked, trying hard to sound like someone who didn't have an ulterior motive.

"I live two blocks from the Lincoln Downs Health Clinic."

"Oh, that's close to my house. I'll walk you," he chirped, a bit more excitedly than he had intended. "You know," he clarified, "just to make sure you get there safely. This can be a tough neighborhood."

"That sure is a gentlemanly act, my kind sir." She played along in a Southern belle accent. "I mean, making sure lil' ol' helpless me gets home safely." She batted her long lashes.

"Nah, I didn't mean it like that. I just—"

"I'm messing with you, dude." She motioned toward the door with her head. "Come on. Walk me home."

D'Melo found himself so intrigued by Zara that he was actually uncomfortable. A million questions jostled in his titillated mind. He didn't know where to begin, so he blurted, "Why are you vegan?"

"It's a pretty rough story," she said.

Zara explained that when she was six, her mother brought her to the pig slaughterhouse where she worked. Not a minute into her visit, Zara burst into crushing sobs. Her tender heart couldn't bear the sight of pigs locked in cages scarcely larger than them, unable to do as much as even turn around. They were forced to eat off the same cage floor on which they excreted their bodily waste. The pigs that succumbed to the dreadful conditions were tossed into a dumpster as thoughtlessly as someone would discard an empty milk carton. The stench from their rotting corpses lurked putridly in the country air. Zara then realized why her town reeked of death.

The pigs that were unfortunate enough to survive to maturity—and therefore ready for slaughter—were suspended upside down on a revolving conveyer belt. Every clink of the metal bearings against the stainless-steel track brought them one step closer to the horrific death awaiting them. The bearings *ticked, ticked, ticked*, like the second hand on the clock in a prison execution chamber. As their trembling bodies rounded the final bend, their executioner, draped in dark plastic overalls dripping warm crimson, came into view. They now knew their misery-filled lives would end at the keen tip of a blood-soaked blade slicing through their throats. Their humanlike cries echoed in vain, bouncing from wall to wall and fading lifelessly into the chilly sterile air before ever finding a sympathetic ear. In a last-ditch plea for their lives, the pigs gazed haplessly into the eyes of the brandisher of the killing blade. But instead of the mercy their instincts must have yearned for, they found only a dark void where a human soul had once lived.

As their motionless bodies continued to clink along the conveyer belt, their bellies were ripped open and insides yanked out. The most tasty pieces of their pale pink flesh were then carved for the market. All that remained was slopped together and flung into a meat grinder.

"From head to hooves," Zara emphasized. To keep her fury at bay, she tried to make light of it. She lifted cupped hands into the air and twisted them. "Get your hotdogs here!" she yelled from the side of her mouth, mimicking the vendors at baseball games. "And if you're not a hotdog fan, no need to fret," she shouted, still in character. "We also have bologna, sausages, and scrapple!"

D'Melo swallowed hard, trying to push down the acid rising from his nauseous stomach.

Over the past summer, Zara had interned at an organization that publicized animal cruelty. She went into the pig factory, pretending to visit her mother. Fitted with a hidden camera masquerading as a shirt button, she surreptitiously videoed the "den of evil," as she called it.

The video was featured on the local news. This led to the livestock company being sued by the people suffering from diseases caused by the factory. The company was also forced to provide more humane treatment to the pigs.

Zara's eyes flared angrily. "I think a better punishment would have been to string the factory owners up and have them experience what the pigs went through!"

D'Melo was jarred by Zara's extreme acrimony. While he admired her verve and righteousness, he found himself distressed by it. A part of him longed to be a rabble-rouser like her, but the thought of upsetting the balance of his life left an anxious pit in his gut.

"Wasn't your mom upset that you exposed her company?"

The fire in Zara's eyes faded into sobriety. "No," she said dismissively. "My mom has always supported me, even when I go overboard." A mischievous grin surfaced on her face. "Which happens on occasion."

Zara stopped at the corner of Cherry and Waldorf. "Okay, this is me," she said.

D'Melo eyed the building, puzzled. "But this is a drugstore."

"Yeah, I live with my grandparents in the apartment above the shop." Zara pointed to the window on the second floor—the same window from where the light emanated when Jeylan was vandalizing the store. D'Melo's heart hammered tumultuously. The world around him imploded in an instant, squeezing oxygen from his lungs.

Meanwhile, Zara launched into the story of her grandfather, Tomáš Zanič (pronounced *Tah mahsh*). Although his family was

German, he was born and raised in Nečzia, a mountainous country in Eastern Europe. He came to America to study pharmacology. After graduating, he worked for years at the drugstore. Without any notice, the store owner abruptly decided to sell the shop. Tomáš bought the store, although the owner cautioned him against it. "The blacks are taking over," he said. To this Tomáš replied facetiously, "Really, I hadn't noticed. It just seems like new people are moving into the neighborhood."

Zara shook her head, admiringly. "My grandparents stayed in Lincoln Downs when most of the other white families fled. Throughout my childhood, my grandfather would often say that if you run from a challenge, you can never be a part of the solution. They love this community. You couldn't drag them away from here.

"You know," she continued, matter-of-factly, "some guys vandalized the shop the other night. They painted 'Racist Nazi' on the wall." She paused to peer through the store window at her grandparents painting feverishly over the hateful scrawl. "I wish I could tell those guys how wrong they are about my grandfather."

Then Zara turned somber, as she recounted her great grandparents' experience with the Nazis in Germany. Tomáš' family spoke out vehemently against the discriminatory treatment of the Jews. Because of that, they were scorned in the streets, even by their own friends. And one night, their house was broken into by masked men, who threatened them at gunpoint. But this only steeled their resolve.

In the late 1930s, Jews were being sent to concentration camps by the thousands. Tomáš' family snuck several dozen Jews out of the city. They hid them in the basement of their farmhouse until they could get them safely out of Germany. One day, Tomáš' father went to Berlin to save more Jews. He never returned; the Gestapo had arrested him. He was taken to a building on the outskirts of the city. After days of being tortured, he was dragged to a courtyard behind the building. They propped his limp body against a wall that held the memory of the others who had also stood up to the injustice. Dried, bloody pockmarks were a sanguine tribute to their final act of heroism.

Upon receiving the news of the execution, Tomáš' family gathered what it could carry and fled. The journey, through the biting chill of winter, took a month. Eventually they arrived in Nečzia, a safe haven for Jews at the time.

"So," Zara said, her eyes misty, "you can imagine how hurt my grandfather was when he saw those words. That was more painful for him than even burning down the store would have been."

Dizzy with guilt, D'Melo murmured, "Zara." His eyes fell remorsefully to the sidewalk, wishing the concrete would open and swallow him whole. "I have to tell you something."

"No, you don't," she said. "I already know."

His head jerked up; he was instantly mortified. He realized that the silhouette at the rear of the store that night had been Zara. He blinked rapidly, trying to fend off creeping faint.

"Are you okay?" She sat him down on a bench.

"I don't know what to say," he sputtered in a low voice. "Other than I'm so sorry." He forced himself to meet her eyes. "You knew this whole time."

Zara tightened her lips and nodded subtly.

"Why didn't you tell the police?"

"Because you guys are just idiots," she said, with a mix of empathy and vexation. "You and Jeylan don't deserve to have your lives ruined over a moment of stupidity. People make mistakes. I should know. I can be a smidge hotheaded at times, too."

"Noooo," he uttered, able to muster a tiny slice of sarcasm through a mouthful of humble pie. "You? Hotheaded?"

Zara chuckled.

"How did you know it was Jeylan with me? It was dark and he was nearly out the door by the time you reached the stairs."

"It wasn't difficult to figure out which of your buddies it was. Marley wouldn't hurt a fly. Kazim is a lover, not a fighter . . . well, in his own mind anyway. And when I heard that my grandfather fired Tyreke, it didn't take much to confirm that he's Jeylan's brother. It all made sense."

Zara locked hesitant eyes with D'Melo. "I understand that Jeylan was angry, but what I don't understand is—" She paused warily. "Well, I've only known you for a couple days, but you don't strike me as a guy who would do something like this."

D'Melo stiffened straight up. "Ohhh, no, no," he asserted, waving his hands feverishly. "You think I did this?"

Zara shrugged doubtfully.

"No way. I was only here to stop him. But I was too late."

Her face softened in relief. "I was hoping my instincts weren't failing me about you.

"D'Melo," she said. "You should know that Tyreke had been stealing oxy for months. My grandfather didn't want to believe it. But Tyreke was caught on camera. My grandfather asked him to return the pills, mostly over concern that something dreadful would happen. When he found out about Tyreke's girlfriend, he understood why Tyreke had been stealing. My grandfather encouraged him to take his job back and even offered to pay for his girlfriend's rehab. But Tyreke turned down the job. He said wanted to get as far away from the pharmaceutical industry as he could. And I don't blame him," Zara finished intensely. "The pharmaceutical industry is . . ." She stopped herself. "Ah, sorry. I can't seem to get off my soapbox."

D'Melo was silent, needing a moment to process everything. He squinted through the store window. Zara's grandparents were jostling playfully with each other as they repaired the store. Shame cascaded through him.

Zara laid a tender hand on his shoulder. "Please don't tell Jeylan that I know. It'll just make things weird."

D'Melo nodded in agreement. Her kindness was a healing balm for his regretful heart.

"I should go in now," she said. "Thanks for getting me home safely in this *tough* neighborhood," she jested. "I don't think I could have made it without you." She leaned over the flower box outside the shop door. She drew the lavender to her nose and took in its soothing sweetness.

When Zara swung the pharmacy door open, the bells chimed festively in D'Melo's heart like they used to. He popped off the bench and hustled over to her.

"Hey Zara," he said, hopefully. "Do you think it would be okay if I helped paint?"

"Well, if you're as good a painter as you are a bodyguard, my grandparents could really use your skills."

D'Melo smiled deeply.

"Come on," she said, towing him by his T-shirt. "They'll love it."

CHAPTER THREE

Deee... Melll... OHHHH

"**D**id you know that ten million pounds of toxic chemicals spew into the waterways in Pennsylvania every year?" Zara trumpeted from behind a portable table through the cool October air. She was wearing a short-sleeve, oversized white hoodie, which contrasted harmoniously with the gold-fringed leaves livening the chilly street.

"Do you know that DunChem is the biggest polluter in Philadelphia? And it has the nerve to put its headquarters a block from the Liberty Bell. That bell is supposed to be a symbol of freedom. How can we be free if we can't even trust the water we drink? Sign this petition and commit to boycott all DunChem products!"

After a full day of educating the mostly oblivious passersby, Zara tossed her handouts into a cardboard box. She lugged the table back to the shop she had borrowed it from, then started for the bus.

"Zara!" D'Melo, Kazim, and Marley scrambled up. "Is it too late for us to sign the petition?"

"Hey! What are you guys doing here?"

"We're part of the Environment Club too, remember?" D'Melo said, as he scribbled his name on the petition. "Whoaaa. You got over three hundred signatures!"

"Yeah, it was a slow day," she jested.

"You didn't even tell us you were doing this." D'Melo passed the petition to Marley and Kazim.

Zara shrugged. "I know you guys were just being nice to join the club."

D'Melo flipped his palms upward, *Give us a chance.*

"Okay, okay," she acquiesced. "How'd you even know I was here?"

D'Melo chivalrously slipped the box from her hands. "I went to the drugstore to see if your grandparents needed help with anything." Unconsciously, he was still exorcising his guilt. "Your grandfather told me that you were out causing trouble again," he chuckled.

They reached the bus stop. "Hey. We're meeting my dad for lunch. Wanna come?"

"I'd love to, I'm starving. But I didn't bring any money," she said with through pouty lips.

Kazim butted in. "I gotchu, girl. They don't call me Pimp Daddy for nothing. I take care of my girls."

"First of all," Marley said, "no one calls you Pimp Daddy. Second, you don't have any girls. And third, you know you're busted and you're just gonna 'borrow'"—he included air quotes—"money from me anyway."

Marley turned to Zara. "Don't worry, my treat. I get a discount at Chubby's anyway. I work there."

"Oh, Chubby's!" she said. "It's only a few blocks from the drug-store. I can stop at home and meet you guys there. Thanks anyway, Marley."

Zara bounced into Chubby's. Immediately she felt conspicuous, like her milky skin was a beacon in a sea of blackness. The steady murmur of the patrons dwindled to a thunderous silence. Zara spotted D'Melo in the back corner. She crossed tensely to the table. She felt like glowering eyes were tracking her with each self-conscious step.

D'Melo introduced her to Baba. She tried to calm her angst with a conscious breath. "It's nice to meet you, Mr. Bantu." She extended her hand, still feeling unnerved.

Baba launched from his chair and took her into a fatherly embrace. "My dear," he said. "There will be no 'Mr. Bantu' from you. You're a friend of D'Melo's. You will call me 'Baba.'"

The boyz dived into their favorite pastimes—jesting and talking basketball. Zara feigned interest. Inside she was a coiled bundle. Her fingertips agitatedly tapped the table.

"My dear," Baba said. "You were a bubble of radiance when you entered the restaurant. Now it's as if your light has been extinguished."

"I just hate that I don't fit in anywhere," she huffed. A glum weight settled forlornly in her stomach. She realized she had never felt at home anywhere.

"Sorry, my dear," Baba said, edging closer to her. "Could you speak up?"

In a hushed whisper, D'Melo informed Zara that Baba was hard of hearing in his left ear.

She raised her voice. "I said, I hate that I never fit in."

"No, you don't fit in," Baba uttered matter-of-factly. Zara furrowed her brow, expecting a more comforting response. "D'Melo has told me a lot about you. You, my dear, are a lioness," he beamed. "And do you know what happens when a lioness reveals herself on the savanna? The other animals become acutely aware that something powerful is in their midst. All attention hones in on her, and for good reason. On the outside, she's sleek and majestic. She's so captivating it's impossible to pull your eyes away. But on the inside, she's a fierce ravager of whatever she sets her sights on. Hence, the saying, 'She has the heart of a lion.' Baba chuckled softly. "I feel sorry for those who get on your bad side."

"Well," Zara felt herself blush, "I don't know about all that, but thank you."

Baba seemed to sense her ambivalence. "Do you believe you're a lioness?"

"Umm . . ." Zara reflected. "Sometimes, I guess."

"Not sometimes," Baba shot back. "You can't be a lioness *sometimes*. You either are or you're not."

"Well, I guess I am, then, because you told me so," she smiled gratefully.

"So now that it's settled that you are in fact a lioness, you must never concern yourself with what other people think of you." He motioned toward the restaurant patrons. "All you have to do is embrace who you are, then others will as well. Then," he concluded, as if having read her mind, "you will be at home *everywhere*."

Zara's eyes glazed moist. An unfamiliar warmth washed through her. Her life had been agonizingly devoid of the firm, tender love of a father.

While they ate, Baba reminisced aloud about the first time he and D'Melo came to Chubby's. On the evening of the day they had arrived in Lincoln Downs, they wandered in the frosty night, exhausted and famished. Suddenly, Baba halted. A man was shooting the breeze animatedly from the sidewalk with a woman propped in a windowsill above a restaurant. Between swigs from a shiny flask, his voice boomed wonderfully familiar sounds through the icy air.

"Let's eat over there," Baba said.

D'Melo was seven years old, half frozen and starving. From the look on his face, he would have settled for eating tree grubs around a campfire.

Baba shuffled up. *"Molo, bhuti"* ("Greetings, brother"). Chubby instantly ceased his conversation with the woman. His eyes shot to Baba, scrutinizing him. His skeptical gaze then dropped to D'Melo.

"It's okay, *bhuti*," Baba assured. "We're not Malungan. We're from Kipaji."

Chubby's face lit up brighter than the Christmas lights framing the entrance to his restaurant. He swallowed Baba in a mirthful bear hug. *"Molo, bhuti,"* he exclaimed, swinging Baba to and fro. *"Karibuni!"* ("Welcome"). He threw the restaurant door open. Except for a single light behind the bar, the restaurant was completely dark.

"Oh, you're closed," Baba surmised disappointedly.

"We're never closed for a hungry comrade!" Chubby clapped Baba on the back.

Chubby was a Malungan of the Shuja tribe. He fought with the Shuja rebel army before being captured by the Malungan military. He was tortured for information about the whereabouts of the rebel leader. After providing his captors with nothing, he sensed his time on this earth was soon coming to an unpleasant end. He needed to act swiftly. In desperation, he slyly promised a hefty sum to a prison guard to leave his cell door unlocked.

Chubby, who wasn't so chubby at the time, slipped out of the neglected prison compound. He found cover in the surrounding dense jungle. By the darkest moments before dawn, he was safely back in the Nyumbani—the homeland of the Shuja tribe.

Early that same morning, the Malungan president, Jaru Amani, was assassinated. The Shuja rebels were blamed. Grisly chaos erupted. Shuja families were ripped from their homes and slaughtered on the streets.

Chubby was able to escape through Nanjier, a neighboring country to the north that was sympathetic to the rebel cause. "And the rest is history," Chubby said, gesturing around the restaurant. His troubled eyes belied the contentment he tried to convey.

"I wasn't planning to be gone forever," Chubby continued dolefully. He planted his flask on the bar with a heavy hand, the scent of whiskey drifting up. "But as long as that rat of a man, Dimka, remains the president of Malunga, I can't go back." He tilted the flask over eager lips a little longer than before.

"I begged my parents to come with me." His glassy eyes dipped to the bar. "But they said Malunga was their home and they would die there." Chubby reached for the flask, but then shoved it away, toppling it. "I think it's true what they say: the soil of Malunga is red from the blood of all the people who have sacrificed their lives there." He blew a distressed sigh. His gaze drifted as he relived that dreadful time.

"So," he said, returning to the moment, "I was in America while my people were being slaughtered." His voice was tinged with guilt. "I naively believed that someone would stop the genocide. But the world sat by and let five hundred thousand Shujas be massacred.

"Those Borutu savages butchered my people with machetes. They didn't even have the decency to kill them quick."

After a moment, Chubby snapped out of his bitter wallowing. He turned to D'Melo with a toothy grin. "You hungry, little man?" D'Melo nodded fervently.

Chubby wobbled into the kitchen. Lights flickered on. He poked his head through the serving window behind the bar. "Have a seat. I'm going to whip up a special Malungan meal for you." He then reintroduced himself to the whiskey flask, which seemed to stoke the fire of his acrimony once again. "One day," he avowed, waving his finger sharply. "We will be victorious!"

Baba wrapped up the story. "Chubby isn't correct yet, but he will be. Tyranny has had its time in Malunga. You can only hold people down for so long. Justice will eventually reign supreme. And in the end, the righteous will be the ones honored, while the tyrants will be brought to their knees and their ill-gotten riches will fade along with any memory of them."

"Truth," the boyz chorused. "Take 'em to church, Baba!"

Baba toasted. *"Kwa uzima."* D'Melo whispered to Zara, "That means, 'to life.'"

"Kwa uzima," the boyz echoed.

Zara sat alone devouring an eggplant sandwich in the school cafeteria. Her eyes were fixed on an article about the melting glaciers in Greenland, wholly oblivious to the typical lunchtime commotion around her.

She didn't make friends readily. In fact, she had never really had a female friend. The girls in her life were focused on things that she couldn't care any less about. She was not into chasing boys; not interested in pop culture; and loathed shopping, although one would never guess that by her stylish way of dressing. She had a single-minded focus: She needed to change the world—today! She knew that to others her age, she came off as aloof. And that, combined with her looks, made her unapproachable for most insecure teenage girls.

Zara tended to do a little better with guys—at least they talked to her, but not the kind of talk she would have preferred. She was burdened with a heavy share of testosterone-driven attention. Their unrequited displays of affection led to encounters that were swift and crushing for her spurious suitors. But the state of her social life was of no concern to her. In fact, she preferred the solitude.

"Hey!" A voice startled her. It was D'Melo. His eyes dropped to her chin, then met hers again. "I've been looking for you."

"I missed most of the morning," she said, wondering why D'Melo's gaze kept dipping. "I arrived just in time for math class; yay for me," she said sarcastically. D'Melo's eyes wandered down her face again. "Dude! What are you looking at?"

"Oh, sorry. You have some sauce on your chin." He offered her a napkin.

"Were you just gonna keep looking at it without telling me?" she snipped. She swiped her chin haphazardly with the back of her hand. D'Melo returned the unused napkin to the table.

"Uhhh," he murmured, trying to ignore the lipstick that was now smeared under her lips. "What's wrong with math?"

"There's nothing wrong with math. There's something wrong with math and me together."

"I could tutor you," D'Melo offered.

"Well, that would be great," she said. "But you'll have to let me help you with something in exchange."

"Um, are you good at chemistry?" D'Melo asked.

"Uhhh, that would be a *no*."

He tried again. "Computers?"

"Nope," she said, pursing her lips. "Keep going."

"Biology?"

"Not so much. Well, thanks for this," she quipped. "Now I realize just how underwhelming my abilities are."

"Nah, there's got to be *something* you're good at. You can't be completely inept."

"Hey!" She smacked his arm. "You don't know me well enough yet to say that."

"How about you just owe me one?"

"Owe you one, *what*?"

"One whatever. I don't know."

Zara gazed skeptically at D'Melo. "Okay, I trust that you're not gonna ask me for anything crazy." She shot out a pinky. D'Melo peered at it, *What do you want me to do with that?* She interlocked his pinky with hers and jolted it downward. "Deal," she said.

"So why were you late for school? You sick?"

"Yeah, I'm sick of big business running roughshod over people. I slept outside the CEO of DunChem's house last night."

"You should have told me you don't have a place to stay," D'Melo jested. "I would've taken you to the homeless shelter."

"Oh, you're a riot, dude," she said deadpanned. "I was there protesting. I wanted to hand the petition to him directly. But he just drove right past me," she said, annoyed. "But I'm gonna keep going until he talks to me." Zara took a bite of her sandwich. A dollop of sauce plopped in her lap. "Aww, man."

D'Melo handed her the napkin. She dipped it in water and scrubbed her jeans. "So why have you been looking for me? Do you need some tips on basketball moves?"

"Now look who got jokes. No, I came to ask you whether you saw today's paper."

"I did!" she said, perking up. She congratulated D'Melo on being selected as a preseason All-American.

"No, not that. Here, look!" D'Melo dropped the newspaper on the table. "There's an article about you in the community section!"

Zara thumbed through the paper warily, wondering whether this was another one of D'Melo's gags. Then she gaped at the page and leaned in for a closer look. "Oh goodness gracious! That's what I looked like?" Zara thrust the paper away disgustedly. "Dang, the lady who took my picture didn't even warn me about how ragged I was looking!"

"That's all you have to say?" D'Melo said. "You don't think it's kinda dope you made the paper?"

"Well, it's great if it creates awareness, but I doubt many people are racing past the sports and entertainment sections to get to the community page. I think people in this town may just be a teensy bit more interested in this other story I saw." She crinkled the paper open and read, "'D'Melo combines qualities that are rare in an athlete.'" He reached to grab the paper from her. She swiveled and continued, loving every minute of the embarrassment growing on his face. "'Watching him play is like breathing in the grace of the ballet great, Mikhail Baryshnikov. He twirls effortlessly and launches high into the air as if the laws of gravity don't apply to him. At the same time, he plays with an aggression reminiscent of Mike Tyson sprinting across the boxing ring because he couldn't wait to see his opponent crash heavily to the canvas.'"

"Okay, okay," D'Melo pleaded, scanning the room to see if anyone was listening.

"Wait, it gets better," she said. "From an NBA scout, and I quote, 'Physically, he's *a perfect specimen.*'" Zara puckered her lips. "Oooh," she warbled. "Has this dude asked you to marry him yet?"

D'Melo was finally able to snatch the paper from her.

"And this is my favorite part." She spouted from memory: "'If he didn't have such a bright future in basketball, I'd say he would have no problem finding work as a model.'" She flitted her eyelashes exaggeratedly. "Oh, my word," she cooed, fanning her face. She leaned over the arm of her chair. "Catch me. I think I just might faint."

"I hate this stuff! I just want to play ball without all this hype."

"Well, my friend, somehow I don't think that's going to happen. According to the article, there will be a ton of scouts and reporters at the game tonight. You nervous?"

"Nah, it's basketball. When I'm on the court, I'm at home. You gonna come?"

"Maybe. I didn't get much sleep last night. On the other hand, how often does one get a chance to see the grace of Baryshnikov and power of Tyson all at once!"

The bell rang.

"Well, I hope to see you there," D'Melo said, scooping up his backpack. "Big-ups on your article! You should be proud . . . no matter how busted you looked," he chortled.

The hype around the first game of the season was always palpable. But this year the buzz in the gym was electric. College scouts with their clipboards and button-up shirts were conspicuous in the raucous crowd. Everyone was anticipating the thrill of watching the best player to have ever come out of the neighborhood. Even spectators from outside Philadelphia had made the trek to Lincoln Downs.

The announcer introduced the starters from Carver High. There was a smattering of cheers from the few Carver fans present. Then the lights dimmed. Spotlights glided across the floor in a random pattern. "Ima Boss" by Meek Mill pounded through the gym: "Look, I be ridin' through my old hood . . ." The frenzied crowd was scarcely able to contain itself.

The announcer boomed: "At center, 6'6", Tashawn Bell! At power forward, 6'4", Asaad Hightower! At small forward, 6'1", Kazim Benga!" The crowd hooted and hollered. "At shooting guard, 6'0", Jeylan Kendrick!" Boisterous cheers rang out. The announcer then paused to build the hysteria. A horn blared. "AND, at point guard, 6'4", give it up for our own Deeee Melloooo!" The cheers redoubled in a deafening crescendo. The crowd tromped the bleachers, shaking the gym. Girls' voices sliced sporadically through the bedlam, "I love you D'Melo!"

D'Melo loped to center court and huddled with his teammates. They gyrated in unison, revving themselves. Before each game, D'Melo closed his pep talk with the same words: "Let's bring it home!" D'Melo scanned the crowd. No Zara.

Performing his typical pregame ritual, he lifted the locket at the end of his silver necklace. His mother gave it to him as a Christmas gift on the very morning of the accident. He kissed the photo of her inside, then pointed heavenward.

As the teams positioned themselves for the opening tip, Zara stepped through the door. D'Melo zealously signaled Marley, who popped off the bleachers and rushed to greet her. He escorted her to the best seat in the gym, directly behind the team's bench.

D'Melo wasted no time in delighting his fans. Jeylan snagged the opening tip and bounced a precision pass to D'Melo in the corner. D'Melo turned his sights to the basket. Silent anticipation descended in the gym.

D'Melo's prolific three-point shooting had inspired a tradition at the school. The crowd took a collective breath, seeming to suck the air right out of the building. As he released the ball and it rotated with promise toward the hoop, the crowd chanted, "Deee . . . Melll . . ." and then, as the ball snapped through the nylon net, the crowd finished in ecstasy, ". . . OHHHH."

That night, the crowd got to chant "OHHHH" eleven times. D'Melo broke the school record with eleven three-pointers and fifty-two points. The scouts had an early night. By halftime, they had seen enough to confirm what they already knew.

The final buzzer sounded. The fans wanted D'Melo to acknowledge his incredible game. But they had grown to understand him well enough not to expect it. As always, he headed straight to the other team. He congratulated them, giving each an enthusiastic handclasp and shoulder bump. The opposing coach told him something that he could never get used to, although nearly every coach said something similar. "When you're in the NBA, don't ever forget where you came from. Congratulations, son."

D'Melo searched the stands. Zara was collecting her stuff to leave. He lifted a hopeful finger, requesting that she wait for him. Four giddy freshman girls corralled him before he could disappear into the locker room. They asked for his autograph.

"You don't want my autograph," he tried. "I'm no different from you. I can just play this game." They cleaved to his arm. "Okay, but only if you give me your autographs too. Because you're all special in your own way." They giggled.

Kazim seized the pen and started signing the girls' notepads. They scoffed. "What?" he jested. "I dropped 12 points tonight."

The girls thanked D'Melo dotingly. As they flittered off, reporters called to him. "D'Melo! D'Melo! Just one minute."

It wasn't in D'Melo's nature to be rude, but he abhorred how reporters put him on a pedestal. He pretended not to hear them. They continued shouting his name from outside the locker room.

Jeylan admonished them as he slipped past. "D'Melo ain't gonna come out until y'all leave. He doesn't want to talk to the press."

"I just want to ask him a few questions," a reporter implored. "I'll be quick."

"It ain't about time," Jeylan replied briskly. "If you weren't gonna write an article about him, he'd chop it up with you all day. He just doesn't want the attention."

"Well, he better get used to it. Reporters are going to be hounding him all season."

"You see," Jeylan snipped, irritation mounting in his voice. "That's why he won't talk to y'all. You just don't get it. He's not like all the other ballers. If you ever just talked with him person to person, you'd realize that as incredible a basketball player he is, he's an even better human being. Until you learn that, you'll never get a word from him. So you need to step and give him his privacy."

In the locker room, D'Melo was fidgeting. He struggled to focus on his coach's congratulatory words. He wanted to get to Zara before she left. Not a second after the coach dismissed the team, D'Melo made haste to the gym.

He bounded through the door. But only the janitor was there, doing the unenviable task of cleaning up after a thousand-person typhoon. D'Melo wilted.

"Hey, Mr. Moses," he called. "Got another broom?"

"Not this time, D'Melo," Moses said, his eyes diverting to the stands.

"Hey, dude." Zara stepped out from the shadows of the wooden bleachers. "Good game."

D'Melo smiled so big he thought his cheeks might pop. "Thanks for coming to cheer me on."

"I came to cheer for the *team*," she corrected. "Go Panda Bears! Woo-hooo!" She flung her leg mockingly and shimmied imaginary pom-poms above her head like a cheerleader.

D'Melo pressed his lips firmly together. "We're the *Panthers*."

"Whatever, dude."

"I didn't know you like basketball."

"I *love* basketball. It was awesome seeing you score all those touchdowns!"

"That's football," he said, shaking his head. D'Melo brightened with an idea. He asked Moses to toss him a ball. He handed it to Zara.

"What do you want me to do with this thing?" she said, examining it. "You want me to bounce it or something?"

"Well, actually, it's called *dribble*."

"Do you mean, like this?" Zara dribbled between her legs, then behind her back. She asked Moses for a second ball. She dribbled both simultaneously, crossing them back and forth. Then, while still dribbling one ball, she shot the other into the basket. "Oh my!" she said, acting ditzy. "Did I just score a touchdown?"

D'Melo realized he had been bamboozled. "Why didn't you tell me you can ball?" he asked, flabbergasted.

"What, you assume I can't play basketball because I'm white? Or maybe because I'm a girl?"

"Well, neither," he quipped. "I didn't think you could ball because you're goofy."

"Oh *shut up*," she countered. "Goofy can take you one-on-one anytime."

"Oh really?" D'Melo found Zara's spunk entertaining. "I'd love to see that!"

Moses propped his broom against the wall and settled on the bleachers. There was no way he was going to miss this.

"Okay hot shot," D'Melo said. "Let's make a deal. If you score on me, I'll treat you to a movie."

"Is that how you get girls to go out with you?" Zara needled, then pretended to vomit. "That's so lame. Also, what if I don't want to go to the movies with you?"

"Then just miss the shot," he smirked.

Zara slipped off her ankle boots and tossed them behind her. She slid out of her olive- green hoodie. She faced him, her uniform now yellow bootcut jeans and an oversized white T-shirt that hung low in the back.

"Are we ready now?" D'Melo said, amused. "Is there anything else you'd like to remove?"

"Just your ego," she jabbed. Zara crouched and dribbled deliberately. She faked left, checking D'Melo's feet for balance. Then she dribbled hard right, crossed left, spun back, and motioned to shoot. D'Melo leapt to block her shot. She ducked under him and reversed the ball into the hoop with her left hand.

"Oooh, scorched!" she yelled, hunching over and cupping her gaping mouth. "What happened? It seemed like you Baryshnikov-ed right by me."

D'Melo grinned, impressed. "I was tired. You know, I *did* just play a whole game."

"Whatever, dude. You got scorched. Own it!" She rolled the balls to Moses. "Thank you, sir." Moses gave her a 'you're welcome' wink.

"So where'd you learn to ball like that, all smooth and shifty. You're like a little Stephanie Curry!"

"I'm from North Carolina, so I like to think of myself more like a Michelle Jordan!"

"You should play for Lincoln Downs. It'd be all like—" D'Melo pretended he was the announcer. "At starting point guard, 5'4", from Hillbilly Redneck, North Carolina, Double Z! Zarrraaa Zanic!"

"I'm 5'7"," she edited. "And it's pronounced, Zan-*ich*."

"My bad. I can't tell the height or names of short people."

"Ha ha," she said. "But if I joined the school team, that would be wrong. I'd take all your glory."

The truth was, Zara couldn't bear the thought of playing basketball anymore. It was too painful a reminder. Her mother had never missed a single one of her games, even when deathly ill with colon cancer. Toward the end, Zara's games were the only thing her mother would leave the house for.

D'Melo dashed to the bleachers. "Let's go." Zara gazed at him, bewildered. "Aren't we gonna camp out at the DunChem CEO's house? Look," he said, unzipping his backpack. "I got my toothbrush, toothpaste, and a change of clothes—because, you never know," he said. "I also brought a book."

Zara tilted her head quizzically. "Do you think we're staying at the Marriott Hotel? It's going to be dark out there."

D'Melo delved into his backpack for a night-light.

Oh, my God. Is he serious? she thought. "What else do you have in there? Maybe a portable stove so you can prepare a four-course meal?"

"Ahh . . . dang. I didn't even think of that." D'Melo wagged a fist. "Next time! But I did bring some beef jerky, bread, and a bottle of Gatorade, in case I get low on electrolytes. Don't worry," he assured her. "I brought something for you, too." Corn bread crumbled in his hands. "Straight from Chubby's."

"Do you realize that corn bread is made with butter? And butter comes from . . .?" Zara paused, rolling out an inviting palm.

"Milk?" he said.

"That's right. And milk comes from . . .?"

"Dang . . . cows," he realized. "My bad, dawg. Well, I guess you gonna be hungry then."

Zara peeked into the backpack. "You're kidding. Are those swim trunks? Are you planning to take a dip in this dude's Jacuzzi and then maybe cool off in his Olympic-sized pool?"

"Well, you never know. Oooh, and I definitely had to bring toilet paper because—"

"Let me guess," she quipped sarcastically, "—because you never know?"

"Exactly! Marls and Kaz are meeting us there. I hope that's okay." D'Melo continued before Zara could even answer. "Are we stopping by the drugstore so you can change?"

Zara raised her arms to her sides. She peered down at her chosen ensemble. "What's wrong with this?"

"Oh, nothing. I just thought you'd want something more, you know, campy."

"Dude, we're not going camping! *And*, this is how I dress. It's casual and comfortable."

Zara hadn't always dressed so fashionably. Growing up, she was something of a tomboy. As long as she could climb trees in it, her outfit was just right. D'Melo's comment triggered a memory of one of her final conversations with her mother.

"*Vezi,*" her mother said, which meant "little angel" in Nečzian, "You're the most vibrant and colorful person I've ever known. Don't use clothes to hide yourself. Use clothes to express yourself. I'm deteriorating by the hour and will die soon. But you're alive! So be alive, every moment."

D'Melo turned to Moses, who was sweeping conscientiously. "Mr. Moses, you sure I can't help?"

"I always appreciate it, D'Melo. But not tonight. I can see you have more important things to do."

"Okay, next time, then," D'Melo conceded. He asked Moses to remind his son about training Sunday morning. "We'll work on his crossover. And don't worry, I'll have him back in plenty of time for church."

"He's getting good, you know," Moses said, gleaming proudly. "You better be careful; he might end up breaking all your school records." Moses glanced at the records board on the wall. D'Melo's name topped most of the categories.

"I hope he does, Mr. Moses. Nothing would give me more joy than to see his name above mine someday."

D'Melo spent much of his free time training kids. He hoped basketball would keep them off the streets, like it did for him. Lincoln Downs was rife with gang activity. But the gang leader, T-Bo, had never tried to recruit D'Melo because of his NBA potential. Instead, he offered him gifts—clothes, the latest basketball sneakers, and jewelry—expecting to one day bask in the glory of D'Melo's NBA stardom. When Baba found out, he nearly lost his mind. D'Melo had never seen his father so furious. He made D'Melo return everything.

As they were leaving the gym, Zara gazed wonderingly at D'Melo. She didn't know what to make of him. He was super smart, had girls fawning all over him, reporters chasing him, and scouts salivating at the thought of recruiting him. And here he was, practically begging the janitor to allow him to clean the gym.

"You truly don't care about playing in the NBA, do you?" she said.

"I mean, who doesn't want to be in the NBA? But," he said, reflectively, "when you watch your mom die right in front of you, your priorities change."

D'Melo offered no further details of that fateful morning, and Zara didn't ask. Instead she sighed empathetically, remembering her own mother.

"Things don't have the same meaning anymore," he said. "Certainly not money or fame. I would trade the NBA for one more day with Mom anytime. I realize that this sounds crazy to people."

Zara thought, *Not to me.*

A sleek black car glided silently along the lengthy driveway. Marley exclaimed, "Oh Sweet Lord; that's a Tesla Model S!" He wriggled out of his sleeping bag. "Do you know that car has an autopilot system that can control the throttle, brakes, and steering. *And* it's electric!" He shot a dubious gaze at Zara. "Which is good for the environment, by the way."

Zara ignored him and grabbed her sign off the grass. The sign read: "Water belongs to all of us; how can one man choose to destroy it?" She thrust another sign into D'Melo's chest. "Here, hold this," she said. D'Melo's sign read: "When all the waters are polluted, only then will you discover that you can't drink money."

"Ohhh, snap," Kazim fretted. "He's stopping!"

The darkly tinted window slid down. "You." The driver pointed in their direction.

"Who, me?" Kazim trembled, jabbing a thumb into his chest. "Hey man, I ain't got nuttin' to do with this. I don't mind pollution."

"Oh, my God, dude. *Seriously?*" Zara nudged Kazim aside and sidled up to the window.

"I hope he ain't callin' the po-po," Kazim mumbled. "I ain't tryin' to get arrested over some dirty water."

The gate swung open. The car passed through. Zara strode back over to the boyz.

"Are we gettin' arrested?" Kazim blurted. "My mom's gonna kill me!"

"No, dude," Zara grimaced. "Get a hold of yourself."

Zara then conveyed her brief conversation with the CEO. Apparently, he had seen Zara in the newspaper. Her passion had resuscitated his long-forgotten love of nature. He had spent much of his childhood in West Virginia, appreciating the purity of the Appalachian Mountains. So miraculously, just before leaving the office, he had actually tasked his head engineer to figure a way to limit the pollutants his company produces. Also, he had invited Zara to give his staff environmental-awareness training.

"Zara, we did it!" Kazim claimed then moved in for a hug.

"Dude, no." Zara repelled him at arm's length.

"*We* did it?" Marley snipped. "Weren't you the fool over there talking about 'I ain't trying to get arrested over some dirty water?'" Zara gave Marley a fist bump.

After a few minutes of celebratory recapping of the evening's events, they took an Uber back to Lincoln Downs. Marley and Kazim got dropped first. They bopped up their shared stoop, arguing about which one of them had helped more that night.

On the ride to the drugstore, Zara's energy flattened. She gazed wistfully into the distance. D'Melo stole a glance or two at her every few blocks. The car pulled up to the store. Zara spun to D'Melo, who quickly averted his eyes.

"Hey, don't forget, you owe me a movie. How about tomorrow? *Queen of Sheba*, 2 p.m."

"The cartoon?" D'Melo balked.

"What, are you too cool to watch an animated movie?"

"Nah, I didn't say that. I'll drop by your spot at 1:30."

Zara plodded to the alley side of the drugstore. She dragged up the stairs that led to the apartment. D'Melo asked the Uber driver to go slowly. He wanted to make sure Zara got inside.

D'Melo found himself fascinated by how Zara didn't seem to be afraid of anything or anyone. She had camped out, by herself, on the driveway of one of the most powerful men in Philadelphia. And somehow, she had gotten him to reconsider how his business operates in practically no time. Until that night, apparently no one else had been able to do that. *But then, why isn't she happy? What happened? Did I do something wrong?*

When he finally climbed into bed that night, D'Melo thought about how he hadn't yet grasped the depth and mystery of Zara. Would he ever get a glimpse, he wondered, into her seemingly tumultuous inner world?

CHAPTER FOUR

Taji Anaru!

Saturday for most high schoolers meant a day of rest after a tax-ing week. But for the boyz, it meant it was time to get paid. Few Saturdays remained to make a quick buck at the Citadel. Winter was fast approaching, and in Philadelphia it could arrive at any moment with unforgiving vigor. Then, graduation would follow on its frigid heels. So the boyz were keen to seize every opportunity.

Usually D'Melo eagerly awaited getting on the court, not for the money, but to do what he loved most. But this Saturday was different. The boyz ambled through his door only to find D'Melo sporting jeans and his favorite Meek Mill T-shirt.

"Come on, dawg! Get ready," Jeylan urged. "Those Whitman Park busters think they can take down the LD Boyz. If they wanna give us their hard-earned cash, who are we to deny them that?"

"I can't ball today," D'Melo said.

"Stop playin', man. Grab your kicks, let's bounce."

"I'm not playin'. I'm going to the movies."

The boyz were flabbergasted, realizing that he wasn't joking. D'Melo had never missed a Saturday at the Citadel.

"Can't you and Baba go to a later flick?"

"I'm not going with Baba." Now D'Melo had everyone's full attention—who else would he be going with besides Baba or them?

It clicked for Kazim. "Ohhh, snap! You're going with Zara!"

"Who?" Jeylan scoffed. "That white girl?"

Although the conversation had turned tense, there was no chance Kazim was going to miss this opportunity to mock D'Melo. "Look at you, Mister 'I'm not messin' with girls until I'm ready to get married.'"

"It ain't like that," D'Melo retorted. "I lost a bet."

"So what y'all gonna see?" Kazim queried with interest, stoking Jeylan's fire.

D'Melo mumbled, *"Queen of Sheba."*

"The cartoon?" Jeylan's voice rose a couple of octaves. "Let me guess, Princess Snowflake wanted to see that? Maybe after the movie she can take you to a Garth Brooks concert and you can square-dance the night away. Don't worry about us, though. We'll be at the Citadel losin' our grad money." The boyz had been saving their Citadel winnings for years to pay for a graduation trip.

"Jey," D'Melo exhorted indignantly. "You need to move on from this hatred you have for white folks."

"Whatever, dawg," Jeylan snipped. "So, if you're not ballin' today, who we gonna get to run with us?" D'Melo directed his eyes at Marley. "Man, you trippin'! You know that fool can't ball."

"Well," D'Melo suggested. "Just don't pass him the rock."

"Heyyy . . . guys," Marley interjected. "I'm right here, and I *do* have feelings."

"Enjoy your cartoon with Snowflake," Jeylan spat. "Let's go, y'all." He stormed out.

Kazim smirked at D'Melo. "You go, playa." He punched D'Melo admiringly on the arm on his way out.

It was an unusually toasty day for October. While the boyz were sweating it out on the court, D'Melo was sweating almost as much trying to keep pace with Zara. His light gray shirt grew darker by the moment. But Zara's loose-fit blouse, tied in the front, was completely dry. There wasn't a bead of sweat on her forehead, as her open-heel booties clicked briskly down the sidewalk.

"Hey, Usain Bolt," D'Melo quipped. "I think we broke the sound barrier back there."

"Sorry, dude. I didn't get my morning run in. So I'm feeling a shade guilty," she reasoned, as she polished off an eggplant and avocado sandwich.

Zara ran six miles every morning. But on the days she needed to work through something vexing her mind, she would easily exceed ten miles.

"Can I run with you sometime?"

"Do you think you'll be able to keep up?" She grinned dubiously. If there was one thing that Zara did well, it was run. She didn't run for exercise or to shed a few unwanted pounds. She ran to survive. It helped her deal with the hyper-intense feelings she suffered on a daily basis. Like D'Melo on the basketball court, for forty minutes every morning Zara was in a world of her own.

Suddenly, Zara's stride tapered.

"You don't have to go *that* slow," D'Melo teased. "I'm not disabled."

Zara closed her eyes and inhaled a steady breath.

"Are you okay?" D'Melo said.

"Yeah. I think it's just a bit of anxiety."

"What are you anxious about?" D'Melo attempted to lighten the mood. "Me leaving you in the dust during our run?"

"Dream on, dude." Zara struggled a smile onto her face. "Let's talk about something else. Thinking about anxiety just gives me more anxiety."

D'Melo had a ton of questions he had been wanting to ask her. Why was she living with her grandparents? Where was her dad? Why did she move to Lincoln Downs just a year before graduating? Why does she stay to herself at school? What does she want to do after she graduates?

But instead, he spouted, "So what's your favorite movie? I'm gonna guess, *Erin Brockovich.*"

"Ehhhh!" she rebuffed, like a buzzer on a game show when the contestant gives an incorrect answer. "Good guess, though. My all-time favorite is *Inside Out.* You've probably never even heard of it."

"What, you assume I don't watch animated movies because I'm black? Or maybe it's because I'm a guy?"

"Touché," she said. "So are you saying you've seen it?"

"Well, let me think. Hmmm . . ." D'Melo gazed insincerely into the distance. "Is *Inside Out* the film about a little girl named Riley who faces mental struggles when she moves to a new city? And, are Riley's emotions portrayed as characters as she navigates her new life?" D'Melo grinned smugly. "Should I continue?"

Zara pursed her lips, realizing she was now the one who had been bamboozled.

"The brilliance of that film," D'Melo continued, "lies in how it manages to fluidly traverse the line of reality. What I mean is, it's able to broach reality and yet be far from it at the same time. It won the Academy Award for Best Animated Feature in 2016. Is that the movie you're talking about?"

"Hilarious, dude. Are you always this ostentatious?" Zara motioned to twist the cap off her invisible good word jar. "Clunk." She tightened the cap back. "'Ostentatious'! Good word," she said proudly.

"Why do you say, 'clunk'?"

"Because that's the sound the word makes when it hits the bottom of the jar."

"Is the word made out of lead?"

"Oh, shut up. Well, what sound do you think the word should make?"

"I think it should be, 'Swish.'"

"Of course, you do. Why did I even ask?"

Zara halted abruptly. Her face blanched, then she doubled over.

"Hey," D'Melo said, alarmed. "Maybe you should sit."

Instead, Zara lifted her weary head. Her unfocused gaze honed in on the white row house at the corner. She staggered toward it, clutching her chest.

"Where you going?" D'Melo shouted fretfully.

Zara peered at the house from outside the chain-link fence that boxed in the tiny yard. She grasped the latch on the fence gate, then snatched her hand painfully back. The metal fence was burning hot from the high sun. She nimbly unlatched the gate, then jolted it open with the bottom of her boot. The gate crashed against the inside of the fence.

"Whoa, whoa," D'Melo said. "What are you doing!"

She hastened along the concrete path and mounted the steps to the porch. The front door was locked. She peered through the porch window, her vision obscured by sheer curtains.

"Zara, please tell me you know these people?" D'Melo said, his voice sounding strained with worry.

Zara ran around the side of the house and down the alleyway to the backyard. D'Melo followed her. "Here, hold this," she said, shoving her purse into D'Melo's stomach. She unstrapped her boots and kicked them off. After hopping the fence, she latched onto a tree branch and dug her feet into the craggy bark. Within seconds she was high enough to vault onto the porch roof.

"Zara!" D'Melo shouted. "You're gonna get us killed!"

Zara cupped her hands against the windowpane. Her eyes probed into the house. She screamed down to D'Melo, "Call 911! Now!" D'Melo dropped the purse and fumbled for his phone.

Zara tried to lift the window. It was locked. She slipped off her blouse and wrapped it around her hand. With a swift jab, she shattered the glass. She punched out the remaining shards from the frame then contorted her nimble body through the window.

On the balls of her bare feet, she navigated through the glass fragments to the elderly woman sprawled on the floor. Zara sat on her feet next to her and rested the woman's head on her lap.

"You're gonna be okay," she comforted, having no idea whether her words were true. Zara patted the sweat off the woman's sweet mocha face. "The ambulance is on its way."

"This is really embarrassing," the woman huffed, each breath a struggle. "I'm lying on a floor in my pajamas in the middle of the day." The lightness of her words stood in sharp contrast to the intensity in her eyes. Zara was momentarily taken aback at how profoundly the woman peered into her, as if boring into her soul.

"You think that's embarrassing, huh? I'm pretty sure I can top that," Zara said, trying to take the woman's mind off her condition. "One time, I dreamt that soldiers were chasing me across a field. Bullets were buzzing past. The forest edge was about thirty feet in front of me. I knew that if I could just make it to the tree line, I'd have a chance. I sprinted as fast as my legs would move. When I reached the forest, the soldiers followed right behind me. I clambered up a tall tree. My shoulder was burning. I'm not sure why. But the pain made it a real struggle to climb."

The old woman got excited, as if she was living the dream with Zara. "Oh no!" she exclaimed. A cloudy white curtain descended over her eyes. "The blood!" she wailed frightfully. Zara sat up, backing away from the woman's sudden outburst. "The blood! Don't let it drop!" the woman cried out.

"Ma'am." Zara caressed her cheek. "Are you okay?" *Where's that ambulance!*

The woman's eyes appeared lucid again. "What happened next?" she said, as if nothing peculiar had just occurred.

"Well," Zara pushed past the woman's bizarre behavior. "One of the soldiers shined his flashlight up the tree. I made myself as small as I could. As the light crawled just beneath me, I woke up."

"That's thrilling stuff," the woman said feebly. "But how's it embarrassing?"

"Oh, sorry," Zara said, rocking forward and smiling under her hand, embarrassed now too. "I got so caught up in the dream that I forgot why I was telling it. Well, my dreams are so real sometimes that I act them out in my sleep. And, unfortunately, this was one of those times. I opened my eyes to my neighbors videoing me in my front yard. I was perched in a tree in my underwear."

The woman laughed into a choking gasp for air. Zara stroked her woolen curls. "I just realized how rude I'm being," the woman said. "You're a guest in my house and trying to save my life, no less, and I haven't even asked what your name is."

"It's Zara."

"Oh! That name fits you perfectly. Do you know what 'Zara' means in my language? Well, silly me. How could you know? It means 'light.' And here you are, just as luminous as you can be." Zara dabbed the woman's forehead. "Your aura is so brilliant. There's light all around you, like an angel."

"Wow," Zara said, trying to sound excited. "And my whole life I thought my name was just the Nečzian version of Sara! I hate to disappoint you, though. I'm far from an angel. But thank you for saying that. And what's your name?"

"Yande Keba," the woman said hoarsely.

"Do you know what that name means in my heart?" Zara said. "It means, lovely woman who I am privileged to have met."

Just then, an ambulance siren blared in the distance.

"They're here!" Zara said. She shot down the stairs. She paused in the foyer; an elaborate fireplace caught her eye. *That's interesting. I've never seen anything like that.*

The ambulance squealed around the corner. D'Melo was in the

street waving it down. Zara frantically led the paramedics to Ms. Keba. They carefully transferred Ms. Keba onto a gurney and carried her out of the house.

Just before they slid her into the ambulance, Ms. Keba sat up abruptly. Her eyes were wild, as if she had seen a ghost. She tried to climb off the gurney toward D'Melo. The paramedics laid her back down.

Ms. Keba slipped a trembling hand out from under the white sheet covering her. She meekly grasped D'Melo's hand. She guided it toward her face and kissed his knuckles. Adoration gushed from her eyes like a cascading waterfall. "I've been searching for you my whole life," she said softly. She lowered her gaze in profound reverence. "And fate would have it that *you* found *me,* and just moments before my great ascent.

"Taji Anaru!" she called out, as vociferously as her weak breath allowed. "Please," she implored the paramedics. "Permit me the honor of bowing before him." Ms. Keba began wriggling out from under the sheet. But the paramedics eased her flat and lifted the gurney into the ambulance.

Zara climbed in behind her.

"The great day has come!" Ms. Keba proclaimed. "I can now die in peace." She gazed at Zara beamingly. "I knew you were an angel. You led me to him! Please beg *Ahadi* (the promised one) to forgive me for not kneeling before him."

"Okay, Miss," the paramedic urged. "We have to go." Zara kissed Ms. Keba's clammy forehead and climbed down from the ambulance.

Ms. Keba raised her arm high and stretched out four fingers. She clenched her fingers into a fist then rested it over her heart. *"Taji Anaru! Taji Anaru!"* she chanted, just before the paramedics shut the doors. The ambulance roared off, sirens wailing.

Zara whispered something under her breath then turned a curious eye toward D'Melo. "What was that all about?" D'Melo shrugged causally, seemingly unmoved by Ms. Keba's excessive reverence toward him.

"When I was in the ambulance, she asked me to request your—" Zara caught herself—"well actually, she said *Ahadi's* forgiveness for not being able to kneel before you. Why would she do that?"

"I don't know. Maybe she's seen me ball," D'Melo quipped.

"How can you make jokes after something like this?"

"Well, what can I say? She was probably delirious. I mean, she *was* having a heart attack or something."

"Maybe, but her mind seemed pretty clear . . . *although*, she did say I'm an angel."

"*You?* An angel?" D'Melo said playfully. "Well, that proves it. She was definitely out of her gourd."

"You know," Zara replied, unamused. "I think you missed your calling as a comedian."

They started to meander aimlessly, the movie having completely slipped their minds. D'Melo reflected out loud on the strange episode with Ms. Keba. "Taji Anaru, Taji Anaru," he repeated in a whisper. "It sounds so familiar. I think it could be Kipaji." Although D'Melo didn't know the language, he remembered how it sounded. His parents would speak in their mother tongue when they wanted to baffle D'Melo's meddling ears.

"But if Ms. Keba is Kipaji, I'm sure Baba would know her."

"Well," Zara said. "There's only one way to find out."

They headed to D'Melo's house. On the way, D'Melo asked Zara what she had muttered to herself when Ms. Keba was driven away.

"Oh, I didn't know you heard that. It's a Nečzian thing. Whenever something important was happening in my life, my mom would whisper '*Edu.*' It always made me feel like everything was going to be alright. Essentially, it means good luck, but in a way of calling on something greater than yourself for help. Whenever my mom was taken to the hospital, I'd whisper '*Edu*' to myself. And she came back every time." A rush of sorrow washed through Zara as she remembered, *except the last time.*

Baba was in the backyard tending to his vegetable garden. When he burrowed his hands into the earth, he was momentarily transported back to Kipaji. Growing food was something he and Diata, D'Melo's mother, cherished doing together. They loved rising with the dawning sun to harvest the fruits and vegetables that grew in the cool, moist air of Amanzi Mountain.

D'Melo and Zara squeaked through the rickety back-porch door. "You two are home a little early, aren't you?" Baba said, as he wiped an itch from his nose, leaving a soil smudge on his cheek. "Dinner won't be ready for another couple of hours." He squinted up at them through the blinding sunlight. "Zara, I'm making something special for you! A traditional Kipaji dish called *Wanjiru Joma*. It's a stew with onions, potatoes, corn, and an assortment of beans in a spicy tomato sauce. How's that sound?"

Zara perked up. "It sounds like I'm going to have a delicious ballet of flavors pirouetting on my tongue!"

D'Melo flipped his palms upward. "Can't you just say, 'That sounds good?'"

Zara creased her lips, *Whatever, dude.*

"Baba," D'Melo said. "I need to ask you something."

"I've been waiting for this moment," Baba beamed. "The answer is yes! You have my permission to marry this lovely young lady."

"No, Baba!" D'Melo said, flustered. D'Melo glanced at Zara, who of course was playing it up. With a hand on her hip, she batted her lashes at D'Melo over her shoulder. "Baba, that's not what I was gonna ask."

"Why not? She's tall enough for you." Zara flattened her hand on her head, as if measuring herself. Baba nudged his glasses up the bridge of his nose, inspecting Zara. "She's a bit on the skinny side, but she'll put on some padding after a couple of babies."

Zara's tune now changed. Her mouth hung open, *Huh?*

"You talk about her all the time," Baba continued, much to D'Melo's chagrin. "It's obvious you—"

D'Melo's eyes shot open nearly wide enough for them to pop out of his head. "BABAAA! Please. I beg." He seized Baba's face. "Pull yourself together. I just want to ask you about something someone said to me." D'Melo explained what happened with Ms. Keba.

Baba sobered in an instant. "Are you sure she said, *'Taji Anaru'?*"

D'Melo nodded.

Baba slid off his gardening gloves. He plunked down pensively on the 10-gallon plastic paint container he used for compost.

"So, *'Taji Anaru' is* Kipaji?" D'Melo asked.

"It is, son." Baba scrutinized D'Melo peculiarly before lowering his gaze, like Ms. Keba had.

"Do you know Yande Keba?"

Baba was quiet, searching his brain. "It's a Kipaji name, but it doesn't sound familiar." While Baba knew most of the Kipajis on the East Coast, there were a number whom he wouldn't know. Many of them had fought with the rebels against the Malungan government. When the rebellion was quashed, they had to leave Malunga or risk being executed. After relocating to their new country, they kept a very low profile. Most even changed their names.

"Zara," Baba said. "You were with Madam Keba most of the time. What can you tell me about her?"

"Umm…." Zara brought herself back inside Ms. Keba's house. "Well, she was really calm for someone who was dying. She had a deepness about her; the way she looked at me. Actually, she wasn't really looking *at* me. She seemed to be looking *into* me, as if she was trying to figure out something about me."

"What about inside the house?" Baba wondered. "Did you notice anything different?"

"No, not really. I was only in her bedroom, and it seemed pretty normal." Suddenly, Zara's voice rose. "Oh, wait a second," she said. She closed her eyes to focus her memory. "When I was waiting for the paramedics, I noticed a small fireplace in her living room. But it wasn't really a fireplace. It was more like a fire *pit*. It was way too small to heat a room. It was only this high"—Zara dropped her hand to just above her knee—"and about a foot wide. It was made of a rock I've never seen before."

Baba reached for his phone as Zara continued.

"It was reddish-brown with tiny crystals embedded in it," she said. "A slab ran across the top with engravings. They looked like—"

Baba showed Zara his phone screen. "This?" he guessed. It was an image of a deep purple flag with a diamond-shaped crest at the center. Golden rays emanated from the quadrantal crest. Each quadrant held a unique symbol. Clockwise from the top, the symbols looked like water, fire, mineral, and air.

"Yes!" Zara exclaimed, tapping the image. "These symbols were engraved in the stone."

"And was there a tall weed-like plant somewhere nearby?"

"How'd you know?" she said, astonished.

"The plant is a variant of *iboga*, which is only found in Kipaji. It's used to induce visions. It's dried and then burned at a very high temperature. The wall surrounding the fire pit was volcanic rock, which absorbs extreme heat."

D'Melo realized how little he knew about Kipaji—and his father, for that matter.

Baba continued, "Madam Keba must be a *Wanaje*. Every now and again, a Wanaje is born in the Choma (Fire) clan, which is one of the four Kipaji clans. Wanajes possess a special gift: they are able to see things that others cannot. So I guess in English "Wanaje" would be something like "seer." Wanajes are highly respected in Kipaji. They often act as special advisors to the Umoja Council, the elected leadership of Kipaji."

Zara suddenly shuddered. Baba noticed tiny bumps on her arm.

"It looks like you have *cutis anserina*," he said.

Zara's face flushed red.

"Don't worry," Baba chuckled. "It's just a fancy name for goose bumps. Are you cold? It's ninety degrees out here."

"I'm fine. It's only a chill. It'll go away in a minute." Baba rubbed Zara's arms to warm her.

"Baba, you still haven't told us what *'Taji Anaru'* means," D'Melo said. "Ms. Keba kept saying it over and over."

"'*Taji Anaru'* literally means, 'Return of the Crown.'" Baba went on to explain, "Legend has it that over two thousand years ago, Kipaji was established by a great king. He unified the four tribes that now make up Kipaji—the Amanzi, Choma, Joto, and Upepo. It was said that during his nineteen-year reign, Kipaji was at the height of its glory. The king infused the culture of Kipaji with a philosophy of life called *Ubuntu*. It's an acknowledgement that we are who we are only through other people. It's the pinnacle of human cohesion.

"So, by saying *'Taji Anaru'*, Madam Keba was probably expressing that you helping her was like *Ubuntu*—a return to how it was at the time of the Spirit King."

D'Melo frowned. "Why have you never told me about this?"

"You're forgetting that when you were young, I recounted many stories about Kipaji. But you scoffed at me. "I think your exact words were, 'Baba, you can't really believe these fairy tales. Why are Africans always making up such ridiculous stories?' After that, I thought it would be best to wait for you to become open to Kipaji. But you never did."

D'Melo lowered his eyes, ashamed. "I'm sorry, Baba. I'm open now. Could you please tell us more about the seers?"

Baba continued. "The last Wanaje left Kipaji before I was born. So I have only heard stories about her. This particular Wanaje had a vision of the Ahadi, the promised one. She said that he was lost and needed help finding his way back to Kipaji. The Council members dismissed her as a heretic. To point out the error in the Wanaje's vision, the Council reminded her of the king's final words:

> "The seed of the will of the Great Spirit has been sown in this hallowed land. Our purpose has been served, allowing for the sun of our existence on this earthly plane to set. In our absence, you must remain ever vigilant against the evil of discord. But if the darksome night descends upon this land once again, rest assured, we will return unto you from the *Walipote*. And with the power of the Great Spirit, we will march together in serried lines to hasten the dawn of the light of unity.

"While the word '*Walipote*' has caused some confusion among Kipaji historians, for centuries it had been widely accepted as meaning 'Unknown Realm.' And that had been interpreted as the 'Spiritual World.' But the Wanaje insisted that the king's final words could be interpreted differently. She conceded that the word '*Walipote*' means 'Unknown Realm'; however, if that same word is not capitalized ('*walipote*'), it means 'a lost world.' And because the king's words were shared with the people only verbally, he could have used *walipote* with a lower case 'w.' So, searching her vision, the Wanaje concluded that the king would return but would be lost in a foreign world.

"The Council didn't buy it. It said that even if the king found himself in a foreign world, why wouldn't he just return to Kipaji?

"The Wanaje explained that when someone is lost, it doesn't have to mean physically lost. The king could be lost from himself—meaning that he may be unaware of who he is. If so, he would need to be led back to Kipaji. There, he would once again unite with his twin brother, as he did two millennia ago.

"The Council members wouldn't listen to any more of 'this sacrilege', as they called it. They branded the Wanaje a charlatan. Life in

Kipaji became unbearable for her. So she left, vowing not to return until she found the lost king. She was never heard from again. It was assumed that she never found the king and died somewhere in the world."

"So, Ms. Keba is this Wanaje and she thinks I'm the lost king?" D'Melo said, chuckling. "The paramedics must have gone way overboard with the morphine. Because obviously Ms. Keba was high."

Baba stared at D'Melo, suddenly transfixed. His body became limp. The paint container he was sitting on wobbled. D'Melo grabbed Baba before he teetered off.

"Baba?" D'Melo said, worried.

"It's just the heat, son," he said woozily. D'Melo and Zara helped him inside. They brought him a moist towel and stretched it across his forehead. They shuffled to the kitchen to pour Baba a cool glass of lemonade.

"You see," D'Melo said. "I told you Ms. Keba was delirious. The king has a twin brother, and I don't have *any* sibling, let alone a twin." He teasingly nudged Zara's head. She swatted his hand away.

"Well, that's good," she retorted. "Because I could never get used to bowing and calling you 'Your Majesty.'"

"After our rematch on the court, and I school you like this," D'Melo dribbled an imaginary ball between his legs and motioned a jump shot, "you'll have no choice but to call me 'Your Majesty.'" D'Melo interrupted himself. "Oooh, that's it!"

Zara glared at him, apparently leery of what he was scheming.

"That can be our next bet," he dared. "If I score on you, you have to call me 'Your Majesty' at school for one full day."

Zara scrunched her face at him. "I am *not* calling you 'Your Majesty' at school or anywhere else. And by the way, there will be no rematch until you make good on the last bet, you big welsher."

"Hey, it wasn't my fault you got all Wonder Woman on everybody," he said, sliding his fists in a circular motion in front of him.

"*Ting, ting!*" He made sounds like he was deflecting bullets with Bracelets of Submission. "Oh, and," he said. "I've been meaning to ask you. Why were you naked when you came out of Ms. Keba's house?"

Baba lifted a judging eyebrow.

Zara bit her lip and narrowed her eyes at D'Melo. "You know I wasn't naked! I took off my shirt to break the window." She turned to Baba. "I had on a *very* modest sports bra."

D'Melo hummed the *Wonder Woman* theme song, as he mimicked Zara in slow motion scaling the tree and smashing the glass.

"Oh, my God!" she said, shoving him. "Baba, how do you have such a jerk for a son?"

"Well, I guess the apple does fall far from the tree sometimes," Baba said, smiling. "And a rotten one, at that."

Zara cupped her mouth at D'Melo. "Oooh, scorched."

As Baba delighted in their playful banter, his emotions swirled like a mighty tornado. He began to piece together the possibility of D'Melo being the lost king. The thought of his son as the King of Kipaji was as monumental as it was preposterous. *But, what if it's true?* His heart sank mournfully. He realized that D'Melo would never live the life he had always dreamed for himself. His world would be turned upside down and inside out. He would never find a moment's peace. The eyes of the world would scrutinize him with laser intensity. Even worse, his life would be in perpetual jeopardy. Pernicious forces would prey upon him incessantly, either to bring his power under their control or to take his life so he didn't hinder them from achieving their corrupt desires.

Baba's eyes misted as he observed how joyful and easy D'Melo and Zara were with each other. Then his stomach knotted in anguish as the Spirit King's covenant to never marry rushed to mind. So if D'Melo *is* the Ahadi, he and Zara would not be able to share a life together. And, perhaps worst of all, D'Melo would never have what he had desired most: children.

CHAPTER FIVE

The Nightmare

After dinner, as had become customary, D'Melo escorted Zara home. A welcome breeze rustled the amber and scarlet-tinged trees, creating an autumn ambience. D'Melo and Zara padded along the leafy sidewalk wordlessly, replaying the day's events in their minds.

Zara broke the silence, pondering out loud about Ms. Keba thinking D'Melo was some sort of king. "As much as I hate to admit it, you were right," she said. "Ms. Keba must have been delirious. At one point, her eyes glazed over and she said something about not letting the blood drop. It was so bizarre!"

"I wonder how she's doing," D'Melo said, concerned. "Maybe we should stop by the hospital."

"She's gone, D'Melo," Zara said delicately. "She died soon after we got to your house. Remember when Baba told me I had that strange disease—goose bumps?"

D'Melo scratched his head, *How did having goose bumps tell her that someone died?*

Zara answered his question without him having to ask it. "It wasn't the goose bumps that alerted me. It was the peacefully frigid sensation that swooshed through my body. I've had similar feelings when people close to me have passed away. Ms. Keba died happy though. Thanks to you."

"Ohhkay," D'Melo said, feeling a tad freaked out. "But how'd you even know that she needed help in the first place?"

"I didn't. I just knew someone in that house was suffering."

D'Melo lifted his hands, *Well, how'd you know that?*

Zara shrugged uncertainly. "I get strong feelings sometimes."

She explained that she was six years old when the first of these mysterious sensations struck. She was climbing trees with her friends in the forest behind her house. Then, for no apparent reason, her throat constricted. She struggled for air, wheezing desperately. In a flash, she sensed that she was experiencing someone else's suffering, and that it was coming from her house. She shot home into suffocating bitter smoke. She found her mother in bed, motionless. Zara shook her frantically. Her mom woke, groggy and coughing harshly. After her mother got her bearings, she scooped up Zara and bolted out of the house.

"So," D'Melo said. "You know when someone's in trouble. That's awesome!"

Zara sighed. "Try to imagine not only feeling your own pain but other people's also."

D'Melo winced sympathetically.

"Okay, now try to imagine that you can't escape it, even when you're asleep.

"There's this one nightmare that's haunted me for years," she went on, her voice quavering. "A woman is in the front seat of a car. Out of nowhere, an SUV blasts into her full speed."

D'Melo unconsciously slowed his gait, hanging onto Zara's every word.

"At first, it was like any other accident, but then the SUV didn't stop."

D'Melo's pulse quickened.

"It actually revved up again. White smoke curled around its furiously spinning wheels. For months after the dream, I couldn't get the smell of burning rubber out of my head. The SUV pushed the woman's car onto the other side of the highway. A truck slammed its brakes but wasn't able to stop in time. Her car was sent tumbling. When it settled, it was nothing more than a heap of mangled metal."

D'Melo's chest squeezed sharply.

"What's horrible is that even though the woman's body was terribly shattered, that pain paled in comparison to the suffering in her heart. I got an image of murky fog descending ominously through her body, devouring the flickering light of her soul. Eerie howls of rage, crushing guilt, and agonizing sorrow echo inside her. A small child's face flashes in the darkness—a child she had previously lost. Then, a desperate heaviness overcomes her when she realizes that she is about to abandon another child. So the woman must have had a second kid." Zara paused, her eyes now burdened with sadness. "I try not to think about it, because when I do, that dark heaviness surfaces in my body."

D'Melo was relieved. Although this sounded strikingly similar to how his mom died, the woman in Zara's dream couldn't have been his mother. *I'm an only child. Just a weird coincidence.*

Zara concluded, "That dream ruined what would have been the best Christmas of my life."

D'Melo's relief was short-lived. "Which Christmas?" he pressed, his heart pounding against his ribs.

"Well, I remember exactly which one."

Zara recounted how, on Christmas mornings, she would usually have hopped with merry anticipation down the staircase. But having just woken from the harrowing dream, the bounce in her step was replaced by a morose trudge. Typically, Christmases in the Zanič home were modest, the tree adorned with a single handmade gift for Zara.

But because her mom had just been promoted at the factory, that particular Christmas was bountiful. The twinkling tree boasted several presents *and* Zara's first bicycle!

"I'll never forget that Christmas. I was seven years old. So, it must have been the Christmas of 2008."

D'Melo's haggard face grimaced at the shooting pain in his chest.

"Are you okay?"

"Yeah," he said stoically. He squeezed his eyes shut, then blinked hard to refocus them.

They plodded the final block to the drugstore. For the first time, they hugged goodbye. It felt natural for D'Melo after experiencing so much together.

"I'll see you tomorrow for your first tutoring session," D'Melo reminded her.

Zara allowed the hug to linger, then maneuvered straight into a dramatic performance. "How can I thank thee, oh great one." She planted a foot in front of her and bowed. "I am but a lowly servant girl. And you are the great King of Kipaji." She swung her arm upward in an exaggerated salute.

"What are you doing?" D'Melo looked around, embarrassed. "Stop being so crazy!"

Zara ignored his plea, frolicking to the apartment entrance. She leapt into a leg stretch, landing nimbly on the balls of her feet. She performed one final curtsy before flitting inside.

For a brief moment, Zara's nightmare faded from D'Melo's mind. He floated along the street, as carefree as a bubble in the wind. He was growing fondly accustomed to the world of Zara. It was distressing but exhilarating. It was edgy but centered on something powerful. It was profound but lighthearted and whimsical. It was frighteningly out of his control . . . but D'Melo had never felt more at peace with anyone.

But before long, D'Melo's bubble burst into sobering thoughts.

Zara dreamed exactly what I've been telling Baba, but he doesn't believe me. Or does he? Is he keeping something from me? But why would the police have lied? Maybe they didn't. Zara's dream had to have been about a different woman. My mom only had one kid. D'Melo's mind twisted with possibilities until it ached.

D'Melo tapped lightly on Zara's bedroom door. Hearing a muffled voice, he tentatively nudged the door open a slit. He peeked in, uneasy with being in a girl's bedroom alone. "Did you say come in?" he murmured skittishly.

"What are you doing?" she snipped. "Get in here."

Zara's voice carried more stress than usual. D'Melo padded in gingerly. Zara sat straight-legged on her bed, propped against the headboard. She had one pencil locked in her clenched teeth, another jutting out of her wildly twisted bun. A math book was planted firmly in her lap, like it had been there long enough to grow roots. There were loose papers strewn across the bed, a few jettisoned on the floor.

"You're twenty minutes late," she mumbled around the gnawed pencil. "I think you *want* me to fail my math test!"

"Sorry, dawg," he said. "I was choppin' it up with your grandfather. He's a trip."

Zara cleared space next to her for D'Melo to sit. But he wasn't at all comfortable with joining her on the bed. He slid a chair to her desk.

"This is a good spot to study." He rattled the desk. "Very sturdy."

Irritated, Zara cobbled her papers into a bunch. She fumbled over to the desk, her math book clamped in her armpit and calculator nestled between her neck and shoulder. The moment she was settled, her phone sounded—the cluck of an endangered bird, the Kakapo.

She sighed as she pushed herself up grudgingly. "I'll be back." She clumped out. After a few minutes, she returned and plopped down at the desk. The air in the room was thick with tension, carrying every sound heavily. Even the cooing of the mourning doves just outside her window sounded strained.

D'Melo attempted to lighten the mood. "So, the key to *chemistry* is you first have to—" Usually that would have gotten D'Melo at least an "Oh, shut up" or "You're such a jerk" from Zara. But not this time.

Zara snapped, "Would you stop screwing around!"

"Whoa, what's up with you?"

"Something has to be up with me because I don't want to fail my math test?"

D'Melo glanced at her apologetically. "You're right. I'm sorry." He opened her math book. Zara shut it back closed.

"No, *I'm* sorry," she said. "I'm taking my frustration out on you. It's just this boy from back home. He keeps asking me to go to North Carolina for Thanksgiving with his family. I've already told him I'm not going. I don't like being pressured."

D'Melo was stunned. "A boy? Or a boy*friend?*"

"I guess you can say he's my boyfriend."

D'Melo's heart dropped, but not because Zara had a boyfriend. D'Melo had no intention of veering from his no-relationship-until-marriage plan. Although he distanced himself from his African heritage, his values were deeply influenced by his Kipaji upbringing. His angst came from suddenly feeling distant from Zara. Over the previous couple of months, they had become really tight—so he thought. *Why is she only now mentioning a boyfriend?*

"We've been friends forever," Zara explained. "Brandon lived a few houses from me. From the time we were in kindergarten, we'd walk to school together. And when my mom got sick, his was the shoulder I cried on the most."

"Well," D'Melo said, concealing his disquiet. "It's nice of you not to leave your grandparents on Thanksgiving." He paused questioningly. "Do they even celebrate Thanksgiving?"

"Ohhh, yeah," Zara said, widening her eyes. "Every year my

grandparents go on a cruise with their Nečzian friends. This Thanksgiving it's the Caribbean. But I'm not going with them. This is their thing. I'm not big on cruises anyway. Do you know how much those cruise ships pollute? I'd be miserable the whole time thinking about how I'm contributing to dumping sewage in our oceans."

"So, if you're not gonna be with your grandparents, why aren't you going to North Carolina?"

"Too many bad memories."

About two years ago, Zara told him, her mother was diagnosed with stage 4 colon cancer. She had surgery to remove a tumor, but the procedure created a hole in her liver. After that, she was in and out of the hospital with various infections.

"I don't know why I'm telling you this," she said. "You don't want to hear about all my issues."

"Of course, I do," D'Melo assured her, longing for the closeness he thought they already had.

"Well, then," she continued. "My mother needed a new liver, but the insurance company denied coverage. It claimed that a transplant wasn't a promising treatment, even though several doctors agreed it would save her life. The surgery would have cost my family over $200,000. We couldn't come close to scraping together that much money.

"Watching my mom deteriorate and not being able to do anything was—" She covered her face with quivering hands. "There are no words to describe it. I'd wake up in the morning and for a second, I'd think it was just one of my horrible nightmares. But then I'd realize it wasn't."

Zara's family had a glimmer of hope when the drug company, Pharma, released a new treatment for colon cancer. It would have extended her mother's life long enough for Zara's grandparents to sell the drugstore to raise enough money for the transplant. But Pharma wanted $40,000 for the treatment.

"We wrote Pharma, pleading for them to reduce the price. But my mom was meaningless to them." Zara's eyes burned with fire. "I will never forgive them!"

"Where was your dad all this time?" D'Melo asked, unwittingly kicking a hornets' nest.

"I don't have a dad," she muttered tersely, leaving no room for discussion.

After a tense silence, D'Melo said, "So you're gonna be alone on Thanksgiving?"

"I don't mind. I can use some quiet time. And you? What are your plans?"

"I have a tournament in Harrisburg," he said. D'Melo hadn't had a real Thanksgiving for three years because of these annual holiday games. He struggled with feeling that the tournament had taken Thanksgiving away from his father.

"That sounds fun." Zara bounced back. "A holiday road trip!"

D'Melo pondered, unsure about what he should say next. *Should I ask whether she wants to come with us? Would it be offensive? She did just tell me she has a boyfriend. But is she saying she's interested? She shouldn't be by herself on Thanksgiving.*

He decided to put the onus on Zara. "Are you saying you'd like to come?"

"Well, I haven't been invited." She squinted her eyes playfully at him. "But if I was invited, I'd love to."

"Wouldn't your boyfriend be upset if you spent Thanksgiving with me and not him?"

"Why would he be upset?" Zara said. "You and I are friends. Am I not allowed to spend Thanksgiving with a friend?"

D'Melo crinkled a brow, questioning her logic; it seemed naive.

"What?" she quipped. "Is D'Melo, the great king from Lincoln Downs, afraid of Brandon from Hillbilly Redneck, North Carolina?"

D'Melo chuckled. "And your grandparents? They may not be happy about you going with me."

Zara brushed off the notion.

D'Melo tilted his head, *I'm not comfortable unless you ask.*

"Dude, seriously?" she puffed exasperatedly. She leaned back in her chair and cracked open the door. "Děda," she shouted, calling her grandfather. "Can I go with D'Melo to his Thanksgiving tournament in Harrisburg?"

Tomáš yelled back, "Of course! I wish I could go with you." Apparently, Zara's

grandmother was next to him, because she slapped Tomáš' arm hard enough to be heard down the hallway.

Tomáš cried out, laughing. "Zara, help! Your Babička is abusing me again!"

Zara pursed her lips at D'Melo, *You see?* "They trust me. So, when do we go?"

"We'll hit the road right after you fail your math test on Wednesday."

"Oh, *shut up.* You're such a jerk!"

D'Melo warmed. *Ahhh, she's back!*

After Thanksgiving, D'Melo was riding high. The Panthers won the tournament for the first time in over a decade, and he and Zara had grown closer by the day. Hardly a day passed that they didn't spent at least some time together. Life was good!

He plopped himself down to watch *The World This Week* with Baba, like he did every Sunday night.

The first story featured a famous documentarian and activist, Kyle Sandersen, who had just released the trailer of his new film, *The Next Colonization of Africa.*

Interviewer: "Let me first congratulate you on your latest film. What was your motivation to make this documentary?"

Kyle Sandersen: "I wanted to raise awareness of the destructive impact that American companies have on other countries. Following the money trail of big business, I was led to Central Africa, where exploitation has reached unparalleled levels. But then, the film took an unexpected turn. The focus narrowed to one company in particular, Pharma.

"While gathering information, we uncovered claims of extraordinary corruption and crimes that Pharma committed in cahoots with the government of Malunga. During our investigation, one name kept surfacing—Wilem VanLuten, Pharma's president of product development for Africa."

"Hey," D'Melo straightened in his seat. "That's the company Zara was talking about!" He texted her to tell her to watch the program.

Kyle Sandersen: "I don't want to give away too much, but we even uncovered information that sheds new light on the assassination of President Amani."

Interviewer: "Wow. Now you're just teasing us. I think this is a good time to play the trailer for those who haven't yet seen it."

The program cut away to the trailer.

Meanwhile, in an almost empty tavern in Nanjier, the trailer played fuzzily on a tiny TV above the bar. Wilem VanLuten was having a drink with his marine buddy, Zachariah.

"Hey, Wilem!" Zachariah piped, gesturing to the TV. "Isn't that you?" Wilem's intoxicated eyes, a bit unfocused, swung to the screen.

"Hey, barkeep," Zachariah shouted over the background music. "Turn it up the TV. My friend over here is a star."

At first, Wilem was tickled to see himself in the documentary, even if only in a few photos. But then the trailer alluded to Pharma's illegal practices in Malunga. His tickle turned into an uncomfortable pang and then searing anger. His face contorted and turned red as he fumed.

Interviewer: "That's powerful stuff, Kyle. You're making some very serious allegations against Pharma."

Kyle Sandersen: "Pharma uses every means at its disposal to create situations where it can continue to exploit the land and people—some legal and some not so legal, but all immoral. We show in the documentary that the civil war between the Shujas and the Malungan government was influenced by Pharma's interests in the Nyumbani. This sacred homeland of the Shuja tribe is the heart of the conflict."

Interviewer: "Yesterday, Henry Stinton, the CEO of Pharma, announced that he's retiring. He cited health concerns as his reason. Do you think his sudden retirement has anything to do with your film?"

Kyle Sandersen: "I hope not. I certainly didn't intend to cause him to step down. I spoke to Henry a couple times for the film. He seems to be a decent human being. I truly believe that he didn't know what's been happening in Malunga. When I questioned him, he genuinely seemed to be hearing it for the first time."

When Wilem heard that Stinton was retiring, he became unhinged. "Stinton's quitting and no one told me? I can't believe I have to hear about this from the TV!"

"Wilem," Zachariah said consolingly. His eyes swept around the bar; there were only a few other patrons, and they were not paying attention. "Relax, man. I'm sure they were going to let you know."

"I've lived on this god-forsaken continent for twenty years and gave up my family for this company. And this is how they treat me?"

The bartender cautioned Wilem to settle down. Wilem looked straight past him. His eyes glued with fury to the TV.

Interviewer: "Some speculate that Stinton's heart condition has worsened because of the protests outside Pharma head-quarters in San Francisco. The commotion had died down recently, but with the release of your trailer, the protests have gained new life. And with it, the drumbeat for Stinton to resign has reverberated loud and wide."

Kyle Sandersen: "Let's see who they replace Henry with. Hopefully, the new CEO will make some much needed change in how Pharma does business in Africa."

Interviewer: "If this film is half as good as your first docu-mentary, *Animal Agriculture: Man's Race to Self-Destruction,* we're in for a special treat. When can we expect the new film to be released?"

Kyle Sandersen: "We're putting on the finishing touches now. It should be available on TruFlix in March."

Interviewer: "Well, as always, it was a pleasure. We wish you all the best with the documentary. And we hope to see many more from you in the years to come."

Kyle Sandersen: "I hope so, too. Thank you, Peter."

As the program ended, the following appeared on the screen:

> "We reached out to Pharma for comment, but it declined our request. A company representative only stated that Pharma was in search of a CEO, and that it hopes the media will respect Mr. Stinton's privacy as he deals with his health concerns."

"I can't believe they're *searching* for a CEO!" Wilem roared. "I've done more for this company than anyone." He slapped his full beer bottle off the table.

"Hey!" the bartender shouted heatedly at Zachariah. "You need to take your friend home, right now!"

"Sorry, he isn't usually like this." Zachariah attempted to calm Wilem down. "Don't worry, man. I'm sure you'll be the new CEO. Look at how far you've come. When we first met, you were a scrawny, wet-behind-the-ears do-gooder. Now look at you. You're running Africa for one of the biggest drug companies in the world."

"Why do they have to search?" Wilem slurred, wobbling as Zachariah practically carried him to the exit. "I'm right here."

"Look on the bright side," Zachariah said. "Even if they don't make you CEO, it's not a big deal. You can make ten times more money in *our* business than you do at Pharma."

"That's *your* business, not mine," Wilem snapped. "I've worked too hard and sacrificed too much to not be CEO."

Wilem hadn't always been so starved for recognition and power. He came from humble beginnings in Detroit. His father was an auto assembly line worker and his mother was a motel housekeeper. Although barely scraping by financially, when Wilem was born, his mother quit her job to be at home with him. Wilem's family couldn't afford for him to go to college, so he joined the Marine

Corps. His first assignment sent him to Nanjier, where he met Zachariah.

At that time, Nanjier was in the midst of a civil war. The U.S. threw its support behind the Nanjier Rebel Front (NRF). Wilem was part of the Marine unit that trained the rebels, working closely with NRF leader Baako Okoye. After the NRF's successful coup d'état, Okoye became the President of Nanjier and Wilem returned to America.

Zachariah, spotting a business opportunity that was too good to pass up, stayed in Nanjier. The war left behind several warehouses full of munitions that the country no longer needed. Zachariah convinced President Okoye to let him "manage" the warehouses—meaning, to sell the weapons. Okoye agreed, but on one condition: Zachariah could only supply the weapons to the Shuja rebels fighting in Malunga.

Back in America, Wilem graduated from college, then went to work for Pharma in San Francisco. Recognizing his great potential, Pharma paid for Wilem to attend Stanford business school, where he met his wife, Helen.

Wilem and Helen got married and had two children right away. Wilem was living the life he had always wanted—a steady job and a growing family. But before long, his life unraveled, beginning with his marriage.

After their second child was born, Helen wanted to get her career moving again. Holding tight to his traditional values, Wilem insisted that she stay home for the kids, just as his mother had for him. At first Helen acquiesced, but as time passed, she grew bitter and defiant. She didn't go to business school to become a babysitter. She had grand ambitions for her career and lifestyle.

On good days, their home was various degrees of tense, but on most days, it was a battleground. Helen communicated in the form of tirades. Then, seemingly overnight, she changed. Her outbursts ended, but nothing filled the void. She became distant and melancholy. Although Wilem was concerned about their marriage, he didn't grasp the extent to which it had deteriorated.

One night, not long after Helen's change in mood, over a typical haphazardly prepared dinner, she casually informed Wilem that she had accepted a job with Zembio. This was a double punch to Wilem's gut, knocking the wind out of him. Not only had Helen ignored his wishes, but Zembio was one of Pharma's main competitors.

From then on, whenever Helen brought up her job, Wilem immediately changed the subject. And every time one of their children did something naughty, Wilem took the opportunity to stick it to Helen. "This would never have happened if the kids had their mother at home!" After a while, Helen no longer even tried to defend her decision to go back to work. Their relationship spiraled. They only spoke when it was absolutely necessary, like deciding who was picking the kids up from day care.

One evening, Wilem came home to an eerily quiet house. Dizzy with anxiety, he instinctively shot to his bedroom. Helen's dresser drawers were bare. He dragged himself to the kids' room, knowing his heart was about to be shattered into a thousand pieces. Not a single artifact of his children remained. Helen had taken everything, even the photo albums. Wilem leaned heavily against the wall, then slid slowly to the floor.

After the longest hour of his life, he carried his weary body to the dining room. Dinnertime used to be the best part of his day. He would come home to vivacious children scooting about and shouting random stuff, Helen scurrying frenetically to cobble a meal together, and Butterbean, their dog, lathering Wilem's face with an excited tongue.

There he found, sitting on the dining table at his seat, a plate full of food. Wilem stared at the plate. He didn't know whether Helen meant it as a gesture of goodwill or a final dagger to his heart, but she had made his favorite meal—pork ribs, mashed potatoes, and asparagus. His eyes slid warily to a note lying forebodingly on a large manila envelope.

Dear Wilem,

I didn't know how to tell you this. I thought about the best way many times, but realized that there's no best way. So I'll get right to it.

Wilem's heart pumped deadened thumps. He shoved the dinner plate away. He had no appetite anyway.

Over the past year, our marriage has really suffered. It was getting worse by the day. I didn't know how to fix it. I started to become despondent, not only at home but also at work. My boss, Ben, took notice of my deteriorating performance. But instead of firing me, like most bosses would have done, he truly cared about me as a person. It started out as him just listening as I shared my feelings. But then our time together became more frequent and lingering, and our calls less and less about work. One thing led to the next and before I knew it, I realized that I had fallen in love with him.

Wilem's head pounded like a jackhammer. He pushed on his temples, trying unsuccessfully to alleviate the mounting pressure.

Ben said we could move in with him. He's taking the kids to see the Giants on Saturday. After the game, I'll bring them over so you can spend some time with them.

I'm so sorry things turned out this way. You and I were madly in love at some point. I don't know where it went wrong, but it did. Now, we must move on and do the best we can for our children.

Love, Helen

A tear stained the note, then another. Wilem slumped numbly in his chair. He brooded, unaware of the hours passing.

Suddenly, he jumped up. He ran to his computer and opened Google. He knew he shouldn't, but he couldn't help himself. Full of apprehension, he entered the name of his wife's new love. He hesitated, then hit Search. And of course, he promptly learned things about Ben that he wished he didn't know.

Benjamin Truitt, three years Wilem's junior, was the youngest CEO ever of a company as large as Zembio. Just the year before, Ben had received a $7 million bonus from his company. If there was one thing Wilem detested about Helen, it was that she made him feel small, as if he and the money he was making wasn't enough for her. Wilem was sickened by the thought that Helen couldn't have a life of luxury with him, so she had found it with someone else. Ben was surely able to give her all the things that Wilem couldn't.

Wilem snatched up a steak knife from the table. With quivering hands, he sliced along the top of the manila envelope. He started to remove the documents, then shoved them back in.

An agonizing week later, he finally raised the courage to look at the papers. They confirmed what he had suspected. Helen had filed for a divorce.

July 5, 1997 was the date the divorce became official and would forever be burned into Wilem's brain. It was the worst day of his life—until, just a month later, he heard from a mutual friend that Helen and Ben were getting married. Wilem spent the few days around the time of the wedding (or "the betrayal" as he called it) in Hawaii, to get far away. When he returned, he became completely unglued.

Wilem was to spend the week that Helen and Ben were off on their honeymoon with his children. He painstakingly planned each day to be packed with fun activities. The highlight was going to be Disney on Ice—the kids loved everything Disney.

He arrived at Helen's new house on the appointed day. Benjamin answered the door. Wilem thought, *Helen doesn't even have the dignity to come and greet me herself.*

"Oh. Hi Wilem," Ben said, seeming flummoxed. "How are you?"

Wilem couldn't bring himself to return the formalities. "Can you tell the kids I'm here?" he said boorishly, as he glanced past Ben into the house.

"Oh, boy," Ben said regretfully. "Helen didn't tell you?"

"Tell me what?"

"When the kids heard we were going to Seychelles for the honeymoon, they begged us to take them along."

Blood coursed violently through the protruding veins in Wilem's neck. "Absolutely not!" he shouted through gritted teeth. "The kids are coming with me!"

It was hard enough for Wilem that they were planning to take away his week with the kids, but Seychelles! Wilem and Helen had always talked about taking a dream trip to Seychelles as soon as they could afford it. They imagined renting a hut standing on pillars over crystal blue water. They would laze on the beach, hike jungle trails, and sip tropical drinks.

"I'm sorry, Wilem," Benjamin said sincerely. "But the kids are coming with us. We already bought the tickets."

Wilem snapped. He shoved Benjamin aside and marched into the living room. "Come on, kids," he said grimly, trying to prevent his rage from seeping into his voice. "Let's go." The children gaped at Wilem, frozen.

Helen stormed in. "Wilem!" she shouted, trembling with anger and fear. "What are you doing here? Didn't you get my message? We're taking the kids with us. You can have your time with them after the trip."

"I'm not leaving here without my children!"

Benjamin calmly clutched Wilem by the arm. "Please, Wilem. You're scaring the kids. When we get back, you can take them for *two* weeks. Okay?"

Wilem ripped his arm free. "Get off me! And no, it's not okay! This is my week with them!"

Benjamin forcefully dragged Wilem toward the front door. Wilem sucker-punched Benjamin in the back of the head. Benjamin dropped heavily in a heap. The kids burst into frightened sobs. Helen comforted them, then called the police.

Wilem closed his eyes, in shock over what he had just done. He turned to his children, his eyes deadened with remorse. "I'm so sorry," he muttered, then slunk out of the house.

When Helen returned from the honeymoon, she went straight to court. She requested a modification to their child custody arrangement. The judge decided in her favor. Helen would have full custody of the children.

Just when Wilem thought things couldn't get any worse, his mother died. Then, his father, who was heartbroken, followed her four months later.

Around that time, Pharma made the decision to expand into Central Africa. Wilem saw this as an opportunity to start a new life and to climb the corporate ladder. He wanted—no, he *needed*—to show Helen that he was on the road to becoming a CEO one day.

Wilem had toiled in Africa ever since. And in those years, because of his extraordinary efforts in discovering new medicines, Pharma had catapulted from the ninth-largest pharmaceutical company in the U.S. to the third.

Nursing a pounding head after his drunken night in the bar that had ended so shockingly, Wilem sat in his kitchen contemplating his next move. The company was "searching" for a new CEO. Wilem believed fiercely that he should be first in line for the job.

But sickeningly, with Kyle Sandersen's unscrupulous portrayal of him, Wilem realized his chances had become slim to none. He needed a game-changing medicine, something that would give Pharma no choice but to make him CEO.

CHAPTER SIX

The Third Guy

Christmas had become a holiday D'Melo could do without. He woke to a flood of gut-wrenching images of that fateful morning ten years before. The devilish eyes of the man who had killed his mother were branded into his brain—the killer's right eye, pure demon; and the left, vacant steel gray, with a slash cutting through it. At times, D'Melo wished, against his better nature, that whoever sliced that guy's left eye blind had finished the job on his right eye. If he had, then his mother would still be alive.

As was the family Christmas tradition, D'Melo and Baba had traveled to Washington, D.C., to celebrate the day with Ameka Bello. Ameka, the aunt of Diata's best friend in Kipaji, selflessly supported D'Melo's family during their early days in America. She had taken them into her home, helped them find jobs, and guided them through an unfamiliar social system that was as foreign as it was mind-boggling.

D'Melo had always dreaded going to Ameka's house. All she talked about was Africa, particularly Malunga. Although he understood that Ameka's job required her to stay on top of the health challenges in

Central Africa, he felt she went overboard. But this Christmas was different: D'Melo sought to satiate his burgeoning curiosity about Malunga and Pharma. When he initiated the conversation, Baba and Ameka shared a surprised glance, tickled by his sudden interest in Africa.

"Auntie Ameka," D'Melo said. He called Ameka "auntie" even though she wasn't his biological aunt, as in the Kipaji culture, friends of one's parents are respectfully referred to as auntie and uncle. "You must have heard about that new documentary about Malunga? What do you know about Pharma exploiting that tribe?"

"*Shujas*," Ameka emphasized, wanting D'Melo to know the name of the tribe. "Well, I don't have the specifics, but I do know that Pharma has been using Malunga's medicinal plants to create new drugs. But you must understand, bioprospecting for medicine isn't the problem. In fact, it's good that companies are bringing new medicines to the world. The problem is that they are taking from us and never giving anything back. And in Malunga, the president is more concerned about lining his own pockets than ensuring that the Shuja people are receiving a benefit from the medicines."

"Well, why do the Shujas allow Pharma to take from their land," D'Melo said indignantly. "Why don't they just stop them?"

Ameka explained, "The Shujas, of which I am one, have tried many times over the years to prevent the desecration of the Nyumbani. But the Malungan government supports the exploitation, even using its military to protect Pharma. Every attempt by the Shujas to fight back has been crushed. So, at the hands of its own government, the Shuja tribe has been rendered powerless against foreign exploiters."

Just then, D'Melo's phone buzzed. "Excuse me, Auntie," he requested. Ameka nodded, giving D'Melo permission to leave. D'Melo shuffled off, his eyes glued to his phone screen.

Zara: Merry Xmas, punk. Hope you're having a better time than me. My GPs have their friends over. I'm engulfed in tales of the old country. Oooh good word, "engulfed." Clunk. But the good thing is, they brought tons of Nečzian food! I'm stuffed!

D'Melo: Actually, that sounds like you're having the time of your life compared to how Christmas at Ameka's usually is for me. But this year, I must admit, I'm having a good time. She's schooling me on Malunga.

Zara: That's awesome! Wish I was there to hear it!

D'Melo: Wish you were here too.

Zara: Aww… you miss me.

D'Melo: Nah dawg, it's just that Ameka and Baba are normal people. I need someone here that's easy to make fun of.

Zara: Jerk!

Zara: Gotta go. Děda just told me it's time to spank some kids.

D'Melo: ?

Zara: Nečzian tradition. We go around whipping the butts of random kids with a willow twig. It's supposed to chase away illness and bring them good health. We have a name for it. We call it *Zdravi.*

D'Melo: We have a name for it too… we call it child abuse!

Zara: LOL

Zara: Later punk

D'Melo: Peace

In D'Melo's absence, Baba and Ameka took the opportunity to quietly discuss the documentary.

"I wonder what information Kyle Sandersen uncovered about President Amani's assassination," Ameka pondered, in a hushed whisper. "Do you think he found the package?"

"That would be the best news I've ever heard," Baba mused.

"Shujas would be off the hook and the country could move on from this horrible legacy. And, best of all, D'Melo and I could be free."

As D'Melo entered the room, they straightened themselves. D'Melo studied them suspiciously. "What are you guys up to?"

Ameka said quickly, "Well, if we told you that, it wouldn't be a surprise now, would it?" She reached under the Christmas tree and revealed a colorfully wrapped gift. D'Melo snatched off the festive paper and beamed at his new basketball sneakers.

Baba gazed at D'Melo, his heart full, feeling a glimmer of hope that the documentary would finally pierce the veil of lies surrounding the assassination of President Amani. It would mean he could finally tell D'Melo everything, a burden he had been carrying for fifteen years. And he would be assured that D'Melo could live his life free of the dark shadow that has been haunting them ever since they left Kipaji.

Not a moment after returning from D.C., D'Melo went to see Zara. He padded through the drugstore entrance. The bells chimed, again creating the ambience of a simpler time in the neighborhood. "Hey Mr. Zanič. What's good?" he said, shaking snowflakes off his long leather jacket.

"It's *all* good, playa," Tomáš greeted.

D'Melo laughed. "You're hilarious, Mr. Zanič. You're the coolest OG I know."

"Original gangster?"

"Nah, old grandfather."

Zara bounced down the stairs. "I thought I heard you down here. What are you guys laughing at?"

"Nunya," D'Melo said.

"Nunya?" she puzzled.

Tomáš chimed in, "Yeah, *nunya* business."

"Ohhh, snap! Mr. Zanič, I didn't know you knew that." D'Melo chuckled. He gave Tomáš a fist bump.

"Děda, you need to stop hanging out with this dude." Zara flicked a thumb toward D'Melo. "He's a bad influence on you." She slid her slender arms into her tan puffer coat. "We're going to Chubby's. I won't be too late."

Tomáš turned to D'Melo. "Keep her out of trouble, huh?"

"I'll try, Mr. Zanič. It's not easy."

"Oooh, you guys are really pushing it." Zara narrowed her eyes at them. "We better go before I change my mind."

Snow glistened and fluttered below the streetlights. The crystal flakes contrasted brightly against Zara's flowing red hair. D'Melo tried futilely to brush them out with his hand. They strolled close enough to inadvertently bump each other every so often. D'Melo blew hard to see his cloudy breath stretch out in front of him.

As they neared Ms. Keba's house, Zara's pace slowed. She struggled for air, her breathing long and ragged. Two young kids frolicked in the yard. They lengthened their arms as wide as they would go and cobbled together just enough of the chilly white powder for one flimsy snowball each. They tossed them at each other, but the snowballs disintegrated into dust before reaching their target. The front door squealed open. A woman beckoned the kids to dinner. They clapped the snow off their wool mittens and scampered up the porch stairs.

D'Melo told Zara how uneasy it made him that the world moved on so quickly. In his mind, that was Ms. Keba's house. And now there was a family living in it. They had their own lives and would make their own memories, but they didn't know anything about Ms. Keba. He was afraid that after Ms. Keba's memory faded in people's minds, it would be as if she never existed.

Zara responded with a different perspective. To her, Ms. Keba would be there forever. Just because people were living in her house didn't change that. Zara could still see Ms. Keba's tender face as clearly as she could see the exuberant kids in the yard. In the short time Zara had with her, Ms. Keba left an indelible impact on her. So, in that way, Ms. Keba's spirit lived on.

Zara bended, resting her hands on her knees. D'Melo rubbed her back. It typically took her a conscious moment to adjust to the powerful sensations that invaded her body, especially when they came from a strong emotion. "I still feel Ms. Keba's suffering," she said, her breath puffing thick, rapid clouds. "But I also feel the bliss she experienced when she saw you." Zara straightened. "It was as if a thousand mountains were lifted off her shoulders."

"Not a day goes by that I don't think about what happened here," D'Melo said in awe. "I know you don't like it, but man, it's like you have a superpower."

"No, dude. I have a super *curse*." Zara revealed that she loved being able to help people using her ability, but it took a hefty toll on her mind and body. She didn't often get to feel people's joy, only their suffering. She wished she could just shut it off. But it didn't work that way. At times, the feelings were so overwhelming that not even running helped. On those occasions, to get as far from the suffering as she could, Zara climbed. Fortunately for her, in North Carolina, a towering Sycamore tree on her farm had offered a safe haven. And on the worst days, when not even the Sycamore provided enough distance, there was a mountain near her house. The higher she hiked, the less she felt. But in Lincoln Downs her yard is bare, not a single tree. And the closest mountain is far from the city.

"So," she explained, "here, to cope, I go to the tallest building in the city and ride the elevator to the top. When I first moved to Lincoln Downs, I was a regular there. The guards all know me now."

"They know you and they still let you in the building?" D'Melo jested.

"Funny, dude. I know it's hard to believe, but some people actually like me. Just not the people at school."

"What do you mean?" D'Melo disagreed. "Lots of folks at school like you."

Zara pursed her lips, *Like who?*

"Well, there's, um . . . no. Let's see . . . um . . .," D'Melo giggled. "Dang girl, you're right!"

She slapped his arm with the back of her hand. "What a jerk!"

"Seriously though, since you're not feeling anything bad right now, does that mean no one on this street is suffering?"

Zara didn't have to be near someone to feel their pain. Sometimes the suffering was hundreds of miles away. But that was usually from people she was really close to, like her family. Also, she didn't feel everyone's pain all the time. Just sometimes. She wasn't sure why or when.

"For instance," she said to D'Melo. "Sometimes your heart squeezes and a pain shoots inside your chest, like when I was telling you about the woman in my dream who was killed in the car accident."

D'Melo halted, stunned. "You can feel that?"

"It's interesting. I've never experienced that particular pain from anyone before. It's like a hot knife digging into your chest."

"Yeah, that's a good way to describe it." D'Melo balked, contemplating whether he wanted to talk about his mother. "Well, your nightmare sounds a lot like how my mom died. So it brought up terrible memories."

Zara slipped her arm under D'Melo's and pulled him close. "I'm sorry." She rested her head against his shoulder.

D'Melo had no idea what caused the episodes when his chest seized into searing pain. It had been happening as long as he could remember. Baba had taken him to several doctors, but not one could find anything wrong with his heart. At first, it was frightening, but over time, he had gotten used to it.

D'Melo's expression turned unusually insecure. "You knowing what I feel is freaking me out. Maybe we can change the subject."

Snowflakes landed on his stubbly cheeks and slowly melted. "How about: what would be your ideal day?"

"Oh! Good question," Zara perked surprisingly. "I thought, at the very best, you'd start talking about how many home runs LeBron James scored."

"Why are you so crazy?—acting like you don't follow basketball. *And* you know I'm a Sixers fan! So why are you trippin' talking about LeBron? Ben Simmons had another triple-double last night—thank you very much!"

"Whatever. That dude couldn't hit an 18-footer if his life depended on it!"

"Yo! Why you throwin' shade at my boy Ben!"

Zara laughed. "Anyway, getting back to a *meaningful* conversation, hmmm." She laid a finger on her lips in careful consideration. "My ideal day, huh?" A snowflake dangled at the edge of her long lashes. "I think I'd start with a long hike up a mountain. At the summit, I'd take in the serene view until my mind was empty and my heart was full. Oooh," her eyes shot open wide, "then, I'd hang glide over a river valley into the setting sun." She was imagining clearly in her mind now. "There's a waterfall, so as I drift in heavenly silence, mist tickles my nose and refreshes my face."

"You know how to hang glide?"

"No. But you asked what my ideal day would be, not what reality is," Zara sniffed, pretending to be peeved that D'Melo was ruining her imaginary day. "Now where was I before I was rudely interrupted? Oh yeah, by the time I landed on the valley floor, I'd probably be hungry."

"Dang, girl. You're always hungry! For someone so slim, you sure do get your grub on!"

"I'd have some traditional Nečzian food, like my mom used to make. Yum!" Zara licked her lips comically. "After that, I'd be too full to do anything but flop on the couch and finish the day with an animated movie. Then in my sleep, I'd see my mom," she cooed, her eyes now a mix of dreamy and somber. "How about you? What would your ideal day be?"

"Same," D'Melo muttered without hesitation. "I mean, not all that hiking and hang-gliding stuff, but seeing my mom again."

D'Melo and Zara sauntered into Chubby's and shook the snow off their jackets. They took a seat in "D'Melo's Corner." The only thing that Chubby loved more than whiskey was basketball. After D'Melo broke the Lincoln Downs freshman scoring record, Chubby hung a large photo of him in the back corner of the restaurant. Since that time, several photos of D'Melo had found their way onto Chubby's walls, but that corner had always been set aside for D'Melo.

The waitress shuffled up to the table. Zara ordered first. "Could I please have—"

The waitress interrupted, "Spicy gumbo soup with no meat and piping hot; and the garden salad with extra beets. Now, the last time you asked whether we had vegan pumpkin pie, but of course we didn't. After that, Chubby said we needed to move into the twenty-first century. So we came up with a small vegan section in our menu. We have vegan pies, corn bread, hush puppies, and other stuff too!"

"Wow. That's so nice!" Zara said. "And it's amazing that you re-membered my order."

"Well, you're a little hard to forget. We were talking about you for days after you put creepy Willie in his place. He had it coming, but we just put up with him because he's old. He's been sittin' on that same barstool for longer than most of us have been alive. He still gawks, but he doesn't say all that foul stuff anymore." The waitress gave Zara a fist bump. "Respect."

The waitress started walking away. D'Melo stopped her. "Uh, you didn't take my order."

"I know your order; you've gotten the same thing for the past ten years—ribs, country fried potatoes, and corn bread."

"Well this time, I'll have what she's having." The waitress tucked her chin and shot Zara a look over her red thick-rimmed glasses, *Girrrl, this guy's really into you.*

"No meat?" Zara asked, stunned.

"Can't a brotha try to eat healthy?"

Then, seemingly at nothing, D'Melo started to giggle. "Remember that time we went to Liberty Steak House?"

"Dude," she said. "Why do you have to bring that up!"

"Because you're probably the only person who has ever gone to a restaurant and brought her own meal. Who does that?" He blew an incredulous chuckle through his nostrils. "What were you gonna do, break out the Tupperware and start eating your wild rice and red beans right there in the restaurant?"

"Yeah, if I had to! Lots of places don't have anything for me to eat," she retorted. "Now, if you'll excuse me, I have to go to the ladies' room. Maybe by the time I get back, you'll have forgotten about the Tupperware incident."

Zara disappeared down the dark hallway. Two guys from the bar staggered over to D'Melo. "What, black girls aren't good enough for the big basketball star?"

D'Melo glared up at them. "It's not like that." His face tensed. "But even if it was, it's not really your business." One guy clamped D'Melo's arm. "Chubby's is for black folks," he snorted. "You see any other snowflakes in here? You need to go find another place to eat."

D'Melo snatched his arm away. "Listen, I don't want any trouble."

The waitress arrived, balancing two bowls of steaming gumbo soup. To ease the tension, she told the guys that drinks were waiting for them at the bar. "On the house," she offered.

"Great," D'Melo simmered. "That's exactly what they need, more alcohol." The waitress shrugged apologetically.

Zara returned. "What happened?"

For a moment D'Melo was surprised by her question, but then remembered that she could feel when he was upset. He played it down. "No big deal. Just some drunken fools flexin'."

"Who? Those knuckle draggers at the bar? They kept looking over here, but I didn't say anything because I'm trying to be on my best behavior." Zara peeked up at them.

"Zara! Don't look over there," D'Melo urged, directing his eyes toward the bar without turning his head.

"Oops, too late," she said. "They're coming."

"Did you have to look at them! I told your grandfather I'd keep you out of trouble. But you make it impossible."

Zara shrugged a shoulder, *What can I tell you.*

The waitress stepped in front of the drunkards, trying to keep the peace. They brushed her aside. Chubby yelled from the kitchen, threatening to call the police if they started any trouble.

"Man," D'Melo groaned. "I just wanted to have a nice quiet meal."

"Don't worry. *I got this,*" Zara winked. "When I say duck, *duck.*"

"What do you mean?" D'Melo asked, then realized what she was planning. "Oh no, Zara. Don't."

Just as the guys stalked menacingly behind D'Melo, Zara shouted, "Duck!" D'Melo dipped his head. She slung her piping hot soup on them. D'Melo followed suit. Then they tore out of the restaurant.

"Run! Run!" Zara screamed, laughing. Slipping on the snow-dusted sidewalk, they stumbled upon a narrow alley. Zara skidded around the corner. D'Melo caught her before she hit the ground. She peeped around the brick building, while D'Melo peered over her with his arm still around her. "They're not coming. We're fine."

D'Melo spun her toward him. "Are you out of your mind! *That's* your best behavior! You could've gotten us killed . . . again! Those guys are lunatics!"

"But I told you," she said, her eyes still crazed with excitement. "*I got this.*"

"Yeah, but I didn't know whether you even knew what you were saying. He put on a slow drawl, trying to imitate her in a Southern hillbilly accent, "Heeyyy, I gottt diisss."

Zara snickered, covering her mouth. "That's the worst redneck impression I've ever heard."

"Well, I couldn't do the impression right because I have all my teeth. I can't get the toothless whistle sound going."

"Oh, my God!" Zara stared wide-eyed at him. "You're horrible!" She slapped his arm. D'Melo caught her hand against his shoulder. He held it there. Their eyes lingered in a tender gaze.

"You know," he said softly. "There's something I've been wanting to say to you."

Zara fixed her emerald green eyes warmly on his. "Yeah," she said, clearly in anticipation. "What's that?"

"You really need to work on your passing. Your soup went everywhere! Did you see how my soup went right in that guy's face?"

"Oh, *shut up*!" She yanked her hand free and punched him playfully in the stomach. He chortled heartily. "Anyway," she said. "I had to throw my soup around you because you didn't duck quick enough!" A smile twinkled on the corner of her lips, as she rubbed something off his cheek.

"Is that soup?" he groaned. "I knew I felt something burning through my flesh!"

Zara flipped a dismissive hand at him. "Oh shush, you big baby."

They waited a few minutes to make sure no one was coming. Zara blew a hot breath into her cupped hands. "Dude, we left our jackets in the restaurant."

"That's alright. Baba will get them for us." D'Melo rubbed her arms up and down to chase the chill away. "Dawg, your grandfather was right. You *are* trouble! Chubby's never gonna let me back in there."

"What! Chubby loves you," she piped. "You could pee on the floor and he'd still let you come back."

D'Melo grimaced disgustedly. "Where do you come up with these things?"

"Hey," Zara suddenly remembered. "What happened to the third guy?"

"What third guy? There were only two."

"No. There was a third guy at the bar staring at us. I don't know how you could have missed him. He had a patch over his eye and a nasty scar down his cheek."

"Are you sure?" D'Melo said, feeling light-headed.

"Why? What's wrong?"

"Nothing. It's just that the guy who killed my mom had a cut through his eye. But it couldn't be him," D'Melo reasoned, shaking off his paranoia. "That was in D.C., and a very long time ago."

Although D'Melo's nightmare had waned over the past few months, it returned with a vengeance that night. This time, after killing D'Melo's mother, the one-eyed shadowy figure slithered to their mangled car. His dark face appeared in D'Melo's shattered window. In a demonic voice, he vowed, "You and your father are next." D'Melo jerked awake, the hairs on his neck bristling.

After completing a magical season at Lincoln Downs, D'Melo was named to the All-American team. It was an honor bestowed on the twenty-four best high school basketball players in the country. He was invited to play in the All-American game at the famed Madison Square Garden in New York.

The day before leaving, D'Melo held a press conference at his school. Reporters from every major news outlet filed into the gym. D'Melo didn't take questions, he simply announced his decision to attend the University of Pennsylvania.

This news sent shockwaves through the gaggle of clamoring reporters. After the raucousness settled, the ESPN reporter's voice rang out above the rest. "D'Melo, I'm not disparaging UPenn, it's a great academic school, but you have the opportunity to go to the best basketball programs. You could have chosen Kentucky, Kansas, or Duke, just to name a few. Those schools churn out NBA players every single year."

"Yeah, that's true," D'Melo responded evenly. "But those schools don't have what I'm looking for. They're not near Lincoln Downs, my home."

After a few hushed moments, D'Melo closed. "I want to thank you all for coming today and showing such interest in my future. Some of you have traveled a long distance to be here. I wish you a safe journey home."

The clip of D'Melo's press conference played repeatedly on the sports networks. It was a feeding frenzy for roused sports commentators.

Steve: "I respect his choice, but does D'Melo really understand what he's doing? Do you know how many players have been drafted to the NBA from UPenn in the last twenty years? That would be a big fat *zero*! Four were drafted from the University of Kentucky last year alone! Now, if you show me a dude that's willing to give up this opportunity, I'll show you a crazy dude."

Mack: "Well, that's a little harsh, Steve. Yes, he won't receive a ton of airtime. And yes, he won't compete against the best talent in college basketball. So yes, it will reduce his chances of being successful in the NBA. But, he's clearly not about money and fame. What's wrong with that? Don't we want to see more of this in today's world? Personally, I admire his choice. I wish others knew that money and fame aren't what they're cracked up to be. Most rich and famous people only realize this after they've become rich and famous. D'Melo has obviously learned this at an early age."

While the boyz were glued to the TV coverage, D'Melo packed for New York. Zara dug in his closet and pulled together outfits for him. He tossed them into his suitcase and walked it to the front door. He poked his head into the living room. "I'm going to bed, y'all."

"Man, it's like eight o'clock," Kazim gibed. "You an old man already."

"Whatever, dawg. I'm the one who's gonna be out there ballin' on national TV tomorrow. You'll just be in the stands trying to push up on every honey in the arena."

Before shuffling off to bed, D'Melo reminded them, "I'll see y'all bright and early. You best be ready!"

"We'll be ready. Just go to bed, grandpa," Jeylan mocked. He cupped his lips over his teeth. "And don't forget to take out your dentures," he gummed. The boyz chuckled.

Just then, brisk thumps rapped against the front door. D'Melo cracked it warily. A couple of T-Bo's thugs loomed on the stoop. T-Bo was street side, leaning smugly against his shiny black Escalade. He gestured for D'Melo to come out.

Although D'Melo saw T-Bo at his games and by chance in the neighborhood, he was thrown to see him at his house. He figured T-Bo just wanted to congratulate him on being named an All-American.

"What's up, T-Bo?"

"How you gonna come out talkin' about 'What's up'!" T-Bo scoffed. "I heard you decided to go to UPenn." D'Melo nodded, rapidly growing concerned about where this interaction was headed. "You think I supported and protected you all these years out of the goodness of my heart? You were supposed to go to the NBA! And UPenn ain't gonna get you there." He jabbed a threatening finger into D'Melo's forehead. "I suggest you reconsider your decision!"

T-Bo drew a gun from the small of his back. He brandished it in D'Melo's face. D'Melo started edging away. T-Bo's thugs snatched

D'Melo by his arms. T-Bo lowered the gun toward D'Melo's knee. "I could end your basketball career right here."

Still inside watching the sports news, Zara suddenly gasped. "Something's wrong with D'Melo."

"What do you mean?" Jeylan fretted.

"I don't know, but something's wrong."

In a flash, Jeylan sprung out the door and down the stoop. He jumped in front of D'Melo, scowling at T-Bo. "Yo! Whatcha doin', fool?"

"Oh, you a tough guy, huh?" T-Bo sneered.

Jeylan brought his face nose-to-nose with T-Bo's. "Put that gun down and we can find out."

"No!" Baba intervened. "We're not going to find out anything tonight." He backed Jeylan up, keeping his eyes fixed on T-Bo. Marley and Kazim pulled the thugs off D'Melo.

"Let's go, y'all," T-Bo commanded. "D'Melo's got his girlfriends out here to save him." He and his ruffians hopped into the Escalade. The dark window slid down. T-Bo glared at D'Melo. "I hope you do the right thing," he winked. "Or I'll see you another day." The car shot off with a screech.

CHAPTER SEVEN

The Hooded Stranger

The All-American players met with the coaches at center court. They gazed around Madison Square Garden in awe. They imagined playing in front of twenty thousand screaming fans. D'Melo was moved as well, but not for the same reasons. He couldn't remember a time when he had felt his mother's presence so profoundly. "Thank you, Mama," he said under his breath, clutching the locket she gave him. "I'm only here because of you and Baba."

As the players headed to the locker room, a brawny man stood at the far end of the corridor. While there were many people milling around preparing for the game, this man seemed out of place. As D'Melo got closer, the man slipped around the corner.

Later, during practice, D'Melo noticed the same man just inside the tunnel that led to the inner corridors. He enquired about the man with a Garden representative. But when he pointed toward the tunnel, the man was gone.

"There was a bulky, dark-skinned guy wearing a black hoodie standing over there," D'Melo said. The representative didn't know of any such person. In fact, this was a closed practice, so no one should have been at court level except the players and coaches.

When D'Melo returned to the hotel, he stopped by Zara's room. Her door was propped open with the metal security latch. D'Melo slid in. She was sprawled across the bed, spent from a hectic day of shopping.

"You know," he cautioned. "It's not safe to leave your door open." He clicked it shut behind him. "Anyone can just walk right in."

"And do what?" Zara popped off the bed into a boxer's stance. She rocked her fists. "I got these to protect me!" She squinted one eye, thumbed her nose, and sniffed. "Who's gonna mess with this, huh?" She jabbed awkwardly, clearly never having fought anyone in her life.

"You're right," D'Melo smiled. "No one's gonna mess with that. The attacker would be in too much pain, having cracked a rib from laughing so hard."

"Oh yeah?" she said. "Will he laugh when I do this?" Zara tried to karate kick D'Melo but missed, smacking her foot against the desk. She bit her bottom lip, trying not to shriek in pain. She clutched her foot and flopped backward onto the bed.

D'Melo burst into a doubled-over guffaw.

"That's not funny, dude," she said, wincing. "I could be seriously injured."

D'Melo stroked her head. "Aww," he feigned sympathy. "Did you hurt your little toey?"

"Jerk." She whacked his hand off her head. "You know, you shouldn't be making fun of your only fan. Oh," she remembered, "how was practice? Did you score any touchdowns?"

"Yeah, and I hit a couple home runs, too," D'Melo jested back half-heartedly, his mind returning to the dark stalker. "You know, it's probably nothing, but I kept seeing this dude in the Garden. He just lurked around. It's weird. I don't know. I'm probably making something out of nothing."

"Yeah, probably," Zara said encouragingly, but not completely convinced. She knew that D'Melo tended to be a worrywart, but his instincts were usually keen.

The game and all its fanfare came and went that evening. It seemed that D'Melo had saved his best effort for his last high school competition. Coaches from the top basketball colleges made a final attempt to convince him to join their programs. But D'Melo was unmoved. Although UPenn was a questionable choice for a player of his caliber, it was a ten-minute bus ride from Lincoln Downs, and that's all that mattered to him.

D'Melo, Baba, and Zara headed to the All-American dinner. A taxi dropped them at a fancy hotel in midtown. Rows of skyscrapers seemed to touch the clouds. The glitter of wealth shimmered opulently from every building. Even the streetlights seemed to gleam brighter than in other places.

They padded unassumingly into the glitzy lobby. A chandelier twinkled overhead like dangling diamonds. They edged their way through the gaggle of reporters to the banquet hall. A tuxedoed server escorted them to their table. "That's a beautiful dress, ma'am," he commented. Zara was wearing a black short-sleeve cocktail dress. It hung above the knee and draped low in the back. Her neck sparkled with a wide rhinestone choker necklace.

Zara's head swiveled, looking for the lady the server was complimenting. Then she realized he was talking to her. "Oh, wow. Thank you," she said bashfully.

Players and coaches filled the tables in the front. Media personnel settled into the rest of the hall, cameras already clicking and flashing. The waitstaff served a steady flow of hors d'oeuvres. D'Melo paced himself so that he had room for the main course. Zara, on the other hand, chowed down on everything that even resembled food.

D'Melo leaned over to her. "You know," he whispered. "There are other people at this table. They may also want to eat something."

"Oh," Zara covered her mouth to prevent food from flying out. "The waiter put it on our side, so I thought it was for us."

D'Melo narrowed his eyes, quizzically. "Do you think he'd bring six plates just for us and nothing for the other folks?"

"I didn't think that deeply about it, dude. I'm just hungry. And this stuff is unbelievable. Here, try this." She dipped a fried broccoli floret into the spicy white sauce, coating it generously, and thrust it toward D'Melo's mouth.

He blocked her hand. "Please," he said, wide-eyed. "You enjoy it."

"Alright, dude. But you're missing out!" She stuffed the broccoli into her mouth. A dollop of white sauce splattered on her dress. "Ahhh, maaan! How does this happen every time!"

D'Melo shook his head. "I wonder," he said sarcastically.

The lights dimmed. A large man took center stage and introduced himself as Dante Gibbons. "I'm astounded by how much things have changed since I was an All-American," he said. "Back then, there may have been three or four reporters and they were all local." He then congratulated the players for being selected to the All-American team. He wished them the best and urged them to never forget the people who helped them get to where they were.

The All-American game MVP trophy was rolled onto the stage. A buzz vibrated through the hall. "I just want to say, every one of you deserves this trophy. But we can only give it to one person. This young man was not only magical on the court but displayed the qualities of true leadership." A muffled chant rang from the players' tables. Zara was the first to make it out.

"Hey." She elbowed D'Melo. "They're saying your name!"

"No," D'Melo said, hoping she was wrong. He listened closely and realized that she wasn't. He dipped his head, shrinking in his seat.

"This year's All-American MVP is . . . D'Melo Bantu!"

Zara screamed. Baba clasped his hands euphorically, overwhelmed with gratitude to the Great Spirit. Chants of "D'Melo!" reverberated through the hall. He lifted himself up and hopped the steps to the stage.

"I—I honestly don't know what to say," he murmured, lowering his gaze meekly. "Like Mr. Gibbons said, I didn't get here on my own. I'm only receiving this award because of the people who've supported me and pushed me to be better." D'Melo lifted an open hand toward Baba to spirited applause. "Also, I can never thank my friends and my community, Lincoln Downs, enough. They've been there for me every step of the way.

"Finally, I recognize that I wouldn't be on this stage if it wasn't for the ballers in this room. So I'm gonna have all of your names engraved on the trophy and donate it to the Citadel, the court I grew up playing on." The room erupted into booming cheers. "I hope that one day you'll find the time to come play there."

On the way out of the banquet hall, D'Melo was swarmed by clamoring reporters tossing questions at him over each other. As he started answering, a slit of space momentarily opened in the mob, revealing the dark man at the back of the lobby. D'Melo halted an answer mid-sentence. He shifted from side to side, trying to get a clear view. But by the time he did, the man had vanished once again. D'Melo thanked the reporters abruptly and headed for the exit.

In the taxi, Zara and Baba bubbled with energy, while D'Melo's mind swirled with thoughts of the hooded stranger.

"The boyz are gonna go nuts when they hear you were the MVP!" Zara said to a vacant D'Melo. "D'Melo." She nudged him. "D'Melo!"

He snapped out of his malaise. "Yeah, yeah. I know. Maybe we shouldn't tell them."

"Dude, they're gonna find out. It's probably all over the Internet already."

D'Melo, his thoughts churning in torment, said nothing.

The day D'Melo, Zara, and particularly Baba had been waiting for had finally arrived: the release of Kyle Sandersen's documentary. Baba seemed unusually anxious as D'Melo connected his computer to the TV. Zara burst through the door and shot straight to the kitchen. "I'm gonna make popcorn," she shouted.

"Watch this, Baba," D'Melo said, his face beaming mischievously. He called to Zara, "Can you bring me a glass of pomegranate juice? Oh, and also a slice of apple pie?"

"Hey, dude," Zara yelled back. "Are we in the 1800s? You need to get off your behind and get your own juice and pie!" Zara must have heard D'Melo and Baba sniggering. "Ha ha!" she shouted. "Baba, I expect this foolishness from your son, but *you* too?" She toddled in, balancing a heaping bowl of popcorn. She quipped, "Aren't you guys gonna make some for yourselves?"

"Funny." D'Melo said, unamused.

"Scooch, scooch," she said, motioning with her head for them to make room for her on the couch. Popped kernels spilled over the rim of the bowl as she wedged between them.

Throughout the documentary, Baba added interesting details not covered in the film. Otherwise, they watched in engrossed silence. The film moved through the history of Malunga, and then focused on the events that led to the assassination of President Amani and the ensuing genocide. The narrator began, the story accompanied by a montage of images of jungles, villages, vintage photographs, newspaper clippings, and portraits of the main people in the story.

Narrator: "Although tension was high at the time we are starting this story, things were still mostly quiet on the streets of Yandun, the capital city of Malunga. The Shujas seemed content to merely grumble among themselves about the injustices heaped upon them. On the rare occasion when violence was used to express their displeasure, it was swift and relatively tame. But one day, this all changed in the flash of a soldier's pistol.

"Yaro Madaki was a beloved fruit merchant in Yandun. He readily won the hearts of market patrons with his kindness and wicked sense of humor. He became known as 'Kila Tuto,' which in Shuja means, 'Makes everyone smile.' But in April of 1999, Yaro would become known for much more than bringing people joy. He would become the flashpoint of an all-out rebellion against the Malungan government.

"Malungan soldiers didn't much like Yaro. While they were bent on dividing the country along tribal lines, Yaro, in a small but profound way, was doing the opposite. Everyone, including the common Borutus, the tribe in control of Malunga, spoke of him with honeyed tongues. So, on an otherwise typical market day, a pair of soldiers decided to turn their hostility into a revolting display of intolerance.

"Luckily for history and justice, unbeknownst to the soldiers, a Malungan spectator captured the incident that day on her camera. Here is that footage."

The soldiers slithered up to Yaro's stand and knocked his fruits to the ground. Before he could collect them, the soldiers squashed the fruits under their menacing boots.

"Oh, sorry," they snickered. "We didn't see them there."

They then taunted, "We heard that you make everyone laugh. So far you haven't made us laugh even once. Why not?"

Yaro shrugged, a nervous smile twitching on his face.

"Come on, make us laugh!"

Yaro's body tensed. He tried to say something, but no sound would come from his quivering lips.

A solider yanked Yaro from behind his stand. "We're not leaving until you make us laugh."

The other market merchants and shoppers watched, horror gripping their faces. Murmurs of disgusted objection buzzed in the crowd of onlookers.

"Look at me!" a soldier barked.

Yaro's body flinched at the soldier's stinging tone.

"I said look at me!" The soldier grabbed Yaro by the chin. Yaro's eyes stayed fixed downward. "I know what you can do to make us laugh. Dance!"

Isolated shouts from the crowd rang out. "Leave that boy alone! He didn't do anything to you!"

The soldier pointed his pistol at Yaro's feet. "Dance, you Shuja cockroach!" He fired into the dusty soil. Yaro jolted at the bullet penetrating the ground inches from his feet.

"Wait, wait," the soldier said. "There's something that's not quite right." He grabbed Yaro's shirt and tore it down. The shirt, now in shreds, dangled at Yaro's waist.

"That's better," the soldier sneered.

The other soldier joined in. He wrenched Yaro's thin cloth pants. The young merchant's rail thin body trembled uncontrollably. The soldiers then unleashed a volley of bullets, forming a dust cloud around Yaro. Yaro hopped in sheer terror, tripping over his pants, which now lay around his ankles. The soldiers cackled.

After firing a few more rounds, the soldiers became bored. They tromped off, but not before taking fruit for themselves. Several onlookers rushed to Yaro. He sat sobbing, scrambling to pull up his pants. He then rose abruptly and ran off.

Narrator: "The woman who shot the video brought it to a news station, hoping the soldiers would be publicly rebuked, if not punished. But the news commentators only weakly condemned the soldiers, while fighting back laughter throughout the clip.

"The following morning, Yaro's fruit stand remained unattended. A concerned merchant went to his home. He found Yaro's lifeless body on his bed, an empty bottle of sleeping pills on his nightstand.

"An enraged Shuja community flooded the streets in protest. Yaro's older brother, Waasi Madaki, arose as the behind-the-scenes leader. Under his command, the uprising quickly spread and swelled bitterly. Then, President Okoye of Nanjier offered to train Madaki and the protesters into a fighting force. This marked the beginning of the Malungan Rebel Front, or MRF."

Baba added, "When I saw the video of the soldiers terrorizing Yaro, I couldn't stop my tears from flowing. During medical school, I would buy fruit from Yaro nearly every day. He was just as the people in the documentary described him—a lovely, light-hearted fellow. But I didn't know that what happened to Yaro sparked the rebel movement. So I'm happy that his death wasn't in vain."

Narrator: "Over the next few months, the MRF launched sophisticated strategic attacks, targeting key Malungan infrastructure. It coordinated a series of bombings where it would hurt most: the economy. Simultaneously, a bomb blasted a government building, a second ripped through the main electrical power plant, shutting down power in Yandun, and a third leveled the headquarters of a British mining company.

"The Malungan economy was in shambles after the attacks. Foreign companies began withdrawing from Malunga. The environment had become too perilous and expensive for them to continue operating. Food and gas prices shot through the roof. Poor Borutus in Malunga could no longer afford to feed their children. They started their own protests against the government.

President's Amani's son, Taj, recounts what happened next.

Taj Amani: "While my father called for calm, his government and military acted against his plea. One day, as he stewed over the swiftly deteriorating situation, I came to his office. I had recently returned to Malunga after graduating from Oxford University. My father lamented that something had to be done to stop the war. He thought that if he could just speak with Waasi Madaki, he could work out a deal. But his advisors would never let that happen. They were monitoring his every move. He even believed that they were tapping his phone.

"I had an idea that I thought would help my father. But, as it turned out, what I did set in motion events that would eventually lead to my father's assassination," Taj's gaze dropped sullenly to the floor. "Late that night, I slipped out of the Presidential Palace and drove six hours to the Nyumbani to meet with Madaki myself. I didn't tell my father because I knew he would never allow me to put my life in danger.

Baba exclaimed, "This is so interesting! I didn't know exactly how the peace agreement was initiated. It was Taj."

"What peace agreement?" D'Melo said.

"Oh, sorry, that must be coming next."

"Oh great! Thanks, Baba," D'Melo jested. "Next time, give us a spoiler alert."

Taj Amani: "I reached the Nyumbani security checkpoint just before dawn. It was manned by a team of armed rebels.

Two rebels approached my car cautiously. One came to the window while the other scanned the area for potential sneak attacks. The rebel shined his flashlight into the car. He asked what my business was in the Nyumbani. I took a deep breath to calm my jitters. I was well aware that capturing the son of the president would be a huge win for the rebels. I told the soldier who I was and that I needed to meet with Madaki.

"The rebel turned to his comrade. 'You'll never guess who I have here, he said. It's President Amani's son!' They laughed skeptically. The soldier told me to stop drinking whatever alcohol I had been consuming, then ordered me to go home.

"I assured him that I was Taj Amani.

"'Well,' he joked. 'If you're President Amani's son, then I'm the Queen of England.'

"'I met the Queen once in Buckingham Palace,' I said. 'And I must say, I *am* seeing a resemblance.'

"I showed him my passport. He studied it, then shined the flashlight in my face.

"'Please,' I said. 'I'm here to meet Madaki on an urgent matter.'

"They ran off to the security booth. When they returned, they ordered me into their jeep and blindfolded me. They drove about thirty minutes, deep into the jungle. The jeep stopped with a screech. They ushered me out of the jeep and into a small tent, at which time they removed the blindfold. After a few anxious minutes, a young man ducked into the tent with a bottle of water for me.

"I told the young man that I was there to deliver a message to Waasi Madaki. He leaned forward in his chair and said, 'Go ahead. I'm listening.' It took me a moment to realize that this youthful man was Madaki. He was in his late twenties, but his slim frame and baby face made him appear like he was just out of high school. No one in the Malungan government knew what he looked like. There were no official documents with his photo. He was a well-guarded secret.

"The first thing out of his mouth was praise for my father. He said my father was a good man but was being hamstrung by his advisors. Then Madaki issued a dire warning. 'The situation will only get more violent if the Shuja people are not provided the same rights as the Borutus.'

"I informed him that my father wanted to negotiate a peace agreement. Madaki scrutinized me suspiciously. He knew that the presidential advisors would never let my father even broach such a discussion with him.

"I explained that the advisors wouldn't know it was happening. The president would meet him in Nanjier. He would tell his advisors that he was going to Nanjier to meet with President Okoye to shore up their economic agreement. And to assuage any concerns that Madaki may have had regarding his security, I told him that the meeting would be monitored and mediated by the United Nations.

"Madaki agreed, but on one condition: the Nyumbani's future as a sovereign territory, just like Kipaji, must be on the table for negotiation. This would mean that the Shuja people would be in complete control of the Nyumbani.

"Madaki then put a firm hand on my shoulder and said, 'It was courageous of you to come here. I'm glad you did.' I was then whisked off and returned to my car.

"When I arrived back at the Presidential Palace, my father was standing stiffly in the doorway of his office. He suspected where I had been all night. He seemed angry, but proud. He told me to get word to Madaki that the sovereignty of the Nyumbani was negotiable and to set up the meeting.

"My father put his hands on my cheeks, and said, 'Son, you may have just saved this country.' He then strode away with the power and confidence he had when he first became president. He strolled into the foyer and disappeared into a cluster of security personnel and soldiers.

"That was the last time I saw my father alive," Taj said, his voice breaking. "They must have bugged his office. That's the only way they would have known what he was planning."

Kyle Sandersen voice-over: "This is where things become unclear as to what happened next. We received information that a top-secret meeting took place that same evening. It was held at a secluded summer cottage deep in the countryside."

The film went into an interview with the taxi driver who drove one of the participants to the meeting. His faced was blurred on the screen and his voice had been altered.

Taxi driver: "I was instructed by my boss to pick up a client at an abandoned building. The taxi they had me take was set up so that I wouldn't be able to see who the client was. The windows in the back were covered with dark curtains. And a wooden board was secured between the front and back seats. I backed into a garage, as instructed. The garage door slid closed, making it pitch black inside. Then I heard someone get into the back seat.

"As directed, I drove a couple hours out of town to a cottage. When the passenger got out, I glanced at the side mirror. I was just too curious. But the passenger used a long black cloak to completely cover himself. As he passed my mirror, I noticed a glint about a hundred feet behind my taxi. It appeared to be the insignia of a Mercedes Benz. Not too many people in Malunga could afford such an expensive car. Usually, only the highest government officials drove a Mercedes Benz.

"Over the years, I've never forgotten about that night. It was just so peculiar. And when President Amani was killed shortly thereafter, I wondered if the events were connected."

Kyle Sandersen voice-over: "Two days after that secret meeting, President Amani left the Presidential Palace for the airport. He would never make it. Just twenty minutes from the airport, on a barren stretch of road, his motorcade of five cars came under attack. A missile whistled out of the jungle through the foggy morning air. It struck the fourth vehicle. The explosion sent the car high into the air and crashing back down onto the road. A second missile was then fired at the same car, shredding it to pieces. If President Amani was still alive after the first missile strike, it was certain he was killed instantly by the second.

"Not even fifteen minutes after the attack, Vice President Dimka went on national radio. He announced the assassination of President Amani. Dimka said the military had determined that the missiles that killed the president were the same type the rebels used. Borutus in Malunga flew into a murderous rage. Those who may have previously supported the rights of the Shujas now wanted revenge against them. Radio personalities fanned the flames. They dehumanized the Shujas, calling them murdering cockroaches. By nightfall, common Borutus were prowling the streets wielding machetes. They hunted down Shujas and hacked their pleading victims to death.

"Over the course of the next ten weeks, over five hundred thousand Shujas were slaughtered. That's nearly thirty percent of the Shuja population in Malunga. This cleansing became known among Shujas as the '*Majira ya Ugaidi*,' the 'Summer of Terror.'

"In 2004, the International Criminal Court initiated an investigation of now President Dimka and his military head, General Nyoko, for the genocide of the Shuja people. If anyone had slowed down and thought for one minute, the ethnic cleansing of the Shuja people could have been prevented. There were basic things that no one seemed to think about.

"First, the position of the president's car in the motorcade was top secret. It was decided only minutes before the motorcade left the Presidential Palace. Whoever was behind the firing of those missiles clearly had knowledge as to which car President Amani would be in; they used both of their missiles on the fourth vehicle. There was only a handful of people privy to this information—the president's driver, the security personnel in his car, and the head of the president's security detail, General Nyoko."

Baba shifted anxiously in his chair. He dabbed a handkerchief to the sweat beading his forehead.

Kyle Sandersen voice-over: "We had the taxi driver take us to the location where he had dropped the passenger that evening. It's now an overgrown empty lot. I went to the National Land Office to find out who the owner of that plot was in June 2001. An employee told me that searching the records would take some time. She said she'd have the information for me the next day. When I returned in the morning, she wasn't there. I was told that she had quit. I was then referred to the manager, who informed me that the office had only started keeping records for that village in 2006. By that time, the cottage had long been destroyed. And since 2006, the owner of the land was recorded as 'The Government of Malunga.'

"This obvious cover-up stoked my curiosity further. I knew then I was onto something. But unless I could find out who had owned that land when the secret meeting took place, I didn't have anything more than flimsy circumstantial evidence. But every angle to the information led to dead ends.

"A week later, in the middle of the night, there was a knock on my hotel door. A tattered envelope was flung under the door. All it said was, 'Ms. Wambuzi.' I didn't recognize the name immediately. But with a little research, my team discovered that Wambuzi was the maiden name of General Nyoko's wife. Now I had something.

"General Nyoko was always very vocal about never allowing the Nyumbani to be a sovereign territory. He said that Malunga had made that mistake once before when it granted sovereignty to Kipaji."

Baba nearly jumped out of his seat. "Granted? You didn't grant us anything! You attacked us and we kicked your—"

"Whoa, Baba!" D'Melo interrupted. "Why are you getting so upset?"

Baba settled back into the sofa. "Sorry. This stuff is very . . . personal to me."

Kyle Sandersen voice-over: "This could explain why a Mercedes Benz was parked at the cottage. We assume that General Nyoko was at the meeting. But who met him there? Who had the most to gain from President Amani's assassination? That much was clear: Vice President Dimka. But could he have been the second person at that meeting?"

Abruptly, Baba excused himself and started for his bedroom.

"Baba, where are you going?" D'Melo said. "This is the best part."

"Continue without me," Baba replied, clearly trying to sound at peace with it all. "I know what happened. Remember? I lived it." He paused at Diata's drawing on the wall and gazed at it intensely. "*Haki inakuja kwako,*" he muttered, then slowly walked away to his room.

"That was strange," Zara said to D'Melo. "Think he's okay?"

"I'm not sure. I'll check on him in a few."

Kyle Sandersen voice-over: "We went to the Government Records Office, where public records are kept on the movements of top government officials. On the night of the secret meeting, Vice President Dimka's whereabouts were not logged into the record. This was quite an irregular omission. Every other evening that month had an entry for him. As for General Nyoko, the records indicated that he was at an official event in Yandun. He was the keynote speaker at an annual charity dinner. His speech was over by 6:45 p.m. The taxi driver said he picked up his passenger in an abandoned building at 7 p.m. The hotel where the event was being held was only a ten-minute walk to that abandoned building. We spoke to several participants at that event. Not one of them remembered seeing the General after his speech.

"So could that top secret meeting in the cottage have been between Vice President Dimka and General Nyoko? In that meeting, did they plot the assassination of President Amani? Did they instigate the ethnic cleansing that followed? Was the genocide part of the plan or did things just spin out of control?"

The film ended. D'Melo and Zara sat speechless, processing what they just saw.

"Whoa," Zara mused. "The situation was so much worse than I thought. It's crazy!"

"I know," D'Melo said. "But I wish it was clearer who killed President Amani."

"True. But the good thing is, all these years people believed the Shujas did it. Now we know that it probably wasn't them."

The wall clock chimed eleven times. "Ohhh, I better get home." Zara hopped to her feet and slid into her coat.

D'Melo offered to walk her home. "I'm okay," she said. "You need to check on Baba. Call me before you go to sleep."

As soon as he saw Zara out, D'Melo went to Baba's bedroom door. It was closed. D'Melo peaked in. Baba appeared to be sound asleep.

As soon as D'Melo was gone, Baba's eyes sprung open. Sleep would allude him all night. The documentary had stirred up agonizing memories that he had desperately tried to leave behind. And worst of all, the one thing he had hoped would be in the film wasn't there. Toward the end when the director posed so many unanswered questions about the secret meeting, Baba knew that Sandersen hadn't found the package containing the evidence of who killed President Amani. And so the ever-present threat to D'Melo and his life would continue.

For the next few days, Zara's texts were less frequent and had less to say. She stopped going to D'Melo's house, which had become a regular part of her day. And at school, as much as she tried to act normal with D'Melo, she knew that he realized something was wrong. But by the end of the week, his patience was worn. He asked her why she was distancing herself. She apologized and explained that she was just going through something.

The following morning, Zara finished her run at D'Melo's house. D'Melo was still asleep. Baba encouraged her to wake him. "The sun is up, so should he be."

Zara quietly entered D'Melo's bedroom. Even though she had been in his room several times, she still marveled at how tidy he kept it. Not one thing was out of place. All his schoolbooks were lined by height on his bookshelf. His notebooks were stacked at the left corner of his desk. His pens and pencils stood orderly in an old metal coffee tin. She didn't even need to look in his dresser to know that his clothes were sharply folded and neatly tucked away.

She parked herself heavily on his bed, intentionally sending a wave through the mattress. He didn't budge. She bounced. He still didn't move. Zara's impatience turned mischievous. She poked her finger in his ear. "Dude, get up!"

He stirred, then flitted one eye open. "Aww, man. I'm trying to sleep, dawg. What time is it?"

"You don't need to know the time. The sun's up, and so should you be."

He sucked his teeth, irritated. "You've been talking to Baba." He turned away and settled back into his pillow.

She rocked him. "Get up, you lazy bum. You're wasting this wonderful day!" She tugged his covers down. "I'll take you to breakfast to celebrate the first day of spring break."

"No thanks," he grumbled. "Every time you take me somewhere, I always end up paying anyway." D'Melo drew his covers back up.

"Oooh, now you're just strumming my nerves." She jostled him. "Get up, punk!"

D'Melo quickly spun and grabbed her. He flipped her over his body into the bed and tickled her. She giggled, half-fighting his tickle attack.

Baba bounded through the door. "Hey! What's going on in here?" he said, feigning anger. "You know you're not allowed to have girls in your bed."

"Baba, it's Zara," D'Melo quipped. "She ain't a girl."

"What!" Zara started tickling him back.

"Zara," Baba chuckled. "I think I can leave now. It seems you've got this under control."

While D'Melo readied himself for the day, Zara sat with Baba at the dining room table. Without her asking, he brought a steaming cup of green tea—her favorite morning drink.

Zara took a breath. "Baba," she said. "Why did you leave before the movie was over that night?"

Baba took a few breaths, too. "It just brought back too many memories of D'Melo's mother. I wish you could have met her. She was a fireball, just like you."

In an instant, Zara felt a deep sadness. Her eyes turned liquid green. "Baba," her voice quivered. "I, I—"

Baba clutched her hand. "What is it, my sweet lioness?"

"I've decided, um—," she paused, wiping her tears. "I've decided to go to Malunga after graduation. I'm gonna intern with Kyle Sandersen's film company."

Baba leaned back in his chair. He drew his hands down his face. "Well, that sounds like a wonderful opportunity," he sighed. "But I assume you haven't told D'Melo. If you had, he wouldn't be singing in the shower right now."

"I don't know how to tell him, Baba. I've wanted to, but I haven't been able to get up the courage."

"Well, my dear, this is not something that will be made easier with time."

"I know. That's why I came this morning. I plan to tell him at breakfast."

"Can I suggest that I leave, and you tell him here? He'll want to be at home when he hears this news."

Zara nodded somberly.

"What about you?" Baba asked, looking at her with concern. "How are you doing?"

"It hurts, Baba. It's hurts really bad."

Baba patted her moist cheeks with a napkin.

"D'Melo's the best person I've ever known. So many times, I've wondered why he chose to be friends with me. And then I'm just filled with gratitude that he did." Her tears turned into sobs.

"Zara, look at me."

Zara lifted her face.

"I will never let you disparage yourself. You are deserving of his friendship in every way. You're amazing in your own right. D'Melo had been broken for years. Since his mother died, he's had a gaping hole in his heart. He tried to fill it with basketball and by keeping himself busy in all kinds of things. Have you ever met anyone who is the president of more school clubs?"

Zara chuckled through her sniffles.

"It's like he's running all the time because he thinks if he stops, he'll get sucked down into the hole. Well, you're filling that hole for him. I've never seen him more at peace than he has been this year."

"Baba, telling me this is only making it harder. I don't want to leave him either. As much as you think I've done for him, he's done even more for me. Besides my mom dying, this is the hardest thing I've ever had to go through. While my heart tugs at me to go to Malunga, my mind just doesn't want to believe it. I'm probably not making any sense."

"No, you're making perfect sense. And that's why you must go. Trust your heart, it'll never lie to you like your mind will. Your friendship with D'Melo is strong. It'll withstand the distance between you."

D'Melo's bedroom door squeaked open. Baba rose to leave. "*Bahati njema*, good luck." He wrapped his arm around Zara and leaned his head onto hers. "It'll all work out. It always does."

Zara hastily dabbed her eyes and straightened in her chair as D'Melo shuffled in.

"Hey. Where's Baba?"

"He stepped out for a few minutes."

"Have you been crying? Your face has that puffy thing happening."

Zara's lips quivered. D'Melo sat apprehensively.

"D'Melo," she murmured, trying to keep eye contact. "You're the best friend I've ever had."

D'Melo seemed to brace himself. He interlaced his fingers and lifted his hands to his mouth.

Zara took a deep, shuddering breath. "After we saw the documentary, I contacted Kyle Sandersen. He's working on a follow-up to his Malunga story."

D'Melo fidgeted nervously in his chair.

"He invited me to Malunga to work for his company." Zara laid quavering hands over her nose. "I leave the day after graduation." She gazed anxiously at D'Melo over her fingers, waiting for his reaction. She was shaken by his silence.

Finally, D'Melo mumbled, "Will you be back in time to start college in the fall?"

She let out a weighty sigh. "It's a two-year internship."

D'Melo's face dropped despondently. Staring vacantly into the distance, he said, "Why are you going? I don't understand. You got into Temple, a great journalism school. Isn't that what you wanted?"

"It was. But after seeing the film, I realized that I can't be content in a comfy classroom in America knowing what's happening to the Shuja people."

"It's messed up there, but—" D'Melo shrugged indifferently.

"'It's messed up.' That's it?" Zara's sadness began to burn away. "You don't care about the injustice going on there?"

"I didn't say I don't care. But what can I do about it?"

"If everyone thought that way, nothing would ever change in this world. What if Nelson Mandela said that? South Africa could still be under apartheid."

"I'm not Nelson Mandela. I'm just D'Melo from Lincoln Downs. My way of helping is to become a teacher. Is there something wrong with teaching kids about the history of the country they live in?"

"Of course not. Teaching kids is admirable, but there are people out there in the world that really need you. *Your* people."

D'Melo stiffened. He glared intensely at Zara. "They're NOT my people!" he said harshly. "I'm an American. And I'm gonna teach *my* people American history. I don't know why you're acting like Africans are your people; they're *black* and you're *white*."

As soon as the words escaped his mouth, D'Melo diverted his eyes. Zara knew he understood how they had pierced her heart.

Zara tightened her lips, trying to stop herself from firing words at him that she would regret. It was a discipline she had learned from D'Melo himself—but one he unfortunately had forgotten in this moment. Zara lifted herself up and walked heavily to the door. As she grabbed the handle, still facing away from D'Melo, she asked gingerly, "You're not going to say anything?"

After a few moments of stony silence, he said coldly, "What do you want me to say? *Edu?*"

Zara's face burned as blood flooded it. She was ready to explode.

Just then Baba returned, pushing open the door behind her.

A deluge of tears threatened to spill from Zara's eyes, but she didn't dare to let even one drop. "You know, D'Melo," she said, her face trembling with rage and sorrow. "You love American history so much, here's a tidbit for you. One of your American heroes said something long ago that is as true today as it was then. So I hope when you're in front of those kids teaching history, you tell them this: 'All that tyranny needs to gain a foothold is for people of good conscience to remain silent.' Thomas Jefferson. But maybe you should teach yourself that first!" She started to leave, then paused. "And by the way, just so you know, *all* people are my people."

"Sorry, Baba," Zara said, as she stormed past him.

D'Melo shut his eyes and sat in silence, his gut churning. He hoped desperately that this was just another nightmare that he would wake up from.

"D'Melo," Baba said sternly. "Go after her!" He held the door open.

D'Melo rose and trudged to his bedroom, and without another word, he slammed the door shut.

CHAPTER EIGHT

Zara's Secret

It was the longest spring break ever. D'Melo and Zara hadn't spoken for a week. For the prior few months, there had been nary a day that they didn't talk. D'Melo hadn't fully realized the extent to which Zara had become a part of his life. Now that she wasn't around, the space she filled was crushingly apparent.

Saturday was the opening weekend at the Citadel. The boyz hoped that basketball would take D'Melo's mind off Zara. It didn't.

"Yo, D. Where you goin'?" Jeylan fretted.

D'Melo strode off the court. "Was that my phone?" He looked at the screen, then sighed, disappointed.

"Come on, dawg. We're in the middle of a game and you're checkin' your phone? Get your head right and let's get our money."

The LD boyz were losing big to the Strickland Heights neighborhood, a team they usually handled quite easily. Typically, D'Melo was upbeat on the court, having fun being unstoppable. Today he was lethargic and unfocused. Basketball had become a chore rather than the thing he loved to do most.

After the game, the Strickland team asked for their fifty dollars.

Jeylan turned to Marley. "Marls, pay the dude."

"What! Why do I gotta pay?" Marley objected. "I didn't even play."

"Cuz you the only one with a job!"

"Well, y'all fools need to start working. Because as long as D'Melo's like this, y'all gonna be losin' a lot of games." Marley handed the Strickland player the cash. "This ain't right," he protested. "This has to be a violation of my human rights or something."

D'Melo started home. He didn't even bother to say goodbye.

The boyz caught up with him. Kazim got straight to the point. "Just call her, man."

"Nah," D'Melo rebuffed, sounding sterner than he intended. "I don't need her."

"I told you about those white girls!" Jeylan butted in. "But I gotta agree with this fool. You need to call that girl."

Kazim had a go at lightening the mood. "Man, if she wasn't your boo, I'd be all like, 'Girrrl, you must be tired, cuz you been running through my mind all day.'"

"I told y'all, she ain't my girlfriend. We're just friends! Well," D'Melo corrected himself, "we *were* just friends."

D'Melo trudged up the stoop to his house. Before he ducked inside, Kazim tried one more time.

"Yo, you should do something special for her birthday. That'll get you back in the game." D'Melo eyed Kazim uncertainly.

"Man, are you kidding?" Kazim chided. "You don't even know that tomorrow's her birthday?"

"Of course, I do. I'm just wondering how *you* know."

"I know all the hotties' birthdays. The school receptionist likes me. She lets me look in the student files. I send each hottie a birthday card with a little *Kaz-anova* note in it. Man, you just don't know how much play I get with that."

"Yeah, I do. None."

"Whatever, dawg. You need to lock away your pride and get right with that girl."

After a full day of wallowing, D'Melo realized that Kazim was right—maybe for the first time ever. The following morning, he woke energized, but also a shade nauseous. *What if she doesn't want to see me? I can't believe I said they're not her people.* He jabbed a finger into his temple, *So stupid!*

D'Melo pushed his fears aside for the moment. He had to at least try. "Baba," he called. "I'm going to Zara's."

Baba let out a grateful sigh, as if D'Melo's words were an answer to prayer.

D'Melo bounded for the drugstore. The bell rang hollow behind the door; Zara wasn't there. Tomáš lamented that she had been leaving early every morning and returning late at night. He had no idea where she had been going.

"I think I know," D'Melo piped. He took out his phone and Googled "the tallest building in Philadelphia." He scanned the results, then bolted.

Tomáš whispered to himself, "*Edu.*"

D'Melo quickly reached the building. The rectangular mountain of glass stretched up into the clouds. He hopped in the elevator and anxiously tapped the button for the sixtieth floor. The flashing floor numbers made it seem as if he was shooting through the sky, but he could hardly feel the motion.

He stepped out into a restaurant with a 360-degree view of the city. His eyes combed the patrons, but he didn't see Zara. He asked the hostess if a redheaded girl had come in.

"There've been a few actually," she said. "Can you describe her?"

"The best way to describe her is, if she was here, you'd know. It's as if there's a spotlight directed on her and the rest of the room exists in her shadow. She has that thing that's just impossible to go unnoticed. And when she smiles at you, you feel like you can't breathe."

"Oh!" The hostess smiled at his outpouring. "You're talking about Zara."

"Yes!" D'Melo's heart leapt. "She's here?" The hostess gestured to the stairwell that led to the roof.

D'Melo scaled the steps two at a time. He halted at the top, taking a moment to calm the butterflies flittering in his stomach. He softly nudged the door open.

Zara was looking out at the city, leaning against the protective metal poles. Her hair whipped in the swirling wind. She lifted strands of her bangs and tucked them behind her ear, but a gust immediately freed them again. She slipped a hairband off her wrist and nimbly wrapped her silky hair into a ponytail. Then she drew her ponytail over her shoulder and tickled her cheek with it—something D'Melo had come to realize she does when she's in thoughtful reflection.

D'Melo allowed himself a moment to drink her in. Then, just as he had gathered the courage to lay his heart on the line, pesky doubts seeped into his addled mind. He was afraid that when she saw him, the sparkle that used to light her smiling eyes would be absent because of the anguish caused by his reckless words. The thought of this possibility constricted his aching heart.

She's better off without me, he convinced himself. He retreated quietly into the stairwell.

Zara called out, "Hey, punk." She turned to D'Melo closing the door. "Where are you going?"

He froze. "How'd you know I was here?"

"I can feel your pain. Remember? And the closer you are, the more it hurts."

He shambled contritely across the roof and sidled up next to her. Side by side, they gazed at the sprawling city below. D'Melo's eyes followed the Schuylkill River snaking around downtown to Fairmont

Park. He realized how few places he had been outside of Lincoln Downs.

Zara positioned herself in front of him. She aligned her straightened arm with his line of sight, then tracked it slowly westward. "If you scan left from the park, you can see LD High. Now if you look to the far corner of the school, you should be able to see it."

"See what?" D'Melo said, squinting.

"The spot where I scorched you on the court!" She bumped him playfully with her hip.

D'Melo's eyes perused the city. "You know, you're right. It's nice up here."

Zara nodded. "It's the only place I've been able to find any peace since our fight. I know people are suffering down there," she bemoaned, gesturing to the thousands of tiny houses below. "But I don't feel any of it. It's so strange that, for me, it's such an incredible feeling to not feel anything at all."

"Well, I even screwed that up," D'Melo said regretfully. "Your chest must have been hurting all week because of me."

"I didn't mind. It's sweet that your heart aches because you miss me. That *is* why your heart was hurting, isn't it?"

"You'll never know." He grinned. "Hey, wait a second. You felt me suffering, and you didn't call me?"

"I wanted to, really . . . desperately, but I couldn't." Zara's gaze dropped. "I was too afraid that you didn't want to be friends anymore. I think my heart would have instantly stopped beating."

D'Melo sighed, feeling a mix of emotions. He was overjoyed that Zara cared so much about him but also devastated that she was afraid he would hurt her again.

D'Melo gazed ruefully into her eyes. "Zara, I'm so sorry. I never should have said those things that day. I didn't mean any of it. You're the first person who has ever really made me face myself, and I got defensive and lashed out like a child."

"You don't need to apologize. You were right. Who am I to tell you how you should live your life? You've done a great job with it. You have friends who treasure you and a father who absolutely adores you. If I had that, maybe everything wouldn't rile me up so much."

Zara then realized that D'Melo had his hand behind his back the whole time they had been talking. "So what do you have there?"

"Where?" He played dumb.

Zara tilted her head. "Ahhh, there," she said, bemused, pointing around him.

"Oh this? It's just a vegan red velvet cupcake. I always carry it with me."

"Oh, really?" she smirked. "You'd think I would have noticed something like that. And do you always carry it with a candle in it?"

"Okay, you got me." D'Melo grinned. "Happy birthday!"

"You know, this is the second-best birthday present I've gotten this year. A card came in the mail yesterday. I'll give you one guess who it was from."

D'Melo inclined his head, *Oh no. Seriously?*

"Yep! Your buddy Kazim. I thought it was really nice," she said. Then she raised her eyebrows. "Until I opened it. He wrote some crazy thing about running in his mind all day." They chuckled.

D'Melo dug a matchbook out of his backpack and snapped up a flame. Zara cupped her hands around it to protect the feeble flicker from the wind. She took a deep breath, her cheeks puffed with air. As she moved to blow out the candle, D'Melo poked his finger into her forehead.

"Uh uh! What's up with the wish, dawg?"

Zara widened her eyes, *Come on, dude. Are we six years old?* She laid a pensive finger against her puckered lips. "Hmmm . . . let me see." She gazed fondly at D'Melo and then said softly, "There's nothing to wish for. This moment is perfect. It doesn't need anything else." She quickly blew out the flame before D'Melo could object and insist she do it right. "Can we eat it now? I'm so hungry, I could eat a vegan horse!"

"Like you need a reason to eat!" D'Melo quipped, as he peeled back one side of the cupcake wrapper. Zara opened wide and chomped down, leaving a coat of red frosting around her lips. D'Melo crammed the rest of the cupcake into his mouth. When the taste registered on their tongues, they grimaced open-mouthed and gawked at each other.

"Can I?" Zara sputtered, cupcake crumbs shooting from her over-stuffed mouth. D'Melo nodded, wild-eyed.

She dashed to the garbage can by the door to spew it out. As her ponytail swung back and forth with her gait, D'Melo caught a glimpse of something on her neck. They emptied their mouths into the can. "That's nasty!" D'Melo spat. "I'm sorry. I should've known when the recipe called for beet juice to color the frosting!"

"You made that? Aww, that's so sweet. Well actually, it wasn't sweet at all. It tasted like tree bark."

"Don't I get any credit for the effort?" D'Melo said, then remembered Zara's neck. "Hey, turn around for a sec. I wanna see something."

"Dude," Zara narrowed her eyes. "What kind of credit are you expecting! Are you getting fresh with me?"

"You wish. Just turn around, dawg. I saw something I never noticed before." He shifted her ponytail to the side. "It looks like a tiny heart."

"It's a birthmark. It runs in my family. My mother had one and my grandfather has one."

D'Melo ran his finger over it. "It's cute." His gentle touch sent a titillating ripple down Zara's spine.

"Oh, snap." He gaped at the time. "We gotta go!"

"Go where? I'm wearing workout clothes, and I'm a messy sweat ball."

"Don't worry, Stinky. You're dressed perfectly for where we're headed."

D'Melo had borrowed a car from Jeylan's father. Before long, he and Zara were out of the bustling city and into the tranquil countryside. As the old-growth trees zipped by, Zara felt more and more at home. After a couple hours of shady country roads, D'Melo pulled into a parking lot in the Pocono Mountains. "It's time to get our hike on."

"What! You? Hike?" Zara raised an eyebrow. "I better get going before you change your mind!" She started for the green trail.

"Hey," D'Melo called. "That trail's for amateurs."

"That's right," she said. "Amateurs—like you!"

"We're going on this one, dawg." D'Melo pointed to the sign for the red trail.

"That trail's three miles and for '*Experienced Hikers Only!*'"

"I sprint around a basketball court for forty minutes! How hard can it be to walk along a trail?"

"All right," Zara shrugged dubiously. "If you insist."

D'Melo dashed off. "Come on, Stinky. You gonna let me embarrass you at your own sport?"

Thirty minutes later, D'Melo felt the pain. "This trail is hella steep."

"Well," Zara said. "Did you think the mountain was going to be flat?"

D'Melo puffed heavily.

"Maybe you should rest with those little old ladies over there," she gibed, gesturing to a bench. "You can exchange cupcake recipes."

"I'm dying over here, and you got jokes."

A bent, elderly woman in a shiny light blue sweat suit tottered past. "What's wrong, kiddo?" she said. "No more gas in the tank?"

Zara burst into red-faced laughter. The old lady then wobbled up to Zara. "Oh, dear," she said, very motherly. She dribbled water from her bottle onto a napkin. "You have something caked on your face." She rubbed around Zara's mouth. "You really should take better care of yourself, dear."

Zara glared at D'Melo, *Unbelievable!* "Dude, I'm just wondering, were you ever planning to let me know that I had beet-juice frosting all over my face?"

He laughed.

When they reached the end of the trail, they gazed for a long moment at the mountain peak across the river valley. "This is . . ." Zara searched for the right words, "just perfect." She slid her arm under D'Melo's and leaned her head against his shoulder. "Thank you."

"You're welcome, but we're just getting started." D'Melo signaled the guys in the sports equipment store in the cluster of shops at the peak. They lugged over hang gliders.

"No way, dude!" Zara's mouth dropped open.

After some exhaustive safety instructions, they strapped in. D'Melo gawked into the valley, which suddenly struck him as an awfully long way down, and a horrible way to die. He swiveled his head toward the instructor strapped in above him. "You know what you're doing, right?"

"I guess," the instructor said facetiously. "It's my first time, too."

"What? Get me off this thing!" D'Melo wriggled, trying to unstrap himself.

Zara guffawed. "He's joking, dude." She turned to her instructor. "You guys *have* done this before, right?"

"I guess we'll find out," he smirked, then shoved off the side of the mountain. They floated out over the valley.

After the initial shock of soaring two thousand feet above the ground, D'Melo settled in. He heard Zara scream, "This is AWESOME!"

They drifted weightlessly in the salubrious air, reveling in the serenity of utter silence. D'Melo pointed toward the waterfall. The instructors redirected the gliders. Mist tickled their faces with hundreds of tiny wet kisses. They swooped gradually, riding gentle winds all the way down. The river glinted tangerine, as the soft sun flickered tinsel across the water.

"Woooo!" Zara exclaimed, as her feet rejoined the earth. "Let's go again!"

"If we could take an elevator up, I'd be game," D'Melo said. "But now, it's time for your favorite activity: eating."

D'Melo drove into town. He had reserved a table at the only Eastern European restaurant in the area, Bistro Nadia.

"I really appreciate you doing all this for me," Zara raved. "I've had such a great time."

A smile twinkled in D'Melo's eyes.

"But," she jabbed, "you still owe me a movie, punk!"

"Dang, girl, what does a brotha gotta do? I take you hiking, hang gliding, and even feed you, and you're still talking about that movie!"

They turned a blissful gaze to the sun, which had just dipped below the horizon between the mountains. "Did you know that the name 'Pocono' comes from the Munsee Indian word, *Pokawachne?*" D'Melo said. "It means, 'Creek Between Two Hills.'"

Zara smirked. "You're such a show-off."

On the ride back to Philadelphia, Zara was unusually quiet. D'Melo knew this meant one of two things: either she had super-glued her lips together by accident or she was wallowing in self-pity. He much preferred the former, because when Zara sank into that dark place in her mind, he had learned she could be a bit of a handful.

Zara stared out her window into the swiftly passing woods. She sniffled, then rubbed a finger under her eye, wiping away a tear. "I'm just thinking about how amazing today was. I don't deserve your friendship," she said sadly.

In his head, D'Melo lamented, *Why couldn't it have been the super glue?*

"You've been so good to me, and I just haven't been able to—" she whispered, "you know, open myself up to you, fully. Do you know what I'm trying to say?"

With Zara, any number of things could have been upsetting her. But this took D'Melo by surprise. "Yeah, but it's cool. We're just friends. I'm good with that. When we got into that fight last week, I realized that I just want you in my life. I don't care in what way. But," D'Melo said, confused. "What about Brandon?"

"Brandon? You think my relationship with him has anything to do with this? Brandon and I are *really* just friends."

"But you said—"

"I said that we became more than friends when my mom was sick. I needed someone to lean on. It was never physical with him. It was emotional. So actually," Zara continued, suddenly shy, "I've never actually had a boyfriend. It's not easy for me to give my heart to someone, let alone anything else."

"So you never, uh . . ." D'Melo swirled his finger around, looking a lot like he was trying to conjure a mini tornado.

"No. I haven't," Zara replied firmly. "And what exactly is that you're doing with your finger?"

D'Melo lowered his hand, embarrassed. "Well," he divulged, "I haven't either."

"Really?" she said. "How is that possible? You have girls swooning all over you."

"It makes more sense than you might think. I was raised with traditional and *strict* Kipaji values." His eyes widened for emphasis. "If I ever even thought about it, I'd see my mom's face. She'd be glaring at me like the time I tried to steal a candy bar when I was five. She swooped down on me like a hawk on a poor little mouse. Her face was so tight, like an overblown balloon. I thought it was gonna burst into shreds right there in the Wawa. My whole body was numb with fear. I never *ever* want to see that face again," he chortled.

"You're so different than anyone I've ever met," Zara said fondly. Then her melancholy quickly returned. "I wish I wasn't so closed off with my feelings," she said. "But I'm always so scared."

"Scared? But you seem so fearless."

"I have to be that way so the fear doesn't swallow me whole. I hate that I'm like this." She burst into tears.

D'Melo pulled over on the shoulder of the highway. He took her hand in his.

Zara's eyes rose, then dropped again. "I've never told anyone this."

D'Melo's heartbeat quickened. He sensed something devastating in her secret.

"When my mom—" Zara's breathing became choppy. "When my mom was sick, I kept asking her about my father. I thought that if he knew, he'd help. My mom would just shrug off the questions. But I kept hounding her." Zara wiped her moist cheeks. "I couldn't just watch her die when all we needed was money. Finally, my mom couldn't take my pestering anymore, and one day she yelled at me, 'He doesn't care about me—or you!'

"She had never raised her voice at me before." Zara sobbed. "I ran to my room. My grandfather came in after me, sat down, and started telling me about my father. My grandmother tried to stop him, but he said that I was old enough and that I needed to know."

Zara then recounted a story about her mother, Tereza. Tereza decided to go to college in Nečzia to reconnect with her roots. During her first week, the dean of the school invited her to his house for a group luncheon. The dean personally met with the foreign students every year to give them an orientation on Eastern Europe. When she arrived at his house, no one else was there yet. The dean offered to give her a tour. He took her to his study, where photos of him buddying up with Eastern European leaders hung on the walls. Tereza started to feel uncomfortable. She asked what time everyone else was coming. He told her that he had decided to make this a special orientation just for her. She insisted that she come back when the other students had their orientation.

"My mom started for the door." Zara's voice trembled. "But he closed it before she could get out. She begged him to let her leave." Zara began to weep heavily. "He threw her down and assaulted her."

"Oh, my God." D'Melo wrapped Zara tightly in his arms. "I'm so sorry," he said, his voice quavering.

Zara burst into a full-blown cry. She pulled out of the hug and stared at him, apparently deciding whether to continue. D'Melo was crying now, too.

Zara took a deep, shuddering breath. "After he assaulted my mom—" She covered her face, slashed with agony. Unable to catch her breath, she paused for a long moment. "I—I," she tried, her voice breaking between sobs. The words hurt so much she could barely squeeze them out. "I was born nine months later." She screamed and erupted into uncontrollable tears. She buried her face in D'Melo's chest. "No! No!" she wailed in anguish, pounding his shoulder. She began to hyperventilate, struggling to breath, but managed to let out an occasional woeful gasp.

D'Melo's mind searched for something, *anything*, to take her pain away. But in this moment, all he could do was sit numbly, his brain wading through agonizing fog. He wiped the tears streaming down his face. "I wish I could say something to make this better."

"There's nothing to say," Zara choked out. She abruptly pulled away again. She grasped his shoulders firmly. "Promise me," she said, shaking him, her green eyes wet with tears. "*Promise* that you won't be different with me now. That this won't change our relationship."

Although D'Melo had been at a loss for words, he had absolutely no problem expressing his heart about this. He leaned toward her, his eyes fixed reassuringly on hers. "Never, Zar. *Never!*" His heart felt like it was about to explode. Now he truly understood why Zara said her ability to feel other people's suffering was a curse. She had enough pain of her own to deal with, more than anyone should ever have to endure.

Other than the occasional whipping sound of passing cars, they sat in silence for several minutes. Finally, Zara tentatively dragged her eyes up to D'Melo's. She looked at him searchingly.

D'Melo hoped she could see all the warmth he felt for her in his eyes. But she wilted in clear dismay, her body wracked from intense sobbing.

D'Melo lifted strands of hair pasted to her sweaty forehead. He tucked them behind her ear. He removed a handkerchief from his backpack and wiped her face. Zara closed her eyes, absorbing his tenderness, a tenderness she couldn't give to herself.

"Is there anything that's *not* in that bag of yours?" she sniffled.

"Yeah," D'Melo quipped, "a change of shirt. So it would be nice if you stopped wiping your snot all over me."

"Oh, my God! You're such a jerk!" She chased him with her drippy nose acting like she was going to slather him with it. "I don't know how you do it," she said. "Even during the worst times, you can make me laugh."

D'Melo set off for home. They rode wordlessly, allowing each other the space they needed to process the moment.

They arrived at the drugstore. Zara lifted her weary body out of the car. She poked her head back in. "Aren't you coming?"

"Are you sure you don't want to be alone?"

Zara raised a cheek, doubtfully. "Trust me, when I go in there, I will definitely *not* be alone."

D'Melo followed her up the stairs to the apartment. Zara's open palm appeared behind her. D'Melo slipped his hand into hers. When she opened the door, her grandparents and their friends belted out, "Happy birthday!" Zara did her best to act surprised, like she always had at her "surprise" birthday parties.

She smirked at D'Melo and whispered, "Told you, dude."

Although Zara never wanted to make a big deal of her birthday, she had to admit that her grandparents and their Nečzian friends looked awfully cute in their party hats, blowing tinsel horns. They snapped hats stingingly onto Zara and D'Melo as they entered.

The apartment was vibrantly decorated in the colors of the Nečzian flag—red, green, and yellow streamers were looped around the ceiling and balloons floated off the floor at each step. Tall bouquets of cheery flowers embellished every corner. And, there was no such thing as a Nečzian birthday without enough food to feed a small country. A long table brimmed with *chlebíčky*, open sandwiches; *jednohubky*, small pieces of bread garnished with egg, cheese, or vegetables; and an assortment of Eastern European baked goodies, including Zara's favorite—*kolaczki*, a crispy vegan cream cheese cookie.

Uneasy about holding Zara's hand in front of her grandparents, D'Melo loosened his grip. But Zara latched on. Tomáš' eyes dropped to their clasped hands. He smiled and gave D'Melo a fist bump.

When Zara ambled off to mingle with the guests, Tomáš whispered to D'Melo, "Thanks for bringing her back."

"It was the best *and* the hardest day of my life," D'Melo sighed.

"She told you?"

D'Melo nodded.

"She's been debating for a while. She treasures your relationship and was afraid something would change between you."

They glanced over at Zara being celebrated by her elderly friends. "They love her so much," Tomáš said. "Through the years, Zara would write letters to each of them. They'd rush into the drugstore waving the envelope. They'd say, 'I got my letter from Zara!' Then they'd tell me what was going on in Zara's life, as if I didn't already know."

The ladies edged their way into a vague line in front of Zara. One by one, they offered words of advice for the coming year. The women were speaking in Nečzian, and Zara seemed to understand. D'Melo wondered how much more there was to Zara that he still didn't know.

"Mr. Zanič," D'Melo said, at a loss. "What's up with the nose twisting?"

"Oh! I guess that *is* a little strange, huh?" Tomáš chuckled. "They twist the birthday girl's nose to make sure she remembers the advice. In the olden days, parents would do this with their children. It doesn't happen anymore, outside of this birthday tradition."

Zara crossed to D'Melo and offered him *jednohubky* from her plate. She snapped a photo of him in his party hat. She threatened to post it on the Lincoln High Facebook group.

"You better not!" D'Melo reached for her phone.

"Hey, it's my birthday. I can do whatever I want today."

"Every day must be your birthday, because you always do whatever you want!"

"All right, you big baby. I won't post the photo, but you have to do something else for me."

"What? That sounds a little ominous."

"You'll find out really soon." Zara paused, listening for it. "It's coming any—"

Before she could finish her sentence, a woman called out, "Zara, it's time!"

Zara tilted her head and finished, "—minute now." She smiled at D'Melo as she backed her way into the space cleared for dancing.

Before the music started, Zara settled into the traditional opening pose—an arm bent over her head and a hand resting on her protruding hip, accentuating the female figure. The sweet shrill of violins pierced the air thick with anticipation. Zara curved her body slowly in waves to the enchanting cadence. She slid her arms side to side before her face, creating an air of mystery. In an instant, she halted and held the position. Then, she clapped her hands twice briskly. Drums entered, reverberating through the apartment. The tempo quickened to a fevered pace. Zara transitioned into rhythmic twirls, heel slaps, foot stomps, and graceful spins. The jubilant spectators snapped their fingers and whistled exuberantly.

D'Melo gaped in awe at Zara. She moved like a sensual angel. He had never seen a dance so poignant and beautiful—a dance of joy, depth, mystery, and allure. A celebration of life. And who better to perform such a dance than Zara.

After a couple of minutes, everyone joined in. Zara grabbed D'Melo's hand and hauled him onto the dance floor. "It's my birthday," she said. "Remember?"

"How can I forget," he jested. "You remind me every five minutes."

D'Melo did his best to follow Zara's movements. He instantly became the center of attention. They all loved that he was trying, although he looked like a fish flopping around, gasping for oxygen. The old folks giggled and cheered him on.

He whispered in Zara's ear, "What's so funny?"

Zara told him that men have their own dance, which was different and a *lot* less feminine than the dance that women do.

"Oh, so everyone's cheering for me not because I'm kickin' it, but because they want me to continue making a fool of myself!"

Zara hunched over in deep laughter. D'Melo couldn't take his eyes off her. When Zara laughed, her eyes creased into a crescent and twinkled like the starry sky. The whole room glowed from her radiance. D'Melo's heart was full.

D'Melo was passed from one elderly woman to the next. He was laughing at himself now, as well. Zara shut her eyes to capture the moment, then mimed to D'Melo that she was depositing the moment into her "happy bank." He knew that just like good words she loved, she saved up these moments to help her cope during the more trying times.

Zara's grandparents broke out the *murzynek*—a traditional Eastern European cake with a chocolate glaze. They asked Zara to make a wish before blowing out the candles. She glanced at D'Melo with a wink. He knew what she was thinking: *There's nothing to wish for. This moment is perfect. It doesn't need anything else.*

A shade tipsy, her geriatric friends sang and danced their way out the door. Tomáš grabbed the broom and started to sweep the crumbs on the floor.

"You know, Tomáš," Babička said. "I'm tired. Let's go to bed." Tomáš was surprised, because everyone knew his wife was a clean freak. Babička shifted her eyes, not so subtly, in the direction of Zara and D'Melo.

"Ohhh." Tomáš caught on. He propped the broom against the stone kitchen wall. They gave Zara a final birthday kiss and shuffled off to bed. Zara fondly watched her grandparents disappear into their room.

D'Melo broke for the broom. Zara's eyes glistened at him. After sweeping and washing the dishes, they plopped down on the couch, exhausted.

"Phew," Zara puffed, inclining her head. "What a day!"

"Well, it's not quite over yet."

"Dude," she said, wearily but excited. "I don't think I can take anymore!"

"Technically, I haven't made good on our bet. So," D'Melo slipped his computer from his backpack. "We're gonna watch *The Queen of Sheba*."

Zara smiled deeply, as she nestled cozily into the couch.

As the movie started, she kissed D'Melo lightly on the cheek and rested gratefully on his welcoming shoulder. Before the end of the first scene, Zara drifted off to sleep. D'Melo replaced his shoulder with a pillow and brought her down gently. He laid a blanket over her and tucked in the edges. He padded gingerly to the door. Just as he was about to turn the knob, Zara said drowsily, "Thanks for the best day of my life."

D'Melo grinned warmly and said under his breath, "Thank you for mine."

As he strolled home, his emotions eddied from euphoric to dread and back again. He had never imagined that he could feel so much for someone. At the same time, he also couldn't imagine life without that someone when she left for Malunga.

In her final lucid moments before falling back to sleep, Zara remembered her fear that telling D'Melo about her father would change their relationship. She realized that she was right, it did change their relationship. A quiet sense of bliss filled her body—they were closer now than ever.

CHAPTER NINE

Haki Inakuja Kwako

Graduation was an eagerly awaited moment for most high schoolers. It held the promise of freedom, independence, and a fresh start in life. But for D'Melo, it had become a day to dread, one he would have gladly postponed for another year, or ten. Graduation marked the end of being cheered by Zara's crescent-eyed laugh, inspired by her passion, and centered by her realness.

D'Melo wallowed on the couch, waiting for Sunday dinner to begin. He noticed for the first time that the wall clock ticked with each passing minute. He was amazed that he had never heard it before. That day, each tick sounded like a tiny trumpet blast, warning that Zara's departure for Malunga was fast approaching.

The boyz arrived. Their jolly clamoring temporarily lifted D'Melo out of his doldrums. As a matter of routine, Jeylan asked him whether he planned to finally make a Kipaji meal. D'Melo shrugged off the question, then tried to nonchalantly drop a bombshell. He knew that what he was about to say violated their unspoken pact that Sunday dinner was *their* time together. "Well actually, we have a guest chef this Sunday."

The boyz eyed D'Melo with reluctant curiosity. Just then the front door swung open. Zara toddled in toting hefty bags of groceries and five chef hats, one hat already topping her head. Marley beamed. He shuffled to Zara and welcomed her with a hug.

Kazim greeted, "What up, girl? You must be tired—"

Zara interrupted, "Let me guess, because I've been running through your mind all day again?"

"No," Kazim grinned slyly, "because you've been carrying those bags. Girl, you need to check that ego at the door."

Zara proudly offered the menu for the evening—*pierogis*, veggie *goulash*, and homemade bread. "And," she turned to Kazim. "We're gonna make *porkolt*. It's a spicy pork stew."

"Now that's what I'm talkin' about!" Kazim gushed. "Y'all need to learn from this young lady."

Zara divvied up the chef's hats. The boyz enthusiastically adorned their heads, except Jeylan. He cast his onto the couch.

Zara always tried not to let on how heavy her heart was over D'Melo's best friend's rejection of her. But D'Melo saw her glance at the discarded hat, and he knew her too well to be fooled.

He pulled Jeylan onto the stoop for a private word. His eyes were burning with rare acrimony. "Why do you treat her like this? What has she ever done to you?"

Jeylan's face tensed. "Who is she to butt into our special Sunday dinners? Man, you just don't know how much these dinners have meant to me over the years. It's the only time I really feel at home. We've all been tight like brothers since we were shorties. And now *she* comes along and, just like that, she's part of our crew?"

"Marley and Kaz don't seem to mind," D'Melo asserted, his voice trembled with controlled anger.

"Those fools accept anyone. I don't want to be around someone like her."

"You mean someone white!" Jeylan's silence affirmed the accusation. "Listen, man," D'Melo said, his tone softening with compassion. "I know your family has had a tough time with white people. But Zara isn't *white people*. She's Zara. Can't you see her for who she is?"

"I see her for exactly who she is. She's the granddaughter of the Nazi who fired Tyreke!"

D'Melo laughed, disbelievingly. "Man, you have no clue. That girl saved your life." Jeylan gazed curiously at D'Melo. "She asked me never to tell you, but I can't let this go on any longer. She saw us that night you vandalized the store. She knew it was you but didn't tell the police anything because she didn't want to ruin your future over a stupid mistake. Not only that, but she's been kind to you all this time, even though you've treated her and her grandfather like trash."

Jeylan released a tense breath. His posture eased. A look of guilt crossed his face.

He peered inside the house. Zara and Marley were sneaking up behind Kazim. They blew baking powder on his neck then burst into childish giggles. Jeylan laid a loose fist over his mouth. "I'm really screwed up, man. I'm just so angry."

"I know you are, and you have good reason to be. But your anger is directed at the wrong person."

D'Melo went back to the kitchen and started preparing the *pierogis*. Jeylan strolled in behind him, donning his chef's hat. "So, Zara," he said. "What am I making?" A smile flitted on Zara's lips. She looked at D'Melo, baffled by Jeylan's change of heart. D'Melo raised his shoulders, *I don't know.*

When dinner was served, Baba began his weekly toast.

"I look around this table and see the love you have for each other, a love that transcends nationality. In this tiny gathering, several nations are represented—Chad, Japan, Sudan, Ethiopia, Kipaji, Nečzia—and South Carolina."

He got some chuckles.

"And I think to myself, if only the world had more people like you, who embrace and cherish our differences, we could finally lay to rest all this unnecessary suffering. One day, the world will wake up and realize that the pain of one is the pain of all. You are a part of hastening the dawn of that day. Don't ever doubt the tremendous impact you can have on the world. Margaret Meade said, 'A small group of thoughtful people can change the world. Indeed, it's the only thing that ever has.'"

"Truth," they chorused. "Take 'em to church, Baba."

They raised their glasses. "*Kwa uzima!*"

This week's dinner discussion centered around everyone's plans for their future. Kazim had received a basketball scholarship to a small university in central Pennsylvania. Jeylan expressed his longing to become a pharmacist, but his father needed him in the family auto repair shop. Marley casually dropped the news that he was not going to MIT, which had always been his dream. The scholarship the school had offered was far too small for him to afford going.

"MIT said that my application lacked 'unique life experiences,'" Marley bemoaned. "I was angry at first, but then I realized that they're right. All I've done is work at Chubby's and hang out with you guys every day. I haven't done anything special. But, one day, MIT will regret that it didn't give me the full scholarship."

"Tru dat!" they agreed, clapping Marley supportively on his shoulder.

As for Zara, everyone already knew her plan to go to Malunga. No one dared to bring it up and reopen old wounds.

Sensing D'Melo's obvious discomfort at the thought of Zara leaving, the boyz skipped to a happier topic: their graduation trip.

"In three weeks, we gonna be lounging on a beach in Jamaica and drinking mai tais," Jeylan said dreamily. Baba cleared his throat. Jeylan chuckled. "Just messin' with you, Baba. *Virgin* mai tais."

Jeylan popped the last *pierogi* into his mouth. Not a moment was wasted before the boyz launched into their ridiculous excuses to shirk cleanup responsibilities.

The boyz gave Zara long goodbye hugs. She cried, of course. They disappeared into the night, their tomfoolery heard all the way up the street.

After cleanup, Zara headed to the door.

"Where you goin'?" D'Melo asked. "The night's not over yet."

"D'Melo, I would treasure spending absolutely every possible moment with you before I fly off in the morning, but I don't want to take away your special time with Baba—*The World This Week*."

"There's a special report tonight about Malunga and Pharma," D'Melo said, hoping to entice her to stay. "You should know what's happening before you go."

Zara said nothing, then started for the kitchen. D'Melo and Baba shared a bewildered glance.

"Popcorn," she called out. "Can't watch TV without popcorn!"

The World This Week opened with a report on Kyle Sandersen's latest accusations against Pharma. In researching his next documentary, Sandersen claimed to have uncovered proof that Wilem VanLuten paid President Dimka of Malunga with stock shares for access to the Shuja homeland. Sandersen also asserted that the culture and health of the Shuja people were being irreparably damaged, threatening a total collapse of the tribe. This had led to calls for a boycott of Pharma products. Wilem was interviewed for his response to the allegations.

Wilem VanLuten: "Well, what you call allegations, I call unsubstantiated rumors. I appreciate you giving me a chance to finally put this to bed. We're bioprospecting in the Nyumbani at the *invitation* of the Malungan government. There is no quid pro quo.

"And in terms of the alleged harm we're causing, I've hired twelve Shuja guides who make sure that we're not trampling upon *any* sacred land. You may not know this, but when I served in the military, I worked closely with the Shujas in Nanjier. I became quite fond of the Shuja people and gained great respect for their way of life. So, I assure you, I would *never* do anything to desecrate their sacred land."

Zara blurted, "You slimy bas—!" She covered her mouth and glanced wide-eyed at Baba. "Oops, sorry." She crinkled her nose. "I didn't mean to say that out loud."

Interviewer: "Why do you think Kyle Sandersen is so certain that Pharma has been colluding with Malungan officials at the highest levels?"

Wilem VanLuten: "Sandersen is a great documentarian. I've enjoyed his films over the years. So I can only believe that he's being misled by people who want to do harm to Pharma. I welcome Sandersen to our operations with open arms. Maybe then he'll put in his documentary how we're actually benefiting the people of Malunga.

"Did you know that we're building a new prison there? The current prison is outdated and deteriorating. Four rebels have escaped this year alone. Having violent rebels running free isn't good for anyone. So I offered to build a maximum-security prison. But not just *any* prison; it's the most secure and harsh prison in Africa. An inescapable fortress. And, we hired psychiatrists to help us design it to break even the most hardened criminals, but within international laws, of course—isolation in ultra-tiny cells, dim and dank all the time, sleep disruption tools, temperature extremes, etc. It will deter anyone from committing crimes! Malungans are so afraid of the prison that they call it, '*Ishogo Gereza*'—'Satan's Lair.'"

Interviewer: "Well. Thank you for being on our show."

"Did you see how the interviewer couldn't hide his shock at that guy's callousness?" Zara spat. "This," she said to D'Melo, pointing a stiff finger at the TV, "is why I have to go."

"I know, Zar. You don't have to convince me."

Zara rose from the sofa and gave Baba a tight hug.

"Wow, that might be the hardest hug I've ever had. I think you cracked a rib," he joked. Baba gazed intently into her eyes. "Go get 'em, Lioness."

Zara nodded, suddenly feeling the weight of what she was about to embark on. She shuffled to the door, kissed her palm, and blew it toward Baba. She laid both hands over her heart and swayed affectionately before exiting with D'Melo in tow.

As D'Melo and Zara walked down the stoop, a glint from the alley across the street caught D'Melo's eye. A tall figure slinked into the dark shadow. As they passed, D'Melo peered into the alley curiously. No one was there.

The stroll to the drugstore was unusually subdued. No joking or teasing. They had a ton to say about their impending separation, but neither wanted to give voice to it and make it real. They arrived at the apartment stairs. D'Melo's cheeks puffed, holding a sigh. He attempted to lighten the somber mood.

"Who knows how much trouble you'll get yourself into over there. And when you do, who's gonna be there to save you?"

Zara struggled to smile. "You know," she said. "It's not too late. You can come with me."

"Even if I could and not jeopardize my scholarship, you know I can't leave Baba. He'd be so lonely without me."

"I know," she acknowledged. Her gaze dropped to her feet. "But you can't blame a girl for trying. Will you call me every night before you go to sleep?"

"That's gonna be like 5 a.m. your time."

"I don't care. You better call me, punk." She rolled out an open hand in front of her.

D'Melo tenderly took it into his. "Always, Zar."

Her eyes misted. "You gave me the best birthday ever," she said, choking back tears. "And I'm gonna miss yours."

"Eh," he shrugged. "Just hearing your voice will be enough."

He loosened his grip. Her hand reluctantly slipped from his clinging fingers. He took a long breath, turned, and started down the sidewalk.

"See ya, punk," she said, with an audible sniffle.

He stuck his hand in the air, as he continued walking away. "See ya, cry baby."

Zara blew a sorrowful giggle.

He shouted from the growing distance. "I know—I'm such a jerk, right?"

"Yeah, you are," she muttered. "The best jerk ever."

The farther D'Melo got from Zara, the wider the hole in his heart felt. As he approached his house, Baba was peering out the window. When he saw D'Melo, he ducked behind the curtains. D'Melo dragged himself through the door wordlessly. He leaned limply into Baba's embrace. Then he pulled away sullenly and headed to the bathroom to ready himself for bed. When he came out, Baba was glued to the window again. He had drawn the curtain just enough to peek through a small slit. D'Melo was too emotionally exhausted to ask about Baba's peculiar behavior. He went to bed.

As he had done every night for months, he rested his head on his pillow and reached for his phone. He shut his eyes in anticipation of hearing her voice. It was always the best moment of his day.

"Hey, punk," she sniffled. "I hope you don't mind, but I think I need to keep this short tonight." Zara went silent, with an occasional scratchy sound. D'Melo pictured her handkerchief brushing the phone as she wiped tears from her puffy red cheeks.

"Yeah, me too, Zar," he said dolefully. "How about you call me before you get on the plane tomorrow?"

"How about I call you before I get on the plane, while I'm in the plane, the moment I land, and then every thirty minutes after that?"

"I wish."

For a long stretch, there were only heaving whimpers on Zara's end and deep sighs on D'Melo's end. Finally, D'Melo raised the courage to say the dreaded words, "Goodnight, Zar." Usually he ended their bedtime call with, "I'll see you tomorrow." The absence of those words echoed agonizingly in his hollowed heart.

Zara closed the call as she always did. "*Dobří duchové dnes večer.*" Her mom would say this to her before sleep. It meant, "May the good spirits walk with you tonight."

D'Melo was a zombie for days after Zara left. The vibrancy of life seemed to have been replaced with a diluted version of itself. Colors weren't as bright, flowers weren't as aromatic, vegan pumpkin pie wasn't as sweet, and even laughter wasn't as joyous.

He pulled his eyes disappointedly away from his phone screen. Before she left, Zara had warned him that it may take several days to get settled with Internet access. Even so, this didn't help D'Melo's ruffled mind. His perception of Malunga was one of lawlessness and violence. Still, he was oddly comforted knowing that they were communicating through the pain in his chest.

The summer months were prime time for the boyz to fatten their graduation kitty. Although they had already saved enough for their trip, some extra pocket money wouldn't hurt. Even with D'Melo not himself, the boyz were winning most of their games. But after the fourth day of not hearing from Zara, D'Melo stopped playing. The boyz didn't try to talk him out of it. They just wanted Zara to call so D'Melo would return to his normal self.

Another day passed. "Still nothing?" Baba asked.

D'Melo answered somberly. "I'm starting to get worried, Baba."

"Son, if there's anyone who can take care of herself, it's Zara. The Malungan government probably shut down the Internet. It does this when it feels under threat. Only certain people are allowed Internet access—government personnel, the military, and some important services, like hospitals. I'll call Ameka to find out what's going on."

D'Melo sulked off to his room. As he stared out the window, distressed, he noticed a strange but oddly familiar man sitting on a stoop across the street. A baseball cap covered much of the man's face. D'Melo shot to the living room. "Baba, did the Bensons move?"

"No. Why do you ask?"

"There's a guy on their stoop. I feel like I've seen him before, but he's not from this neighborhood."

Baba drew the curtains a sliver. The man was gone. "He was probably just resting. It's hot out there today." For the moment, D'Melo was satisfied.

The next day, D'Melo woke to no calls or messages from Zara. He dragged himself to the bathroom. Baba was speaking on the phone in hushed tones, sounding quite upset. As D'Melo went to knock on Baba's door, he heard him say, "I think we may be in trouble again." A searing pain ripped through D'Melo's chest. When he raised a hand to clutch at it, his elbow brushed a framed photo just outside Baba's room.

"Hold on." Baba paused. "I think I just heard something." He quickly changed the subject. "Okay," he said, speaking in his normal tone. "So the Malungan government *did* shut down the Internet. Thanks, Ameka. That's good to know. So, we'll see you for your Fourth of July cookout."

When Baba emerged from his room, D'Melo cornered him. "Baba, I'm sorry. I overheard something. What did you mean when you told Auntie Ameka that we may be in trouble again?"

"Oh, um . . .," Baba stammered. "Well, it seems I was right. The Shuja rebels have become active again, so the Malungan government is reacting like it's under siege. Whenever that happens, it spells trouble for not only Shujas, but Kipajis and everyone else in the region."

D'Melo wasn't convinced that was what Baba was talking about. The same feeling he got when Baba told him that a drunk driver killed his mother now churned in his gut. But he had no reason not to believe Baba. Plus, at that moment, he had a single-minded focus. "So is Zara safe?"

"I'm sure she's fine, son. The Malungan government does this frequently. They put the country on alert to give the impression that they're taking measures to protect their citizens, even when there's no real threat. Ameka said she would let us know if Zara was in any danger."

D'Melo retreated to his room for another sulking session. When he rejoined the world at lunchtime, Baba was again peering through a cleft in the curtains.

"Baba," D'Melo said.

Baba jolted and hastily shut the curtains.

"Are you looking for that guy? Are you worried about him?"

"No," Baba replied automatically. "I'm just curious, that's all. If we have a new neighbor, it would be good to welcome him to the neighborhood."

D'Melo scrutinized Baba's face. *Why is he constantly at the window?*

And why is he acting so skittish? D'Melo's mind rumbled like a runaway train for the rest of the day. None of this was sitting right with him. *Who's that guy? Why is he in our neighborhood?*

By the time Sunday dinner rolled around, D'Melo was racked with worry about Zara, and now also Baba. D'Melo had never seen his father so on edge. For much of the day, Baba stood glued to the window, like he was on a police stakeout. He even started locking the doors during the daytime, something he had never done. And his dinner toast didn't ease D'Melo's concerns even a smidge.

"Soon you will be on your own in the world," Baba started, "stretching your wings and flying along the path you choose for yourself. Make that path one of service to others. If you do, you will live a meaningful and fulfilling life. Life doesn't last forever. It's precious. Don't waste even a moment. None of us are promised another day."

Baba raised his glass and turned to D'Melo. "Always know that my spirit will surround you at all times."

The boyz raised their glasses—D'Melo hesitantly. "*Kwa uzima.*"

The typical brotherly jesting and shenanigans ensued. But it all felt very distant to D'Melo, like he was observing it through a fog. His mind eddied anxiously all evening.

Even before the boyz finished their meal, Baba left the table and slunk to the window. He drew the curtains, then quickly closed them. He returned hurriedly to the dining room. He told the boyz that he wanted to give them a little gift. He handed D'Melo money for the movies.

D'Melo's concern now reached new heights. Baba had never missed *The World This Week* with him. "Baba, what are you talking about? We have to clean up and then it's time for the news program."

"Not tonight, son," Baba said, his eyes darting furtively to the window. "Soon you will all go your own ways. So please enjoy your last days together." Baba nudged them to the door.

D'Melo handed Jeylan the money. "You guys go. I'm staying here."

"No, D'Melo," Baba insisted. "You must go, as well." He practically shoved D'Melo out the door. He grasped each of the boyz one at a time. He gazed intently into their eyes, smiling, and hugged them longer than usual. "Please, you must go now."

"I don't want to go, Baba," D'Melo pleaded, sensing something was very wrong. "Please don't make me."

"You're going with your friends!" Baba said sternly.

D'Melo took a step back, jarred by Baba's uncharacteristic tone.

Baba's eyes then went tender. "I love you, son." He embraced D'Melo, holding him for a long time. "I've been immeasurably blessed to have you as my son." A look of peace washed over his face. Baba glanced around D'Melo to the street. "Please go now."

D'Melo plodded away obediently, glancing back at Baba every few seconds. Baba waved from the stoop.

In spite of D'Melo's deep concern, he tried to shake off his thoughts while his friends debated what movie they should see. Marley made his case for the latest Marvel film. Jeylan and Kazim pushed for the new Dwayne Johnson movie. They asked D'Melo to chime in, but his mind was far away.

Just as they reached the theater, D'Melo's phone buzzed. It was an unknown number. His heart leapt hopefully.

"It must be Zar!" He pressed the phone against his ear. "Shhhh, I can barely hear her."

The boyz mimicked him. "Shhhh, it's Zarrrr. Ohhh Zara, I miss you sooo much."

D'Melo ducked out of hearing. "Hey. Where've you been? I've been really worried."

"I'm so sorry. I tried to call but it wouldn't go through. And the Internet was shut off."

D'Melo realized what time it was in Malunga. "Are you okay? It's almost 4 a.m. for you."

"I'm fine. I'm on a computer at the hospital. It's one of the few places that has Internet."

"You're at the hospital! What's wrong?"

"Nothing. I faked being sick. I waited in the emergency room until some lady left her office, then I got onto her computer. I don't have much time, though. I think she just went to the bathroom."

"Can't you get in big trouble for this?"

Zara skirted the question. "Hey, is everything okay with Baba?"

"I don't know," D'Melo said warily. "Why are you asking that?"

"Aren't you guys about to watch the news together?"

"No. I'm at the movies with the boyz."

"What! D'Melo, something's wrong. Please go check on Baba, right now!"

D'Melo's heart thumped so rapidly it felt like he was going to pass out. He sprinted home, leaving the boyz wondering what was happening. The front door was ajar. He bounded inside to a waking nightmare. Baba was slumped on the floor, leaning against the living room wall.

"Baba!" D'Melo rushed to him. "Baba, no. Please. Please."

Baba's face was swollen, a thick gash under his eye. Crimson seeped from two small holes in his white shirt. D'Melo pressed hard on his chest, trying to stop the bleeding. His friends ran up the stoop, panting.

D'Melo screamed, "Call an ambulance!"

Baba's eyes flitted open. He looked at D'Melo with concern. "Are you okay, son?"

"Me?" D'Melo said. "Please Baba, save your breath." D'Melo told him the ambulance was on the way. "Please, Baba. Don't leave me alone. I beg you."

"Yabo," he said, gazing at D'Melo with fading eyes. "You're not alone. You've found your light. Follow the light, Yabo."

D'Melo realized that Baba was losing touch, calling him 'Yabo'. He screamed at the boyz, "Where is that ambulance!"

"Yabo, listen carefully." D'Melo lifted his head, his eyes wet with tears. "You have to leave tonight. It's not safe for you here anymore. They found us again. Go, and never look back. Take the bus to Ameka's. She'll know what to do."

"Safe from what, Baba?" D'Melo pushed out the words between sobs. "*Who* found us?"

"There's over forty thousand dollars in the wall behind my desk. Take it and use it to settle somewhere very far from here." Baba, now laboring to breathe, continued, "I'm so sorry, son. I wish you could have lived the life you wanted. But it's not to be. Your path was chosen for you."

Baba's eyelids closed briefly. He leaned his head against the wall and chuckled painfully to himself. "They didn't even know what they were looking for. Your mother was a smart woman." His gaze turned toward the drawing. "*Haki inakuja kwako.*" He lifted four fingers atop an outstretched arm. He clenched them, then brought a fist down to his chest.

Baba's glassy eyes darted to beyond D'Melo's shoulder. "There's your mother!" He grinned. "She's waving. Do you see her, Yabo?"

D'Melo turned to the empty space behind him. "Yes, I see her, Baba," he said, feigning joy. "She's beautiful."

Baba smiled feebly. "Yes, she's the most beautiful." Blood dripped from the corner of his lips. "Son," he said, struggling to raise his hand. He caressed D'Melo's cheek. "Always remember one thing."

Dong, dong, dong . . . with each chiming of the clock, D'Melo's heart sank like an anchor deeper into the darkest depths of a sorrowful sea.

Baba waited for the ninth chime, then continued hoarsely. "You've never truly lived if you don't have anything in your life that you're willing to die for." Baba's eyelids fluttered, then slowly shut for the final time.

"BABA!" D'Melo wailed.

The ambulance arrived, followed by the police. The paramedics tried to revive Baba, but they were too late. They zipped his lifeless body into a shiny black bag. D'Melo stared vacantly at the plastic enveloping his father. Jeylan stepped between D'Melo and Baba's body to protect his friend's shaken mental state.

The police cordoned off the crime scene and made a cursory sweep of the ransacked house. All the drawers were flung open. Clothes were strewn across the floor. The couch cushions were sliced to shreds. The dish cabinet was toppled.

"This wasn't a typical robbery," the police officer said to a dazed and listless D'Melo. "The thief left your father's wallet with two hundred dollars sitting on his desk. This guy was looking for something in particular. Do you have anything of unique value the thief may have wanted?"

D'Melo shook his head.

"Do you have any idea who may have done this?"

Jeylan raged, "It had to be T-Bo! He threatened D'Melo a couple months ago." Jeylan stormed for the door.

D'Melo grabbed his arm. "Jey, it wasn't T-Bo." D'Melo told the officer about the man who had been lurking around the neighborhood and how Baba had been acting oddly, peering suspiciously out of the window.

The officer scribbled on a small pad. "What makes you think it may have been that man?"

"Something just wasn't right about him." D'Melo said reflectively. "I think he's been watching us for a while. He may have even been the guy I kept seeing at the All-American game in New York."

"Okay. We'll follow up on that and any other leads we find." The officer laid a consoling hand on D'Melo's shoulder. "I'm sorry. Your father was a good man. My wife is a doctor at the LD clinic. She has only great things to say about him."

D'Melo's eyes were blurred with tears as he watched the paramedics removing Baba's body from the house. The policeman offered to take D'Melo to the hospital. "You can have as much time as you need with him there."

"We'll come with you," Jeylan asserted.

"Jey, it's okay. I'll be fine. But I need you to do something for me." Jeylan listened intently. "I have to go away. Please tell everyone that I appreciate what they've done for me."

"What! Where are you going?"

"I can't explain right now. But I'll reach out soon." D'Melo group hugged the boyz. "I love y'all." He started for the door. Jeylan clasped the back of D'Melo's shirt, not ready to let him go. D'Melo halted, allowing Jeylan the time he needed. Jeylan reluctantly released his grasp. D'Melo scanned the street, then headed to the police car.

After the hospital, D'Melo returned home. He shut the police car door. The sound echoed in the lifeless, empty street. He climbed the stoop as he had thousands of times before. But this time, he wouldn't be greeted at the top by Baba's loving embrace. He numbly entered the house, hoping this was just another one of his gruesome nightmares. But the blood-stained floor where Baba lay dying just hours before jarred him into the reality that he was truly alone. He averted his eyes, trying not to relive the scene.

He trudged to Baba's room and pried free the wood paneling behind the desk. A manila envelope was propped just inside the wall. As D'Melo held the bulky package in his weary hand, he realized, *Baba's been preparing for this day for years. Why would he think someone would kill him?*

He headed to his bedroom and mindlessly packed some necessities. Leaden with mourning, he looked around his room one last time. He paused at the trophies lining the shelves—trophies that, at one time, symbolized accomplishment and conjured treasured memories. Now they were nothing more than dusty, twisted yellow metal—except for one. D'Melo picked that trophy off the shelf, which seemed tiny in his adult hands. He wistfully revisited the moment he received it.

When he was seven, D'Melo brought home his first report card with straight A's. Baba wasn't at all pleased that the school didn't acknowledge his academic achievement. So he and Diata bought a trophy for D'Melo. The only non-sports trophy they could find was one with a figure wearing a crown. The inscription read, "To D'Melo. You're the King of the World"—the famous line from *Titanic,* Baba's favorite film.

Memories of Baba overran the banks of D'Melo's brimming mind. There was hardly a day that he hadn't learned an important lesson from his father, either through the abundant gems of wisdom Baba delivered or from simply observing how his father lived his life.

D'Melo tugged on the locket at the end of his necklace. "Mama, please take care of Baba." His words trailed out heavily in the still midnight air. He lifted himself off the bed, knowing that Baba would want him to get started with his new life, whatever that may be. Just before clicking off his light, he noticed a hastily scrawled note on the nightstand. His heart thumped to life. He read Baba's final words.

"Son, I don't have much time. So please don't take the brevity of this note as a measure of my love. There isn't enough paper in the world that could hold how much love I have for you. Now that I'm gone, there is something I always want you to carry with you: *Haki inakuja kwako.*"

"That's it?" D'Melo groaned. "Baba, why would you use your last moments to tell me something that you said all the time?"

D'Melo trudged toward the front door. As he passed the living room, he glanced at his mother's drawing on the wall. He paused, then murmured, "*Haki inakuja kwako?* Were you trying to tell me something, Baba? Please, talk to me."

After a moment of no answer from Baba, D'Melo grew frustrated. He cried out, "Wasn't it enough to lose my mom, now you take Baba too? What did they do to deserve this? They were wonderful people. Where's the justice in that!"

D'Melo pounded his fist angrily against the wall. With the impact, the drawing slid down and crashed to the floor, shattering the glass. When D'Melo picked up the drawing, he noticed something for the first time. It had a distinct shape when rotated—left side at the top. "I've seen this shape before," he said out loud. He opened his phone and searched Google maps. "This is Kipaji!" *Am I seeing things?* D'Melo creased his brow, confounded. *Why would Mama hide Kipaji in her drawing?* Baba's note flashed in his mind like a New Year's Day firework.

"Now that I'm gone, there is something I always want you to carry with you: *Haki inakuja kwako.*" *Did he want me to take this drawing? Why? And why wouldn't he just say that?* D'Melo slid the drawing out of the frame and rolled it up. He peered out the door, sweeping the area for the dark stranger. He hurried clandestinely to the bus station, full of questions and no answers.

D'Melo arrived at Ameka's house just before dawn. She dashed out to greet him. D'Melo melted into her motherly arms.

"I'm so sorry, D'Melo. When I got your message, it felt like the world had ended. I loved your father so much." Ameka led D'Melo to the room she had arranged for him. He crashed onto the bed, nearly asleep before his head even hit the pillow.

Nightmares marred his long but agitated sleep. He awoke with a start in a pool of sweat. For a moment, he could hear Baba's voice, "Time to catch the worms, son." He sighed painfully when he remembered that Baba was gone—a paralyzing sadness washed through him.

Ameka poked her head in. "I thought I heard you. You must have been so tired, my poor boy. It's almost dinnertime. Come down when you're ready."

"Okay, Auntie." D'Melo switched on his phone. It buzzed repeatedly for several seconds. Dozens of texts awaited him from people expressing their condolences. His eyes shot down the list of messages until they reached Zara's name.

> **Zara:** Internet's back on! Plz tell me what's happening? How's Baba?
>
> **Zara:** I'm getting worried. Plz let me know if everything's ok.
>
> **Zara:** OMG! Something's terribly wrong. I can feel it.
>
> **Zara:** I'm sooo sorry, D'Melo. Baba was the best man I've ever known. He was like a father to me. I wish I could be there with you right now.

"Me too," D'Melo said under his breath. "I don't know if I'm gonna make it through this."

> **Zara:** I know you're thinking that you're not going to make it thru this, but you will. We'll get thru it together. I'm coming back as soon as I can get a ticket.
>
> **Zara:** I'm scared, D'Melo. Are you ok? I haven't heard from you and I can feel a terrible heaviness in my chest. I can barely breathe. Plz let me know how you're doing.

D'Melo thumbed his response.

> **D'Melo:** I'm living the worst nightmare I can imagine. I can't believe Baba's gone. I feel like he's gonna walk into the room any minute, but he won't.
>
> **D'Melo:** I'm at Ameka's. Baba said the LD isn't safe for me anymore. I can never go back. I have no idea what's going on or where I'm going next.
>
> **D'Melo:** I'm gonna talk to Ameka now. Baba said she knows

what to do. You're not blue-ticking. You must be asleep. Plz call when you wake up.

D'Melo's weary legs wobbled down the stairs. A traditional Shuja dinner awaited him, and not a second too soon. He was famished.

Ameka let D'Melo settle into his meal before gingerly breaking the news to him. "D'Melo," she uttered softly. "Baba requested to be laid to rest in Kipaji."

D'Melo took a moment to process this. "Okay," he said. "When do I leave?"

Ameka sighed. "I'm sorry, D'Melo. You can't go."

"What do you mean? I didn't get a chance to say goodbye to my mom. I'm not gonna miss Baba's funeral too!"

Ameka gazed at him intently. "Baba was hoping you would never have to know this."

"Know what?" He straightened in his chair, waiting with bated breath.

"Baba was wanted by the Malungan government. And—"

"What do you mean, *wanted*?" D'Melo said incredulously. For what? There's no way Baba was a criminal."

"The government believes he has, or had, some information that if released would destroy some very powerful people."

It suddenly dawned on D'Melo, "That's what the thief was looking for." He rubbed his forehead. "Well, did Baba really have it?"

"No. They're barking up the wrong tree."

D'Melo paused, relieved. "So what does this have to do with me being able to go to the funeral?"

"Well, it isn't just your father they're after. It's your whole family. It's the reason you guys left Kipaji. So going back there will be too dangerous for you."

A thought struck D'Melo like a battering ram into his chest. "Oh, my God." He inclined in his chair. "I was right about my mom all along. It wasn't an accident. That guy *was* trying to kill her . . . trying to kill all of us!"

D'Melo stared reflectively into the distance. "The last thing Baba said to me was, 'You've never truly lived if you don't have anything in your life that you're willing to die for.'" D'Melo turned a resolute gaze to Ameka. "I don't care what danger I'm in. I'm going."

"Your father suspected that I wouldn't be able to talk you out of it. I'll do my best to make your journey as secure as possible. But you have to understand, I can't guarantee your safety."

D'Melo nodded slowly, considering her grave words.

"Kipaji doesn't have its own airport and the one in Malunga is out of the question. The Malungan secret police will be on the lookout for you. The government doesn't have food or jobs for their people," Ameka said with disgust, "but they have millions of dollars to spend on state-of-the-art security technology." She shook her head. "I'll arrange for you to be picked up by my niece, Chipo Kayode, at the Nanjier airport. She'll take you to the Hasira Bridge, which leads to Kipaji.

"You may not know this, but Chipo and your mother were best friends in college. They were birds of a feather, both fighters against injustice. Chipo hasn't stopped. She's still smuggling rebels across the Nanjier-Malunga border. So you'll be in good hands. Once you make it into Kipaji, you'll be safe. Malungans aren't allowed to enter Kipaji without permission from the Kipaji Council. And the Council would never grant them access while you're there.

"Chipo will approach you as you exit the airport. Malungan spies are everywhere. So for safe measure, Chipo will say to you, '*Hatimaye itakuja*.' It means, 'Your fate awaits you.' She'll then shake your hand with only four fingers. If this doesn't happen, the person isn't Chipo. Run as fast as you can back into the airport and take the next flight out of there. Also, a couple of years ago your father asked me to bring Chipo a flash drive to keep for you. He thought this day would eventually come.

"There's a flight for Nanjier tomorrow morning. I'll get your ticket. Now, when you return to America, you'll go directly to Miami. I've arranged for you to live with friends there. The money Baba saved will sustain you for a while."

Ameka then threw a cold wet blanket of reality over D'Melo. "You'll have to change your name and you won't be able to play basketball anymore." D'Melo gawked at her, numb and sickened. "They know you're a star basketball player. So if you play, they'll find you. You'll be in the newspapers, and even on TV."

D'Melo's world was collapsing around him. He forced himself to divert his thoughts from his future . . . if he didn't, he would lose his mind. At that moment, his sole focus was getting to Kipaji for Baba's funeral. He dropped his house keys on the table. "In case I don't make it back," he said soberly. "Baba would want you to have everything in the house."

He trudged back up the stairs, his mind and body weighed by utter exhaustion. It didn't help that there were no messages from Zara on his phone. He texted her.

D'Melo: Hope you didn't buy your ticket yet. I'm coming to Kipaji for Baba's funeral. I leave tmrw morn. Arrive Wed evening. If you can, plz come to the funeral."

His phone buzzed.

"Zar?"

"Hey," she said, her voice faint and scratchy. "It's so great to—" Static.

"I can't hear you. The connection's really bad."

"I *said*, it's great to hear your voice."

"You have no idea how much better it is to hear yours."

"How are you holding up?"

"I'm mostly numb. It still doesn't feel real. Are you able to come to the funeral?"

"Nothing could keep me away." The connection continued to fuzz in and out. "I'll be in Kipaji Thursday morning."

"Great. See you then."

"*Edu.*"

Dead air. The call dropped.

D'Melo tossed restlessly in bed. His addled mind twisted and spun, swaying his emotions wildly. He was anxious about being in Malunga, a country that wanted him dead for reasons he didn't even know; afraid that he'd be killed before even making it to Baba's funeral; overjoyed that he may see Zara soon; enraged that whoever killed Baba and his mother had gotten away with it; warmed that Ameka was so lovingly caring for him; devastated that he would no longer be able to play basketball; heartbroken that he may have seen his friends for the last time; but, most of all, overwhelmed with grief that he was about to say goodbye to his father forever. With fits and starts, D'Melo slipped into a tormented sleep.

Soon, his nightmare returned, with a haunting twist. It started out as it usually did, with his family driving to Ameka's on Christmas morning. But this time, D'Melo's mom turned around to him. A sparkly emerald dangled in front of her forehead. Her face was unfamiliar, a shade darker and more narrow. D'Melo saw the other car barreling toward them. He screamed, "TURN AROUND!" But his mother continued to gaze at him, her eyes teary and gleaming with infinite love.

"Don't worry, Yabo. I'll see you again," she said, as serene as a lucid pond on a windless day.

As the final word fell from her lips, the other car transformed into a keen metal spear just before ramming them. D'Melo shut his eyes tight. He couldn't bear to watch his mother die, again. The spear sliced through the passenger door and pierced her back and chest. D'Melo felt a liquid splatter over him. Strangely, it wasn't warm or red like blood. It was cool and clear. Then, a jolt sent them tumbling. When everything settled, he opened his eyes. He could see his mother, but his vision was blurred and wavy, as if looking up through rippling water. "Always remember one thing—" she murmured. *Dong, dong, dong* . . . Her voice morphed into Baba's, who finished the admonition.

"Later. Later." Baba's voice echoed faintly in the distance.

"Baba!" D'Melo shouted. "We can't say goodbye like this. Come back!"

"Later. Later," Baba repeated, fading into nothingness.

PART II
King of Kipaji

"Africa isn't something you will ever be able to understand sitting on a couch in Lincoln Downs. To really know Africa, you have to touch it, you have to breathe it, taste it, smell it. It's a place of spirit. So to understand it, you have to lead with your soul. Once you do, you'll realize that Africa is pure magic."

—*Baba*

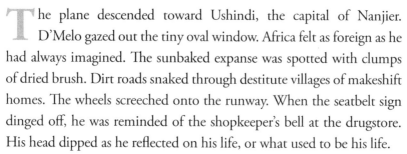

CHAPTER TEN

Haya – The Tree of Life

The plane descended toward Ushindi, the capital of Nanjier.
D'Melo gazed out the tiny oval window. Africa felt as foreign as he
had always imagined. The sunbaked expanse was spotted with clumps
of dried brush. Dirt roads snaked through destitute villages of makeshift
homes. The wheels screeched onto the runway. When the seatbelt sign
dinged off, he was reminded of the shopkeeper's bell at the drugstore.
His head dipped as he reflected on his life, or what used to be his life.

A flight attendant jogged him. "Excuse me." D'Melo snapped
back to attention and realized no one else was on the plane. "Sorry,
but we must finish clearing the aircraft."

As he stepped off the plane, he was walloped by suffocating heat.
His lungs worked extra hard to take in oxygen. Heat waves rose from
the blistering concrete tarmac. As he entered the baggage area, Ameka's
caution crept to mind: "There are Malungan spies everywhere." His eyes
probed the sweltering airport, although he had no idea what a Malungan
spy would even look like. He tried to blend in. But that wasn't easy
for a 6'4" young man in a Meek Mill T-shirt in a country where most

people are diminutive and wearing traditional garb. He felt like an underdressed giant. He walked quickly, avoiding eye contact with anyone. As he reached the exit, someone grabbed him. His heart leapt.

"Hatimaye itakuja." A slender woman, whose face was worn beyond her years, extended four fingers. D'Melo could now breathe. As he clutched Chipo's hand, he remembered the story that Ameka told him. A few years ago, Chipo had been captured by the Malungan government. She was accused of smuggling rebels and guns into Malunga. She denied it. Her captors severed her right thumb to dissuade her from continuing her smuggling business, or to discourage her from starting one. It didn't work.

Chipo ushered D'Melo into her ramshackle pickup truck. When D'Melo closed the creaky door, caked mud broke off. The truck rattled down the bumpy road, kicking up a brown cloud behind it. The sun, a glowing orange orb, was now just below the desolate horizon. As they ascended an incline near the Malungan border, the landscape became more verdant and the air cooler. Chipo made a call that lasted but a few seconds. She spoke in a low, clandestine voice, rousing D'Melo's anxiety.

Chipo stopped the truck. "This is the Hasira Bridge," she told him, "and that is the Hasira River below."

D'Melo looked out his window at the raging river.

"It creates a natural border between Nanjier and Malunga. The Malungan side of the bridge is officially the Kingdom of Kipaji.

"A Kipaji Council representative will be on the other side to greet you," Chipo assured him, gazing across the bridge. D'Melo felt like he was in one of the many spy movies he had watched over the years. He hoped it wasn't one of the films with a sequel. He just wanted to say goodbye to Baba and never return.

"Oh," Chipo exclaimed. "I can't believe I almost forgot." She snapped open a secret compartment in the truck and handed D'Melo the flash drive.

"What's on it?"

"I don't know. I'm only the messenger. But for your father to go through the trouble of getting it to me, it must be quite important." D'Melo tucked it into his backpack.

"When you want to leave," Chipo instructed, "make arrangements through Milpisi. He's the Kipaji Healer." Chipo wished D'Melo luck, *"Bahati njema."*

D'Melo shook Chipo's damaged hand gratefully. He took a settling breath before exiting the truck for the bridge. He attempted to look natural, but it was impossible. This was the most unnatural situation he could have ever imagined.

As he approached the border patrol booth, he noticed it was empty. Two cups of tea were steaming next to half-eaten meals on paper plates. D'Melo realized that Chipo's call must have been to ensure that the guards would make themselves scarce when he arrived. Although the guards were Malungan, they were apparently motivated more by the money Chipo paid them than any loyalty they had to the Malungan government.

A light blinked from the brush on the Malungan side of the bridge. D'Melo quickened his step toward it. Just as he passed the patrol booth, loud bangs and shrieks of terror resounded in his jarred ears. A searing pain ripped through his chest, forcing him to a knee. His head swiveled as he heard bullets whizzing by and his mother screaming. He yelled, "Mama! Mama!"

He looked back and saw Chipo gaping at him with horror. She darted onto the bridge.

"Hey," she said, softly but urgently. "You have to be quiet. The guards will return any minute."

D'Melo felt like he was at the epicenter of the chest pains he had been experiencing his whole life. He took a moment to gather himself. "I'm sorry," he panted. "I don't know what happened."

Chipo helped him to his feet, her eyes sweeping the area. "You have to go. Quickly!"

D'Melo scuttled hastily across the bridge, as Chipo scampered back to Nanjier. Just as he reached Kipaji soil, a high-pitched ululation full of deep emotion rang from within the dark brush like a beacon of joy. A woman materialized from the untamed thicket. Her smile gleamed almost as brightly as her elegant white Kipaji dress. She absorbed D'Melo into her arms.

"Welcome home, son of Kipaji. I am Bamidele. I have been bestowed the great honor of greeting you." Bamidele led D'Melo along a path worn from centuries of use. It wound up the north face of Amanzi Mountain. It was surprisingly well lit by peculiar illuminated stones perched atop bamboo poles. As they neared the summit, the cool mist of a double waterfall made him think of whooshing through the Pocono Mountains on Zara's birthday, which now felt like a lifetime ago.

As they ventured under the falls, the water gushed overhead and splashed heavily into a pool fifty feet below. The pool, glistening in the moonlight, jutted out flat from the mountainside. The overflow spilled down into the river.

Suddenly, D'Melo felt wonderful. A rush of tranquility, which had been elusive in his life, cascaded through him. It was as if the water was purging the disquiet in his mind and invigorating his spirit. At the edge of his consciousness, he sensed that there were intrinsic natural forces at work in Kipaji.

As they descended the south side of the mountain, the soft prattle of crystal water gurgled along stony brooks. Its placidity ran in juxtaposition with the clicking and screeching of wild animals all around— not exactly noises D'Melo had come across in the big city. The sounds harmonized like a perfectly conducted orchestra, wafting nature's melodies through the sweet woodland air.

They reached a small clearing. Here D'Melo was greeted by the chief of the Amanzi clan. "It's an honor to meet you, son of Kipaji."

D'Melo lowered his eyes humbly.

"Bamidele, I'll take it from here," the chief said.

Bamidele's smiling eyes lingered on D'Melo as she slipped off into the forest. Her ululation echoed from deep in the woods.

The chief escorted D'Melo to a large cottage-like hut—a circular structure made of mud, with a conical thatched roof. They climbed sturdy wooden steps to a charmingly furnished porch. D'Melo ducked through the doorway, clearly not made for someone of his height. It was pitch black inside. D'Melo searched along the wall for a light switch.

The chief chuckled. "*Nuru,*" he said. The darkness was chased from the room by the soft light of exquisite indigenous lamps. D'Melo was surprised at the sophistication.

"We put you in Rondeval *Ukuu*. A rondeval is what we call this traditional kind of dwelling. And 'Ukuu' means 'Majesty.'

"I think you'll find your quarters suitable. You have a busy day tomorrow. By midday, Milpisi will collect you for a special luncheon. If you have any questions about Kipaji, Milpisi knows more than the rest of us combined. And then tomorrow evening is the Festival of Lights. There, you will meet the other three clan chiefs."

Before leaving, the chief took a long, doting look at D'Melo. "*Amani ndoto.* That just means I'm wishing you peaceful dreams."

D'Melo dropped onto the cozy, rustic living room sofa. "Yo! This is most definitely suitable." Intricately hand-carved wooden side tables sat at either end. Exotic flowers decked the plentiful space and colorful vines draped the walls, bringing the jungle into the ambience. An overhead fan broadcasted the fragrance of the flowers. The floral scents were familiar and conjured sweet nostalgia; his mother had always made sure fresh jasmine graced their house. D'Melo toured the rest of the exquisite earth-toned rondeval, discovering that the dining area, two bedrooms, two bathrooms, and kitchen were equally divine.

He headed to the master bedroom and familiarized himself with his new digs. Before long, the rhythmic sounds of a babbling spring sent D'Melo into an exhausted trance. He tossed himself onto a bed fit for a king. His mind slipped between consciousness and semiconsciousness. The deluge of thoughts that typically overwhelmed him at night were whittled down to just one: *Kipaji is nothing like I had imagined*. Within moments, he drifted into deep slumber.

D'Melo's dream was much tamer that night. His mother still wore the emerald on her forehead, but no sinister SUV screamed toward them. His mother simply smiled at him and mused, "You're home now, Yabo." She playfully brushed the tip of his nose. When D'Melo wiped away the tickle, uproarious laughter startled him from his sleep. He lifted his heavy eyelids to see Zara doubled over, enjoying a red-faced guffaw. To his amazement, Jeylan, Kazim, and Marley were there too. He did a doubletake at Marley, who was wearing new, odd-looking glasses. The boyz were howling and clapping each other like they had just won the NBA championship.

D'Melo, still foggy, wondered if this was just another sweet twist in his dream. He tried to blink the haze from his mind. His vision still clouded, he rubbed his eyes, only to realize he had just lathered a palmful of shaving cream onto his face.

Zara sidled onto the bed next to him. "Aww, poor baby," she chortled, wiping him clean with a towel.

"That's funny, huh?" he responded playfully. He smeared shaving cream onto her face. She pulled away, laughing.

"What are you guys doing here?" he marveled. "Is this for real?"

Jeylan chimed, "Did you think there was any chance we wouldn't pay our last respects to Baba?"

"But it's so expensive to—." D'Melo then realized that the boyz had used their grad money. "Ohhh . . . you guys," he said warmly. "I love y'all, man."

"We can always go to Jamaica," Kazim said. "This is Baba we're talkin' about."

The room fell silent while they acknowledged the heartbreaking reason that brought them back together.

Jeylan ogled the room, then broke the somber mood. "Dang, dawg. They hooked you *up*! This is lit!"

"Ohhh, check this out!" D'Melo depressed a button on the technology control panel above the nightstand. The wall across from the bed became translucent.

"Oh, snap!" Marley cooed. "That wall's a window!"

The wall tint faded, revealing the sun blossoming over the alpine horizon. The reflection of a rainbow shimmered on a pond at the foot of a pristine waterfall.

"Hey, look at that funky looking horse," Kazim observed. "It has zebra stripes across its behind! It looks like Marley's butt that time his mom caught him turning her water heater into a rocket. She whupped that fool up and down the street."

"Come on, dawg," Jeylan said. "Please don't embarrass us like this. You've never heard of an okapi?"

"Yeah, man. But I didn't know it was real. I thought it was a myth."

"Kaz," Marley couldn't resist a comeback. "I think your brain's a myth."

"You think the wall's dope?" D'Melo warbled. "Peep this!" He pushed another button on the panel. The roar of the waterfall poured into the room.

Marley leapt into the air wildly. "This is too much!"

"You need to chill, dawg," Jeylan said. "You gonna hurt yourself."

"You don't understand, man. This is futuristic! It's called ANC— Active Noise Control. I've read about scientists working on it, but I didn't know it existed!"

"I knew we should have left this nerd at home," Jeylan jested.

Marley prowled the room. "Ahh, here it is." He approached the ANC device delicately, as if he had discovered some rare endangered species. "The speaker emits a sound with the same amplitude but with an inverted phase, which neutralizes the original sound."

"Yo Einstein," Kazim exhorted. "How about some English?"

Jeylan tried. "Kaz, it's simple. There's something positive and then something negative comes and cancels it out. You should be able to understand this. It happens to you every day." Jeylan paused for effect. "It's like when there's a hottie doin' her thing, then you come and try to throw some game at her, she ignores you and then walks away."

"Oooh, scorched," Zara reveled, cupping her mouth.

"Man, y'all just haters," Kazim said, pushing down a smile.

D'Melo got around to asking Marley about his new glasses.

"Oh, these ain't just any old glasses," Marley puffed proudly. From his phone, he replayed D'Melo slathering the shaving cream over his face. They howled with laughter all over again, even harder this time.

"Everyone back home wanted to be here," Jeylan explained. "But, you know, folks is broke. So we gonna make a video for them."

"But so far this fool's only been recording silly stuff with his glasses," Kazim grunted. "He even recorded me going to the bathroom on the plane. Now why would folks back home wanna see that!"

"I told you," Marley defended himself. "That was for my blog."

"Why you gonna blog about me using the bathroom?"

"My blog's about daily life. By the way, I'm up to eighty-three followers!" Marley said proudly. "And guess what? They *all* use the bathroom. So they can relate."

"Then why didn't you video yourself using the bathroom?"

"What! Why would I do that? That's embarrassing."

Kazim pursed his lips at D'Melo, "You see what we've been dealing with? It's gonna be a long trip."

D'Melo washed up for the day, then sauntered into the living room. His eyes fell upon a familiar and warming site. Marley was tinkering with all the new technology, trying to figure out how it worked; Kazim was leering in the mirror, fluffing his Jheri curl; Jeylan was reading a book about the Shuja struggle for independence; and Zara was in the corner doing her morning stretches and calisthenics.

A rapid clacking snatched their attention. Their eyes combed the rondeval for where it might have been coming from. *Clack, clack, clack.* Zara identified it. "That's a woodpecker."

"Good morning," an angelic voice called from behind the front door. A glowing young lady let herself in. "Sorry to intrude, but you didn't respond to the doorbell. I'm Jua," she said, balancing a heaping breakfast tray on her head. She rested the tray on a circular board hovering over the dining table.

Marley investigated. He slid his hand leerily under the board. "How's it floating?"

"Oh, it's just magnets. It makes it easy to pass the tray of food to each other." Jua demonstrated. She spun the board, then slid it effortlessly over the table. Observing the dumbfounded faces of the guests, she enquired, "How do you do it in America?"

Kazim piped, "We just say, 'Yo dawg, pass the jammy-jam!'"

"Oh," Jua recoiled. "That's a little, um—" she clearly was trying not to offend, "coarse."

As she started for the door, Kazim pranced over to walk her out. From the dining room, they heard him say, "Girrrl, you must be tired—"

"Kaz, no!" D'Melo shouted.

Kazim proceeded, "cuz you been running through my mind all day." They heard Jua giggle. Kazim returned bearing a toothy grin.

After a delectable breakfast, D'Melo suggested a dip in the hot mineral pool in the master bathroom. The boyz grabbed their shorts from their suitcases. They slid into the revitalizing water, hooting with delight. Zara sashayed in wearing a white two-piece, crop top, with a thin purple crochet cover around her waist, knotted on the side. Not even its modest style could hide Zara's physical attributes.

Kazim squeezed D'Melo's arm. "Oh. My. God." He averted his eyes, then said without moving his lips, "I can't do this. I gotta get out of here, dawg." He pretended to remember something. "Ohhh, yeah," he said dramatically. "I gotta text my moms to let her know I got here okay. She worries." He sloshed hurriedly out of the pool, dousing the tiled floor.

Jeylan lowered his gaze and shaded his eyes. "Oh snap," he feigned, blinking rapidly. "I think I got something in my eye." He excused himself and hopped out.

D'Melo glanced over at Marley, whose mouth was locked half-open. Liquid gathered at the corner of his lips. D'Melo hoped that it was water and not drool. He slid his hand under Marley's chin and closed his gaping mouth.

"Marley, are you okay?" Zara said. "Your face looks like when you saw that CEO's Tesla."

"I'm uh—" Marley jutted his lips and sort of twitched. Failing to finish his sentence, he rose to leave. As he stepped on the rocky edge of the pool, his foot slipped back inside, splashing water onto D'Melo. "My bad, dawg." He tried again. This time he planted his foot firmly on the tiles. When he shifted his weight, his foot slid out from under him. His leg stretched across the floor into a semi-split. His crotch smacked down on the rocky edge. "Oooh," he squealed, "right in my naughty bits."

"You all right, Marls?" D'Melo winced.

Marley blew out his cheeks, waiting for the throbbing pain to become bearable.

Zara crinkled her nose empathetically. "You need some help, dude?"

"Nah, I'm good," he peeped from quivering lips. "This happens all the time."

Zara shot D'Melo a dubious glance.

"I fall in the bathroom a lot," Marley said in a very high pitch. "Dang nearly every day."

D'Melo tightened his lips, trying not to burst into laughter.

"My mom says it's because I'm special. My feet are stiff and smooth, like marble. She said I'm like a superhero. That's why she calls me Marbleman."

D'Melo raised his eyebrows. "I thought that was because you got that marble stuck in your nose and had to go to the emergency room."

"Nah, man," Marley objected, grimacing, still riding the pain. "I just didn't want to tell y'all the truth; you know, and make y'all all jealous and what not."

D'Melo chuckled through his nostrils at Marley's delusions of grandeur.

Marley lifted his other leg from the pool and up righted himself. For balance, he waved his arms at his sides like a high-wire artist. He took a cautious step toward the towel rack behind the door. He slipped, then managed to latch onto the granite counter, but not before slamming his knee thunderously against its thick wooden base. He yelped in agony. He gingerly hobbled along the counter, using it as a crutch all the way to the door.

Zara squinted an eye at D'Melo and tilted her head, *WHAT in the world is going on here?* She untied her crochet waist cover and slid her long, creamy-skinned legs into the steaming pool. D'Melo tried desperately not to look, but found himself stealing glances out of the corner of his eye. Zara dipped her hands into the toasty water and ran them through her silky hair. Her red strands shone brilliantly in the golden morning sun. Matted tightly to her head, the longest strands flowed between her shoulder blades. D'Melo swallowed hard. Then she did it again, this time beads of water rolled down her taut, round forehead. A few settled on her lashes over her glistening emerald eyes. She let the droplets dangle for a tantalizing moment, then blinked them off.

"Okay, that's it," D'Melo murmured abruptly. "I'm done." He practically leapt from the pool, causing a small tidal wave to overflow onto the floor. He took one glance back as he shuffled out of the room. Zara was staring at him, completely bewildered.

Just before lunch, the woodpecker clacked again. An elderly man poked his head around the door. His shiny dark skin contrasted splendidly with his white goat-like beard and the white-rimmed glasses resting toward the tip of his nose. He was surprisingly virile for a man of his years.

"Lady and gentlemen, it gives me great pleasure to make your acquaintance," he greeted them, his eyes lowering with the utmost humility. "But first let me offer my deepest apologies for my tardiness." He laid a gentle hand on his chest and bowed, a gesture to beg forgiveness. "I was called to attend to a young boy with a high fever. As the guests of the *Umoja*, the Unity Council of Kipaji, you are welcome to whatever we can humbly provide. Your very whims are our command."

Everyone looked at D'Melo, obviously thinking the same thing. *Who's this dude?*

"My apologies," he said. "I've been remiss. I am Upendo Akachi, but everyone calls me Milpisi. And I am here to escort you to a banquet. In the master bedroom closet, you will find several outfits that are fitting for this occasion. D'Melo, yours is on the top shelf. For Madam, an outfit will arrive shortly."

Zara raised her brows at D'Melo, *Did you hear him? He called me Madam.*

Just then, the woodpecker doorbell sounded. "Oh, it has arrived in a timely manner . . . unlike me." Milpisi chuckled.

Jua came in and handed Zara a rectangular box made of intricately woven palm fronds. The box was sealed with banana leaves tied in a bow.

"For me?" Zara's face beamed. She snatched the box as politely as her excitement would allow and bounced off into the guest bedroom. Jua followed.

Within minutes, the boyz emerged wearing homespun traditional Kipaji attire. Loose silk trousers enriched with stylish slits along the sides were paired with sleek V-neck tops designed with elegant stripes running past the waist. A matching cap graced their heads—called a *kufi*, by tradition six inches in height and flat on top. Jeylan's outfit was cocoa with tan trim; Kazim's was scarlet with yellow; and Marley's, white with crimson.

D'Melo was styled in garb reserved for a native Kipaji. His pants were comparable to the boyz, but his purple and gold top was robe-like and composed of a richer material. Also, his taller *kufi* was adorned with a gold tassel.

They strolled proudly into the living room. Kazim modeled his outfit like he was on the runway, turning on a dime and striking a pose. "Not even I thought I could look *this* good," he said.

Then Zara walked in. The room suddenly went silent. Awed, everyone paused for a moment to drink her in.

While her normal attire was quite fashionable, this African style was a world apart. Her features were accentuated perfectly. It was as if the ensemble had been delivered from heaven especially for her. The dazzling emerald hue of the dress and the artistically styled eyeliner drew out the mesmerizing qualities in her eyes, making them more striking than ever before. The bright orange streaks on the wrapped piece that crossed her torso seemed to be an extension of the fiery light that burned within her. And the ornate gold choker hugging her neck reflected her lively personality. D'Melo had never seen her so beautiful—scratch that, he had never seen anyone so beautiful.

But alas, the moment was fleeting. All it took to break the spell was for Zara to open her mouth.

"What are you guys looking at? It's the head wrap, right? I look stupid, don't I? I knew I wouldn't be able to pull it off. Ohhh no," she covered her mouth. "Do I have seeds in my teeth? I shouldn't have eaten those strawberries!"

And just like that, everyone snapped back to reality. Zara was Zara, no matter what she was wearing.

Milpisi's eyes creased into a smile. "It is most pleasing to see how well you all clean up." He then offered his elbow to Zara to escort her to the luncheon. The boyz followed.

Together they walked through the forest along a winding path through trees hundreds of years old. D'Melo could tell Zara was blissfully taking in the woods. She seemed to be noting every kind of flora and fauna.

Kazim, on the other hand, had his head on a swivel—listening for feral creatures. Suddenly, a bullfrog bellowed a boisterous croak. "What was that?" he cried, halting.

Zara teased, "Is Pimp Daddy afraid of a little frog?"

"Kaz ain't afraid of frogs," Marley jabbed. "Have you seen the girls he's been hitting on?"

They wound their way down to a picturesque clearing in the valley. Long wooden tables of gleaming oak were arranged in concentric semicircles. The tabletops were low to the ground and colorful seat cushions decorated each place setting. A special table faced the others; it was covered with a diamond-shaped fabric with silver tablecloth weights dangling along the edges. Lavish flowers embellished each end.

Milpisi signaled Jua, who ululated toward the Amanzi forest. Within minutes, scores of Kipajis in vibrant garb, maybe more than a hundred, materialized at the forest's edge. They paused at the semicircle of tables.

D'Melo was confused. "Why did they stop?" he asked Milpisi.

"They won't take their seats before the *Maalum*—our honorable guests," Milpisi explained.

"Oh, great," D'Melo said. "Special guests. Who's coming?"

Milpisi extended an open hand toward D'Melo and his friends.

"Us?" Marley piped.

Kazim lightly punched Marley's arm. "He's just messin' with us, dawg."

"I assure you that I'm not—," Milpisi paused, apparently struggling to drop the words from his polished and eloquent tongue, "'messin' with you.'"

He gestured to the grand table. "You'll find a special trinket located at each place setting. Your seat will be the one with the trinket that most resonates with your heart."

Jeylan found a wooden pendant on a natural-fiber necklace. It was a carving of the continent of Africa. "Oh, this is me, y'all." He sat.

Kazim eyed a rock of tan-colored stone sculpted into an African man clutching the hand of a boy that seemed to be his son. Kazim's eyes became sullen. "Is it okay if I have this seat?" No one objected. He sat deliberately, his eyes fixed on the sculpture.

Zara knelt next to him. "That's beautiful, Kazim," she said compassionately. She laid a hand on his shoulder. She knew Kazim's father had left his family soon after Kazim was born. Kazim hadn't seen him since.

Zara was immediately drawn to what looked like a petrified twig. Curious, she leveled it with her eyes.

"Rub it," Milpisi said.

Zara swept her fingers along the twig. The perfume of lavender lifted gloriously into the air. The aroma immediately reminded her of better days—those she'd had with her mother. From an early age, Zara had trouble sleeping. Her mother knew that lavender was a powerful natural remedy, so she would always put fresh lavender in Zara's room.

"Thank you so much, Milpisi," Zara said, her eyes misty.

D'Melo scanned the table. Milpisi watched him attentively. D'Melo stopped abruptly when his eyes fell upon a silver ring, engraved in Kipaji. Milpisi offered the translation: "Your life as a man has just begun. May you take your rightful place among the heroes of Kipaji who have come before you and will come after you." Serenity flowed from the ring into D'Melo's heart. He could feel Baba's presence for the first time since he was killed.

"This was your father's ring," Milpisi explained. "Fathers bequeath it to their children when they return from the *Ibada*—a rite of passage. All Kipajis at fifteen years old venture into the forest for nineteen days with a spiritual teacher. It is a time to delve deeper into themselves than they ever thought possible. That's when they first begin to grasp their true connection to a mysterious power outside of themselves, a consciousness that binds everyone and everything together—the Great Spirit. Baba's father died before he was born, so I gave him the ring when he returned from the Ibada."

"Thank you," D'Melo murmured, teary. He kissed the ring and slid it onto his necklace next to his mother's locket. Then he looked up suddenly, upset. "But Milpisi," he said. "What if one of my friends chose this? Then I wouldn't have received it."

"Ah, son. You are seeing with eyes fixed in this realm—the realm of substance and disintegration. When you see things from the realm of the spirit, you will understand that it would not have been possible for anyone else to have chosen that ring. Its spirit has attractive power for you only."

D'Melo didn't understand what Milpisi was saying, but he trusted him.

"Ahhh, man," Marley griped. "Y'all left me with the rock! That's messed up." He examined the glossy stone from every angle. He dropped it on the table then spun it. "Man, it doesn't even do anything. How'd y'all get all that dope stuff, and I ended up with this rock?"

"Mr. Marley, this is a *daima* stone—*daima* means 'always,'" Milpisi explained consolingly. "Do you have an electronic device?"

Marley took out his cell phone, his Lumalink, his power bank, and pulled off his glasses. He reached back into his pocket for more.

Milpisi stopped him, chuckling. "That's more than enough." Milpisi pushed the power bank aside. "You won't need this anymore. Please look at the charges on your devices."

Marley's cell phone was down to 32 percent; the Lumalink to 7 percent; his glasses to 44 percent.

Milpisi tapped each device once with the stone. "Now look at the charges," he said.

Marley lifted his phone skeptically.

"No way!" All the devices were charged to 100 percent.

Marley eyed the stone again. "But how do I keep the rock charged?"

"How do you keep the sun charged?" Milpisi responded rhetorically. "How do you keep the wind and water moving? The rock has perpetual energy. It will never be exhausted—well, certainly not for at least the next thousand years."

"Oh, my God! I can't handle this." Marley fanned himself. "I think I'm gonna pass out."

Milpisi rose from his seat and addressed the community. "We are the proud people of Kipaji, sons and daughters of the Great Spirit Mungu, the bearers of the banner of Kipaji, born of *damu udongo*, the blood red soil of Africa. We, together, are the Wapendwa, 'the loved ones of the Great Spirit.'"

The Wapendwa ululated.

"We welcome our native son back home, and with him our honored Maalum." Milpisi raised his glass. "This is a blessed day! Our Kipaji family has grown by five! *Kwa uzima!*"

At his cue, food servers emerged from the woods, carrying a feast fit for a royal family. Balanced on their heads with seemingly impossible grace were large wooden trays. They carried the trays to the central table and arranged them on top.

The Wapendwa sat motionless. They waited for the Maalum to approach the sumptuous buffet first. A soft breeze carried the tantalizing aroma of exotic foods—an array of colorful salads, succulent tropical fruits, spicy pea soup, potato stew, *jollof* rice, *githeri*, fried plantain, and an assortment of other savory dishes.

"I'm gonna get my greez on!" Kazim said, licking his lips. "Are they bringing the meat next?" he asked Milpisi.

"We don't eat animal products in Kipaji," Milpisi said.

"For real?" Kazim whined. "I gotta get some meat soon, or else I'm gonna shrivel up and die!" Kazim eyed an okapi with containers of water strapped over its back. "That horse-zebra thing is lookin' tasty," he joked. "You think it tastes like sausage?"

D'Melo was genuinely curious. "Milpisi, it seems like you have everything in Kipaji. But you can't get meat?"

"It's not a matter of not being able to. The largest animal farm in Africa is less than ten kilometers from here, in Malunga."

"So you choose to be vegan?" D'Melo asked.

"Not exactly. We *are* vegan, and so are you, you, and you," Milpisi said, looking at each of them. He reached over and cupped Jeylan's chin. "Open," he said.

Jeylan complied, with a furrowed brow.

"What do you see in his mouth?"

"Crooked yellow corn kernels," Kazim quipped.

Marley added, "And gingivitis!"

"Besides that?" Milpisi laughed. "Do these look like omnivore teeth to you?"

"Omni-who?" Kazim said.

"Animals that eat both plants and other animals. The omnivores you would be most familiar with are bears, raccoons, and skunks. Their teeth are long with a keen edge, particularly the canines, right?

Jeylan's are short and blunt." Milpisi pushed his fingertip against Jeylan's canine teeth. "And the rest are flat—a very poor design for shredding flesh, don't you think? Our canines are similar to those of animals that use those teeth to crack nuts and break the skin of fruits.

"Also, the human digestive system is not designed to process animal meat. Because of this, there is undigested red meat in your bowels right now, festering."

Jeylan made a disgusted face, his mouth still open.

"So we don't *choose* to be vegan; we *are* vegan," Milpisi concluded. "You choose *not* to be."

Zara pointed at the boyz and said, as she so loved to say, "Oooh, scorched!"

Milpisi continued. "But it is not just about health. We recognize animals as creations of the Great Spirit, just as we are. They are our earthly companions. I would even go as far as to say that they are our friends. Would you eat your friend?"

Kazim said briskly, "If he was a pork chop, you're darn right I would!"

As the boyz descended upon the food table, Milpisi asked Zara to remain behind.

"My dear," he said. "I hope my intrusiveness is not off-putting. But curiosity has gotten the best of me. I have never had the pleasure of meeting any soul with the name 'Zara.' From where does it originate?"

"It's Nečzian," she said. "I was born there."

"Please forgive my ignorance, but wasn't Nečzia at one time known as Nečsláva?"

"Yes," Zara said, surprised. "Not many people know that. It was Nečsláva until the revolution in 1959. After that, it split into two countries, Nečzia and Sláva."

"And your surname?" Milpisi asked, looking at her searchingly.
"Zanič."

"Ah huh," Milpisi uttered, stroking his beard. "My dear, at the festival tonight, would you do me the honor of accompanying me? I would like to show you something about Kipaji that very few people know about."

"That would be awesome!" Zara said.

When Zara caught up with D'Melo he asked, "So what was that about?"

"Milpisi invited me to hang out with him!" she said, bubbling with excitement.

"Whaaat? Why doesn't he want to hang out with me?" D'Melo said, teasing her. "After all, I *am* a son of Kipaji."

"Sorry, dude. Obviously, that's not enough. You need to be special, like *moi*," Zara teased back.

Zara lifted a forkful of the beet and carrot salad to her mouth and closed her eyes in ecstasy. "It's like my taste buds have come alive for the first time! I wish I brought my Tupperware. I could take some back to the rondeval with me."

D'Melo shook his head. "I never realized how ghetto you are."

"Well, I'm learning from the best." Zara motioned toward Kazim and Marley. Kazim's plate was so full that he had to use his thumbs to keep his food from sliding off the sides. While they were watching, Marley reached onto Kazim's plate and snitched a slice of fried plantain.

Kazim swatted his hand. "Whatcha doin', fool?" The plantain tumbled along the plush grass.

"I forgot to get some of that," Marley said.

"You got legs. Go up there and get yours," Kazim mumbled, bits of carrot shooting from his mouth.

Marley jerked backward, trying to avoid Kazim's spittle. "Man! Look what you did!" Marley brushed carrot from his shirt.

"It was an accident, dawg," Kazim said, laughing more carrots out of his mouth.

Zara turned to D'Melo, "Need I say more?"

"Point taken."

Dessert was a chocolate-coconut swirl cake, which the Maalum were devouring. Marley looked as if he was about to cry. "This cake is like what I always hoped heaven would be. I've never had chocolate like this. It's so smooth and creamy. It melts in your mouth."

"You know, cocoa trees are not native to Kipaji," Milpisi said. "Cocoa was brought here decades ago by one of our scientists who visited Guatemala. One day, he was offered hot chocolate. He couldn't believe his taste buds. He called it a miracle. After that, he was determined to bring cocoa to Kipaji. But non-native agricultural products were not permitted in Malunga. So he swallowed some cocoa beans before flying home."

The boyz gazed at Milpisi, perplexed. "How did that help?" Marley mumbled around a mouthful of cake.

"Well, when he arrived in Kipaji, he excreted the beans, then planted them. A few years later, Kipaji had its first cocoa pods. We now have thousands of cocoa trees in the Choma forest."

Marley stopped chewing. "You mean," he muttered, "this chocolate came out of that dude's butt?"

Milpisi chortled, "Well, I guess you could say that."

The boyz smiled nervously as they nudged their dessert plates away.

Milpisi addressed the Wapendwa to close the banquet. "Thank you all for showing the utmost hospitality to our esteemed guests. I hope everyone filled their bellies to contentment with this fabulous food." He motioned to the chefs with gratitude. The Wapendwa ululated. "We will see you all again this evening at the Festival of Lights." The crowd dispersed, gradually vanishing into the forest.

"As for the Maalum," Milpisi said. "Jua will collect you at the rondeval just before sunset. She will escort you to the festival."

Back at the rondeval, Kazim was glued to the window, waiting for Jua to arrive. He planned to impress her with a piano piece.

"His mom spent every free penny she had to get this dude piano lessons," Marley observed disapprovingly. "And this is how he uses it!"

"Here she comes!" Kazim shouted. He scurried to the piano and started playing Beethoven's *Für Elise*.

But just as Jua entered, the piano went silent. She looked at Kazim, puzzled, wondering why he was tapping the keys like he was playing something. Kazim tapped harder in frustration. Still nothing.

"Just my luck!" Kazim moaned. "The honey gods are against me!"

Marley mischievously waggled the Active Noise Control remote at Kazim.

"Oooh, you—" Kazim said through gritted teeth. "You're gonna pay for that!"

Soon after, the Maalum were escorted to the main clearing—the *Moyo*, which meant "Life." Thousands of big colorful cushions were arranged in concentric circles. Intricately designed bamboo poles were topped with glowing stones in woven reed lamps. Jua explained that the illumined rocks were called "wazi stones,"—clear minerals that capture the sun's energy during the day and become luminous after sunset. Wazi-stone lamps lit the perimeter of the clearing and the four pathways that led to the center. The paths sliced the concentric circles into four sections, organized by clan. The color of the cushions in each section represented one of the colors in the Kipaji flag—gold, red, green, and purple.

The Wapendwa filtered into their clan sections: Amanzi gold, Choma red, Joto green, Upepo purple. Enthusiastic chatter filled the clearing. As Milpisi made his way down the pathway, not a single soul missed the opportunity to greet him.

Zara elbowed D'Melo. "Milpisi's like a rock star."

Milpisi reached the centermost point of the concentric circles, called the Tabernacle. Only the Milpisi and the King of Kipaji could access this medium between this world and the realm beyond. His frame became momentarily obscured, as if passing through a membrane. Just as he entered, the Wapendwa became illuminated in rings of light, progressing outward from the innermost circle. They offered the Kipaji salute—raising four fingers, clenching them into a fist, then laying their fists over their hearts. Within the Tabernacle, Milpisi faced all directions so each of the Wapendwa sections could see him. He lifted an open hand. The chatter ceased instantly. Only the natural sounds of the forest remained. The Maalum were awestruck by the brilliance of the circles, the otherworldly technology, and the discipline of the Wapendwa.

"My dearly beloved friends." Milpisi's serene voice floated down from the bamboo lamps. "As always, it is a true joy to see each and every one of your radiant faces illuminating the circles of light. I am once again honored with the privilege of commencing the Festival of Lights. For our esteemed Maalum, I will take a moment to explain this occasion.

"Every nineteen days, the Wapendwa gather to discuss community affairs. It is an opportunity to consult upon concerns, ideas for improving community life, and whatever may be in the heart of any Kipaji. The only way we can truly be a community of strength is for all of us to feel free to allow the tongue of our hearts to speak.

"Today is a special Festival of Lights. The newly elected Council members will be announced. While it is an honor to serve the community as a Council member, it is no different from every other service in the community.

For the benefit of the Maalum, do I have your permission to introduce the different service areas?"

The Wapendwa clicked from the back of their mouths, signaling the granting of permission.

"Thank you. The food-growing servers, will you please stand?" About a third of the community rose, ululation greeting them.

"Will the natural-energy servers please stand?" About a fourth of the community lifted off their cushions.

"The peace servers." Forty-eight warriors rose.

Milpisi continued through another ten or so cohorts of servers— health and nutrition, enlightenment, natural innovation, culinary, and others. Then, when everyone was standing and the invocation seemed complete, suddenly the assembly started flicking their wrists rapidly, snapping their index fingers against their middle fingers.

"Oh, you're right. I forgot one." Milpisi dipped his head, embar-rassed. "Will the Healer servant please stand?" He lifted his arms to his sides and chuckled.

Milpisi then announced the newly elected members of the Council, after which he opened the festival to consultation. Each of the four sections were to discuss a topic of concern amongst them-selves. The outcomes of the consultation would then be reported back to the full community as recommendations for the Council to decide upon.

First to speak was the Upepo clan from the purple section: "We humbly offer the Council our thoughts on the selling of our excess energy. The deal with Malunga to supply them with energy at a very low cost was made decades ago and under different Malungan leader-ship. The current Malungan government is not our friend, or even a friend to most Malungans. We recommend renegotiating the deal so more revenue will be made for the Kingdom of Kipaji. We know that we have more money than we need, but a rainy day can come. We should be prepared."

Next was the Joto clan, from the green section: "We would like the Council to discuss greater accessibility to the Internet. We feel that we are falling behind the rest of the world. Our access at the library is grossly insufficient. Thank you."

The Amanzi clan spoke next from the gold section: "Our recommendation is that Kipaji move toward becoming an independent country. Although we are a sovereign region, we are still in the dark shadow of Malunga. Perhaps it is time to come out from under its tyrannical cloud."

And finally, the red section spoke, the Choma clan: "We request the Council to consider offering Kipaji's special natural resources to the world." A hush came over the listeners, then a growing murmur. The Choma representative continued, "With the money that would pour into Kipaji, we could modernize our emergency healthcare system."

Milpisi thanked the Wapendwa for their thoughtful recommendations. "I assure you the Council will give each and every one of your recommendations the careful consideration they deserve." With that, he closed that portion of the festival.

"It is now time for the *Kinfuna*, the Reunion. Our ancestors await us," Milpisi told the Maalum.

The drummers at the edge of the clearing began beating on the taut skins of their drumheads. Before long, the pounding built and increased in tempo. The Wapendwa sang and danced their way into the forest.

Milpisi started off down the pathway toward the foot of Amanzi Mountain. He motioned for Zara to accompany him. He then looked at D'Melo. "You too." D'Melo smiled and joined them.

Milpisi walked nimbly through the low-lying undergrowth of the forest. About a hundred feet from the clearing, he stopped. He lifted his hands flat before his face and began to chant, as if in a trance.

The forest in front of them began to blur. Zara rubbed her eyes, then blinked hard. She edged closer for a better look. Milpisi raised his hands above his head. The blur lifted like a curtain, revealing a humble tree standing alone. The other trees and brush of the forest vanished. The earth beneath their feet vibrated, alive with burgeoning energy. Twinkling lights ran along the roots of the tree, up the veiny trunk, and along the branches. The tree's flowers opened, pulsing brilliant colors. Zara was mesmerized, trying to fathom what she was witnessing.

An orange aura glowed and flickered around the tree, like it was on fire but with no heat. The back of Zara's neck suddenly burned, like a hornet had stung her. She caressed it unconsciously.

Milpisi jolted in his trance. Though his eyes remained closed he seemed to know that Zara was stroking her neck. When she removed her hand, her birthmark radiated light.

Milpisi let out a grateful sigh, then gazed up beyond the tree, as if observing something. Joyous ululation rang out from around the forest. For perhaps ten minutes, a murmur of voices filled the surreal woodland.

Milpisi chanted again. The tree dimmed and the blurry curtain drew down.

He turned to D'Melo and Zara. "This was for you only. You must never tell anyone what you saw here. Not even your friends."

They nodded in enraptured silence.

"But . . . but, what was that?" D'Melo managed. "Why was the tree blurry and then clear? How did it light up like that? Where—"

"One thing at a time, son of Kipaji." Milpisi's eyes were still glazed with intensity. "Haya, the Tree of Life, is a portal for the extraordinary energies of the Great Spirit to pour into this world. What you witnessed tonight is only one of its many gifts to humanity—allowing us to commune with our ancestors. But for now, the only things you need to know is that the Tree of Life exists. The rest will be revealed to you as the need becomes manifest."

"Do you mean I can talk to Baba—and my mom?" D'Melo said hopefully.

"You can, but only at the time the Great Spirit has destined for you."

Zara asked, "Is this the special natural resource that the Choma section recommended to the Council to share with the world?"

"It is, my dear one," Milpisi said, clearly not wanting to delve further into the subject. He thanked them for gracing the festival with their presence, then directed them back to D'Melo's rondeval.

Their ten-minute trek up Amanzi Mountain was mostly reflective. There was much to say, but neither could find words adequate to convey what they had just experienced.

When they reached the rondeval, they greeted Jua on her way out. As Zara started to head inside, Jua gently asked her whether she knew where her rondeval was.

"Oh, I have a rondeval?"

"In Kipaji," Jua explained, "unmarried women and men cannot share the same quarters unless they are family. It is a protection for everyone."

Zara nodded appreciatively.

"If you continue along the path," Jua said, "in five minutes you'll come to Rondeval *Mwanga*, which means 'Light.' We took the liberty of relocating your belongings. You will find them inside waiting for you. *Amani ndoto,* peaceful dreams."

"Did you hear that?" Zara looked at D'Melo, bright-eyed. "I got my *own* rondeval, all to myself!" she gloated, in a singsong fashion.

Just as Zara was heading off, D'Melo said, "Baba left me a flash drive. I was thinking about going to the library to see what's on it. Wanna come?"

"Do banana trees have bells?"

D'Melo lifted his brows. "Is that a yes?"

Zara's cheeks turned red trying to contain her laughter.

"Do spring peeper frogs hibernate in logs?" she managed, through growing giggles.

"Okay, stop. You coming or not?"

"Is broccoli a flower?" She burst into laughter.

D'Melo shook his head. "Something's wrong with you."

Zara was now hunched over, guffawing. "Let's go, dude."

D'Melo couldn't have known that with this simple stroll to the library, he would be crossing the Rubicon. There would be no turning back. What he learned there would upset the balance of power in Central Africa, nay, the world.

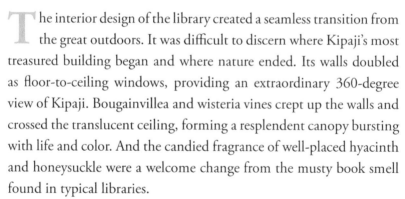

CHAPTER ELEVEN

The Assassination of President Amani

The interior design of the library created a seamless transition from the great outdoors. It was difficult to discern where Kipaji's most treasured building began and where nature ended. Its walls doubled as floor-to-ceiling windows, providing an extraordinary 360-degree view of Kipaji. Bougainvillea and wisteria vines crept up the walls and crossed the translucent ceiling, forming a resplendent canopy bursting with life and color. And the candied fragrance of well-placed hyacinth and honeysuckle were a welcome change from the musty book smell found in typical libraries.

A handwoven rug with the Kipaji crest commanded the floor of the central room. Bookshelves fanned out from the circular tapestry in nine directions. Golden runners lined the rows of books, like rays of the sun—a theme that D'Melo was starting to realize was common throughout Kipaji.

A multitude of crafted nooks spotted the library. Each seemed to have its own unique personality and decor, perhaps to make a visit to the library a deeper experience in the acquisition of knowledge.

As D'Melo and Zara weaved their way to the computers, they passed the art nook. Before he knew it, D'Melo found himself powerfully gravitating to a particular painting. He edged up for a closer look. A deep sense told him that this was one of his mother's paintings. He squinted at the signature, but the initials at the bottom were "DJ."

The painting depicted an oddly familiar woman poised on Amanzi Mountain above what he now knew was called the Ukuqala Pool. She was gazing into a glittering sky, as if embracing heaven. Two babies, nestled in a single white cloth, hovered radiantly above her raised hands. D'Melo's eyes fixed on the bright emerald dangling from a headlace wrapped around the woman's cornrowed hair—much like the emerald his mother had been wearing in his recent dreams. He was suddenly filled with comforting feelings.

"The library's closing soon," Zara said, then started toward the computer nook. D'Melo lingered, pondering his vague sense of kinship with this woman. Just as he was leaving, he noted the engraved placard beneath the painting. It read, "Leda, Mother of Kipaji."

D'Melo joined Zara at the computer. He inserted the flash drive and scrolled to its only file—an audio labeled, "Yabo." D'Melo tucked one earbud into his ear and offered the other to Zara.

She raised a brow, *Are you sure?*

He shook the earbud, *Of course.*

He inhaled a conscious breath before opening the file.

"Please enter the password" appeared on the screen.

D'Melo flipped his palms upward, *How would I know the password?*

"Baba made it password-protected so only you can see what's in the file," Zara suggested. "So you must know it. Think."

D'Melo drew a blank.

"Was there something that only the two of you shared?" Zara asked.

"There are probably a thousand things we shared."

D'Melo dug a frustrated elbow into the table and squeezed his forehead. "I can't believe this. Baba left me something, and I can't even listen to it."

D'Melo removed the flash drive and rose to leave, disappointed.

"You're giving up that easily?"

"Well, no, but I can't think of what the password could possibly be. Maybe it'll come to me later."

They wandered through the library aisles, mulling.

Just as they reached the painting that reminded D'Melo of his mother's artwork, Zara tried again. "Well, was there anything that Baba would always say to you?"

D'Melo halted in his tracks. "I think I know it!"

They scurried back to the computer. He typed, "*Haki inakuja kwako.*" He closed his eyes hopefully and tapped the enter key.

"Incorrect password" appeared on the screen. He leaned back heavily in his chair, rankled.

"Hey," Zara said. "Try, 'Justice will find you.'"

D'Melo frowned.

"Just try it," she exhorted.

D'Melo typed it and pressed "Enter."

"It worked!" she screamed.

"Shhh, dawg." D'Melo scanned the hushed library. "How'd you know that?" he whispered.

"Well, dude, if you ever took the time to learn Kipaji, you would have known it too. The night we watched the documentary, Baba said it when he looked at your mother's drawing, so I looked it up. *Haki inakuja kwako* means, 'Justice will find you!'"

D'Melo clicked open the audio.

"My beautiful D'Melo, I want you to know that my love for you has no bounds. The Great Spirit blessed this most undeserving soul with the bounty of being able to call you my son.

"The fact that you're listening to this means my earthly life has come to an end. Please know that I did everything I could to protect you from what I'm about to reveal. I never wanted you to be involved. But clearly, I failed. Now, for your safety, it is imperative that you know the whole truth.

"Years ago, like an unwitting fly, I became entangled in a most formidable web of corruption and deceit. Like any other day, I was doing my rounds at the Malungan hospital. A woman named Jasiri was rushed into the emergency room. She was suffering from violent abdominal pains and vomiting. After some testing, we discovered that she had eaten a deadly mushroom called Death Cap. We were mystified by how it could have gotten into her system. These mushrooms don't exist in Central Africa.

"By the time my shift ended that evening, Jasiri was recovering well. I told her that I was leaving for a medical conference the next day, but I would check on her before going. That's when things became strange. Suddenly, her attention was drawn to the hallway. She turned ghost white. Her eyes swung back to me, terrified. She grasped my wrist tightly and begged me not to leave. I assured her that she would be fine and that I'd see her in the morning. Then she said, 'They're going to kill me.' I turned toward the hallway. There was no one there. I thought that maybe the lingering effects of the poison was affecting her mind."

D'Melo felt a gentle tap on his shoulder. The librarian whispered, "The library will be closing in five minutes. If you need to save your work, please do so."

"Jasiri asked where the medical conference was. When I told her San Francisco, the fear in her eyes melted. She thanked me for helping her and offered me a gift. I graciously declined. I was simply doing my job. But she insisted.

"She stumbled to the closet and returned with a small box. Inside the box was a cassette sealed in an airtight bag. Apparently, her company used those bags to preserve medicinal plants for transport overseas. I took out the recorder that I used for listening to my medical notes and opened her box. She snapped the box shut. Her eyes shot to the hallway. She said it was a precious live recording and that I should only listen to it at home. I assured her that I love music and would treasure the cassette.

"When I arrived home, I started packing for the trip. As I reached for my medical bag, I remembered Jasiri's cassette. I grabbed your mother and told her we were going to dance. I played the cassette—but it wasn't music. It was two people talking. We drew the cassette player close to our ears. When I heard what was being discussed, my body went numb. The two people were plotting the assassination of President Amani. We stood there petrified, because we recognized one of the voices; it was—"

The computer screen went black.

"What happened?" D'Melo scrambled under the computer desk to see if any cords were disconnected.

The librarian ambled up. "The library is now closed."

"Just five more minutes, *please*," D'Melo implored.

"I'm sorry, there is nothing I can do. The central computer shuts down all the computers at exactly 11 o'clock to save energy. You can come back in the morning. We open at 9 a.m."

D'Melo remained statuesque for a stupefied moment. He finally stood, his legs rubbery.

"For Baba and your mother to be so frightened," Zara said, "the voice on that recording must have belonged to someone with a lot of power. Well, I guess so—whoever it was had enough power to kill the president."

Zara's voice was mere background static to D'Melo. An anxious tornado of questions churned relentlessly in his mind. *"Who was behind the assassination? Was the recording what made Baba a wanted man by the Malungan government? Were he and Mama killed because of it? Does the Malungan government think I have it?*

D'Melo jerked out of a fitful sleep, images of his mother's dreadful murder marring his dreams. Beads of sweat tickled his forehead. He lay back down, but too afraid to close his eyes. Then the rondeval phone tweeted. He checked the time: 3:17. He reluctantly answered, worried that only bad news came at that hour.

"Hello?" he whispered.

"Hey, dude." Hearing Zara's voice immediately soothed him. "Are you all right?"

"Not really. But I'll be okay."

"I'm coming over," she said. "Meet me outside in five minutes."

D'Melo settled on the divan in the porch, crossing his arms to fend off the crisp night air. He fidgeted agitatedly until his weary eyes glimpsed the starlit sky. He fondly remembered the times Baba would drag him outside on clear nights to revel at "the handiwork of the Great Spirit." He could never understand why Baba was so enamored by the near starless night over Philadelphia. But now he understood. When Baba gazed into the sky, he was imagining the glorious vault of heaven that glittered spectacularly above Kipaji.

A glowing orb crossed the thick woods. It pulsed glints of moonlight filtering through the forest canopy. D'Melo squinted for a better look. As the light flicked closer, he realized it was just Zara. She made her way to the porch and wordlessly slipped onto the divan, clutching his chilly arm.

"It seems you have a severe case of *cutis anserina*," she said, showing off that she remembered the medical term for goose bumps that Baba taught her. She raised a finger, *I'll be back*. She scooted inside and returned with a throw blanket. She stretched it over them and nestled her head on his shoulder. In an instant, D'Melo's eyelids grew weighty. He struggled to stay conscious, not wanting to miss a second of the tender moment. But alas, his body was no match for Zara's calming influence.

He arose. "I'm okay now. Thanks." Before ducking inside, he glanced back at Zara, who was now spread snuggly across the divan.

She yawned, "*Amani ndoto*, punk."

The delicate light of dawn trickled through the awakening forest. Zara headed to her rondeval and changed into workout clothes. After shaking loose her morning mental cobwebs, she loped along the Trail of Unity. This primal path circumambulated Kipaji, connecting the four mountain ranges that offered a natural protective rampart around the region. Within minutes she reached the summit of Amanzi Mountain. A river gushed over the ledge and drummed the Ukuqala Pool on its northern face. She paused briefly, running in place, to absorb the vista of the Hasira River and Nanjier across the bridge.

Zara's eyes swung down into the valley. She was awed by the precision of the landscape design. The library was the most prominent rondeval in the Moyo. It was the central point around which nine elliptical paths connected the forested valley. Along the paths, clusters of rondevals dotted circular clearings. From her vantage point, Kipaji looked like a colossal atom.

Intrigued, she continued her run. Before long, she entered a fresh microclimate. A faint whistle shrilled through the dense woodland.

She veered off toward the sound. As she trudged upward, she was greeted by a gale that was as passionate as she was. Her hair whipped wildly behind her, nearly horizontally. With her muscles tested to capacity, she took strategic cover behind the thick strength of ancient trees. They became her ally as she battled to the summit. Atop Upepo Mountain, thousands of wind turbines whirled vigorously. At their center, a generator converted the wind into usable energy. *That's awesome!* she thought.

Zara quickened her pace, eager to see what else this extraordinary land had to offer. At the southern edge of Kipaji, she descended rapidly into a region that looked like how she imagined Mars to be. Unlike the other mountains, Joto Mountain had a significant plateau and was considerably warmer. Wet sulfuric heat rose from the harsh raw earth up Zara's sweaty calves. The ground beneath her began to rattle, then quickly intensified into a rumble. She slowed to a stop, wondering whether she was experiencing her first earthquake. Suddenly, a burst of steamy water blasted a tower into the azure sky. It peaked three stories high, paused midair, then plummeted back to the earth, slapping down heavily against the craggy landscape.

The final leg of Zara's run was Choma Mountain on Kipaji's eastern border. It was the most ecologically diverse of the mountain regions. While it was largely forested, patches of rocky black surfaces swept over treeless portions along the mountainside. The petrified lava was the only visible evidence of an eruption that was said to have occurred at the time of the Spirit King. In time, it too would be weathered into the fertile reddish soil bursting with life like the other areas of Choma Mountain. Orchards of coffee, cocoa, orange, and lemon trees lined terraced rows down the western face of the mountain. The eastern side boasted nuts, herbs, and spices. The more tropical climate at the foot of the mountain was colored brilliantly by kiwi, mangoes, papaya, and other delectable fruits.

Zara marveled. *Kipaji is the coolest place in the world—massive waterfalls, powerful wind tunnels, geysers, volcanoes, and all within three miles of each other.*

As she circled back to Amanzi Mountain, kids frolicked in the clear streams. Their little faces beamed gregariously at the sight of Zara. A gleefully overzealous band even attempted to keep pace with her until their feeble legs gave way. One bright-eyed boy continued to trail her. Zara turned to let him catch up. He leapt into her arms. She swung him around until dizziness overwhelmed her.

Zara completed the loop, having traversed ten glorious miles. She sprung into D'Melo's rondeval, feeling amazingly energetic, like she could go another ten. Jua had just dropped off the morning's breakfast tray.

Their greeting was cut short by D'Melo shouting, "Hey! Hey!"

They raced into the dining area. An elephant was reaching its giant trunk through a window, curling food off a plate. D'Melo waved his arms frenetically above his head, while keeping a healthy distance from the elephant.

"Shoo! Shoo!" he yelled.

The elephant ignored him, of course. Zara and Jua broke into laughter.

"You're laughing?" D'Melo said, eyeing the elephant with horror. "There's a huge creature eating my breakfast!"

"Well actually," Jua corrected, "she's eating *her* breakfast. We feed Msada and her family every day. We help them, they help us. As you may have noticed, there are no vehicles in Kipaji. So the elephants offer rides and do some heavy lifting for us."

Jua extended a reverent hand. "Msada, meet D'Melo, son of Kipaji." Msada lifted her enormous trunk. D'Melo furrowed a brow at Zara, *What do I do?* Zara gestured for him to shake "hands." D'Melo stretched his arm out as far as he could without having to move even an inch closer to the elephant. Msada dropped her thick prickly trunk into D'Melo's hand. Then she padded off in graceful silence—a baffling quality for a creature so huge.

"*Siku ya heri,*" Jua excused herself.

"*Siku ya heri,*" D'Melo and Zara replied, clearly feeling good about having learned at least a basic Kipaji phrase.

After another bountiful breakfast, Zara waddled to the living room. She collapsed on the couch, massaging her stuffed belly.

"I don't know how you can eat so much," D'Melo asserted with a tinge of jealousy. "If I ate like you, I'd weigh three hundred pounds."

"Dude, don't start with me," she retorted, her arm resting over her droopy eyes. "I ran ten miles already today. What did you do? Brush your teeth? And from the smell of things, you probably didn't even do that."

"Yo! That's just wrong. Is that how friends do each other in Country Bumpkin, North Carolina?"

The woodpecker clacked. D'Melo went to the door as Milpisi ambled in.

"Ahh, the son of Kipaji. *Siku ya heri,*" Milpisi said. Then he asked, "Was someone sleeping in the porch last night? There is an untidy blanket on the divan."

"I had an awful dream. So Zara came to comfort me."

"It's beautiful that you call her for consolation in tough times. Life is a blessing when you have such a friend."

"That's true, but I didn't call her. She called me."

"*She* called?" Milpisi was puzzled. "How did she know?"

D'Melo shrugged. "She's amazing."

"Hmm…," Milpisi pondered, tugging his beard pensively before broaching the reason for his visit. "If you have time, I can take you to your parents' rondeval."

"Sounds great." D'Melo scratched a note for the napping Zara; he would meet her at the library at 9 a.m.

"Very well, then. Let's go see Mujiza and your mother's home."

D'Melo's expression must have given away his confusion.

"Oh," Milpisi said softly. "You don't know your father's birth name?"

On the way to the rondeval, Milpisi explained that Baba never knew his parents. His father fought with the Shuja rebels in Nanjier and was killed only weeks before Baba was born. Then Baba's mother died giving birth to him. She had a genetic condition that prevented her from bearing children. She lost four babies in the span of six years. Milpisi warned her that every time she got pregnant, she was putting her life at risk. But she insisted that the Great Spirit was impelling her to have a child. So she kept trying until she finally gave birth to Baba.

"So, your father was a miracle," Milpisi said, the look in his eyes a mix of pride and anguish. "Hence, his name—Mujiza Mdogo. It means 'the Little Miracle.' You know, technically, you and I are related," Milpisi added. "But not by blood. Baba's mother and my wife were cousins."

Soon, a humble rondeval came into view. It was tucked cozily among towering trees and a party of manicured flora. D'Melo was disappointed that he didn't remember it. He wandered around, hoping to jog a memory.

"The people living here are doing a great job keeping it up," he said. "It looks brand new."

"No one lives here," Milpisi said. "In Kipaji, your home is forever. We held out hope that your family would rejoin us one day. And you see, the son of Kipaji has returned. This rondeval is yours now."

D'Melo felt a surge of excitement, but it was quickly tempered when he recalled his difficult situation. "But I'm not staying. So I guess you should let another family have it."

"Well, you never know. If the Great Spirit wills it, you may once again return home to Kipaji."

D'Melo remembered he was supposed to meet Zara at the library. "Milpisi, I'm so sorry," he said hastily. "Zara's waiting for me."

Milpisi's eyes smiled softly. "You must never make a friend like her wait."

"Thank you so much for showing me my parents' home—" D'Melo corrected himself, "*my* home." He dashed for the valley.

D'Melo chugged up to Zara, out of breath but on time. They hurried inside, anxious to find out who killed President Amani. D'Melo clicked open the audio and skipped to where it left off.

> "When I heard what was being discussed, my body went numb. The two people were plotting the assassination of President Amani. We stood there petrified because we recognized one of the voices; it was Vice President Dimka."

D'Melo gulped. Now he understood why Baba went to such great lengths to keep his family hidden in America.

> "The voices on the recording were discussing how to stop President Amani from signing the peace agreement. They thought that if they could somehow remove him, Dimka would become President and would cease the peace process. But they had a couple of problems. First, President Amani was beloved by the citizens of Malunga. And second, the peace agreement was wildly popular among common Malungans. So they had to devise a way to get rid of Amani and at the same time turn the Malungan people against the peace agreement. So the plotters decided to assassinate him and make it appear as if it was at the hands of the Shuja rebels. The Borutus would turn their anger of losing their President against the Shujas. And, in one fell swoop, both problems would be solved.

"They decided that the opportune moment to kill Amani would be the morning he was to fly to Nanjier. On his way to the airport, Amani would be vulnerable. They only needed to know which vehicle in the motorcade he would be in.

"Within fifteen minutes of the president's car being blown to pieces, Dimka announced that the Shuja rebels were to blame. The Borutus reacted just as Dimka had hoped. They flew into a murderous rage. They killed any Shuja they could find. The slaughter escalated, leading to the mass extermination of the Shuja people. All the while, Dimka did nothing to stop the genocide.

"After hearing the recording, your mother ranted about how this was finally our chance to bring down the corrupt government of Malunga. She wanted to take it to the International Criminal Court. Although I knew she was right, I didn't want to have anything to do with the recording. If it was discovered that we had it, Dimka would have our whole family tortured, then killed. I wasn't willing to take that chance. I planned to return the recording to Jasiri the following morning, but the Great Spirit forced my hand.

"As you can imagine, I couldn't sleep that night. Every little sound—sounds that I had heard my whole life—startled me. I would get out of bed and prowl around the house with a broom." Baba chuckled at himself. "What was I planning to do, sweep the Malungan assassins out of the house?

"Against your mother's insistence, the moment the sun rose, I went straight to the hospital. When I arrived, it was swarming with military personnel. I was immediately ushered to the cafeteria where the emergency care staff was being confined.

"I asked the hospital administrator what was happening. She told me that Jasiri had died in the middle of the night and within minutes soldiers appeared and cordoned off her room. The military claimed that Jasiri had come into contact with a person infected with the Ebola virus. Jasiri did not have Ebola. Our tests clearly indicated that she had consumed poison. But maybe the strangest thing of all was, the head of the military, General Nyoko, led the investigation. There was absolutely no reason for someone at his level to be involved with something like this.

"Soldiers started interviewing the staff one by one. They rummaged through purses and emptied pockets. At that point, I knew for sure this had nothing to do with Ebola. Sealing off the emergency-care wing was just a ruse. They were looking for the recording that was sitting in my medical bag.

"My heart was beating so fast. I couldn't think straight. The only thought my mind could hold was finding a way out of there. I told the administrator I had to use the bathroom. She urged me to hurry because my turn to be questioned was coming. I slipped into the bathroom and climbed out through a window. I shot through the woods and didn't look back.

"I reached our house, frantic. We wildly threw clothes into a couple sacks and started for the Nanjier border. Now, what I'm about to tell you is going to be a bit of a shock."

D'Melo's chest clenched apprehensively. What could be more shocking than Baba being wanted as a traitor because he had evidence that would bring down the president of the country? Zara clasped D'Melo's hand, preparing for the worst.

"I hope you can find it in your heart to forgive me for not telling you sooner." Baba paused, then said in a low, contrite voice, "You have a brother. His name is Kavu. He's your twin."

D'Melo stared blankly at the computer screen. His body immediately started to brew furiously with emotions, like the waves of the sea during a violent storm, colliding harshly against one another—anger that his parents never told him; sad that he grew up without a brother, when he actually had one; and peculiar joy that he was not alone in the world.

> "Please try to understand. Telling you would have put all of our lives in danger, including Kavu's. If you knew, you would have wanted to contact Kavu. But that wasn't possible without the Malungan government finding out. So we decided it was best not to say anything. We were going to tell you when the situation changed in Malunga, but it never did."

D'Melo stopped the audio. He staggered out of the library and slumped down on a bench. Zara followed, and asked if she could sit with him. He didn't respond. She took a seat anyway. After several ponderous minutes, D'Melo muttered, "Why me? A few days ago, I had everything. I don't understand!" He repeatedly pounded his leg with a heavy fist. Zara clutched his hand and held it down.

"My life is over, Zar," he said, sobbing, bitter tears burning his cheeks. "Everything I wanted, everything I planned, won't happen. But you know, that doesn't even matter. What makes this impossible is that I don't have Baba anymore. What am I going to do without him?"

D'Melo buried his face in his hands.

Zara was devastated for D'Melo, but glad that he was finally allowing himself to process his emotions. Before this moment, she worried that he had been suppressing his feelings about Baba. But now she wondered, *Why isn't D'Melo talking about the assassination? The recording? Or his brother?*

Zara drew long, even breaths, hoping D'Melo would follow. He did.

After a few settling moments, he rose from the bench. "Okay. Let's go."

Zara started for the rondeval.

"Where you going?" he said.

"You said, 'let's go.'"

"Yeah, back into the library to finish the audio."

Zara was blown away by how much D'Melo could absorb. He had internal levels of strength that went far beyond anyone she had ever known, including herself. She would have been paralyzed with sadness, unable to get out of bed for days. But here he was, ready to take on more.

"I packed the cassette and recorder into my bag. Just as we were leaving the rondeval, Milpisi appeared. I'm sure you've met him by now and have already discovered that he is a very special person. Milpisi informed us that President Dimka had requested permission from the Council to allow some Malungan soldiers to enter Kipaji. Dimka told the Council that a Shuja rebel had escaped from their prison and was hiding in Kipaji.

"As much as I wanted to, I couldn't tell Milpisi that Dimka was really looking for me. We hugged him and said we would be back in a few days. It broke my heart that we would never see each other again, and I couldn't even tell him why.

"Your mother arranged for Chipo to smuggle us over the Hasira Bridge. We were to meet her there in twenty minutes. We weren't far up Amanzi Mountain before the soldiers reached our rondeval. We had only a few minutes lead on them.

"As we neared the bridge, the border patrol officers were scurrying about. They must have been alerted because they were securing the border with extra barriers. And, if that wasn't bad enough, we also noticed that Chipo hadn't yet arrived at the bridge and we could see the Malungan soldiers at the summit of Amanzi Mountain. We were trapped. Our only hope was to get over that bridge, but we wouldn't be able to with the recording. So we buried the box with the cassette on the mountain.

"When we reached the border, the officers peppered us with questions. With each question, I became more restive. I knew it wouldn't be long before the Malungan soldiers on the mountain would see us on the bridge.

"I explained that I was traveling to America for a medical conference and we had decided to turn it into a family vacation. Just as they were about to let us pass, a phone rang. An officer dashed to the patrol booth. He returned with his gun drawn. 'So, you're Dr. Jakanda. Yes?' D'Melo—it is hard to tell you all of this at once, but Jakanda was our family name before we changed it to Bantu.

"Before I could even answer his question, the border officer started searching our bags, but came up empty.

"'Where is it?' he grunted.

"'Where is what?' I said, playing dumb.

"He pointed his gun at your head and said that he would only ask one more time. 'Where is it?' We stood in silence. His face tensed as his finger tightened on the trigger.

"I couldn't just stand there and let him kill you. So I started to tell him, 'It's—' Just then there was a pop. Then another, and another. The officer buckled, then collapsed before me. The other officers turned and fired into the brush on the Nanjier side. Chipo and some rebels were hiding in the jungle. Three of the six border officers were killed instantly. The other three ran for cover in the patrol booth. A gun battle ensued.

"We ducked behind one of the concrete barriers. Bullets were ricocheting off the metal railings of the bridge and sparking on the concrete. The Malungan soldiers scrambled down the mountain. Our time was running out. We needed to get across the bridge. But we were in the middle of a fierce firefight. It was the scariest moment of my life.

"The Malungan soldiers had now made their way to the Kipaji end of the bridge, a hundred yards behind us. Your mother said we had to go, but it would mean running through the crossfire between the border officers and the rebels.

"When I stood up, a bullet clanked off the barrier just next to my head. The Malungan soldiers had positioned a sniper on the mountainside, waiting for us to come out from behind the barrier. The soldiers were now bearing down on us, fighting their way across the bridge. So we had no choice but to take our chances. I grabbed you and your mother snatched Kavu. We stayed low to the ground and as close to the edge of the bridge, as possible.

"But the sniper wasn't the only problem. There was no way we would make it past the officers in the booth; we would have to come directly into their line of sight. But then the Great Spirit showered his grace upon us. Just as we approached the booth, there was a flash in the Nanjier jungle. Then a missile screamed out. I yelled, 'GET DOWN!' Your mother and I dived flat to the ground, shielding the two of you with our bodies. There was a tremendous explosion. The bridge shook and debris crashed down around us. My left ear was ringing so savagely that I thought my head was going to crack and just crumble off my neck. I was half wishing it would, so I could be rid of the pain. While the smoke and confusion from the explosion were still providing cover, we darted toward Nanjier. It was like the most horrifying dream

I could imagine. I wanted to run fast, but I couldn't. I was too dizzy from my ruptured eardrum.

"Just when I thought we might make it to Nanjier, the sniper's bullet clipped your mother's leg. She dropped Kavu and stumbled forward several feet before floundering to the ground. I turned to see Kavu frozen with terror, crying. Your mother started crawling back to him. But then, a bullet ripped through Kavu's back and out of his chest."

D'Melo winced, clutching his heart. Zara laid a consoling hand over his, clearly struggling with the pain she felt in her own chest.

"A rebel soldier scooped up your mother before she could reach Kavu. He flung her over his shoulder like a sack of potatoes. She flailed her legs and punched his back, screaming for him to take her to Kavu. But the rebel carried her away. I will never forget his words as he shot past me. He said, 'There's nothing you can do for him. He's gone.' I can still hear his voice. It was calm, as if his words weren't a knife slicing the desire to live out of our hearts.

"As we carved our way through the jungle, bullets from the Malungan soldiers tore bark from the trees around us. But the deeper we got into the forest, the more the rebels' tension eased. They knew the Malungan soldiers wouldn't dare to enter Nanjier.

"Chipo led us to a military compound in the jungle. A medic attended to my bloody ear while another bandaged your mother's leg. At that moment, I realized that I hadn't just lost a son, but I had also lost my wife. Her eyes were vacant, as if no one was inside her. One of the things I loved most about your mother was how full of life she was. Unfortunately, you never got to see her that way. She never recovered from that night.

"Nanjieri soldiers then whisked me away to Ushindi. Military security officers met me inside the gate of the presidential compound. They were very intimidating, brandishing machine guns and wearing full body armor. The head officer flung the car door open and commanded me to follow him. The other officers surrounded us as we practically ran toward the presidential headquarters.

"They ushered me into President Okoye's office. Moments later, Okoye entered, flanked by a pair of guards. A career's worth of medals dangled from his chest. Although he had a slender and nonthreatening frame, he held an unmistakable aura of power and authority.

"The guards swept the office for threats, then stood at attention inside the doorway. Instead of taking his place behind the presidential desk, Okoye sat beside me on the couch. I had no idea what this was all about. I was only hoping that he wasn't going to send us back to Malunga.

"He scrutinized me shrewdly, his eyes intense. He conveyed how sorry he was to hear about Kavu. He, too, had lost a son. His son died fighting for the rebels against the Malungan government. Time clearly hadn't quelled the agony weighing his heart.

"Okoye then informed me of the reason for my presence. He had received a call from President Dimka. My heart raced until he said, 'Do you know that that man had the nerve to threaten me?' Okoye pretended to spit his disgust on the floor. 'Dimka said Nanjieri rebels killed some of his soldiers and he considered that an act of war. I told him he could consider it whatever he wanted. He knows he's in no position to threaten Nanjier. I told him that he should be more concerned about saving his own filthy Borutu skin.'

"Just then, there was a tap on the door. A soldier marched

in and whispered in Okoye's ear. Okoye left abruptly, then returned with a piece of paper. He said, 'It appears that you have escaped the fate that I will have to live with for the rest of my life. Dimka said he saved the life of your son.'

"Okoye handed me the paper. It was an image of Kavu sitting up in bed. Dimka was at his side with an empty smile on his devious lips.

"I barely had a moment to process that Kavu was still alive, when Okoye cautioned me. 'You know,' he said, 'there is a chance that this evening's event will lead to a war between our countries. So you better have a good reason to have caused this international incident.'

"I wanted to tell him about the recording. He surely would have been able to retrieve it and bring Dimka to justice. But if he did, Dimka would have no reason not to kill Kavu. It was obvious that he only saved Kavu to ensure that I wouldn't release the recording to the public. So I searched my mind quickly for anything that would keep Okoye on my side. I knew that Chipo was wanted by the Malungan government for her smuggling activities. So I told Okoye that Dimka had found out that your mother was friends with Chipo. He sent his soldiers to capture us and force us to give her up. So we ran.

"'I know Chipo very well,' Okoye said. 'She's one of the rebel's greatest assets. Without her, I don't think the rebels would have a chance.'

"President Okoye then clapped me on the back. 'You and your wife are courageous and admirable. I'm sure I can find a place for both of you in my military,' he joked. 'Anyone who is an enemy of Dimka is a friend of mine!' As he rose to leave, he said, 'As soon as your wife is able, my men will take you anywhere you want to go. After that,' he said, 'it's probably best if you never come back here. Good luck to you, comrade.' The following morning, we were on a plane to Washington, D.C.

"When things settled down, I returned to Kipaji. Through Ameka, I made an arrangement with Dimka. I agreed to turn over the evidence and myself in exchange for Kavu. But when I arrived at the Nanjier airport, Chipo sent me back. She had discovered that Dimka wasn't going to hold up his end of the bargain. He was never going to release Kavu. Kavu had become too important to his political aspirations. When Dimka became president, he wasn't popular like Amani. So he used Kavu to gain the admiration of the Malungan people. He had made it widely known that he had saved, then adopted, the son of a traitor. Many touted him as the most magnanimous leader of the century.

"Please understand that this has never been easy for me. Over the years, there have been times when I've questioned my decision to take the recording instead of handing it over to Dimka. But, although I lost a son, a wife, and my own life, I would do it again. I have to believe that all the suffering this has brought upon our family is for a greater good that will eventually win out.

"If you choose to pursue this, you will need to find the recording and make it public, while ensuring your brother's safety. It will be no simple task, and terribly dangerous. I'm so sorry that you have inherited this. No one will blame you if you choose to walk away. You still have a chance to return to America and patch a life together—well, the best you can while staying hidden. Just know that, no matter what decision you make, I love you beyond words."

The audio went silent.

"Baba, Baba," D'Melo said in a panic, as if his father could hear him. "You didn't say where it is! Where's the recording?" D'Melo threw his hands up in exasperation. Then suddenly the audio sprang back to life, with Baba laughing.

"You're probably wondering where the recording is. I didn't forget to tell you. I can't risk saying it, in case this drive falls into the wrong hands. The recording is the only thing keeping Kavu alive—*and,* let's not forget, the future of the Shujas, Malunga, and even Kipaji depends on getting the recording in front of the world.

"What I can tell you about its location is that you, and *only* you, have everything necessary to find it." He laughed again, "I knew you would make this choice. I'll see you soon, son."

CHAPTER TWELVE

The Zodiac

As D'Melo slouched through the rondeval doorway, he halted abruptly. "Zar, we can't tell the boyz about this," he realized. "It's too dangerous. It's bad enough that I got you involved."

"Agreed. But, for me, I wouldn't have it any other way."

When they went inside, the boyz were busy devouring brunch and clowning with each other. D'Melo and Zara slipped into the living room to avoid questions about where they had been.

"What did Baba mean when he said I have everything I need to find the recording?" D'Melo sighed, painfully frustrated. "I have no idea where it is."

"Well," Zara said. "Did he mention anything before he died?"

D'Melo scratched his head. For the first time, he allowed himself to relive his final moments with Baba. "Most of what he said sounded like the ramblings of a dying man."

"He had to have said something. That was his last chance to pass information to you. Think," Zara urged. "Did he say anything that seemed out context?"

D'Melo shut his eyes to visualize every detail. Suddenly, he shifted to the edge of the couch. "Baba started talking about how smart my mom was." D'Melo swept his hand over his hair. "How did I miss this?"

"Miss what?"

"Baba laughed and said, 'They didn't know what they were looking for.' Then his eyes shot upward along the wall behind the TV."

D'Melo and Zara scanned that wall in their minds, trying to figure out what Baba could have been looking at. Then they spun toward each other, eyes wide. Together, they turned their gazes to the drawing in front of them on the coffee table, lying in silent anticipation.

Just then, Marley came in. He flopped onto the couch across from them. "Ah man, too many vegan pancakes," he lamented. After a few very still moments, he shot D'Melo and Zara a suspicious glare. "Hey, what's up with you guys? You're being way too quiet."

They shrugged, then murmured simultaneously, "Nothing."

A skeptical crease appeared between Marley's brows. He rested an arm over his drooping eyes. "You know, your mom was a dope artist," he yawned. "It's amazing how she was able to create drawings within drawings. That ain't easy."

"What are you talking about?" D'Melo said, piqued.

Marley peeped out from under his forearm. "Are you serious? You didn't know?" He pushed himself up with a grunt. "When I got out of the mineral pool this morning, the drawing was on your dresser, upside down. I had never seen it from a perspective other than how it was hanging in your living room. It's fascinating. I've been studying it all morning." Marley centered the drawing for D'Melo. "This was how it was in your house." D'Melo nodded breathlessly, wondering whether Marley had unwittingly uncovered the location of the recording. Marley rotated the drawing ninety degrees. "What do you see now?"

"It's a map of Kipaji," D'Melo mumbled, disappointed. "I already knew that."

"Okay, but did you know this?" Marley turned the drawing another ninety degrees. "It's funny," he said, "I've seen it in your house a thousand times, but I never noticed this." D'Melo and Zara leaned in for a better view but had no clue what they were looking at. "Come on, y'all," Marley grumbled impatiently. "Look!" His finger traced several dots on the drawing. "This is Aries . . . and here's Gemini." D'Melo and Zara remained bewildered. "The constellations!" Marley said. "Don't you guys know nothin'!"

Marley went to his room and returned with an astronomy book. He flipped to the Aries and Gemini constellations.

"You brought an astronomy book with you?" D'Melo realized that Marley's nerdiness truly knew no bounds. He examined the images against the drawing. "Oh, my God," he said gawking at the pages. "Marls is right!"

"It has to mean something. But what?" Zara said. D'Melo flashed her a silencing stare.

"What do you mean, 'It has to mean something'?" Marley said.

Zara cringed, clearly realizing that her slip could put Marley in danger.

"Of course it means something," Marley said. "Aries and Gemini are two of the twelve constellations of the zodiac." Zara let out a relieved sigh. Marley didn't catch on to her faux pas.

Marley explained that in Greek mythology, Aries is the ram. Its golden fleece is a symbol of kingship and gives its wearer confidence and fierceness. "Jason—"

D'Melo and Zara exchanged blank looks.

"You know, *Jason,* from Jason and the Argonauts?" Marley clarified, still receiving vacant stares. "Well anyway," he proceeded. "Jason set out to find the fleece. With the help of his future wife, Medea, he recovered it and rightfully claimed the throne.

"As for Gemini, it represents the twins Pollux and Castor. They had the same mother but different fathers. Pollux's father was Zeus, which made Pollux immortal. But Castor was the son of a mortal man, the king of Sparta. So when Castor was killed, Pollux begged Zeus to let him share his immortality with Castor, to keep them together forever. Zeus granted the request by placing the twins in the night sky for all time."

D'Melo glanced at Zara and shrugged. He didn't know what any of this had to do with the recording. D'Melo rotated the map another ninety degrees, hoping for more clues. "It looks like another constellation."

"Yeah, it looks like that—to an astronomical fool," Marley said, clearly amused with his play on words. "But it's not."

"Are you sure?"

Marley flipped his palms upward, *I'm the president of the astronomy club. Of course I'm sure.*

D'Melo wordlessly snatched up the drawing and book from the table and bounded for the door. Zara followed.

"Where you guys going?" Marley called after them. "There are ten other constellations of the zodiac. They're just as interesting!"

D'Melo and Zara hurried out and descended into the valley. They knew that if there was anyone who could help them make sense of this, it was Milpisi.

D'Melo and Zara found Milpisi outside the library. He was teaching the week's Enlightenment Lesson—The Legend of the Spirit King. A cluster of riveted children was seated in front of him on the cushiony blue-green grass. Milpisi lifted a hand. "*Kuja,*" he said to D'Melo and Zara, beckoning them to join the group.

Jonju, the boy who had chased Zara during her morning run, stole a doting glance at her. She returned a cross-eyed, goofy face. Jonju swiveled back to Milpisi, full of giggles. Milpisi, having lost the attention of his star pupil, motioned Jonju to his side, away from the great distraction of Zara.

Milpisi began recounting the legend with Leda's journey to the mysterious man to find a cure for her husband's illness. After the mysterious man blessed her into the Akhtiar—a corps of special healers— Leda returned to Kipaji at a time when her tribe was on the brink of annihilation at the hands of the Choma and Joto tribes. The Amanzi chief demanded that Leda use her healing abilities to save the lives of the Amanzi warriors. Before long, the tide of the war shifted in favor of the Amanzi. Upon discovering that Leda was responsible for the Amanzi's good fortune, the Choma tribe hunted her down to kill her. But before they could, Leda sacrificed her newly born twin sons into the Ukuqala Pool. In the pool, animated by the Great Spirit, the babies merged into a youthful king, who wielded extraordinary power.

Milpisi then delved into how the Spirit King's wisdom laid the foundation upon which current-day Kipaji was built.

"Astride a hippo, the Spirit King emerged, luminescent, into the Moyo. From his cloak, dazzling rays were cast into the purple sky."

Jonju said enthusiastically, "And that's why our flag is purple with gold streaks!"

"That's correct, Jonju." Milpisi said, pleased. "In the centermost point of the valley, the king dismounted from his fleshy throne and entered the Tabernacle. From there, he addressed the Wapendwa, united the tribes, and established the homeland of Kipaji.

"His first act was to create the *Umoja Mkutano*, a council of nine members. He ordained equal representation, two members for each of the four tribes. The ninth member of the Council was the Milpisi. Milpisi then offered a little trivia, "D'Melo's father was the youngest person ever to be elected to the Council." D'Melo managed a faint smile over his somberness about Baba.

"Then," Milpisi continued, "the Spirit King uprooted a deeply held tradition. He declared all leadership positions, including the chiefs, be determined by election and not blood-right. The king was then asked about the succession of the crown. His response was received with great apprehension. What no one could fathom at the time, we now credit as the cornerstone for the preservation of Kipaji's enduring unity.

"The king proclaimed, 'The establishment of the Umoja Mkutano annuls the need for kingship. The Wapendwa are bidden to follow the guidance of this supreme elected body, just as they would a king.' Then, to ensure that kingship did not persist, the king declared, 'The nature of humankind is to turn to the king's offspring or wife for leadership when the monarch's earthly life ends. So, as a safeguard, we, the king, vow never to marry. This kingdom was established through the Spirit, not the flesh, and, for the welfare of Kipaji, it must continue as such. Blood or marital relations can never confer the right of kingship.'

"Since that day, over two thousand years ago," Milpisi concluded proudly, "Kipajis have been living in peace and harmony."

He then opened the lesson to questions.

"Sir, why did the king say 'we' when he was talking about himself?" Jonju asked.

"That's a wonderful question. Not even our scholars know for sure. Some theorize that he was speaking for both himself and the Great Spirit. Others speculate that it was because he saw himself as one with all people. So when he spoke, he was representing the collective will of humanity. But most believe it was because he was composed of the merged twins from the Ukuqala Pool."

D'Melo lifted a tentative hand. The children giggled.

"D'Melo," Milpisi said, amused. "You are free to speak whenever your heart is so moved. You must just seek the right moment."

D'Melo lowered his hand, uncomfortable with this disorderly process. His eyes flashed to and fro, trying to tell whether it was the right moment. The children giggled again; Zara joined them.

"Well," D'Melo finally said. "Not that I don't trust that you believe what you're saying, but how do you know that these things actually happened? I mean, it's quite an extraordinary story."

"Leda and the Spirit King kept meticulous notes for posterity," Milpisi assured, peering over his tiny spectacles. "If you are interested, the translations are displayed in the archives in the library."

A tiny voice piped, "When Leda dropped her babies into the Ukuqala Pool, the young king emerged. But how? Where did this king come from?"

"Thank you, Zanu, for asking such an essential question. But unfortunately, my answer cannot match its import. I can only tell you what has been passed down from our ancestors. A further explanation is outside my realm of understanding, as are so many things. The legend is that Leda's sanctified blood blessed the pool with unimaginable and celestial power. The water, animated by the unbounded grace of the Great Spirit, merged the babies, giving birth to the Spirit King."

A bright-eyed young girl asked, "What were the other women of the Akhtiar like? You have only told us about Leda."

"The extent of my knowledge on this matter lies within the four corners of Leda's journal. She made only one brief mention of the other women of the Akhtiar.

"When the mysterious man led her to the Akhtiar, Leda was captivated by their wildly varying hues of skin and the color and texture of their hair. Seeing them under the acacia tree was like gazing at the most gloriously vibrant flower garden. A few of the women had hair like her own—tightly coiled—while others had hair as straight and shiny as a horse's tail, and still others had flowing curls. The array of colors ranged from jet black to stark white. In between were assorted shades of brown and yellow. One woman even had reddish-orange hair. Leda noted that it was as if flames of fire poured from her scalp, like an erupting volcano."

The kids peered at Zara and giggled. Zara lifted a tuft of her hair, *You got me.*

"Leda was magnetically drawn to the red-headed woman. She curiously caressed her fiery strands. The woman was tickled by Leda's fascination. Just before the mysterious man began to address the Akhtiar, Leda whispered in the woman's ear.

"Are there any other questions?" Milpisi said, scanning the assembly. There was an unsettled murmur among them. "Is there something amiss?" he asked.

"Well, sir," Jonju offered politely, "you didn't say what Leda whispered to the woman."

"Oh," Milpisi acknowledged apologetically, rocking back in his cross-legged position. "That was not quality storytelling, was it?" he chuckled. "That section of Leda's journal was damaged by water. So no one knows what she whispered." The kids slumped, disappointed. "But I can tell you what the red-haired woman responded. She said, 'I hope so. That would be a blessing.'

The kids pursed their lips, wondering what Leda had said that would have drawn such a response.

"Sir," Jonju said next. "Could you please tell us about how one becomes the Milpisi?"

"Jonju, do you have your sights set on my job?" Milpisi chortled. "Well, I'm sorry to inform you that this would be not possible. The mysterious man explained to the Akhtiar that when they passed from this world, the fruit they bore from their wombs would follow them as the Milpisi. He also warned that, even though their bloodlines had been purified, they must choose wisely from their children. Not all would be worthy to administer the elixir of Haya. The only other guidance he gave was that the Milpisi would possess an unusual capacity that enhanced her or his ability to heal others. For instance, for me, it is my zany sense of humor," Milpisi joked.

The kids remained expressionless.

"So Leda's third child," Jonju deduced, "the baby the warriors didn't know was still in the alcove, must have become the Milpisi."

"That's very astute, Jonju," Milpisi affirmed. "And if not for that third child, I would not be here before you. She is my ancestor."

"But Milpisi," Jonju said, "you have no children. So then who will be the Milpisi when you pass to the eternal realms?"

Milpisi released a weighty breath. "I don't know, Jonju. But rest assured, the Great Spirit has a plan. By the time I complete my earthly journey, I have faith that your question will be answered."

Zara chimed in. "Milpisi, if I may."

"Of course, my dear."

"Haya is the most magnificent and precious resource in the world. How does Kipaji ensure its protection?"

"At the bidding of the Great Spirit, the king trained twelve warriors from each clan in the art of elemental conjuration. They were endowed with the ability to manipulate the natural elements prominent in their regions—water, fire, mineral, air. We call these spiritual warriors 'conjurers'—our Army of Light. The conjurers train new recruits to ensure that Kipaji maintains an army of forty-eight."

"Ohhh, that's why!" D'Melo said under his breath.

"What's why?" Zara whispered back.

"I have this recurring dream that has always seemed so strange. In the dream, I'm play-fighting with a boy in a field of wildflowers. We're pretending to command the elements, like these conjurers Milpisi's talking about. I'm controlling minerals, like rocks and dirt, and the other boy is controlling fire. But then I pick up a real rock and throw it. It hits him just above his eye. The boy drops to his knees, blood pouring down his face. I'm so scared. I think I killed him." D'Melo mused. "Now I understand why I have this dream. Baba must have told me the legend when I was little. Thank God. I'm not as weird as I thought I was."

"Ahhh," Zara said sarcastically, "let's not close the book on that so quickly."

D'Melo pursed his lips. *Ha ha.* They turned their attention back to Milpisi.

"The king commanded that the conjurers use their capabilities for the protection of Kipaji and Haya only. Also, they must act with stealth, ensuring that their abilities remain hidden from the eyes of the world beyond Kipaji."

"Do you think this is real?" Zara said to D'Melo. "I mean, about the conjurers having special powers and all?"

"Well, if you would have asked me that before seeing a tree summon ancestors, I would have said no." He shrugged. "Now, I don't know what to believe."

D'Melo resisted the urge to raise his hand, then asked, "Milpisi, what ever happened with the king?"

"Without warning, the Spirit King's reign ended on the nineteenth anniversary of the birth of Kipaji. He was meditating on the summit of Amanzi Mountain, as he did every sunrise. His spirit, donning the golden fleece, lifted from his body and drifted to the bank of the summit river. He gazed heavenward and then spoke these words into the hearts of all Kipajis:

"'The seed of the will of the Great Spirit has been sown in this hallowed land. Our purpose has been served, allowing for the sun of our existence on this earthly plane to set. In our absence, you must remain ever vigilant against the evil of discord. But if the darksome night descends upon this land once again, rest assured, we will return unto you from an unknown realm. And with the power of the Great Spirit, we will march together in serried lines to hasten the dawn of the light of unity.' Then the king's final words were, 'O Wapendwa, know of a certainty that we are never further from you than your own hearts.'

"The king's spirit then floated down from the riverbank into the rushing torrent. It was carried over the mountain ledge and into the Ukuqala Pool, returning to its birthplace. The pool rejoiced, dancing and swirling around his spirit. At the spot where the king was meditating, nothing remained. His body had vanished.

"In just a couple of days, on the fifth of July, our grandest festival celebrates the anniversary of the Spirit King's ascension to the Hidden

Realm. So," Milpisi's eyes shifted to D'Melo and Zara, "this is an aus-picious time for you to be here."

Zara nudged D'Melo. "Hey, that's your birthday!"

With Baba gone and his life in tatters, D'Melo couldn't care any less that he was soon turning eighteen.

"For next week's lesson," Milpisi closed, "we will venture to the alcove. There, we will visit the *Mwanzo Mpia*, a monument to a 'New Dawn,' erected where Leda birthed the triplets."

The kids bounced to their feet and immediately began play-fight-ing, imagining themselves to be conjurers. All, that is, except Jonju. He was enchanted by something else, or more accurately, *someone* else. He made a beeline for Zara and leapt into her lap. She dipped him, planted her lips on his neck and blew, making bubbly sounds. He giggled hysterically. The other kids rushed over, hoping to have a turn.

"Well," Milpisi grinned, "it seems you have won the hearts of the children of Kipaji with astonishing ease. I wish I could get them this excited about my lessons."

"It's just my hair," she said, as the kids tugged a few strands, mar-veling at its glistening hue.

"They've never seen anyone with hair like yours," Milpisi ex-plained. "I've only seen it once myself, years ago. So red hair runs in your family?"

"Actually, no. My mom and grandparents have brown hair. But apparently one of my ancestors was a redhead."

Milpisi looked to the sky. Then he said gratefully, "It's my time." Before Zara and D'Melo could ask him what he meant, Milpisi re-quested a private moment with them. The children ran off to the wild-flower field. Only Jonju remained.

"You too, Jonju," Milpisi prodded.

Jonju's shoulders dropped glumly.

"I'm sorry, my love," Zara comforted. She smooched his forehead.

His pouty eyes instantly brightened into a twinkly gleam. He breezed off, his euphoric feet hardly touching the ground.

The moment the kids were out of sight, D'Melo's thoughts returned to Baba's audio.

"Son," Milpisi said. "You look troubled. Is there something you want to tell me?" They settled on the bench outside the library.

D'Melo told Milpisi everything about Baba's message on the secret flash drive. Milpisi gazed reflectively into the distance, listening.

"It all makes sense now," he said. "I never knew why your parents left so abruptly. For weeks, I replayed our final encounter in my mind. I wondered woefully about what happened to your family. But, about a month later, a tiny box appeared on my porch. Inside was Baba's Ibada ring."

D'Melo fondled the ring on the chain around his neck.

"That was his way of letting me know you guys were okay," Milpisi said, his eyes moist.

Milpisi's attention then returned to the matter at hand. "So where is this recording?"

"We don't know." D'Melo unrolled the drawing across his lap. "But we think this has something to do with it."

Milpisi slipped his spectacles from his shirt pocket and positioned them toward the tip of his nose. "It's a lovely piece," he said. "But I don't see anything to help locate the recording." Just then a stormy wind kicked up. D'Melo turned the drawing ninety degrees, struggling to keep it flat.

"Ohhh. Look at that," Milpisi said, leaning in. "It's Kipaji."

D'Melo rotated the drawing another ninety degrees.

"I had no idea that Diata was so mystical with her art." Milpisi pointed out Pollux and Castor. "These stars are the twins." His finger moved contemplatively over the drawing. "And here is Hamal. It's the most luminous star in the Aries constellation. In Arabic it means, 'the head of the ram.'" Milpisi wrinkled his brow, as if discovering something. "The way Diata overlaid the constellations, Hamal lies directly on Pollux, the immortal twin. Why would she do that? What is the relationship between the head of the ram and the immortal twin?" Milpisi inclined his head, stroking his beard. "Ahhh, Diata!" he said, straightening. "You're brilliant!"

"What is it?" D'Melo asked.

"The ram, headed by Hamal, had a golden fleece—the representation of kingship. And the Spirit King lives forever in the hearts of Kipajis. So, in this sense, he can be said to be immortal, like Pollux. These two things converge at the Ukuqala Pool, where the Spirit King arose wearing the golden-fleeced cloak. The recording must be there."

D'Melo said warily, "But the recording can't be in the pool."

"That's true," Milpisi said, deflated. "I must be missing something. How about rotating the drawing the final ninety degrees?"

Milpisi helped D'Melo flatten the drawing, as more strong gusts lifted the edges. A dark shadow crawled across the valley floor from the thick gray clouds creeping over Choma Mountain. Milpisi observed the swiftly darkening sky. "A mighty storm is brewing," he said.

Zara reached into her handbag, dug out a shawl and wrapped it around her neck. Next she pulled out a slouchy beanie cap and tugged it onto her head. A tuft of hair danced in the breeze over her eye.

D'Melo raised a brow at her. "We'll just wait for you to finish preparing for New York fashion week. Because we have nothing more important to do right now."

Zara narrowed her eyes at him, *Was all that sarcasm really necessary?*

"Milpisi," D'Melo said. "We looked at the drawing from this angle, too. There doesn't seem to be anything significant."

"There has to be," Milpisi insisted. "Otherwise, it would be incomplete. Three sides with meaning and one without? That would not make sense." A raindrop splashed on the drawing. D'Melo quickly rolled it up. They hastened into the library and spread the drawing out on a table in the art nook. While D'Melo thumbed through Marley's astronomy book, Milpisi ventured off to examine Diata's other pieces of art for clues.

Zara took some photos of the drawing on her phone. While she was framing her shots, she zoomed in on a particular area of the image.

"You know," she called out, "I didn't notice this before."

Milpisi returned to the table.

"This star right here isn't part of the two constellations," she said. "It's faint, but if you look closely, it's there."

Milpisi's eyes darted between the book and the drawing. "You're right," he said, "This star doesn't belong to either constellation. Diata must have put it there for a reason. The rest of the drawing is meticulous. She wouldn't have made this mistake. Plus, Baba would have spotted it immediately. He studied astronomy before going to medical school.

"Wait a minute." Milpisi slid his finger in a circle, outlining Kipaji. "Look where Diata placed that star." He tapped the northern end of Kipaji. "Do you see how this area of the drawing is a shade darker than the rest?"

"Uhhh, yes . . ." D'Melo and Zara said together, waiting for the punchline.

"This star isn't a star at all. It's a marker—you know, like X marks the spot. It's pointing us to the recording!" Milpisi paused, stroking his beard. Suddenly, he murmured, "The final side must tell us exactly where the recording is." Milpisi turned the drawing. "Here," he said, running his finger along the darkened area. "It's a U shape, but upside down.

"We're a little dense, Milpisi." Zara squinted an eye and shrugged. "We need more."

"Think about it. What on Amanzi Mountain is shaped like an upside-down U?"

"The entrance to the alcove!" D'Melo exclaimed.

"Exactly. But knowing it's in the alcove is insufficient," Milpisi said. "We need to know specifically where it hides. You will be afforded but a few minutes to retrieve it."

"I'm sorry," D'Melo said, disconcerted. "Did you just say that I'll be 'afforded but a few minutes'?"

"Well," Milpisi hesitated, then sighed. "It seems my mouth got ahead of me. I don't want to frighten you, but now you need to know. I'm sure the Malungan government is tracking your every move."

"Tracking me? But how? I thought I was safe in Kipaji!"

"You are . . . mostly," Milpisi said, in a less than assuring voice.

"Milpisi, you're not exactly filling me with confidence with that response."

"The truth is, we know Dimka has obtained information that could have only come from within Kipaji. So we have suspected for a while that there is a spy among us. And I would be surprised if you are not at the top of this spy's list of priorities."

D'Melo blew a tense breath. "Okay then," he said, absorbing what he had just heard. "So we better pinpoint the exact location of the recording before I set foot in the alcove. I won't have time to be digging around in there."

They resumed their attempt to crack Diata's code. "This is weird." Zara zoomed in on the extrinsic star. "It's pixelated, but you can see that this non-star is green."

"Yes," Milpisi agreed. "But why?" Then he brightened as he focused on the darker area of the drawing. "The outline of this U-shaped region could also be seen as sort of a necklace, right?" Milpisi theorized. "And what's at the end of the necklace? The green dot."

D'Melo and Milpisi lifted their gaze to the "Mother of Kipaji" painting above Zara's head "Ohhh," D'Melo murmured, having an epiphany. "In my dream, Baba wasn't saying 'Later.' He was saying 'Leda.' He was leading me to the recording."

Zara spun toward the painting. Her eyes immediately fixed on the emerald dangling from Leda's forehead. "That's helpful," she acknowl-edged, "but we still don't know exactly where the recording is. Only that it has to do with Leda."

"On the contrary, my dear," Milpisi replied. "We do. There was something I failed to mention during today's lesson. Remember Leda had challenges getting pregnant? Well, when the mysterious man re-leased the Akhtiar to return to their homelands, he had Leda remain behind. He gave her a gift—an emerald strung on a leather headlace. As he crowned her head with it, his face became luminescent. Leda was forced to turn away lest the brilliance of his countenance damage her eyes. 'Oh Kipaj,' the mysterious man implored. 'I beseech Thee by Thy power and might to allow this faithful handmaiden to bring forth children, the most sublime pearls.' His brightness then dimin-ished, though his eyes continued radiating. 'My child,' he assured her. 'You are now relieved of the malady that has been the source of much anguish to your soul.'

"As you know from the legend, the night Leda returned to the alcove, she became pregnant with the triplets."

Satisfaction filled D'Melo's heart. "It's at the Mwanzo Mpia mon-ument… the spot where Leda gave birth!" he said.

"Well, actually, it must be *inside* the monument," Milpisi clari-fied. "The monument was created with an interior chamber to protect our most precious artifacts. Only Council members are aware of its existence. If Kipaji is ever overrun by an enemy, a Council member will remove the artifacts and carry them to safety.

"Atop the monument, there is a bust of Leda. A replica of the em-erald is embedded in the bust's forehead. One revolution of the replica opens the chamber. I'm sure that's where Baba stashed the recording. It makes perfect sense. The chamber is the most well-guarded secret in Kipaji."

"Now what?" Zara said, ready for action.

Just then, a hummingbird pecked the library window.

"Someone needs help," Milpisi muttered, then quickly ducked outside.

D'Melo and Zara trailed after him, sharing a dumbfounded glance. *Did a bird just communicate with Milpisi?* The hummingbird darted off toward Joto Mountain.

"I apologize," Milpisi said. "We will have to consult upon our next steps at a later time. I have an urgent medical matter to which I must attend."

"Milpisi, before you go," D'Melo said. "The story you told the kids today, is it just legend or is it true?"

Milpisi's eyes creased into a smile, "Can it not be both?" He mounted the okapi waiting to transport him up Joto Mountain.

"Komba, *twende*!" He clicked and Komba trotted off. Suddenly, Milpisi pulled the reins. "*Kata*," he commanded. Komba obediently halted. Milpisi turned around and looked at Zara. "My dear one, would you like to join me? You can witness firsthand the healing power of Haya's nectar."

"Well," Zara said, "I *am* a bit busy right now. I haven't had my morning coffee yet."

"Okay. Perhaps another time."

D'Melo sighed at Zara's ill-timed attempt at humor.

"Hey!" she called, "I was joking. Do you think there's anything in the universe I'd like to do more than to see the most awesome phenomenon in human history?"

"Very well, then. We must move with dispatch. My satchel is empty of nectar. I had planned to fill the vials after the lesson this morning. Once again, I have been remiss."

D'Melo cast an expression of disbelief at Zara. "What are you thinking? Have you not noticed that Milpisi is the most sincere person in the world? He's not gonna understand your whack sarcasm."

"Whoa, dude. I know I screwed that up, but '*whack*'? A tad harsh, don't you think?"

Milpisi, several paces ahead, shouted, "Zara is not whack. She just needs her coffee."

Zara whispered to D'Melo, "Was he just being sarcastic?"

"Yes," Milpisi called out. "But it wasn't whack sarcasm!" He laughed boomingly.

Zara's eyes widened, surprised at Milpisi's uncharacteristic amusement with himself. She dashed over and nimbly hopped onto Komba behind Milpisi.

"Am I really riding an okapi to save someone's life with nectar from a tree?" Zara called back to D'Melo, bouncing in rhythm with Komba's gait. "Could my life be any more awesome!"

On the way to Haya, Milpisi explained Kipaji's emergency system to a mystified Zara. The forest animals are one with the spirit of life. When the light of that spirit threatens to flicker out, they are keenly aware of it. They communicate through each other to the hummingbird and the okapi. The hummingbird, called a '*Malaika*' in Kipaji, which means 'hovering angel', tracks down Milpisi and leads him to the fading light, hopefully before it extinguishes.

"It's simple," Milpisi concluded matter-of-factly.

"Yeah, of course," Zara muttered. "Silly me. What could be more simple than animals working together to save the life of a human being? This is amazing beyond words."

"I agree, but I must admit, it's not foolproof." Milpisi's spirits seemed to dampen. "Not long ago we lost the Choma chief's wife. Three events converged to create the perfect storm that prevented me from saving her. It seemed as if the universe was leagued against me. Minutes after the Malaika's alert, a brutal storm swept into Kipaji. By the time Komba and I reached the base of Choma Mountain, the wind was whipping mercilessly, and rain was pummeling us in sheets. It slowed our progress significantly. Even so, we still would have reached her in time. But then a most unfortunate accident occurred.

Streams of water were gushing down the mountainside, making the path to Choma village treacherous. Komba lost her footing and fell heavily into the mud, breaking her leg. If I had been carrying two doses of the nectar, as I typically do, I could have administered one to Komba. But when the Malaika alerted me that night, I had just given a serving to an Upepo boy who had a lethal reaction to a bee sting. And, with the unaccommodating weather, I couldn't risk taking the time to replenish my supply at the Tree. So I set off with only one vial of nectar.

"Without Komba, I trudged the remaining distance to Choma village on foot, only to arrive a minute late. The chief was sick with grief and aflame with fury. I don't blame him."

Zara put two and two together. "Is that why the Choma section of the Festival of Lights recommended selling the elixir to the world, so Kipaji can modernize its healthcare system?"

Milpisi hesitated. "You are sharp, my dear. You don't miss a thing. Well, there had been rumblings about improving our technology for some time. But with the death of the chief's wife, who, by the way, was also the daughter of the Joto chief, the rumblings gained a couple of very influential voices, adding fuel to the fire."

In his lifetime, Milpisi explained, he had never seen Kipaji more divided. The Choma and Joto chiefs had become bedfellows. Together they were increasing the pressure to open Haya to the world, creating a stark split within the Council. On critical Council votes, the clan members started sticking together—Choma and Joto on one side and Amanzi and Upepo on the other. This created endless four-to-four-vote stalemates. So Milpisi, as the ninth member of the Council, was the deciding vote. Until Milpisi was convinced that the proper safeguards for Haya would be put in place, he would continue to vote against revealing the Tree. This intensified Choma and Joto distrust. They felt Milpisi was biased because he was of the Amanzi clan.

Milpisi paused his story as they reached the forest edge nearest Haya. With the wind stirring stronger and drizzle now tapping their faces, they hopped off Komba and scuttled through the underbrush. Zara knew the Tree was close but didn't see it. And then—thump, she thudded into it.

"*Umf.* What the—?" Her disbelieving hands groped a tree that was not there.

Milpisi chuckled softly, then raised his palms. Accumulated moisture from the forest canopy dripped onto his hands. In the Kipaji tongue, he invoked, "Oh Great Spirit, please unmask your glory to this lowly one." With an air of mystery, he slid his hands apart like a celestial magician. As the gap widened, Haya unveiled gradually, until finally it was revealed in its full splendor.

"Oh, my God," Zara murmured unconsciously. "I don't think I can ever get used to that. It's, it's—"

Milpisi finished her thought, "The opposite of whack?"

"Exactly," Zara giggled, amused with Milpisi's expanding command of slang.

With the utmost care, Milpisi took a dangling flower into his hand without detaching it. He settled into a supplicating posture before Haya. "Oh, Great Spirit," he intoned, "I beseech Thee to grant this humble servant the least measure of your life-giving elixir."

The flower opened and emitted a sparkling purple light. Milpisi reached into his satchel for a wooden vial and a *chombo*—a toothpick with a tiny bowl at the tip. He inserted the *chombo* into the center of the flower with the precision of a brain surgeon. A bead of glittery liquid appeared in the bowl. Milpisi slid the *chombo* into the vial.

"This is *definitely* the opposite of whack!" Zara marveled, as they remounted Komba. "What did you say to Haya to get her to give you the nectar?"

"It is not *what* you say, dear one, it is how you say it that matters. The only requirement is humility. But that is simple."

Here he goes with that "simple" stuff again! Zara thought. *Everything is simple to this dude—I mean, to Milpisi.* Zara corrected herself, out of respect for Milpisi.

"When you feel the tremendous weight of being the Milpisi, you have little choice but to be humble. On a daily basis, I am reminded that my power compared to that of the Great Spirit is like a light bulb to all the suns in the universe."

As they approached the Joto plateau, Milpisi prepared Zara for the scene she was likely to encounter. "For our forest friends to alert me, it means that the injury is life threatening, and, on the geyser field, injuries can be gruesome."

And just as he had warned, the horrifically burned body of a young man appeared through the sweltering mist. He lay motionless on the coarse landscape. His training to become a conjurer had taken a fateful turn when he slipped into one of the boiling pools. The jolting smell of cooked flesh permeating the wet air halted Zara in her tracks. She gathered herself so she wouldn't vomit.

Milpisi opened the young conjurer's mouth very gently, but still he shrieked in absolute agony. It seemed that every movement sent searing pain ripping through his body. Milpisi lifted the *chombo* from the vial and smeared the nectar under his tongue.

Zara watched, transfixed. Within moments, the conjurer's flesh began to regenerate. Fresh layers of skin weaved over the charred areas. Zara gasped. She would never have believed this was possible if she had not witnessed the phenomenon with her own eyes.

Amazingly, soon after Milpisi's ministrations, the young conjurer teetered to his feet. He fixed a grateful gaze on Milpisi, laid a fist over his heart, and bowed with great reverence. Joyous ululation from the other conjurers cut through the steamy air.

Milpisi and Zara started back for Amanzi Mountain, where they knew D'Melo was devising a plan to recover the secret recording. After several minutes of bobbing silently on Komba as she trotted along, Milpisi said to Zara, "I don't think I've ever seen you so quiet. You have not uttered a syllable since the plateau."

"I—I just don't know what to say. Haya is the most amazing medicine that's ever existed. It seems it can literally heal the world. So why isn't it?"

"You have touched on a uniquely sensitive topic in Kipaji. You must know that we wholeheartedly embrace the fact that Haya does not belong to us alone. Every Council since I was born has grappled with the question of whether to unveil Haya to the world. And every Council has decided against it.

"It is an unfathomable responsibility to have the fate of humanity in our hands. Although Kipajis have a profound desire to heal everyone, protecting the Tree is paramount. As far as we know, our Tree is the last of its kind." Milpisi let out a distressed sigh. "The Council feels the world cannot be trusted to care for Haya. And we have yet to conceive of a way to ensure its safety.

"Humankind has shown time and again that gaining control over the earth's most vital and precious resources eclipses whatever universal benefit they were created to have. Take for instance, the immense power in the nucleus of an atom. Instead of it being used to bring energy to all, it has become the source of division and imbalance in the world. America and the Soviet Union raced feverishly to be the first to use atomic energy for mass destruction. Since then, a handful of nations have prevented other countries from developing a similar weapon. They say it is because the more countries that have nuclear weaponry, the more precarious the world becomes. While that is logical, I do not believe it is the real reason. You see, the holder of a nuclear weapon wields tremendous power. And the wealthy countries want to maintain that power for themselves so they can dictate their self-serving whims to the rest of humanity.

"Now I ask, how much more valuable would be a technology that heals the diseases plaguing humankind? The nation that commands this natural technology will rule with a power and ironclad authority to an extent that the world has never before witnessed. So, countries with the strongest militaries would stop at nothing to seize control over Haya. And the truth is, Kipaji does not have the means to thwart an invasion. The weapons of war today are far too sophisticated, even for our conjurers. It is an agonizing dilemma that I face—I mean, the *Council* faces."

Zara nodded sympathetically.

"But don't fret, the day is approaching when the way forward will be revealed. Haya's ultimate purpose is to heal the world. It is the will of the Great Spirit." Milpisi paused. He gazed into the forest canopy, where the leaves rustled below an increasingly ominous sky. He murmured prophetically, "The winds of change are stirring."

CHAPTER THIRTEEN

Kavu –
The Golden Boy

An impassioned D'Melo greeted Milpisi and Zara at the door of his rondeval. He ushered them into the living room, then beckoned the boyz to join them. The boyz piled in with their usual boisterous melee. But sensing D'Melo's mood, they instantly settled in, matching his sober attitude.

D'Melo had desperately tried to devise a plan which didn't involve the boyz, but he just couldn't think of another way to get the recording safely out of Kipaji. After bringing them up to speed on what's happened, he delved in.

"The Malungan government will do anything to keep the evidence from being revealed, including kill all of us," he said gravely. "So if you want out, I understand. This is not something you signed up for when you came here."

"I'm in!" Jeylan declared, without hesitation.

"I didn't even tell you the plan yet."

"It don't matter. You're my brotha. I'll always have your back. If you go down, I go with you."

D'Melo pulled Jeylan into their customary handshake hug, adding a few grateful claps on the back.

"Me too," Kazim said.

Kazim glanced at Marley, then nudged him.

"What?" Marley shrugged.

"You in, fool?"

"I wanna hear the plan first!" Marley declared. "I ain't jumpin' in on no half-baked idea. This thing's gotta be tight." Then his straight face melted into a wide grin. "Just playin'. Y'all know I'm in." He bellowed, "LD in the house!"

D'Melo gazed at them, flooded with emotion. He then began to lay out the scheme. It was to unfold during the funeral. When he reached Zara's part, he pinched her nose and twisted it.

"Ow!" she yelped, slapping his hand away. "Dude! What are you doing?"

"It's the Nečzian tradition, right?" he said. "You know, to help you remember what I'm saying."

"Are you kidding? You think that really works? *And*—we don't twist for real! Just tell me the plan, dude."

D'Melo explained her role, which involved many details.

Her eyes glazed over at the complexity. "You're right," she said, yielding. "I'm not gonna remember that. Twist my nose." Much-needed laughter filled the room.

D'Melo hesitated before revealing the final piece of the plan—securing the recording. Then he started in, spelling out each step warily, anticipating all the while the sting of Zara's opposition.

"What?" she burst, just as he expected. "Are you saying that *we*," she motioned between the boyz and herself, "are retrieving the recording, while you stay in the valley?"

D'Melo lowered his eyes.

"You must be kidding!" Zara raged. "They're going to kill you the first chance they get! There's no way I'm leaving you behind. We all go together, or we don't go!"

"Listen, Zar," he sighed. "I wish I could go with you guys. But that would jeopardize the mission and put your lives in danger. The Malungan spy is watching my every move. Let's use that to our advantage. Jey, remember that game against Madison? Coach knew that they would double-team me all game. So he used me as a decoy."

Jeylan lifted his chin, acknowledging where D'Melo was going with this.

"The strategy worked. You scored thirty-six that game and Kaz got twenty-eight. And we won. We can do the same thing here. While the Malungans focus their attention on me, the four of you can slip away to the alcove. You'll be gone before they even know what happened."

Zara wasn't buying it. "This isn't a stupid basketball game! We're talking about your life. The boyz can get the recording. I'm staying with you."

"Zar," D'Melo exhorted. "You *have* to go with them. They don't know where the alcove is. And it's too risky to take a practice run before the funeral."

"Well, I don't know where it is either."

"Yeah, you do."

Zara squinted at him, dubiously.

"You know how to get to the summit, right?"

She nodded suspiciously.

"From there, you'll easily find the alcove, by feeling it."

The boyz' faces contorted.

"Excuse me?" Jeylan asserted. "Maybe you want to run that by us one more time. Are you saying we're gonna rely on Zara using the force? Is she a Jedi and no one told me?"

"Trust me. Zara knows what I'm talking about." D'Melo turned to her. "Leda suffered so much on that mountain. Her pain will lead you straight to the alcove, where her suffering was the most intense."

"But," Zara retorted, "I've never felt the pain of a person who isn't alive."

"Yeah, you have," D'Melo disagreed. "Remember that day those kids were playing in the snow outside Ms. Keba's house? You could still feel her."

Zara inclined her head, realizing D'Melo was right. "Even so," she said, "I hate this plan."

D'Melo lifted his brows at Milpisi, seeking his blessing. A confirming and subtle grin sparkled in his eyes.

"Okay then. It's settled." D'Melo gazed intently into their eyes. He tapped his chest and shot out a fist. "LD Crew forever!" The boyz met his fist.

"Come on, Zara," Jeylan urged. "Ain't you part of the LD Crew?"

Zara felt a rush of warmth cascade through her at Jeylan's words. Her eyes glistened with grateful tears. She tapped her chest and joined her fist.

D'Melo accompanied Milpisi outside. Out of earshot of his friends, particularly Zara, D'Melo made a request. He wanted to meet Kavu. It would be his only opportunity to see the brother he never knew he had.

Milpisi told D'Melo that it had been more than a decade since he last saw Kavu. Kavu was a young boy when the prime minister of Turkmenistan presented him with a gift, an Akhal-Teke. This majestic horse is known for its speed, intelligence, and golden coat. The first time Kavu rode it, he was thrown off. He broke two ribs and punctured his spleen. Milpisi was summoned to administer the elixir. Oddly, Kavu didn't improve after ingesting the nectar. Milpisi realized the healing power of the nectar was being thwarted by unnatural substances tainting the area. Nearby, soldiers were rolling barrels into a storage shed. The barrels contained caustic material used to develop chemical weapons. Milpisi demanded that the soldiers lock them in a sealed room. Once the barrels were secured, Kavu immediately began to recover.

"But," D'Melo inquired, confused. "Isn't the elixir a secret for Kipajis only?"

"Well," Milpisi said, shaking his head. "A few years before that incident, I used the nectar and Dimka found out about it."

D'Melo was stunned. "That was you! You saved Kavu that night he was shot on the bridge."

"Yes," Milpisi muttered tentatively, seeming to question whether he made the right decision. "A soldier was carrying Kavu's blood-soaked body through Kipaji to Malunga. Kavu surely would not have survived the journey. And I couldn't just let Baba and Diata's child die. So I told the soldier I would treat Kavu. The soldier phoned Dimka, who gave his consent. Dimka emphasized that Kavu was a valuable asset to Malunga, and so the soldier must not leave my side. When Kavu was revived, the soldier dragged me to Malunga with him. He knew Dimka would want to know about the 'miracle medicine' I used.

"Dimka pressured me to administer the elixir to Malungans. I refused. It would have been too risky. Information about Haya would have surely leaked to the world. So Dimka offered a compromise. The elixir would be used for him and his family only, and, in exchange, he would keep Haya a secret. I agreed, but told him that if anyone ever found out, the deal was off."

"Well, what about the soldier?" D'Melo asked. "He knew."

Milpisi lowered his eyes somberly. "That soldier never made it out of the presidential compound that night." He shuddered. "There was really no other choice."

After a remorseful moment, Milpisi said to D'Melo, "I debated whether to tell you about your brother. My fear that you would want to see him compelled me not to. But here I am, faced with it anyway.

Meeting Kavu is much more complicated than you can imagine. It could put you, and all of Kipaji, in jeopardy."

Kavu had become a high-ranking soldier in the Malungan military, Milpisi explained. He headed a special anti-rebel unit composed of the country's most elite fighters. So even though Kavu was technically Kipaji, Milpisi doubted the Council would grant him access into Kipaji. At the very least, the Council would want time to thoroughly vet Kavu and devise a protection protocol. That would take time.

D'Melo couldn't hide his disappointment. "But I don't *have* time. Are you sure there's no other way? Please, he's the only family I have left."

Milpisi pondered. "Well, there is one possibility."

Milpisi recounted a story of Kavu's heroism that had made him something of a celebrity among the Choma. About two years ago, Kavu and his special regiment were in hot pursuit of the rebel leader, Waasi Madaki, and one of his soldiers. They were attempting to flee to Nanjier through Kipaji, which set off internal alarms. Conjurers found them hiding in Choma village. To protect himself and his soldier, Madaki took the Choma chief hostage.

Just then, Kavu rode into the village, the coat of his beautiful horse gleaming. He was flanked by his elite fighters, wearing their signature maroon berets. Madaki raised a blade to the neck of the Choma chief. He threatened to open his throat unless the conjurers killed Kavu and his soldiers.

Kavu calmly proposed a different solution. He suggested an exchange, himself for the chief. Kavu knew that, as the adopted son of President Dimka, he was a much more valuable hostage than the Choma chief. He started to explain to Madaki who he was.

"I know who you are," Madaki said. "You're *Kijana Dhabu*, the Golden Boy."

"Oh, that's flattering," Kavu smiled inscrutably. "I didn't know I had a special name among the Shujas. Let the chief go, and President

Dimka will give you whatever you want for my safe return. This way, no one will have to get hurt."

Madaki agreed. Kavu dismounted and laid his rifle at his feet. He ordered his fighters to do the same. The rebel soldier secured Kavu's hands behind his back.

But Madaki didn't release the chief.

"Hey!" Kavu howled. "The deal was, me for the chief!"

"Well, I changed my mind. For now, we will hold on to the chief. He is our insurance that these Kipaji warriors won't try anything stupid."

Madaki commanded one of Kavu's soldiers to call Dimka. "Tell him we got his Golden Boy. No harm will befall him as long as we are allowed safe passage to Nanjier. Oh, but there is one other thing we want," Madaki added. "We will require the release of the fourteen Shuja rebels he imprisoned. Once these rebels are in Nanjier, we will let the Golden Boy go."

The Malungan soldier looked at Kavu, awaiting his instructions. Kavu nodded his approval.

The soldier communicated Madaki's proposal to Dimka. Judging by the shock on his soldier's face, Kavu surmised that Dimka declined the deal. He would never free the rebel prisoners, not even to save his adopted son. With a clandestine wink, Kavu conveyed to his soldier not to worry. He had a plan.

"President Dimka guarantees your safe passage to Nanjier," the soldier lied. "And he will set in motion the release of your rebels from prison."

Madaki cautioned the Malungan soldiers and the conjurers against following him. He crossed a tense finger over his throat, threatening what he would do to Kavu and the chief if they didn't heed his warning. With aggressive shoves, Madaki and his rebel steered Kavu and the chief through the thicket. A few minutes into their walk in the jungle, Madaki halted abruptly at the sound of branches crackling overhead and falling leaves. He peered up into the canopy. Red colobus monkeys frolicked in the treetops.

"Now," Milpisi noted, "the way the Choma chief recounts this part of the story, you would think Kavu is some sort of superhero. Kavu used Madaki's moment of distraction as an opportunity to end the abduction."

With lightning speed, Kavu vaulted backward over the rope that bound his hands. He swiftly struck the rebel with tremendous force on his windpipe. The rebel collapsed to the ground, gasping for air. And, seemingly all in one motion, Kavu leapt into the air, wrapped his legs around Madaki's neck, and snapped it. On his acrobatic return to the forest floor, he drove his heel into the chest of the rebel, crushing his sternum.

"For obvious reasons," Milpisi said, "Kavu became an instant hero to the Chomas. The chief held a festival for him, where he made Kavu an honorary Choma."

D'Melo was silent, unsure how to feel about this. Part of him was proud to have a brother with such special skills. At the same time, he was sickened by how easy it was for him to just kill another human being.

"So," Milpisi continued, "if you really must see Kavu, I will ask the Choma chief to call a meeting with him. You could join them in Choma village."

"But," D'Melo protested, "we can't talk freely with other people around. Can he not come to my rondeval?"

Milpisi pondered. "Okay," he said, his face strained. "I will do this for you. But understand, it is contrary to protocol. Meeting Kavu is clearly such a deep need for you, I trust it is aligned with the will of the Great Spirit. But—and I will not budge on this—two conjurers will escort Kavu for the entirety of his visit. Also, his invitation extends for one hour *only*. After which he will be treated as any other intruder."

D'Melo was delighted. "Thank you so much, Milpisi! Oh and—"

There's more? Milpisi looked at him incredulously.

"Would it be okay if I invite Kavu to Baba's funeral?" D'Melo requested humbly.

Milpisi glared at D'Melo like an annoyed but doting grandfather. But apparently not even Milpisi could resist D'Melo's sincere gaze. "Okay, I'll see what I can do with the Council." He grinned, clearly in disbelief at all he had compromised for D'Melo.

D'Melo scrambled around the rondeval, making sure everything was tidy. He found dirty dishes in the kitchen sink and was instantly irritated. "These guys never clean up after themselves!"

Zara had never seen him so anxious. Not even T-Bo's threat had rattled D'Melo's characteristically level demeanor.

"Hey dude, are you okay? You're acting a bit neurotic. Maybe I'm rubbing off on you," she joked.

"Well, let's see," he said, heated. "I just found out that both my mother and father were murdered because they had evidence that Dimka killed the former president. The life I've always dreamed of was within my grasp but now, in a blink, it's in shambles. And, oh yeah, I have to find a secret recording and slip it out of Kipaji while being tracked by a Malungan spy . . . *and* do it before getting us all killed. So, yeah, I'm great. Thanks for asking."

"Whoa, dude," Zara said. "What's going on with you? I understand you have a lot happening right now, but—"

"*A lot?*" He laughed bitterly. "You think?"

"But," Zara finished, clearly trying to remain composed. "That's not what's agitating you. You were fine before you knew Kavu was coming."

Their conversation was interrupted by the clacking of the woodpecker doorbell.

"He's here!" D'Melo scurried about, taking a final look around the rondeval. D'Melo clutched the door handle. He took a calming breath before swinging the door open. For a second, he thought he was looking in a mirror. But closer scrutiny revealed where the difference in their physical appearance was the most obvious. Although D'Melo had an athletic build, Kavu's physique was far more developed. His veiny muscles bulged from years of intense military training. Also, Kavu lacked D'Melo's stylish twists; he maintained his naturally tight curls low to his scalp in conformity with military regulations.

D'Melo's sight blurred briefly, as an electric wave zinged through his tremulous frame. His thoughts were hijacked by a flurry of images of people he had never met and events he knew nothing about. The images flicked too quickly to see anything clearly, but not quickly enough for him to escape the emotions associated with them. He was wading through a murky cloud of desperate loneliness and torment-ing conflict.

"Hey brother!" Kavu greeted.

A jolt zapped D'Melo's chest. The feeling in his legs deserted him. He dropped to a knee. Zara dashed over, seizing her chest, apparently with her own pain. She and Kavu helped D'Melo to the couch.

"Hey," she said to D'Melo. "What's wrong?"

"I'm okay," D'Melo said groggily.

From a slight hunched over position, Zara excused herself from the room. "I think I need to lie down for a bit," she said hoarsely.

D'Melo blinked to regain focus. He turned to Kavu. "Sorry. I don't know what happened. Maybe I was so excited to see you, my body got overloaded." His eyes dropped to Kavu's waist.

Kavu peered down. "Oh," he said. "It's a tranquilizer gun. Don't worry, it's not for you," he chuckled. "They're standard issue for Malungan soldiers. We're required to carry them at all times. Apparently, there were a couple of incidents when soldiers were killed by dangerous animals in the jungle."

"But the soldiers have rifles," D'Melo said, puzzled.

"That's true, but most Borutus believe that forest animals represent the spirits of their ancestors. So they avoid killing them as much as possible. Instead, they tranquilize the animal. By the time it wakes, the soldiers are far out of harm's way."

Kavu scrutinized D'Melo's face. "This is mind-blowing. Even though we aren't identical twins, it feels like I'm talking to myself."

"I know. It's amazing," D'Melo concurred, his smile tempered by the loss he felt having missed out on his brother all these years. His gaze drifted to a spot above Kavu's left eye. It reminded him of his dream. "Hey, how'd you get that scar?"

"You don't remember? We were in the wildflower field." Kavu paused to see whether he had jogged D'Melo's memory. "You threw a stone at me."

"I knew it!" D'Melo exclaimed. "That really happened! All this time, I thought it was just a dream."

Kavu continued, "The funny thing is, I wasn't even in pain. But then I made the mistake of looking at you," he laughed. "I had never seen anyone with such sheer fright on their face. It was like you had seen a *Mabaya*—umm," Kavu searched for the English translation— "an evil spirit. I started screaming because I thought there was something terribly wrong with me for you to have been so scared." They laughed heartily together.

"Yeah, I panicked, man! I thought Mama was going to whack me good!" D'Melo and Kavu were now doubled over in a roaring guffaw. "Then, I tried to heal the gash."

"I forgot about that!" Kavu bellowed, clutching his stomach in joyous pain. "You smeared dirt in my cut! What made you think that would stop the bleeding?"

"I was three years old! What did I know?"

While they were in hysterics, Zara returned.

"Well, D'Melo, I guess you're feeling better," she said. "I'm gonna leave. You guys have a lot to catch up on."

D'Melo barely acknowledged her. "Okay," he said. "See you later."

Kavu chimed in, "You should stay. I want to get to know my brother's girlfriend."

"She's not my girlfriend," D'Melo swiftly replied.

Zara shot her hand out to Kavu. "It was a pleasure meeting you."

Kavu stood and moved straight into an embrace.

Zara's body shuddered. Her limp arms struggled to return Kavu's hug. Then, bent at the waist, she took long, quieting breaths.

"Are you okay?" D'Melo asked.

"I'll be all right," she said, as she staggered out.

"That day wasn't the only time I almost died," Kavu chuckled. "When I was six, I was given a horse. I was enraptured from the moment I saw her. I didn't do much else besides eat, sleep, and be with Safiri—that's her name. It means 'sapphire.' She has a reddish tint to her golden coat. She is my most loyal friend. I've tried to let others ride her, but she bucks them off. Her heart belongs only to me.

"The president wouldn't permit me to ride her at first. He said I was too young. So, one morning I woke just before dawn. I slipped out of the main house to the stable. I wanted to at least sit on her. She was completely serene, so I decided to let her out of the stall. It was incredible to feel her power under me. Then a light came on inside the house. So I rode her back into the stable. Just as Safiri was entering her stall, our cat tried to pounce on a chicken. The chicken flew up and toppled a metal bucket of feed. The bucket slammed onto the concrete floor. Safiri was startled. I couldn't control her. She shot back out of the stable and leapt over a watering trough. When she landed, I lost my grip on her mane and fell onto a large jagged rock. I could hardly breathe, let alone move. The pain in my ribs was unbearable. Then I thought that even if I survived, the president was going to beat me to death."

D'Melo laughed. Then he realized Kavu wasn't joking.

"Because I was on the far side of the trestle, no one in the house could see me. I was for sure going to die. But then, I could feel Safiri connecting deeply with me. I couldn't talk, so I begged her in my mind to pull me from behind the trestle. She immediately cantered over and offered her hind leg. She dragged me beyond the trestle and toward the house. One of the workers saw what was happening and ran over.

"The next thing I remember was a doctor dripping medicine under my tongue. Even as a young boy, I wondered how a tiny dose of liquid was going to help. But within minutes, I was up and running around again. The president didn't beat me or even yell at me. Instead, he was proud of the courage I showed—such a small boy trying to ride a huge horse. He never said anything about me almost dying or my miraculous recovery. The following week, he sent me to the military academy. I was the youngest cadet ever. Usually they don't accept anyone under ten."

"Wow. You've had such an exciting life," D'Melo observed, without even a trace of envy. "My life has been the opposite. But I like it that way. The calmer, the better. I've always had the only three things I need—basketball, my friends, and my family." As soon as 'family' fell from his lips, a sick twinge crept into D'Melo's stomach. He realized Kavu had grown up without his family.

"I never had family, not really," Kavu responded, outwardly unbothered. "The president and Madam Dimka did their best, I guess. They were busy. The other cadets at the academy became my family. We would die for each other," Kavu declared, his expression betraying his words. "Those guys got me out of many sticky situations."

"That's great," D'Melo said, trying to sound enthusiastic. "There's nothing better than having such close friends." But not even D'Melo was buying his thinly veiled attempt to smooth over his thoughtlessness.

After a long moment, Kavu said, "Well, I have family now. You're here!" This made D'Melo feel even worse. He didn't have the heart to tell Kavu he would only be in Kipaji for a couple of days.

Kavu's attention shifted to the drawing on the table. "What's this?"

"Oh, that's nothing," D'Melo said dismissively, sensing he should steer Kavu away from it. "Just one of Mama's drawings."

"It looks like a map of Kipaji." Kavu slid the drawing off the table and started examining it. D'Melo wondered anxiously, *Does he know something? How could he?* Kavu rotated the drawing.

D'Melo tried to divert Kavu's attention. "Hey, the people here must have really loved Baba. They're doing so much to honor him at his funeral."

Kavu brushed off D'Melo's comment. He continued to study the drawing, flipping it upside down.

D'Melo gently slipped it from Kavu's hands. "You'll be there, right?"

"The funeral?" Kavu said, suddenly cold. "No. Why would I be there?"

"What! You're not coming to your father's funeral?"

"He's not *my* father. He's *your* father. He abandoned me, remember? He took his favorite son with him."

"He didn't abandon you," D'Melo objected. "What have you been told?"

"The cold hard truth," Kavu spat. "Your mother and father were traitors. When soldiers came to question them, they fled and left me here. And no Kipaji wanted me, so the president and Madam Dimka adopted me."

D'Melo retorted defensively, "Does that even make sense to you? Why would no one in Kipaji want you? You're Kipaji!"

"They weren't willing to take a boy from a family of traitors. They were ashamed of your parents and their actions against the Malungan government."

"That's ridiculous!"

"*That's* ridiculous?" Kavu hissed. "You know what's ridiculous?

That my so-called parents just forgot about me. What kind of people do that!"

D'Melo's patience was wearing thin hearing his parents being disparaged so unfairly. He leaned back into the couch, debating whether to tell Kavu the truth.

Kavu continued, "So now you're asking why I'm not going to your father's funeral? Why would I honor a traitor who abandoned his child? He can rot in hell for all I care."

That sent D'Melo over the edge. "Those are all lies!" he burst. "That's not what happened! I can't believe you think Baba and Mama would abandon you. Your beloved President Dimka," D'Melo jabbed with venom in his voice, "tried to kill you, and almost succeeded. Baba and Mama had evidence against Dimka that would have landed him in prison for the rest of his life. Dimka was doing everything he could to make sure that didn't happen, including killing our whole family. So Baba and Mama took *us*," D'Melo stressed, "and ran for the Nanjier border. At the bridge, the Malungan soldiers shot you."

Kavu clutched the left side of his chest, seemingly unaware of his own movements.

"Mama ran back for you, even though the soldiers' bullets were flying all around her. But a rebel pulled her away because he thought you were already dead."

Kavu shook his head, reluctant to believe what D'Melo's was saying.

"Only after we were safely in Nanjier did Baba find out that you were still alive. The same Kipaji doctor who saved your life after falling from your horse saved you that night too."

"But that doesn't make sense," Kavu said. "Why would the president try to kill us and then raise me as his own son?"

"I'm sorry to tell you this, but Dimka used you as a bargaining chip. You were a pawn—his insurance that the evidence wouldn't be released. Dimka never stopped trying to finish our family. He had Baba and Mama killed, looking for that evidence."

Kavu stared off, apparently adding up what he had just heard with what he thought he knew. He rose suddenly and headed for the door.

"Hey, where you goin'?"

"I need some time to think," Kavu muttered, without turning to face D'Melo. "If this is true, then I'm fighting for the wrong side." He raised an impassioned fist to his gritted teeth. "It means my whole life has been a lie." Kavu dragged himself outside, where the conjurers were waiting to escort him to the Malungan border.

D'Melo cupped his face with regretful hands. *What did I just do? What if he questions Dimka about this? Who knows what Dimka will do to him?*

Zara went to find Milpisi. She needed to know more about Kavu. Why did her body react so aversely when she was around him? Was he deceiving D'Melo? Was D'Melo in danger? On her way to the valley, she was nearly bowled over from behind.

"Hey, Jonju!" She lifted him into the air.

"Madam Zara," he chirped. "Can we play the bubbles game?"

Zara was stumped.

"You know, when you blow bubbles on my neck."

"Ohhh. I wish I could, Jonju. But I must find Milpisi. Do you know where he is?"

"With Haya. He meditates there at midday."

"Thank you!" Zara 'bubbled' his neck quickly. He giggled in pure delight. She dashed for Haya, then yelled back, "We'll play more later. I promise!"

Milpisi sat cross-legged in front of the Tree of Life in a deep meditative state. Without turning, he greeted, "*Siku ya heri*, my dear one." As if he knew what was weighing on her, he advised, "Appearances can be deceiving, no? Thank the Great Spirit for giving us a third eye—the eye within. It detects what our outer eyes fail to capture. Everyone has a third eye, but some have become blind to its powers. Like any living organism, if it is not exercised, it withers until rendered impotent. You, my dear, have a keenly developed inner eye. Now, you must only learn to trust it."

Zara remained silent, wondering whether Milpisi could read her mind. She felt both impressed and vulnerable. In any case, she received the answers to her questions about Kavu.

"I've been meaning to ask you," Milpisi said, stroking his beard. "At the banquet, you mentioned that you were born in Nečzia. Do you have a family member named Magdalena?"

"Yes, I think I do," Zara narrowed her eyes, searching her memory. "I've heard her name. I think she was my great grandaunt. "How'd you know that?"

"Well, you can say I met her once."

"What? Wow, what a coincidence!"

Milpisi smiled. "There are no coincidences, my dear one, only the Great Spirit linking the most improbable things together for our benefit . . . and for the Great Spirit's amusement." He chuckled.

Milpisi recounted a vision he had many years ago. That day, the weight on his shoulders was threatening to crush him. The Kipaji medical clinic had confirmed that his wife suffered from a genetic disorder that made it impossible for her to bear children. She spiraled into a dark depression.

Milpisi went to Haya to beg the Great Spirit to grant his wife a child. When he unveiled the Tree, a woman was sitting before it. She had blazing red-orange hair. Eyes wet with tears, she introduced herself as Magdalena Stromová—Healer of Nečsláva. She informed Milpisi that his Tree would soon be the last remaining Tree of the original eighteen. Some had been destroyed by war, and others by the ignorant who feared the power of Haya as the work of the devil. Also, several of the Akhtiar had been declared witches when they returned to their regions. They were burned at the stake, never having borne children. So while there may have been a few trees still standing, the knowledge of Haya had been lost.

"Magdalena visited me that day to deliver a message—the future of the world depended on this Tree." Milpisi gently handled a branch. "I promised her that I would protect it for as long as I could, but the Healer bloodline in Kipaji would end with me because of my wife's genetic defect. Magdalena then shared knowledge about the Tree that must have gotten lost over the centuries, as it had not been passed down to me.

"She said, 'Hidden within the Tree is the Heart of Seeds. Locate the Heart, slice the membrane, and remove a seed, only *one*,' she emphasized. 'Have your wife swallow it. The seed contains enormous power. It has the ability to alter the very foundation of organisms—its genetic material. A seed should never *ever* be removed unless it is absolutely necessary for the preservation of the world. The Heart membrane will regenerate, but the seed can never be replaced. And each Heart has only nineteen seeds. Also, without the Heart of Seeds inside, the Tree can survive only one day of sun. And Milpisi,' she urged, 'tarry not. The transformational power of the Seed doesn't last long. It could be an hour, a day, or a week. No one knows for sure. The only thing that is known is the more pristine the environment around its host, the more potent and lasting will be the effect.'

"Magdalena then turned abruptly, as if hearing something. Several tiny flames flickered in her eyes. 'They're coming,' she said tranquilly. Then she muttered one final word. She said something like, '*Edo*' or '*Idu*.'"

Still trying to process that there was a Healer in her family, Zara muttered, "Umm, I think she probably said, '*Edu*.' Essentially, she was wishing you the best of luck."

"Not knowing the last thing Magdalena said to me has nagged me all these years." Milpisi released a satisfied sigh. "What a *coincidence* that you are here now to tell me," he said with a wink.

"So, what happened to her?" Zara asked urgently.

"Magdalena calmly admonished the people coming to kill her. I'll never forget her words. She said, 'You think you are victorious, but your victory is as foolhardy as it is illusory. What you do now, you do against your own best interests, and the interests of your descendants.' She embraced the Tree and, in a flash, she and it were set aglow.

"Her body gradually disintegrated. The last part of Magdalena that was visible was a heart-shaped mark on the back of her neck."

Zara reached over her shoulder and rubbed her birthmark.

"Yes," Milpisi affirmed, "just like the one you have. When the flame subsided, she was gone. I wasn't sure what to feel. Knowing that I was the world's last Healer with a Tree weighed heavily on my heart. But finding out that the Tree could cure my wife's genetic defect brought me hope.

"I rushed home and bounded through the door. I called for my wife. She didn't respond. I thought maybe she was having an afternoon nap. I was barely able to contain my excitement. I swung the bedroom door open, ready to rouse her from her slumber. But my eyes fell upon an empty bed. Then, the shadow of a figure swayed ever so subtly on the floor. I looked toward the window." Milpisi paused, wiping the moistness from his eyes. "I was too late. Her limp body was hanging from a ceiling beam. She couldn't bear the guilt of not being able to continue the Healer bloodline. She knew I would never divorce her and marry another woman. So she thought that if I was relieved of this dilemma then I would feel free to remarry." Milpisi's voice quaked. "But she was wrong." He closed his eyes, tears rolling down his cheeks. "She will always be my wife. We are wedded through all the worlds of the Spirit. And so, I never had a child to become the next Milpisi."

"I guess that means you'll need to live forever," Zara jested gently.

"Well, I used to think that." A soft smile glinted in his eyes. "But not anymore."

Just as Zara was going to ask him what he meant, a buzz vibrated in his shirt pocket. It was a sound Zara hadn't heard since arriving in Kipaji. Milpisi appeared equally surprised to receive a call. He covered one ear and pressed the phone against the other. He sighed deeply, excused himself, then hustled toward Choma Mountain.

Zara returned to the rondeval. D'Melo was still on the couch, not having budged since his meeting with Kavu. "Hey, dude," she said, trying to muster some cheerfulness.

D'Melo lifted his hand wordlessly.

She slid up next to him. "What's up? Something happen with Kavu?" Zara probed, hoping for the best but fearing the worst.

D'Melo rubbed his forehead. "Well, I'm not sure. Everything was going great, but then I asked whether he was coming to the funeral. He went off on Baba, saying all this messed up stuff. Dimka brainwashed him into believing that Baba and my mom were traitors and horrible people who abandoned their child. That was really hard for me to accept. I wanted to set the record straight so bad. But I kept my cool."

"Good." Zara nodded thankfully. "It'd be a huge mistake to tell Kavu what really happened."

"Well, but then," D'Melo murmured, his face flattened.

"Oh no," she gasped. "You didn't?"

"But, I didn't tell him *everything*," he said quickly, before Zara could flip out. "He doesn't know anything about the recording. I only told him that Baba had evidence against Dimka. But," D'Melo said, releasing a long breath, "I did mention that Dimka tried to kill him and then used him as a pawn."

"What!" Zara screeched. "What if Kavu confronts Dimka about it?"

"I know, it was stupid," D'Melo lamented. "But I've thought more about it. As long as Dimka believes I have the recording, he can't do anything to Kavu."

"Yeah, but what happens after we release the recording to the public? Then there will be nothing to stop Dimka from killing Kavu."

D'Melo lowered his gaze. "I know. But that was always a risk. The silver lining is, Kavu may now question his loyalty to Malunga. If so, maybe I can convince him to escape with us. One way or another, I have to save Kavu."

"Have you completely lost your mind? Kavu escaping with us would mean that he'd have to know our plan, *and* that the recording is in Kipaji. That puts all of us at risk." She paced fretfully. "Whether you like it or not, Dimka is the only father Kavu has ever known. How do you know he won't go straight to Dimka and tell him about our plan?"

"I'm the only *real* family he has," D'Melo shot back. "He wouldn't do that to me."

"I think you want family so bad that it's clouding your judgment. I've never seen you so out of sorts. What if Kavu's the spy? What if he was sent here to get information out of you? Has that even crossed your mind? You barely know him, and yet it seems like you lose all sense of reason when it comes to him."

"Well, I'll take my chances," D'Melo said, his voice tight with irritation. "I can't leave Kavu's life in the hands of that madman. Dimka sat by and watched half a million people be butchered!"

"You'll take *your* chances?" Zara bristled. "You're willing to risk having Dimka get the recording *and*—"

D'Melo cut her off. "He's my brother! He's the only family I have left in this world." He rose rigidly. "Of all people, I would have thought that you'd understand what it's like not having any family."

Zara took a calming breath, then tried to reason, "Baba and your mother protected this secret and sacrificed their lives for it. They understood how much was at stake. If Dimka gets that recording, he'll get away with the Shuja genocide and continue his tyrannical rule over the people of Malunga. Have you thought about that?"

"You're seriously asking whether I've thought about my parents?" D'Melo said, his voice shaking. "That's pretty much *all* I think about! And I'm pretty sure that Baba and my mom would want me to save their other son. Have you thought about *that?*"

CHAPTER FOURTEEN

A Change of Plans

On an okapi, Milpisi trekked over Choma Mountain to the Malungan border. A small prop plane awaited him there, its propellers stirring clouds of dust off the makeshift runway. A Malungan soldier ushered Milpisi into the plane. Thirty minutes later, the plane touched down at a deserted airport on the outskirts of Yandun. Milpisi was met by three presidential vehicles. The motorcade raced down cleared roads toward the Presidential Palace.

Meanwhile, President Dimka lay in his large, ornate bed. His sweaty, sallow face floated atop silk sheets and a lavish duvet. Wilem VanLuten stood in the doorway. Having received word of Dimka's failing health, he had immediately chartered a private jet from South Africa.

He slid a chair to Dimka's bedside.

"Ahh, look who it is!" Dimka choked out, his voice gravelly. His doctor offered water to quench his parched throat. "So, I have to die to get my friend to visit me, huh?" Dimka said, half jokingly.

"Apparently, I have stage four pancreatic cancer. The doctors at the hospital were delicately preparing me for my demise. Do you know what I told them?"

Wilem scooted closer, as Dimka struggled to push the words from his lips.

"I said I've had worse and that I'd be back on the squash court by week's end, beating all of them, as I've done for the past thirty years." Dimka's cackle broke into a dry, ragged cough.

Wilem forced a laugh, figuring he could humor Dimka during what seemed likely to be his last moments on earth. He slumped in his chair, pondering his suddenly dubious future. He knew that when Dimka died, his free pass to exploit the Nyumbani went with him.

A presidential guard whisked into the room and whispered in Dimka's ear.

"You can speak freely," Dimka rasped. "This man—" He tilted his head toward Wilem, "knows all my dirty secrets." He laughed, then revealed what the guard told him. "Wilem, apparently my *real* doctor will be here in a few minutes."

Dimka lifted his head wearily and addressed the people in the room. "Why such gloomy faces? You're starting to make me feel like I'm sick or something. This is nothing more serious than a cold. I'll be back and ordering you around first thing tomorrow morning."

Wilem forced a dubious grin to his lips. Wilem knew that no medicine could help Dimka now. His death was imminent.

The presidential motorcade screeched into the palace grounds. A guard rushed to meet Milpisi. They hustled him into the palace and up a winding staircase to the president's bedroom. Along the way, the guard briefed Milpisi on Dimka's condition.

"Dr. Akachi," Dimka sputtered when Milpisi entered. "Glad you could make it."

Dimka ordered everyone out of the room. Wilem, however, didn't budge. Milpisi's eyes darted insistently to Dimka, *The elixir has to remain a secret.*

Dimka asked Wilem to allow them a private moment. During the few encounters Milpisi had had with Dimka, he had never heard him use such a respectful tone with anyone. Wilem rose stiffly, straightened his suit, and sauntered out.

Dimka's years of heavy drinking had taken a toll on his body. "As you can see, I need a dose," he said, struggling for breath.

Milpisi stared at him, battling sickening regret that he had made a deal that required him to save Dimka—a man who had committed the most heinous acts of cruelty the region had ever endured. Worse still, this was the third time he had administered the nectar to Dimka, who treated the elixir as a license to lead a destructive life, for himself and others. Milpisi slid the *chombo* from the wooden vial, trying to mask his reluctance, and kept his end of the bargain.

When Milpisi emerged from the bedroom, he was whisked back to the motorcade. As he settled in the car, he heard a familiar voice. A presidential guard ordered the gate open. For a

moment, he thought he was seeing D'Melo. But he quickly realized, *Oh, Great Spirit! That's Kavu! He's now the president's top security officer!*

Soldiers were only elevated to such a high position after years of exemplary service and unshakable loyalty to the country. The security officers' only responsibility was to protect the president. And, being the head of presidential security, Kavu was without a doubt the president's most trusted officer.

The sweet scent of morning dew wafted into Wilem's immaculate quarters. Whenever he visited the palace, he was given the room reserved for Dimka's most honored guests. In the prior two weeks alone, the room had been graced by the king of Eswatini and the prime minister of Nečzia.

Rapid thumps vibrated the dense wooden door. Wilem's presence was requested in the presidential study. He checked his appearance and departed from his room, readying himself to hear the news of Dimka's death.

He entered the study to a sight he could scarcely believe. Dimka was sitting behind his desk smoking a cigar, soaking up his pre-break-fast whiskey and jovially chatting up his doctor, the Vice President, and General Nyoko.

Wilem narrowed his eyes skeptically. "Mr. President?" He murmured, unable to contain his astonishment.

"Did you think you'd get rid of me that easily?" Dimka chuckled, behind a haze of smoke.

The doctor shrugged, grinning. "He must have nine lives."

Although no one else seemed to think much of Dimka's miraculous recovery, Wilem knew it just wasn't medically possible. His mind flew back to the evening before. *Who was that guy? Dimka's "real doctor"? What did he do?* Wilem's ambitions thrust his thoughts from bewildered to opportunistic.

Wilem requested a private audience with the president. With a flick of Dimka's hand, everyone vacated the room.

Wilem got straight down to business. "How?" he asked gravely.

Dimka reclined in his oversized presidential chair. He puffed out a defiant cloud of smoke.

"Come on," Wilem pressed. "I know your so-called 'real doctor' gave you something. What was it?"

Dimka took a lengthy drag on his cigar. "I don't know what you're talking about."

Realizing that Dimka wasn't going to divulge the secret without motivation, Wilem resorted to his deal-making philosophy—everyone has their price. "Would $25 million help you know what I'm talking about? All I want is access to whatever medicine that doctor gave you. Then, if my technicians confirm that it can do for others what it did for you, another $25 million is yours."

Dimka blew smoke rings in Wilem's direction.

Wilem grew impatient. He knew that whatever Milpisi gave Dimka would revolutionize medicine. Bringing this miracle drug to Pharma's board of directors would definitely lock up the CEO position for him. The cockles of his heart warmed as he imagined heading the wealthiest pharmaceutical company the world had ever seen. Visualizing his photo on the cover of *Fortune* magazine, which Helen and her new husband would certainly see, spurred Wilem to land this deal at all costs.

"Listen, I don't think you understand. What that doctor has could be the greatest medical breakthrough in nearly a century."

"Oh, my friend," Dimka said, waving a finger enticingly. "Do you mean penicillin? That's child's play compared to this!"

Wilem leaned forward, nearly salivating at the thought of controlling this medicine. "You drive a hard bargain, my friend. How about $100 million in Pharma stock, on top of a $50 million cash payment. Once we announce this new drug, our stock price will shoot through the roof. You'll be a billionaire overnight."

Dimka's silence returned.

"Okay." Wilem rose tensely. He straightened his suit jacket. "I can't offer more than that," he grumbled, his throat tight with ire. "I'm trying to make you one of the richest men in the world." He stalked toward the exit.

"My friend, do you give up so easily in all your business deals?" Dimka said, chuckling. "I can tell you what you want to know, but you won't be able to access it anyway."

Wilem returned to his chair. "What do you mean? Is it in another country?"

"I wish it was that simple."

Dimka told Wilem about the Tree of Life. However, he neglected to mention his agreement with Milpisi to keep it a secret. "It produces a medicine that has no equal. But the problem is, warriors with special capabilities make Kipaji impenetrable."

Wilem didn't believe for one second that any country was impenetrable. As a marine, he had seen firsthand the firepower of modern-day weaponry.

"You don't understand," Dimka said. "It's a place that is protected by a power that we cannot fathom. I've witnessed it myself. I was part of an attempted invasion of Kipaji after Malunga gained independence from the Brits. Every time we attacked, some sort of natural phenomenon wiped out our soldiers. Most of us couldn't even get halfway up Choma Mountain. We were swept down by flash floods and tremendous wind gusts. The unfortunate ones who reached the summit perished ingloriously. There were hurricanes, volcanic eruptions, lava falls, and tornadoes . . . but not ordinary tornadoes. These tornadoes whirled with steam that seemed to be directed to targets, and literally melted our soldiers' skin.

"I know you're thinking that we were defeated because our military wasn't up to Western standards. Well, I've got news for you. The Brits tried before us with even less success. If they know you're coming, you won't get anywhere near the Tree. Why else do you think we haven't already taken the nectar?"

"So, that's it!" Wilem brightened. "We get through without them knowing. All we need is one person to slip in and get a sample of the nectar and a clip from the Tree. We can easily reproduce the nectar in our labs. And who knows, we may even be able to grow a genetically modified tree, one that can generate ten times or even a hundred times as much nectar."

Dimka lifted his chin questioningly. "But how could someone get to the Tree unnoticed?"

Just then, there was a rap on the door. It was Kavu.

"Sorry, sir. I don't mean to interrupt, but your motorcade is prepared to take you to the military parade."

Dimka's eyes beamed. He interlaced his fingers and propped his elbows on his desk. He whispered to Wilem out of the corner of his mouth. "The answer is standing in the doorway."

Dimka gestured for Kavu to join them.

Kavu obediently came to attention. "Yes, sir!" He saluted, standing tall and stiff.

"Kavu, you recently entered Kipaji without the Council's approval, right? How did you manage that?"

"Well," Kavu explained, "I am given privileges because I saved the Choma chief's life some time ago. The Chomas, therefore, invite me to certain special occasions. But I'm not permitted to go any farther than Choma Mountain without a warrior escort."

Dimka shot Wilem a glance, *What do you think?*

Wilem nodded.

"Kavu," Dimka said, with an air of formality broaching a proposition. "You've been my top security officer for three months now. I suspect that at least a part of you misses field missions. I mean, you *were* the best young soldier this country has ever had."

A faint smile animated Kavu's otherwise stoic face. "Well, thank you, sir. That is quite a compliment coming from Malunga's most celebrated soldier."

"Would you be interested in a special operation? It's dangerous, but if successful, it would catapult Malunga into world leadership. Finally, those pompous Western countries will be begging *us* for help!"

"Absolutely, sir! And thank you for trusting me. There is nothing I wouldn't do for you or this great country."

Dimka then summoned General Nyoko. He explained the situation but omitted the part about him becoming a billionaire. "We must do this for the people of Malunga who are suffering unnecessarily," he said, putting a spin on the story as usual. "The answer to their suffering is just across the border. Kipajis have selfishly used the nectar for their own people for centuries and have shared it with no one. They are officially a part of Malunga, yet they thumb their noses at us."

Dimka began to outline his plan, but then Kavu humbly chimed in.

"Sorry, sir. If I may."

Dimka gestured for Kavu to continue.

"Even if I can get into Kipaji," Kavu said, "I wouldn't be able to find the Tree. I've heard it's invisible."

Wilem's face contorted. "It's what? How can that be possible?"

"I don't know," Kavu responded politely. "But one time, the Choma chief, a big fan of homemade palm wine, had too much to drink. His lips began to move freely and independent of prudence. He told me many things about Kipaji that are difficult to believe. But now that the president has confirmed the power of the Tree, it's all starting to make sense. The chief complained about the Tree being controlled by a single person. Apparently, the only one who can make the Tree appear is—"

Wilem completed Kavu's sentence. "Let me guess: the 'real doctor'?" He rubbed his chin intensely. "There has to be another way."

"Well, maybe there is," Kavu said. "I've been invited to Mujiza Jakanda's funeral in two days' time."

"Okay," Dimka said, wanting more. "But how do you get a sample from an invisible tree?"

"When I saved the chief, a villager was killed by the Shuja rebels. I wasn't permitted to attend his funeral, but the chief requested that I come to the celebration afterward. At the celebration, I overheard people talking about the ascension ritual that happened at the Tree. I was curious, so I waited for the chief to be sufficiently drunk, then asked about it. I thought he would have his warriors escort me straight out of Kipaji, never to be invited back. But he didn't. He seemed happy to tell me. He said Milpisi—the 'real doctor,' as you call him—unveiled the Tree after funerals so that everyone could summon their ancestors to welcome the new soul into the eternal realm.

"This would be the only opportunity to get to the Tree," Kavu said. "I just need to be close enough when Milpisi unveils it."

"I like that!" Wilem said, worked up. "So, you think this can work?"

"I believe so, sir. But I can't imagine that I will be able to get the sample in secret. I would probably need to fight my way out of Kipaji. And honestly, although I'm confident in my skills as a soldier, I won't be able to fend off several Kipaji warriors by myself."

"General," Dimka asked Nyoko, "do you have any trusted soldiers who could help Kavu escape Kipaji?"

The general seemed apprehensive. He explained that most Malungan soldiers wouldn't even consider fighting anywhere near where Kipajis commune with their ancestors.

Wilem scoffed, "What's up with you people and this ancestor stuff? First the Shujas, now the Borutus too! They're not even *your* ancestors. Why would your soldiers care about them?"

The room fell uncomfortably silent. Dimka knew that Wilem's callousness, particularly regarding the immense reverence that Malungans have for ancestors, would halt the operation before it even began.

"Wilem," Dimka said, attempting to smooth things over. "You've been in Africa long enough to know that it doesn't matter *whose* ancestors they are. Our people have great respect for those who have come before us. We are only here because of them. Their spirits protect us and influence the prosperity of our lives. The soldiers will not upset the Kipaji tradition, *especially* during a funeral."

General Nyoko added, in his deep raspy voice, "Even if some soldiers agree, it's unlikely they would be able to get Kavu out alive. The Kipaji warriors are said to possess extraordinary abilities."

"Well, what if we can get some of the Kipaji warriors on our side?" Kavu floated. Skepticism surfaced emphatically on Dimka's and General Nyoko's faces. Kavu continued, "I know it sounds crazy, but I may be able to swing it."

"How?" Nyoko croaked. "There is no one more loyal to Kipaji than its warriors. Why would they ever turn against it?"

"You're right. The warriors will never turn against Kipaji," Kavu acknowledged. "But what if they didn't realize that's what they were doing? What if they thought they were protecting Kipaji?"

Wilem chimed excitedly, "I like this kid! Say more."

"Since the Choma chief's wife died, he's been trying to change how things are done in Kipaji. According to him, Kipaji is way behind the times, still using archaic methods like animals for transport and agriculture instead of machinery. He wants Kipaji to become technologically advanced, on par with Western countries. He believes that if it was, his wife would still be alive. I didn't understand what he was saying at the time, but now I do. Somehow his wife must not have received the nectar.

"So, what if Pharma promised the chief a certain percentage of its profits from the medicine? He could convince his warriors that the money will modernize Kipaji so no more of their kin suffer and die needlessly. If the warriors are true to their sworn duty, they will recognize that their oath of loyalty to Kipaji compels them to help bring about this advancement."

"Well, I'm convinced!" Wilem asserted. "We can offer the chief five percent. If he balks, you have my permission to go as high as ten percent, but no more."

Dimka liked the plan as well, but cautioned, "Kavu, this is an extremely delicate matter. If you're wrong about the chief and he informs the Council, Kipaji will cut off our energy supply." Dimka had an even graver concern, which he elected not to mention: Failure of the mission would also mean that he would have seen the last of the elixir. Milpisi would surely never administer it to him or his family ever again.

Kavu took a sobering breath. "I understand what's on the line, sir. I won't fail you."

General Nyoko and Wilem exited the presidential study, energized by the thought of having the world's most precious resource within their grasp. Kavu remained seated. He had been debating all morning whether to ask Dimka about what happened that night on the bridge almost fifteen years ago.

"Sir, could I please have a word?" He unconsciously rubbed his chest where the bullet exited. "There's something I need to ask you."

"Of course, son. But before you ask, I want you to know how proud I am of you. You're a first-rate soldier. You know, one day you'll be sitting right here." Dimka padded the armrest of his chair. "This country will achieve its greatest heights with you at the helm."

Kavu beamed. "Thank you, sir." He tightened his posture, saluted, and headed for the door.

"Kavu, aren't you forgetting something? What is it that you wanted to ask me?"

"Oh, it's nothing important, sir." Kavu marched out with a bounce in his step.

General Nyoko waited just outside the study. He drew Kavu into a side room. "When you're in Kipaji, I want you to capture D'Melo and bring him to me."

"With all due respect, sir," Kavu said. "Why is this necessary?"

Nyoko stiffened. He didn't take well to subordinates challenging him. "D'Melo has information that's detrimental to the future of Malunga. That's all you need to know."

Kavu remained silent, realizing this was about the evidence against President Dimka that D'Melo had mentioned.

"I know D'Melo's your family," Nyoko said. "You have my solemn promise that we won't hurt him. We only want to find out what he knows. This may be our only chance. Once he returns to America, he'll disappear again."

"Sir, he's not my family. The president and Madam Dimka are my family." Kavu glanced toward the study. "Does the president know about this?"

"No, and we must keep it that way. If this goes sideways, the president can't be blamed for something he knew nothing about."

"Makes sense, sir." Kavu saluted. "Rest assured, I will bring D'Melo to you."

D'Melo stretched lazily toward the control panel and switched off the ANC. The rumble of the waterfall flooded the room. D'Melo's "morning person" energy was eluding him. Typically, he rose early, eager to "catch the worm," as Baba always said. But today, he dawdled. Being at odds with Zara weighed on him. "But he's my brother," he contended to himself, repeating his case for why he was on the right side their quarrel.

He grudgingly peeled back the covers and dragged himself to the bathroom. The doorbell clacked. He freshened his breath hastily and shuffled expectantly to the door. He hoped to find the glimmer in Zara's emerald greens had returned. Instead he found an empty porch. His eyes canvassed the forest for who may have sounded the bell. As he started back inside, his foot skated on an envelope. Cautious curiosity quickened his pulse. He slipped a handwritten note from the envelope.

The note read: "I will come to the funeral."

D'Melo shook a delighted fist. "Yes! I knew it!"

The note continued: "But first, I need to talk to you in private. Please meet me at Warriors Rock at 10 a.m. You can't miss it. It's a huge boulder with the Kipaji crest engraved on it. It sits at the eastern foot of Choma Mountain, near the Malungan border. I'll be there waiting for you." The note was signed, "Your brother."

D'Melo scrambled to get ready for the day, then dashed for Warriors Rock. When he arrived, there was no sign of Kavu. He peered around the boulder into the Malungan forest.

"Rrrrr!" Kavu grabbed him. D'Melo jerked, letting out something of a squawk.

"You . . . you should have seen . . . your face," Kavu laughed raucously, barely able to get the words out. "It was like you thought there was a real lion behind you." Kavu's immensely amused gaze dropped to D'Melo's traditional pants. He reached for them. "Let me see if you wet yourself."

D'Melo couldn't help but to join Kavu's howling laughter. "You scared me, man. I don't know what's in these woods!"

Kavu finally composed himself, then said gravely. "Listen, I don't have a lot of time." His eyes darted suspiciously with each sound. "President Dimka is planning to take a sample from the Tree."

"What!" D'Melo's heart raced in panic.

"There's this businessman who's planning to develop medicine from it. They're sending soldiers into Kipaji after the funeral for when Milpisi unveils the Tree."

"Wait a minute," D'Melo said. "How do you know about the Unveiling?"

Kavu's eyes lowered apologetically. "There's a person in Kipaji who's been feeding me information."

D'Melo inclined his head incredulously, rain misting his face. "It's the Choma chief, isn't it?"

Kavu confirmed with a slight nod.

"Well," D'Melo said confidently. "They'll never get past the Kipaji warriors anyway."

"They won't have to. The chief has convinced his warriors to allow the soldiers passage."

D'Melo squeezed his forehead anxiously. "I understand the chief wants change in Kipaji, but," his face hardened, "why would he risk its future for Dimka and this businessman?"

"He's not doing it for them. He's doing it for Kipaji. The chief doesn't want any more Kipajis to die because of antiquated technology."

The depth of Kavu's knowledge of Kipaji was unsettling. D'Melo suddenly remembered Zara's caution. *Could Kavu be the spy? Is he trying to gain my trust to get information out of me?* D'Melo blurted, "Why are you telling me this?"

"Why do you think?" Kavu exhorted, with a tinge of irritation. "You're my brother! And your life is in danger. Do you think they're only coming for the Tree? They're coming for you, too. You'll be tortured for information about the evidence you have against the president." Kavu paused. "D'Melo," his voice quivered, "they'll never let you out of here alive."

Kavu took a measured breath. "I've thought a lot about what you said Baba and Mama did that night on the bridge." The sound of "Baba and Mama" coming from Kavu's lips rang melodiously in D'Melo's ears. "I knew what you were saying was true, but I just didn't want to believe it. How can I accept that my supposed father tried to kill me and then adopted me just to save himself?"

"You know," Kavu fingered the scar on his chest, "the nectar healed my body, but it didn't heal the scar in my mind. I often have this dream where I'm running frantically to Mama. She's holding out her arms and crying. But strangely, the harder I try, the farther I get from her." Kavu released a shuddering breath, his eyes moist. "Suddenly, I can see the terror in her face, as if she is right in front of me. She stretches a desperate arm toward me. Just before she latches on, a lightning bolt rips fire through my chest."

D'Melo wordlessly wrapped him in a tender embrace. He could feel Kavu absorbing the warmth between them, as if he had been yearning for it his whole life.

Kavu abruptly backed out of D'Melo's clinging arms. "D'Melo," he cautioned, his eyes intense. "Be ready for them, and please be careful. They're dangerous people."

"I'll be okay," D'Melo said confidently. "I'll alert the Council. They'll make sure the warriors are prepared."

Kavu pressed his lips together. "Yeah, you could do that," he said tepidly.

Kavu's lukewarm response made D'Melo realize the flaw in informing the Council. "Dimka will know that you warned me," he deduced out loud.

"Hey," Kavu replied. "But if that's what you think is best, then so be it."

"They'll kill you. I'm not gonna let that happen." D'Melo puffed his cheeks pensively, then decided, "I won't tell the Council. We'll let it play out." D'Melo devised a plan on the spot. "Before the Unveiling, I'll have Milpisi pulled away on some fake emergency. While everyone waits for him to return, I'll alert the warriors that I saw Malungan soldiers in the forest. The warriors will easily handle the soldiers, *and* no one will suspect that we knew in advance. What do you think?"

Kavu nodded, impressed. "You're really good at strategizing. You'd make a great general."

D'Melo smiled. "A week ago, I would never have imagined that I'd be concocting plans to save Kipaji."

Kavu froze. His eyes jerked toward the Malungan forest like an antelope sensing a prowling lion. "I've been away too long. They'll start suspecting something."

D'Melo clutched Kavu's arm. "Hey, come with us."

"To America?" Kavu said doubtfully. He looked away, gazing with reverence at the pristine woodland, flourishing with the energy of life, then at the majestic summit of Choma Mountain. He exhaled absolute contentment. "This is my home," he said. "There's no place like it in the world. I will never leave here. Instead of me going, how about you stay?"

"You know I can't do that. It's not safe for me."

"Well, one day, I'll make sure that it is." Kavu grasped D'Melo's shoulders. "When that day comes, you must return home. We will join forces and together make peace in this region."

Just the thought of reuniting with his brother washed away, but for a fleeting moment, the tension mounting in D'Melo's mind. "That sounds like the best plan I've ever heard." They clasped hands, sealing an unspoken promise.

"Okay, brother," Kavu said. "I'll see you tomorrow." He lifted his gaze to the darkening sky. "I hope the weather turns in Baba's favor." Like the superiorly trained soldier that he was, Kavu weaved stealthily through the drizzle to the Malungan forest. Just as he was about to enter, he spun back to D'Melo. He raised a fist of solidarity, then vanished into the thicket.

D'Melo absorbed the moment, relishing having his brother in his life. But the bliss was short-lived. His mind pivoted to the impending attack on Kipaji. He hastened to the rondeval. When he arrived, Zara and the boyz were mulling the fine details of the plan. Their execution and coordination would need to be flawless. Their lives and the fate of Kipaji were at stake.

"Hey guys." D'Melo's eyes fixed on Zara, seeking assurance that their relationship wasn't in tatters. She returned an emotionless gaze, not exactly the response he was hoping for. He sighed before launching into what would surely stoke Zara's ire even further.

"There's been a slight change of plans," he announced. "We need to move the timing up. You guys will slip away during the funeral instead of after." Zara narrowed her eyes, skeptical.

"But," Jeylan said, "if we leave while the funeral is still happening, it'll be obvious that somethin's up."

"Maybe," D'Melo acknowledged. "But there will be thousands of people there. If you guys spread throughout the crowd and position yourselves toward the back, it'll be less noticeable, especially if you sneak away at slightly different times."

"Alright," Kazim acquiesced. "But why the change?"

"It's just the best way to keep everyone safe."

The boyz shrugged, accepting the new plan. But Zara wasn't as easy to persuade. She waited for the boyz to leave the room. "So what's the real reason?"

"Like I said," D'Melo replied, avoiding her eyes. "It's safer for everyone."

"You saw Kavu, didn't you?"

D'Melo attempted to defuse Zara before she exploded. "I was right, though! Kavu's legit."

"How do you know that?" Her cheeks burned pink.

"I just know," he shot back in knee-jerk fashion.

Zara bit her lip, clearly struggling to hold back the verbal missile firing up on her tongue.

"Kavu asked to meet," D'Melo explained. "He wanted to warn me that Dimka is sending soldiers into Kipaji."

Zara's eyes widened.

"After the funeral, when Milpisi unveils Haya, they're planning to steal a sample from the Tree. That's why you guys have to retrieve the recording and get out of Kipaji while the funeral is still happening."

"Oh, my God," Zara's breath shallowed with anxiety. "We have to let the Council know."

D'Melo shook his head regretfully. "We can't. If we do, Dimka will know that Kavu warned us. He'll kill him."

Zara stood abruptly and paced the living room. "Well, we have to at least let Milpisi know. He can help us figure something out."

D'Melo slumped in his chair. "Can't do that either."

"Are you kidding me? You're not planning to tell Milpisi?"

"Believe me, I've thought about this." D'Melo let out a plagued sigh. "Even though my plan will ensure that nothing happens to the Tree, Milpisi won't risk it. He'd warn the conjurers. I can't let that happen. Kavu put his life on the line for me."

"You do realize that when the soldiers come for the sample, they'll kill Milpisi."

D'Melo said vehemently, "I would *never* put Milpisi in danger. When it kicks off, he'll be safe and sound, nowhere near the Tree. The conjurers will easily take care of the Malungan soldiers, and it will all be over before Milpisi even knows what happened."

"You can't know that for sure! Things may not go as smoothly as you're envisioning. And, how do you know that Kavu isn't telling Dimka right now what your plans are?"

D'Melo's jaw muscles tightened.

"You're putting Kavu ahead of Milpisi, the boyz, and me!" Zara spat, fire in her voice. "What did he do to deserve that place in your life?"

"He didn't have to *do* anything." D'Melo glared. "He's my brother! Why can't you understand that?" He rose brusquely, toppling his chair, and stomped away.

CHAPTER FIFTEEN

The Darksome Night

The stillness in the rondeval was unnerving. Usually by midmorning, the boyz' antics were in full swing. But that morning, they mulled anxiously over the plan while packing. They left a change of clothes in the closet and a few unlaundered shirts strewn about—a tidy room would have made their early departure too conspicuous.

D'Melo should have been packing too, but instead he sat motionless on the side of his bed. The weight resting on his shoulders was paralyzing. Hanging in the balance were the future of Kipaji, his friends' lives, and one other little thing, the preservation of the world's most precious resource. And none of this was made any easier by it all unfolding on the day he was to say goodbye to his father forever.

Zara entered the rondeval. She brushed the rain off her backpack. Outside, a steady drizzle was falling.

"That's it?" Jeylan observed. "Just one backpack? Remember the Thanksgiving tournament? You brought like seven suitcases!"

"Dude," she shot back, lips pursed. "It was only three."

"But still, girl. It's an improvement."

"Not really," Zara confessed. "I still have five suitcases in Malunga." She chuckled. She added her backpack and a change of clothes to the boyz' pile in the closet.

"I'm gonna miss this place," Marley mused.

"Word," Jeylan and Kazim concurred.

Zara swiveled toward the doorway thinking, or perhaps hoping, that she heard D'Melo coming, but he wasn't there. Her heart sank.

"Yo, girl," Jeylan said. "I don't know what's goin' on with you and D, but y'all need to squash it. That dude ain't been right since yesterday. We need both y'all with clear heads for this plan to work."

Zara headed toward the door, feeling glum. "I'll see you guys at the funeral," she muttered, her voice wobbly.

The moment D'Melo was dreading had arrived. Under a twilight sky, he descended into the valley, his heart heavy with thoughts of life without Baba. But as he entered the Moyo, his spirit was uplifted. The jovial energy of the Wapendwa was a welcome surprise. In Kipaji, a funeral was a joyous occasion. It was a celebration of the life of service that had been lived and the soul's reunion with the ancestors. In honor of the festive spirit, the Wapendwa dressed in their most vibrant and colorful Kipaji attire. The Moyo was transformed into a veritable human rainbow.

Baba's body, elegantly wrapped in fine white cloth, rested on an elevated platform of tightly woven natural fibers. Four thick pillars secured the structure. Each clan's symbol was meticulously engraved on one of the pillars. D'Melo approached, anxiety rising in his chest. The last time he saw Baba's body, it was on a cold metal slab in the hospital morgue. He lifted his gaze reluctantly to the platform. The peace on Baba's face was a balm for his shattered heart. If he didn't know better, he would have thought that Baba was just enjoying a nap.

A lump rose in his throat. He was not prepared for this moment. What final words could he offer a man whose entire life was devoted to serving others? Who made the ultimate sacrifice for his family and Kipaji. Who protected him from the world and from himself. Who molded him into the person he was. In short, to a man he owed everything.

D'Melo was relieved of this impossible task before he could formulate a single word.

"Son," Baba's voice rang in his ears. "There is nothing you need to say. I've heard your soul."

The voice was so crisp that for a moment D'Melo forgot that Baba lay before him. He closed his eyes to listen keenly with his heart. He swooned in the melody of Baba's voice, a sound he thought he would never hear again.

"Please know that the world awaiting me is one of pure joy," Baba assured him. "I will soon reunite with our ancestors and once again be able to embrace your mother. So you must never be sad for me."

"Baba, life is so hard without you. You said you'd always be here when I need you. Well, I need you now."

"Son, I'm with you at all times. You need only look into your heart. You will find me there. Then, when the Great Spirit wills, we will once again be together. But first, there are things you need to do."

"Yes, Baba," D'Melo said somberly. "I'll try."

Milpisi approached the platform to open the ceremony.

"Baba, I must go now." D'Melo choked back tears. "Please help me finish what you started. And please protect my friends." D'Melo kissed two fingers and lifted them heavenward. "I love you, Baba."

D'Melo joined the innermost ring of the crowd. He craned his neck, searching for Kavu through the thickening raindrops. Suddenly, Kavu seized him from behind. "Are you looking for me?"

D'Melo jerked. "Man, you gotta stop doin' that." They hugged. "So glad you made it."

"Of course, I made it. I'm not going to let you send Baba off alone." Light twinkled in Kavu's smiling eyes.

Milpisi began. "Today we assist our Kipaji brother with his glorious ascent to the realm of lights. Only a thin veil separates our world from that realm. When we lift the veil with eyes of faith, we will see Mujiza being welcomed home by his ancestors. They will embrace him with the love he showered upon everyone while he was on this earth.

"Some of you never met Mujiza. If you had, I assure you that your life would have been enriched. His warm smile was as abundant and undiscriminating as the rays of the sun, basking all in its radiance. I have many stories about Mujiza, but I only need one to convey the pure heart of the man we honor this evening.

"When Mujiza decided to make medicine his life, it was no surprise to anyone." Confirming clicks echoed in the crowd. "From a young age, it was obvious that his only desire was to serve others. Once, while he was still quite young, just inside the forest, Mujiza almost died." Milpisi pointed toward the edge of the clearing. "At the tender age of fourteen, he happened across a baby bird. It had fallen from high in a tree. He gazed upward and saw that another baby was in peril, dangling precariously over the edge of a nest. Mujiza wasted not a moment. He hurriedly scaled the tree. He lifted the motherless nest and started down. But then a branch snapped under him. He plummeted down and crashed heavily onto a protruding root. He broke three ribs, ruptured his spleen, and was rendered unconscious. Do you know that Mujiza never let go of that nest? When we found him, he was covering it with his hand to make sure the bird didn't fall out on the way down.

"If you are unconvinced of the size of this man's heart from what I just told you, I doubt you will remain so when I recount what happened next. When Mujiza regained consciousness, his glazed eyes fluttered slowly open. He looked up at me and the first thing he said was, 'Is the bird okay?'

"Many of you may be wondering why Mujiza left Kipaji. All I can tell you is that he did so with a heavy heart. He was called to a special mission by the Great Spirit, which required the sacrifice of his life. Although he never would have chosen to leave the homeland that he loved so dearly, he courageously and selflessly followed the path laid before him. Now he returns to us, not as a lifeless body, but as a guiding light of spirit.

"Of all the services Mujiza offered in his life, none was greater than raising a son of Kipaji." Milpisi gestured toward D'Melo. The Wapendwa snapped their fingers, the sound of joyous approval. "It is apparent that Mujiza never forgot the Kipaji ways, because D'Melo is an embodiment of them." D'Melo lowered his eyes, both dreading the attention and feeling sensitive about Kavu not also being mentioned as Baba's son. But his heart was warmed to see Kavu snapping with the others.

As Milpisi continued his eulogy, D'Melo scanned the crowd to make sure Zara and the boyz were in position. They were perfectly situated away from each other and along the outer ring of the crowd. Zara stood with Jonju, flashing a thumbs up. They all watched D'Melo intently, awaiting his signal.

"As we bid our special son a glorious journey to the realm of lights," Milpisi concluded, "let us honor him with our deepest gratitude." He raised four fingers high above his head, then brought a fist down over his heart. The Wapendwa followed, making the same gesture in unison.

"*Uzima wa milele.* To a life that never dies," Milpisi intoned.

"*Uzima wa milele*," the Wapendwa chorused.

The pillars supporting the structure slowly lifted the platform. Milpisi raised an unlit torch. He swirled it magically into a blaze.

A drum thumped a heartbeat, symbolizing that Baba's life wasn't over, but had merely taken on a greater and eternal form. Along the outer ring, another drum joined, then another and another, until the Wapendwa were encircled by rhythmic vibrations. The beat built to a fevered pace, stirring the Wapendwa into a frenzied euphoria.

D'Melo saw this as an opportune moment to set the plan in motion. He signaled his friends, rubbing two fingers against his temple. Zara and the boyz stealthily disappeared into the forest, one by one.

D'Melo surveyed the crowd, making sure his friends had slipped away unnoticed. *It's on now.* He breathed deeply. *Edu.*

The drumbeat quieted to a hum, mixing with the patter of an intensifying rain. Milpisi touched the torch to the hollowed bamboo shoot that crisscrossed beneath the platform. Blue flames rolled toward the corners. The pillars crackled disturbingly, as the fire climbed to the fiber bed and began to consume Baba's body.

D'Melo cringed, orange light flickering on his face. Kavu laid a comforting arm around him.

Embers glowed red, then orange as flames danced upward into the dark, stormy sky. The drumbeat quickened once again.

Realizing that the ceremony was closing, D'Melo initiated the next phase of the plan. He turned toward Jonju and raised his arms as if stretching. Jonju immediately scampered to Milpisi.

"Milpisi! Milpisi! Come quickly," he fretted, tugging on Milpisi's shirt. "It's Zara, she's really sick."

"What!" Milpisi's eyes scanned the crowd. "Where is she?"

"She left the funeral early and went to her rondeval."

"Where is Komba?" Milpisi seemed to expect to see Komba but remembered that this wasn't a Malaika alert. He started for Amanzi Mountain with hurried feet. Then he drew to a halt, realizing that D'Melo wasn't following him. "Are you not coming?" he puzzled.

"Nah," D'Melo said. "She's in good hands."

"*Zara,*" Milpisi emphasized suspiciously, "is ill, and you are not going to her bedside?"

Jonju tugged Milpisi's arm. "Milpisi, we must hurry!"

Milpisi took a longish look at D'Melo over his spectacles before scurrying off. Once Milpisi was out sight, D'Melo corralled a conjurer. He informed him that he had seen Malungan soldiers in the Choma forest.

"That is not possible," the conjurer responded. "The alarm would have sounded."

"Yeah, you're probably right," D'Melo said, feigning agreement to avoid suspicion. He searched his mind for a more convincing way. "Umm, but most of the community was here at the funeral, so isn't it possible that the soldiers could have slipped in unnoticed?"

"It is not the friends who monitor the border. The animals are our eyes. Nothing can slip past them."

"Oh," D'Melo said, surprised and dismayed by this revelation. His anxiety bubbled up. *If I can't convince this guy that soldiers are in Kipaji, this could get really dangerous. I have to do something!*

"You know," he said, playing dumb, "the person was carrying a rifle. Guns aren't allowed in Kipaji, are they?"

The conjurer's face tensed. "Are you sure you saw a gun?"

"Absolutely. I can even describe it. It was one of those rifles with the wood handle, curved magazine, and shoulder strap."

Kavu chimed in to assist. "It sounds like an AK-47, the gun that Malungan soldiers carry."

D'Melo continued, "Maybe you should go, just to be sure everything's okay. It couldn't hurt, right?" The conjurer nodded and headed toward Choma forest.

Kavu turned to D'Melo. "I will join him."

"What!" D'Melo exclaimed. "If Dimka finds out you helped Kipaji, he'll kill you. Plus, a Kipaji warrior will easily handle a couple of soldiers."

"Yeah, but only if he finds them. What if he doesn't? We can't let them get to the Tree. Also, I'm not going to put your life in the hands of someone else."

"But I just found you," D'Melo said. "I don't want to lose you again."

Kavu clutched D'Melo's shoulders. "Don't worry. This is what I do best. I track people. And these are *my* people. I know exactly how they operate. Also," Kavu gripped a bulge at his waist. "I have my walkie-talkie. I'll hear all of their communications."

"If you do this, you definitely won't be able to stay here. It's too risky. You'll have to come with us."

Kavu smiled with gratitude, seeming to acquiesce.

D'Melo glanced at the time on his phone. "Meet me at my ronde-val in one hour."

Kavu clasped D'Melo's hand and pulled him into a hug, then shot off to catch up with the conjurer.

The next few minutes were the longest of D'Melo's life. Nothing was happening in the forest. He paced, trying to keep his nerves at bay. The lingering crowd was getting antsy, wondering why the ascension ceremony hadn't started. *How long will they wait for Milpisi?* D'Melo squeezed his forehead. *Oh, my God. What if the soldiers come into the Moyo with all these people? That would be a catastrophe. I have to get the Wapendwa out of here.*

D'Melo cleared his throat. He shouted, "Excuse me everyone." The murmur of the crowd ebbed to silence. "Milpisi had to rush off for an urgent health matter. He wanted me to tell you that he may be a long time, so you should just go home." No one budged.

An elderly woman shuffled up to D'Melo. "Don't worry about us, son," she said adoringly. "We will wait for as long as it takes. We have to make sure your father is welcomed by our ancestors."

A few more excruciating minutes passed. There was still nothing in the forest. *What's happening in there? Come on! Why isn't the conjurer catching them?*

All at once, the natural noise of the forest silenced. A tremulous hush descended on the crowd. Many of the Wapendwa were old enough to remember the last time the forest went silent—it was right before the Malungan invasion, decades ago. Then, like someone had flipped a switch, the forest returned to life. In a blink, its natural sounds returned, then built momentum like a tsunami. Thousands of birds suddenly shot through the canopy and soared above the Moyo, squawking frenetically. All the wazi stones suddenly de-illumined, plunging Kipaji into darkness. There wasn't even a trace of moonlight. The thick storm clouds absorbed every lunar ray. The Wapendwa let out a collective gasp. They knew the blackout was a security measure in the case of an invasion. An unlit forest provided the conjurers a tactical advantage, as they knew the terrain better than any intruder ever could.

The darkness broke when a fiery alert launched from Choma Mountain. The pulsing orange light streaked overhead, like a meteor. At its zenith, the fireball exploded into brilliant colors. Screams resounded throughout the valley. The Wapendwa scattered into the forest, taking cover in its darkness.

Several conjurers sloshed briskly past D'Melo. *The conjurers must have finally found the soldiers,* he surmised, letting out a relieved sigh. *This will be over soon.*

A volley of gunshots echoed deep in the woods. Then what sounded like a deluge of water thudded heavily against something.

"What the heck was that?" D'Melo exclaimed. After a few moments, he realized that the gunshots stopped. The fighting seemed to be over. "Yes! The conjurers must have gotten 'em!"

Almost before he could finish his thought, the forest sparkled, the way it does when fireflies fill a dark summer night. But with each flash, the valley floor trembled beneath his feet. Flickers of orange dotted the forest. The bitter smell of smoke wafted ominously into the clearing.

Then, the forest began to whistle with wind. Branches whipped to one side. And, in an instant, all the fires were extinguished, leaving the forest black once again. But the whistling continued, growing intensely, as if a freight train was rumbling through the forest toward the Moyo. The trees at the edge of the clearing quaked. Some snapped under the pressure. D'Melo squinted through the rain, trying to see what was coming his way. Suddenly, he was smacked by a huge gust, heavy with moisture. It threw him backward. He slammed with a splash into the muddy earth, sliding several feet. He lay there, momentarily stunned.

Still dazed, he heard a rapid pounding vibrating in the distance. His foggy mind was momentarily comforted, believing that the celebrants had returned and resumed drumming. But the violent tremble of the earth beneath him, like subterranean thunder, dashed that hopeful thought. Cold drops of rain stung his forehead, then rolled down his face. He lifted himself up to a sitting position. Fires again were raging in the forest. *What's going on? This was supposed to be over quickly.* His thoughts shifted to concern for Kavu. *What if the conjurers mistake him for one of the intruders?*

Meanwhile, Milpisi had reached Zara's rondeval. He bounded through the door and called for her. No answer. He searched the rondeval. She wasn't there. He paused, sensing something was terribly wrong. Just then, the light from all the wazi stones in Kipaji de-illumined. Inside the rondeval was black but for a flickering orange light reflecting on the floor. "Oh, Great Spirit! The Darksome Night is upon us!" He ran to the window just in time to see the alert flare burst at its peak above the valley. "The Tree!" he cried.

Milpisi raced out the door. Komba appeared outside the rondeval. He mounted her and she galloped straight for Haya.

Just as Zara and the boyz neared the summit of Amanzi Mountain, the world around them went dark. Although within arm's reach, they could barely see each other. A fiery flash zipped across the valley and exploded high in the air. They gazed in frightened awe at the brilliance that momentarily dispelled the darkness. When the sound and tremor from the explosion finally reached them, it sent shivers up their spines.

"Oh, my God," Zara said, her heart pounding. "We better hurry!"

The light from the alert fizzled out. Marley scrambled for his phone. He tapped the flashlight app.

"Yeah, Marls!" Kazim said. "I'll never make fun of your nerdiness again!"

The light dulled and then went out.

"Marley!" Kazim retracted his compliment. "What kind of nerd forgets to charge his phone?"

"Well, y'all could have brought your phones. But nooo," Marley mocked, "you didn't want them to distract you from your Kipaji experience. Now look at us! Soaking wet, running for our lives, and now in total darkness. I don't know about y'all, but that's dampening my Kipaji experience a bit! I'll never forgive y'all for not bringing your phones."

Jeylan chimed in, "What about that stone Milpisi gave you? Your phone will charge in like a second."

"Yeah, yeah," Marley remembered. "Okay, I forgive y'all." He pulled the *daima* stone from his backpack. It promptly slipped through his wet fingers. "Uh oh."

"Uh oh, what?" Jeylan asked, afraid of the answer. "Please don't tell me—"

"I dropped the rock." Marley fell to his knees. He frantically searched in the mud. "Oh, thank God! I got it!" He tapped the rock against his phone. Nothing happened. He tried again, tapping repeatedly. "It's not working."

"Give me that rock, fool." Jeylan found Marley's hand and snatched the rock. "Man, this ain't even it! This rock is way too big."

"I know," Marley replied. "But it felt like the same *kind* of rock."

"Are you a geographist now?" Kazim said, irritated. "You can't use just *any* rock!"

"I think you mean geologist," Marley muttered sheepishly.

"Man," Kazim gritted his teeth. "You lucky I can't see you. I might just throw you off this mountain!"

"Oh, my God!" Zara interjected. "Will you little old ladies quit your bickering? Forget the stone. We're just gonna have to do this without light." She closed her eyes and focused her feelings inward, trying to lock into Leda's pain.

Another massive explosion shook the mountain under them. They clung to each other.

"Okay, Zara," Kazim said, his voice quivering with terror, "I'm not sure what you're doing, but this would be a good time to find the alcove."

Zara's breathing became shallow. She clutched her chest and doubled over, panting heavily.

"Zara?" Jeylan said. "Are you okay?"

She had honed in on Leda's suffering. "It's just part of the process," she replied. "Everyone grab someone and let's go."

They headed blindly for the far side of the mountain. The Mapacha Waterfall rumbled faintly through the pounding rain. They shuffled in a clump along the north face. The roar of the waterfall was growing. A wet wind pushed steadily against them. Zara's hair whipped behind her.

They leaned into the wind, fighting it with each step. The waterfall became deafening as they got closer, drowning out the persistent explosions in the distance.

Zara stumbled. Jeylan offered himself as a crutch.

"I'll be okay," she shouted over the noise. "I just need a minute to adjust." She swallowed hard. "I've never felt anything this intense." She took a long breath, then trudged forward. After a few steps, she swung to the side and vomited.

Kazim hopped back. "Yo!" he bellowed. "You need to point that thing the other way next time."

"Oh really?" Zara said gruffly. "Well, how about I point my foot into your crotch instead!"

"Whoaaa," Kazim mumbled. "Someone's gettin' a little testy."

They made their way under the first of the twin waterfalls. "Here it is!" she screamed over the roar.

"How are we gonna find the monument?" Jeylan asked. "I can't see a thing in here."

They groped around, feeling helpless.

"Oof!" Marley squealed. "I think I found it," he said, his voice very high pitched. "I just barreled into a solid block. And right in my naughty bits! Why always me?"

Zara explored the smallish monument with her hands. It was a three-foot-tall rectangle sculpted out of the stone wall. A few divots marred its otherwise smooth, glossy surface. As she was told to expect, a bust sat atop the monument. Zara's searching hands found the emerald replica embedded in its forehead.

Zara rotated the gem clockwise, as Milpisi had instructed. It instantly illuminated with a green glow. The front of the monument grated open, stone against stone. At the same time, a twinkling light appeared at the alcove entrance. They watched in wonder as the twinkle floated to Marley.

"It's the rock!" Marley exclaimed, flabbergasted. He tapped his phone with it. When his flashlight came on he was squatting in agony against the wall. The others burst into laughter.

"Thanks guys," he said sarcastically. "I may never have children, but your laughter makes me feel so much better about it."

"Awww, Marley," Zara crouched next to him. She rubbed his shoulder with giggly sympathy.

Marley reached into the monument and pulled out a padded manila envelope. "This must be it."

Zara steadied the light as Marley groped inside the package.

"There's nothing here!" he said with dismay.

"What!" Kazim exclaimed. "We did all this for nothing!"

A mischievous grin spread across Marley's lips. "Gotch'all!" he snickered, as he removed a cassette from the envelope. "Now we're even!" He inserted the recording into Baba's cassette player.

"What are you doing? We gotta go," Jeylan urged. "Chipo's probably at the bridge waiting for us."

"Don't y'all wanna hear what this is all about? What we've risked our lives for?" He tapped the cassette player with the *daima* stone. They crouched down around Marley to listen.

"Wow!" Zara said, in awe. "Dimka's going down!"

"Real talk," Jeylan agreed. "That fool's toast!"

The boyz rose to leave. Jeylan returned the cassette to the package and slipped it into his backpack.

When Zara turned around to close the monument, a greenish glint deep within the dark compartment caught her eye. She stretched her arm inside as far as it could go. The edge of an angular stone was just beyond her grasp. Pressing her face painfully against the side of the monument, she coaxed the stone with her fingertips into her palm.

"Oh, my God," she whispered, cupping her mouth. "It's Leda's emerald." Her eyes glowed green, reflecting the brilliance of the gem.

The boyz shuffled back into the alcove to hasten her exit. When they saw what she was holding, they stared. For a moment, they forgot the peril they were in.

"Great googly moogly," Marley cooed. "Is that an emerald? It's huge." Marley lifted it from Zara's hand. He bounced it lightly in his palm. "And heavy. You know how much this must be worth?" he mused dreamily. "I wouldn't even need that stupid scholarship to MIT."

"What's wrong with you!" Jeylan plucked the emerald from him. "We're not taking this!" He returned it to Zara.

"I wasn't gonna take it. What kind of person do you think I am?" Marley said self-righteously, gazing longingly at the emerald. "But maybe we can just borrow it for a little while."

Zara shook her head at him, then secured the emerald back in the monument.

"Let's bounce, y'all," Kazim urged. "Chipo's gonna leave us if we don't get a move on."

Zara lingered, shining the light on the bust. Having experienced the depth of Leda's suffering, Zara teared up in appreciation for her sacrifice. She then caressed Leda's cool, polished face. The touch sent a jolt of energy through her. Vibrant images suddenly filled her mind's eye, swirling, like through a kaleidoscope. Finally, she was able to bring a single image into focus.

A group of women are sitting wordlessly with Zara by a river under the leafy branches of an acacia tree. She counts sixteen faces. Each woman breaks off a chunk of bread from a hearty golden-brown loaf. Peculiarly, when the loaf finally reaches Zara, it is no smaller than before the first woman had taken her share.

Heavy thumping pounds in Zara's ears. She lays a concerned hand over her heart. She's relieved that the thumps aren't coming from her. Then she notices that with each passing moment, her heartbeat is aligning more with the thumping. Soon, they share the same frequency. An ethereal universe now surrounds her. Colors have taken on intricate hues that her eyes were never before able to discern. Smells are so keen that she can detect an approaching storm miles away. All matter has been stripped down to its elemental parts, yet remain connected as one. There is no separation between the river and the sky, the lizards and the insects they consume, the sand and the tree she is sitting under—a tree that is buzzing with the energy of all things.

A man approaches, gliding along the riverbank. A dark, smooth-faced woman trails him. Her clothes are tattered. Her hair is curled tightly to her scalp. She spots Zara and settles beside her, gazing deeply at her.

The woman's dark brown eyes lift to Zara's hair. She runs several silky red strands through her fingers. The woman speaks almost hypnotically. "This is the most beautiful fire I have ever seen."

Just before the man begins his address, the woman whispers in Zara's ear. A ribbon of sunlight filters through the leaves of the acacia tree and makes her blink with its glistening.

The man begins to speak in a language unknown to Zara, yet it seems she has been speaking it her whole life. After a time that has no time, his words slow to a warp. The image freezes, whirls rapidly, then gets sucked into the vortex of Zara's mind.

Zara jerked her head and blinked her eyes open. She was back in the alcove, kneeling before the monument. While she was still readjusting to reality and staring at Leda's stone face, suddenly the bust came alive. Dark brown seeped into the gray stone. Its coolness melted with human warmth. The bust's stony eyes softened to a tender glow. Zara shook her head, unsure whether this was real or another vision. Leda's lips began to move. "Remember what I whispered to you that glorious day under the tree?" she said. "I told you that I would see you again one day… and here we are."

Zara smiled brightly, realizing that these were the words lost in the damaged section of Leda's journal. "Yes, I remember. And I was right, it *is* a blessing."

"You have now born witness to another reality—the oneness of all things," Leda said. "Hitherto, you have merely glimpsed this world, the world of all-encompassing truth. You have paid brief visits and yet have remained unaware. It is why, at times, you have been able to feel what others cannot, to know things to which others are oblivious.

"You were chosen by the mysterious man for a reason. So root out all trace of doubt from your heart, and tarry not. You are the

Daughter of the Akhtiar. Never forget your station nor the monumental responsibility it carries."

"Come on, Zara!" Kazim shouted from outside the alcove, penetrating her consciousness. "We have to go!" Zara snapped back into the moment. The bust was now cool stone once again.

For the first time, Zara had felt total acceptance of herself, and that her abilities were a gift, not a curse. In spite of the current danger, she walked on light feet to join the boyz. Before exiting, she spun around for one last glimpse of Leda. She pressed grateful hands to her heart.

CHAPTER SIXTEEN

Follow the Light

A steady cavalcade of explosions continued to rock the valley. D'Melo watched, sickened, as a bevy of fireballs lit up the forest dangerously close to Haya. Then, once again, the trees at the edge of the Moyo began to rattle. Having learned what follows this sound, D'Melo hit the ground flat on his belly. A wet gust swept through, sliding him along the valley floor. But this time the blazes were too many and too intense for the moist wind to extinguish.

Milpisi galloped on Komba along the northern rim of the clearing. He dismounted from Komba and ducked into the thicket.

D'Melo yelled as loud as he could, straining his throat. "Milpisi! No!" But Milpisi was unable to hear anything over the jarring blasts and raging fires.

D'Melo leapt to his feet, only to dive back down, as a fireball blazed out of the Choma forest. It screamed by and exploded against Upepo Mountain. His heart pounding, he gazed toward the summit of Amanzi Mountain. It was quiet. He sighed, relieved. *At least Zara and the boyz are safe.*

He managed to balance his wobbly legs, then darted over the soggy earth quaking with every explosion. He hurtled into the forest, hopping over clumps of brush with the agility that made him a great basketball player. When he reached the Tree, Milpisi was deep into the Unveiling.

"Milpisi, please stop," he implored. "That's exactly what they want. If you unveil the Tree, they can take a sample."

Milpisi proceeded, undeterred. And to D'Melo's dismay, the veil was lifted.

"Son," Milpisi said, "there is something I haven't told you about the Tree. When veiled, it is invisible, but it is not indestructible." Milpisi motioned to the infernos devouring their way toward them. "This Tree may be the last of its kind. I cannot risk it being destroyed. I need only a few minutes to extract the Heart of Seeds. After all of this is over, we can regrow the Tree." Milpisi started the extraction process.

D'Melo heard swift footsteps approaching. He swiveled abruptly, terrified. He wiped rain from his eyes and focused in the direction of the sound.

"Milpisi, you have to hurry!" he cautioned. "Someone's coming!"

A fireball sizzled past Haya, singeing its leaves. It exploded, setting several trees ablaze. D'Melo protected his face from the fiery debris. By the time the blast settled, the footsteps were upon them.

D'Melo's eyes then fell upon a sight that brought him both overwhelming joy and horrifying dread. It was Zara! She was dashing through the heat and glow of the fire.

"What are you doing!" he exclaimed, squeezing her tight. "You're supposed to be in Nanjier. It's too dangerous here."

"I don't care how dangerous it is. And I don't even care how much of an idiot you are! I'll never leave you behind. Who knows how much trouble you'll get yourself into. And when you do, who's gonna be there to save you?"

D'Melo smiled, remembering that those were the very words he had said to her before she left for Malunga.

"The boyz got the package and should be safe in Nanjier by now," she said.

Before D'Melo could take a moment to rejoice, they paused, listening to a whistling sound in the forest. It was growing louder by the second. D'Melo leapt protectively in front of Zara just before a sulfuric ball of steam burst and splattered, scalding his back and neck. He stiffened, yelped in anguish, then crumbled to the forest floor. The steam was so intense that it burned through his muscles. D'Melo writhed on the ground.

"Milpisi!" Zara cried out.

Milpisi snapped out of his trance. "Oh, Great Spirit!" He hurriedly implored the Tree for nectar. A flower blossomed, incandescent. Milpisi held D'Melo's mouth open and placed the nectar under his tongue.

Almost instantaneously, D'Melo rose to a sitting position. "Thank you, Milpisi," he beamed. "Do we have the Heart of Seeds yet?"

"I nearly had it, but something came up that needed my attention," Milpisi said with a wink, then chanted back into his trance state.

Not a minute too soon, a saving mini tornado churned toward them. Its funnel zigged and zagged in a furious whirl, extinguishing the fires nearest the Tree.

"What's happening?" Zara asked nervously. "Who's out there fighting?"

D'Melo shook his head, baffled by what could have gone wrong. "If the conjurers were fighting the Malungan soldiers, this would have been over a long time ago. But by the way the fire and steam and the water and wind are going back and forth, it seems like the conjurers are fighting each other." D'Melo dipped his head. "And because of me, Kavu's in the middle of it."

Suddenly, a stray bullet whirred past. It stopped with a sickening thump behind them. They spun around and saw Milpisi curled up in a puddle, crimson seeping into his shirt.

"Milpisi!" Zara screamed. She scrambled to find the bullet wound.

Oh, God no! Not again! D'Melo was reminded of Baba. "Milpisi," he exhorted. "Tell me how to get the nectar." They ducked as a fireball scorched by, narrowly missing the Tree.

"There's no time, son." Milpisi blinked through the raindrops. "Get the Heart and run. And," he said emphatically, "no matter what happens, you can never, *ever* let them have it."

"D'Melo," Zara pleaded, sobbing. "We can't let him die."

The battle edged closer. Whoever was defending Kipaji was clearly losing.

"They will be here any minute," Milpisi grimaced. "Saving me won't help. They will kill me anyway, because I will never assist them."

D'Melo closed his eyes. He couldn't believe he was about to let Milpisi die.

"What do I do to get the Heart?" he said solemnly.

"What!" Zara snatched D'Melo's arm. "We have to save him!"

"Oh, my dear one," Milpisi hummed tranquilly. "The time has come. My soul can finally break free of its earthly cage and reunite with my beloved." Zara buried her face in her quivering hands and wailed.

"Yabo, follow the light," Milpisi echoed Baba's words to D'Melo, blood dripping from his lips.

D'Melo had no idea what it meant when Baba said that, and still didn't. *What light? There's no light . . .*

"There is a new Milpisi now." Milpisi peered beyond D'Melo. "My dear one," he choked out. "You were born for this very moment."

A wave of heat blanketed D'Melo's back. He turned around. Zara was aglow with spirit, radiating fiery brilliance.

Milpisi lifted his satchel from his neck. He squeezed Zara's hand around it.

"But—" Zara shuddered.

"Why do you think you are here in Kipaji at this exact moment, oh great grandniece of Magdalena Stromová? A coincidence?" He chuckled into a wince. Milpisi's expression turned wondrous. He gazed at the Tree. Perfectly still, he listened intently. "My dear one, someone wants to remind you to 'root out all trace of doubt from your heart, and tarry not.'"

"Leda?" Zara murmured. She peered toward the Tree but saw only pulsing light.

"Look inside," Milpisi said. "In there, you have a universe yet unexplored. Trust that it contains everything you need." Milpisi coughed, sputtering blood.

"Why me?" Zara howled.

"It's your destiny, my dear." Milpisi released a long, tapering breath. A nebulous light rose from his breast. It drifted upward toward the Tree. With a flash, it merged into Haya's luminescent aura. Zara buried her face in his chest, sobbing.

As D'Melo watched helplessly, a fireball streaked toward the Tree. Just before it hit, a protective wall of water materialized from the drenched soil. The fireball was swallowed into the wall and then dropped to the ground, reduced to a large, steaming rock.

"Zara," D'Melo appealed. She didn't budge. "Zara!" He jogged her. "You're the Milpisi now!" She stared blankly at him, quailing at the responsibility. "You have to extract the Heart!"

"But," she gulped. "I don't know what to do." D'Melo shaded his eyes from her brilliance. He hoped that he was the only one who could see her light. If not, it would lead the enemy straight to the Tree.

"Think. Think." She finger-jabbed her forehead, urging herself. "Okay." She dropped to a knee, tapped her right shoulder, left shoulder, then her forehead, tracing the shape of a cross on her body.

D'Melo spouted dubiously, "The Tree isn't Catholic!"

"Well, neither am I."

"So what are you doing?"

"I told you, I don't know!"

"Milpisi said you were born for this."

"Okay. Give me a sec to think." She exhaled from puffed cheeks. "Milpisi said I just need to be humble."

"Alright, then do that!" D'Melo needled. "The soldiers will be here any minute!"

"Hey," she said, lifting a stern finger. "Don't pressure me, dude!"

D'Melo rolled his eyes.

Zara tried, "Umm, Dear Tree." She shook her head. "No, that's stupid," she acknowledged. "I'm not writing it a letter." She shimmied her body, readying herself for another go. "Oh, Great Tree." She turned to D'Melo, delighted with her new start.

"Yeah, that's great," D'Melo huffed sarcastically. "Can you hurry, please!"

She narrowed her eyes at him before turning her attention back to the matter at hand. "This humble servant begs thee to provide us your most wonderful, most magical, most unbelievable—"

D'Melo swirled a finger in the air. "The Tree knows it's great. Can you get on with it!"

"Do you wanna do this?" she chided. "Then be quiet." Zara resumed, "—and most amazing Heart of Seeds. You are in danger and we want to make sure the world continues to be graced with your generosity."

To their amazement, a circular area of the bark began to thin.

D'Melo gaped. "Keep going! It's working!"

A fire now raged within fifty feet of the Tree. Charred branches crackled and crashed onto the forest floor.

"Umm, these seeds will provide the healing remedy for generations to come, as willed by the Great Spirit."

"Clunk," D'Melo said under his breath.

Zara creased her lips and threw her hands to her sides, *What are you doing?*

"What?" he shrugged. "You said 'remedy.' That's a good word."

"You interrupted the extraction to tell me that's a good word? I know it's a good word, that's why I used it!"

"Well," D'Melo mumbled, "you like good words."

"Dude, not when I'm trying to save the world!"

"Oh, Great Spirit," she continued. "Please bless this world, although we probably don't deserve your mercy."

The bark became translucent. A heart-shaped sack the size of a small nut hovered inside. Its seeds sparkled, radiating energy. Zara and D'Melo were mesmerized, astonished by how something so small could hold such tremendous power. Just then, a bullet clipped the Tree. The cry of a thousand souls echoed within.

Zara extended her hand under the floating Heart. It wafted into her palm. As she extracted it, the valley quaked with sorrow and the forest creatures whimpered in an anguished chorus.

The Tree's glow dimmed. Its branches cracked with a brittle sound, and its flowers shriveled and dropped lifelessly into the puddled undergrowth.

"I'm so sorry," Zara sniffled tearfully, as she placed the Heart of Seeds in the satchel. "I promise you; we will return your Heart." She wrapped her arms around the Tree. It quivered with the chill of death. "Thank you for your sacrifice."

She kissed Milpisi on the forehead. "I won't let you down."

They began the trek up Amanzi Mountain to join the boyz in Nanjier.

As they neared D'Melo's rondeval, Zara broke off toward the summit.

D'Melo clenched her arm. "I'll meet you in Nanjier."

"What! Where are you going?"

"I told Kavu to meet me at the rondeval."

"What are you talking about? Can't you see what's happening down there?" She pointed at the chaos of war engulfing the valley.

"I'm not abandoning him again."

Zara inclined her head and sighed. The rain pattered her exasperated face. "Okay," she relented. "Let's go."

"No, Zara. It's not safe."

"I told you," she said sternly. "I'm not leaving without you." Zara shot down the path to the rondeval.

The rondeval was faintly lit by the blazes in the Amanzi and Choma forests. They ran inside, calling for Kavu. He wasn't there.

D'Melo looked at his phone. He took a tense breath. "He's twenty minutes late."

Violent flashes lit up Kipaji. Much of Choma Mountain was an inferno. "D'Melo," Zara said mournfully. "It's hell down there. It's possible that Kavu didn't make it."

"He's crafty and well-trained," D'Melo protested, desperation tingeing his voice. "He'll be here. Just five more minutes, please."

Unable to withstand D'Melo's hope-filled eyes, she agreed. "But not a second more. If I have to, I'll drag you to Nanjier myself!"

Suddenly, Zara dropped to a knee, clutching her stomach.

"What's wrong?" D'Melo asked, concerned.

"He's coming," she replied, wearily.

D'Melo peered out the window like a child hankering for his lost dog to return home. He smushed his face against the cool glass for the best vantage point.

"I see him!" he shouted.

Kavu sprang through the door, out of breath. "Oh, my brother. You don't know how happy I am to see you. I didn't think I'd survive!" He drew D'Melo into a fraternal embrace.

"Okay, let's go," D'Melo exhorted.

Just then, several sets of boots splashed nearby. "*Nuru*," Kavu commanded. The lights in the rondeval illumined. He calmly strode to the window.

"Are you crazy?" D'Melo exclaimed. "Get down, they'll see you!"

Kavu slid the window open. He yelled, "We're in here!"

D'Melo's chest caved in, like a ton of bricks had fallen on him. His eyes dropped closed in disbelief. He realized he had been horribly fooled.

"I'm sorry it has to be this way," Kavu said. "Under different circumstances, we would have been great friends. But your father got you caught up in something that is way beyond you. The good news is, because you're my brother, your life will be spared as long as you turn over what belongs to President Dimka."

D'Melo's heart tightened. "I don't have it," he fumed.

"Where is it?"

"I don't know."

"Well, General Nyoko seems to think that you do."

D'Melo stared defiantly at Kavu.

Six soldiers rushed into the rondeval, AK-47s strapped over their shoulders.

"Perfect timing," Kavu said. He glanced at one of the soldiers, then motioned toward D'Melo. The soldier slammed the butt of his rifle into D'Melo's ribs. D'Melo buckled.

"Are you sure you don't know where it is?" Kavu prodded.

D'Melo remained silent. The soldier smashed the rifle across his face. White light flashed in D'Melo's head and blood splattered onto the hardwood floor.

"No!" Zara cried, hoarsely. Too weak to stand, she leaned listlessly against the couch.

The soldier raised his rifle to strike D'Melo again. Kavu stopped him.

"D'Melo, trust me, you don't want me to take you to General Nyoko. He'll torture you in excruciating ways. Can't you see I'm trying to help you? Just tell me where it is."

D'Melo jutted out his swollen, bloody lips and shook his head.

"Well," Kavu said, "if he's not going to tell us, then we have no use for him." The solider pointed his rifle at D'Melo's face.

"Stop! Stop!" Zara begged. "He doesn't know where it is, but I do. Our friends—"

D'Melo cut her off. "Zara, no!"

"I can't sit here and let him kill you," she muttered. Tears ran down her face. "Our friends took it to Nanjier."

"Okay, now we're getting somewhere," Kavu said. "D'Melo, call your friends and tell them to bring me the package."

"Ahhh, I'm so sorry," D'Melo muttered insincerely. "I can't. Our cell phones don't work here."

Kavu gritted his teeth. "Okay," he sighed angrily. "You forced me to do this." He snatched a military field phone from a soldier.

"Good evening, sir," Kavu said. "Yes, I have him. But he doesn't have the package. His friends from America took it to Nanjier. Oh really? That's great news, sir." Kavu looked smugly at D'Melo. "Okay, sir. Will do."

"It seems that no one has gone over the Hasira Bridge tonight," Kavu gloated. "And it would be impossible to cross the river by boat. It's too fierce with this storm. So your buddies are still somewhere in Kipaji."

D'Melo looked at Zara, his gut roiling anxiously. She was so weak her eyelids barely quivered open.

"I'm sorry it has come to this," Kavu said. "The General has requested your presence. But before we go, there's one more thing. You know, I went to the Tree." D'Melo's heart raced. "It's dead. There are no flowers, and that means there is no nectar. At first, I thought it was destroyed during the battle, but then I noticed a hole in the trunk. When I looked inside, there appeared to be something missing." Kavu's eyes probed the room searchingly. "Do you know what may have been in there?"

D'Melo, desperate to protect the Heart, appealed to Kavu's humanity. "Kavu," he pleaded. "We're family! Why are you doing this?"

"Well, let me think," Kavu snarled, tapping a sarcastic finger on his temple. "You guys abandoned me, leaving me for dead. And, on the other hand, President Dimka took me in and has been grooming me to replace him one day. So I think the question should be, 'Why wouldn't I do this?' Did you think I was going to get all mushy inside and run off to America with my long-lost brother? Outside of Malunga, I'm nobody. But here, I'm the king of the world," he exclaimed, throwing his hands to his sides. "And by the way, that may be literally true soon. With the power of the nectar in my hands, the world will be my playground. So whatever you took from the Tree, you're going to hand over to me now."

D'Melo locked eyes with him. "Never."

"Oh, look at you," Kavu said, showing surprise at D'Melo's mettle. "A true modern-day American hero. You obviously don't value your life. Well, let's see how much of a hero you are when it comes to your girlfriend's life." Kavu gestured toward Zara. A soldier marched over and leveled his rifle at the back of her head. "It would be a real shame to turn that beautiful face into a bloody pulp."

Zara lifted her drained eyes. She nodded weakly at D'Melo and mouthed, "It's okay." She squeezed her eyes tight, waiting for the bullet to burn through her brain.

D'Melo's heart pounded like it was trying to break free of his chest. "All right! All right!" he relented. "You win." He slid over to Zara and unbuttoned the satchel.

Zara's weary hand tried to stop him. "D'Melo, don't."

"Don't worry," he whispered. "*I got this.*" He carefully removed the Heart of Seeds. "Is this what you're looking for?"

Kavu was mesmerized by its sparkling glow. "You're finally wising up."

D'Melo moved to place the Heart in Kavu's hand, but then suddenly tossed it into his mouth and swallowed it whole.

"What the—" Kavu seized D'Melo by the chin.

"You're too late." D'Melo grinned obstinately.

"You're an idiot! Do you think that's going to stop us from getting it? You just condemned yourself to a horrible death. Now we're going to have to gut you like a fish."

Zara's face burned red. She mustered her energy and lunged at Kavu. He easily knocked her to the floor, then cackled.

D'Melo set himself to pounce, his jaw muscles pulsing. The soldiers readied their rifles.

Kavu snickered. "I think you may want to reconsider what you do next."

D'Melo balled his fists so tight that his hands went numb.

"It's a pity our budding brotherhood has to end this way," Kavu sneered. A pair of soldiers laid their full weight on D'Melo, pinning him to the floor. Kavu slid a serrated blade from his belt. He knelt down, angling the knife above D'Melo's abdomen. He paused, blowing a long breath. He then handed the blade to one of his soldiers. "You do it."

Just then, the military phone buzzed.

"Yes, sir. We tried. The Tree is dead. D'Melo removed something from it. We're in the process of retrieving it right now. Yes, but it's not that simple. He swallowed it. We're going to have to slice him open. Oh. Okay sir." Kavu clicked off the call, sounding almost relieved.

Kavu bent down to D'Melo's ear. "Today's your lucky day. The General says he wants you alive until we find your friends and recover the package. Just in case they somehow slip away, they won't make it public as long as we have you, and your little girlfriend. That's ironic, isn't it?" Kavu smirked coldly. "Now who's the pawn?"

D'Melo mumbled something inaudible.

"Excuse me?" Kavu scoffed. "Did you say something?"

"Yeah," D'Melo laughed insolently. "I said, how many times do I have to tell you, she's *not* my girlfriend."

"You think this is some sort of joke?" Kavu motioned to a soldier, who slammed his rifle into D'Melo's stomach.

D'Melo curled into a fetal position. He thrashed in agony—but not from the soldier's blow. He felt electric bolts radiating from his midsection, setting afire every nerve in his body. He began to convulse violently. The blood vessels in his eyes burst in rapid succession, until the whites of his eyes were pools of red. A thousand needles of energy tried to poke their way out from under the surface of his skin. The soldiers watched the spectacle in sheer horror.

Zara blazed at Kavu. "What did you do to him? He's your brother! He loves you!"

The chill in Kavu's eyes momentarily thawed.

Then, as suddenly as it began, the freakish episode ceased. Everyone stood petrified, hoping that whatever had just happened was truly over. D'Melo rose from the floor, as if lifted by an invisible force. His eyes, now piercing orbs, gleamed white. The energy surging within him revved turbulently. The soldiers took a terrified step backward.

Kavu yelled, "Why are you backing up? He's just a man! Shoot him!" The soldiers raised their rifles in trembling hands. D'Melo stood before them, unperturbed. A barrage of piercing bangs reverberated through the rondeval. Zara covered her ears and shrieked. D'Melo lifted a hand. He moved it in a circular motion. The bullets halted. They lay suspended in the air motionless in front of him. With a flick of his wrist, the bullets winged off and clattered against the floor, sliding to the wall.

D'Melo raised his arms to his sides. The earth rumbled, rattling the rondeval. Kavu and his soldiers latched onto anything they could find that would support their weight. The lights dimmed and glowed in and out, then sizzled and popped. The ceiling cracked, chipped wood falling at their feet. The windows shattered, sending shards across the room. Kavu and the soldiers darted in a frenzy for the exit.

The rondeval support beams snapped. D'Melo blanketed Zara with his body.

Outside, Kavu and his soldiers waded through the flooded ground, water seeping into their muddy boots. They stood in the downpour, watching the full weight of the rondeval collapse on D'Melo and Zara. Just to be sure D'Melo was dead, one of the soldiers lobbed a hand grenade into the rubble. Debris from the blast smacked against the soldiers' soaked uniforms. Kavu squinted through the rain and smoke. He could scarcely believe what he saw. The silhouettes of two figures rose from the ruins.

D'Melo raised his arms above his head, bent at the elbow. Water from the saturated earth stirred, then elevated. Swirling waterballs materialized in his palms. Without moving his hands, D'Melo launched them. They blasted into two soldiers, propelling them off their feet. The soldiers landed in an unconscious, sodden heap. Aghast, the remaining soldiers dropped their guns and scattered into the woods, screaming things about the devil. Kavu stood speechless and alone, rain pouring down his defeated face.

D'Melo's eyes slowly returned to tender brown. He peered up at his hands in awe. "Zar, what's happening to me?"

"I don't know," she replied. "But Milpisi said the seeds have a special potency and can change a person's genetic makeup."

"It's like there is no separation between me and the earth. Like I can control the elements as if they are an extension of my body. When those bullets were coming at me, they were moving in slow motion. I could even see them spinning. I communicated with the lead and copper. I told them to stop. And they did!"

"But," Zara said, concerned. "Milpisi said that only one Seed should ever be taken. You swallowed the whole Heart!"

"Great," D'Melo quipped. "Now you tell me."

"Well, I didn't think you'd *eat* it!"

D'Melo chuckled. "Don't worry. I feel awesome. My energy is off the hook!" he raved, flexing his biceps. "This is dope. Now I have a superpower like you."

"That's true," Zara said sarcastically. "I feel people's suffering, while you get to control the earth's elements. Yeah, that's fair."

D'Melo started ogling Zara, his eyes perusing her up and down. "Mmmm, girl . . . I'm sayin'—"

She crinkled her brow suspiciously. "What exactly are you doing?"

"The seeds must have given me X-ray vision," he cooed salaciously. "I can see right through your clothes."

"What!" Zara hunched, wrapping one arm across her chest and jabbing the other between her knees.

D'Melo doubled over with laughter.

"Oh, my God! You're such a jerk!"

They crossed the demolished rondeval toward Kavu. Zara checked, just to be sure, "So you don't really have X-ray vision, do you?"

"You'll never know," D'Melo said with a devilish grin.

"I hate you."

Kavu stiffened as D'Melo approached. He readied himself for D'Melo to finish him. "Just make it quick," he said, defeated.

D'Melo and Zara sauntered past, paying him no mind other than a pitying clap on the shoulder.

As Kavu watched them stroll away toward the summit, he reflected on what had just happened. He thought back to the time he fell off his horse and Milpisi saved his life. He never thought much about it, but in this moment of desperation he realized that the nectar's healing power didn't work when the unnatural chemicals were nearby. *Can unnatural elements be its Achilles heel?* he thought.

Kavu seized the tranquilizer gun from his belt.

D'Melo's eyes began to radiate again, signaling danger. He spun around to see Kavu leveling the gun at him.

"You should have killed me when you had the chance," Kavu spat. He fired the tranquilizer dart. D'Melo lifted his hand to redirect it, but it continued unabated. The dart pierced his chest. He immediately became woozy. His legs leaden, he dropped to his knees.

"D'Melo!" Zara screeched. "What's happening?"

D'Melo removed the dart, his eyes already heavy. "The dart. It's plastic," he slurred. "I couldn't communicate with it."

Panic threatening to smother her, Zara instinctively smeared mud over D'Melo's body. "Oh please, let the earth's natural elements revive him," she implored the Great Spirit.

D'Melo felt the energy begin to percolate within him. He teetered to a standing position. Kavu quickly reloaded and fired another dart. D'Melo's body crumbled, splashing back into the sodden soil.

Kavu slapped his soldiers conscious. "Get up!" he shouted. "Kill the girl and bring D'Melo to me." They tried to shake their heads clear, then started firing wildly.

Zara crouched down as low as she could. Bullets hissed by.

"Run, Zara," D'Melo exhorted.

"I didn't come back here to leave you!" Zara scooped her hands under his arms. She dragged him, bullets narrowly missing. But with each step, the slick earth bested her.

"Zara, stop," D'Melo pleaded, his eyelids fluttering. "There's nothing you can do for me. You have to go! Tell the world what's happening here," he said, his voice tailing off. "You can still take down Dimka."

Zara buried her face in her hands, inconsolable. Suddenly, she clutched her shoulder. Watery blood seeped between her fingers where a bullet grazed her. The soldiers were now only a couple hundred feet away.

She placed a fretful hand on D'Melo's cheek. "I'll be back for you."

Zara sprinted for the forest. Bullets hummed past, clipping branches in front of her. She leapt into the thick undergrowth, clambered up a tree, and perched on a high branch. She gripped the trunk for balance, her shoulder throbbing burningly.

The soldiers prowled beneath her. "She couldn't have gotten far." Their flashlights probed the dark woodland. Just as they were about to head off, Zara felt a trickle down her arm. In a flash, she realized she had been here before. It was the dream she recounted to the Seer, Ms. Keba. Ms. Keba's seemingly incoherent response at the time rushed alarmingly to mind.

"The blood!" Ms. Keba had ranted. "Don't let it drop!"

No! No! Zara reached to cup the blood running down her elbow before it dripped, but was too late. A droplet hurtled down and splattered on the lens of one of the flashlights. The soldier swung his light upward. Zara stiffened, making herself as small as possible. The beam climbed searchingly up the trunk. As it neared Zara's hands, she released her grip. She tottered, then balanced herself. The light halted on the trunk where she stood. She breathed evenly to calm her nerves and fluttering legs. The light continued mercifully upward. A relieved breath seeped from her tense lips.

The soldier examined the lens just as another scarlet drop splattered on it. He then realized his nose was bleeding, apparently from the blow he endured from the waterball. The soldiers went deeper into the forest to search for Zara but soon returned, again passing under the tree in which Zara was hiding.

When they were gone, Zara slinked down and positioned herself at the forest edge. She cleared wiry branches from her line of sight.

The soldiers returned to Kavu. "You lost her?" he barked. "You idiots! If she gets to Nanjier, she'll tell everyone what happened here. Go find her!"

Kavu hoisted D'Melo over his shoulder and trudged toward Malunga. Zara trailed, navigating the dense brush. The drubbing downpour and thundering sky drowned out the noises made by her untrained feet. After nearly an hour, Kavu emerged from the jungle to a clearing just inside the Malungan border.

A boxy compound stood in ominous contrast to the tranquil natural environment surrounding it. Formidable wooden pillars, linked with webbed wire fencing, enclosed the overgrown cage. Four guard towers topped the pillars. From the towers, aggressive flood-lights illumined the grounds, sliding mechanically to and fro. The only guard-controlled floodlight settled on Kavu as he approached the gate. Guards in the west and south towers targeted their rifles at him. Kavu waved a hand nonchalantly. The gate swung open.

Zara surveyed the compound from the jungle. Two decrepit L-shaped cement block structures faced each other in the center. Farthest from the gate, on the east side, there was a horse stable. Soldiers attired in distinguished military fatigues and maroon berets led horses from the paddock into the stable. To the south was the grandest and most modern of the buildings. It appeared to have been modeled after the heavily fortified castles of medieval times. At each corner of the edifice, a cylindrical tower rose above the tan block walls. Above its cone-shaped roof, the Malungan flag flapped sluggishly in the soaking rain.

Zara's mind harkened back to Wilem's interview. *That must be the prison that Pharma was bragging about building.*

Kavu hauled D'Melo into the vacant fortress prison. Moments later, a light went on in a window on the west wall. *Okay, at least I know where he is. But how do I get him out before they find the boyz? Think Zara!* she urged herself, daunted by what she was up against.

Her searching eyes halted at a temporary construction shed not far from the lighted window. She scrutinized the compound, trying to devise a way in. Squinting upward through the driving rain, she concluded fearfully that scaling the twenty-foot-high fence was her only chance.

Zara studied the roaming floodlights crisscrossing along the ground and fencing. She observed momentary blind spots, but they didn't follow any discernible pattern.

I can make it. She tried to convince herself. *I have to make it.*

She steeled nerves, then scurried clandestinely out of the jungle to the fence. She peered to the top, which suddenly seemed a lot higher than she had estimated. Her pulse raced as she grasped the metal links, slick from rain. She climbed quickly, stopping just below a passing floodlight.

"Okay," she groaned, her shoulder pulsing with pain. "You're halfway." She proceeded, scrambling to beat the next light. It passed beneath her, as she mounted the top. She flipped one leg over, then the other. As she tried to secure her foot, it slipped from the links. The sudden jolt of weight made her lose her grip on the rail. Her body swung and slammed against the fence with a resounding rattle. Clinging desperately with one hand, she spied wide-eyed for any movement in the nearest guard booth. There was none. She was once again saved by the hammering storm.

But her relief was fleeting. A floodlight slid along the fence toward her. She scrambled to secure her footing, then started down frantically. A force tugged against her. Her T-shirt was snagged in the jagged ties atop the fence. The light was now within a few feet. Wild with fear, she looked at the long drop to the ground.

Just as the light was about to reveal her, she let go and yanked her shirt, tearing it from the fence. She careened to the soaked earth, biting back a scream. Landing with an emphatic thud, it felt like an electric shock was zapping every nerve. But there was no time to register the pain arcing through her body, as another floodlight moved in her direction. She staggered to her feet and hobbled to the shed. She cracked open the rickety door and slipped in. Passing floodlights flashed between the wood panels. It wasn't ideal, but it was enough for her to spot what she needed—two buckets and a brick.

On the cold concrete floor, D'Melo teetered on the edge of consciousness. He focused on the sound of the rain battering the window to keep his mind awake.

A soldier bumped clumsily into the room carrying plastic drop cloths. Kavu ordered him to tape the cloths along the walls and ceiling. The soldier was bewildered by the order. "Just do it!" Kavu barked.

D'Melo felt his senses starting to stir. He peeked through quivering eyelids at the soldier hanging the plastic.

"The tranquilizer is wearing off!" the soldier gulped, backpedaling.

"Don't worry," Kavu reassured him confidently. "He's as harmless as a baby in here."

A burly man decked in military fatigues stalked in. An abundance of shiny medals clanked on his chest.

Kavu straightened and saluted, "General."

General Nyoko browsed the room. "What's happening here?" he queried in his low raspy voice.

"Sir, when D'Melo swallowed the seeds from the Tree he obtained extraordinary powers," Kavu explained. "But I've discovered that his abilities are neutralized by unnatural elements, like plastic."

"Good work, Kavu." Nyoko stomped over to D'Melo.

Nyoko blurred in and out of D'Melo's vision. Nyoko slapped him. "Wake up!" D'Melo's eyes darted around, then finally settled on the General. "I've waited long enough," Nyoko said gruffly. "Where are your friends?"

D'Melo was groggy, but alert enough to revel in Nyoko not having yet found the boyz. He gazed wearily at the general and said nothing.

Nyoko thrashed D'Melo's face with the bottom of his heavy boot. Blood splattered from the congealed cut on his lip. He shook it off, then stared obstinately at Nyoko.

"So you're a tough guy, huh? Just like your brother here." Nyoko gestured toward Kavu. "Okay, have it your way. But it's only a matter of time. Before long we'll win the battle and wipe those Kipaji cockroaches off the face of the earth. How long do you think your friends will be able to hide after that? All that will remain to make Malunga the most powerful country in the world is slicing you open."

Kavu scuttled to join Nyoko on his way to the door. "Sir, you're not serious about killing all the Kipajis, are you? The mission was only to get the package and the nectar."

"Are you getting soft for your fellow Kipajis?" Nyoko said, clutching Kavu's shoulder. "They abandoned you, remember? They discarded you like they would a piece of rubbish. So you should be happy to rid the world of those filthy insects."

"No sir. I'm not concerned about them." Kavu paused pensively. "It's—it's just that, another genocide would bring a lot of international heat on us."

A sinister smile crept onto Nyoko's face. "Kipajis have reserved the healing nectar for their own people, while Malungans and everyone else have suffered. To do this, Kipaji had to keep itself a secret, completely isolated. So in the eyes of the world, it's just another worthless region of Malunga. Do you see the irony?" he said with an ugly laugh. "With the hands of selfishness, Kipaji has constructed its own coffin. But even if anyone took notice, like that cockroach-loving Kyle Sandersen, we'll just say the Kipajis were killed in another Shuja uprising." Nyoko mused, "We're *Africans*; the world won't lose a minute's sleep over fifty thousand of us dying. They never do."

"That's brilliant, sir," Kavu muttered, with a hint of melancholy in his voice. "But why wasn't I informed?"

"Soldier," Nyoko scowled, irked by being questioned. "You were told the part of the plan that we needed you for."

"Yes, sir!" Kavu shot, stiffening. "I understand, sir."

"Door!" Nyoko bellowed to the guards positioned outside the cell. "I'll return with the doctor when we've recovered the package."

D'Melo squinted up at Kavu. "You're not a monster like he is, you know." Dark red dripped from his mouth. "I've seen who you really are. I don't think it was all an act."

Kavu remained silent, his gaze falling to the floor.

Sensing an opening, D'Melo pressed on. "I know you don't want harmless Kipajis to be slaughtered. Think about the children. They've done nothing to deserve to die like that. They're just like we were—innocent, playing in the wildflower field. Don't you even care?"

"Of course, I care!" Kavu snapped. "But I'm a soldier. This is all I know. It's all I have."

"That's not true. You're a whole lot more than a soldier. You're a human being." D'Melo demanded, "Look at me."

Kavu glanced up momentarily, then lowered his eyes again.

"You can put an end to this craziness. All you have to do is let me out of here."

Kavu took a wistful breath. "I'm going to be the president one day. Then I can do whatever I want. I'll make things right, my way."

"How can you make a *genocide* right!" D'Melo pleaded. "There's already been one in this country, are you going to let—"

"Listen," Kavu shouted. "I can't help you! Stop talking to me!"

CHAPTER SEVENTEEN

Rise!

Soaked and shivering, the boyz squatted in the ferny vegetation along the Hasira River, waiting for the signal from Chipo. They had become numb to the seemingly endless explosions. The jarring sounds were now almost as natural as the croaking of the tree frogs or screeching of the colobus monkeys.

They spied six border guards keeping vigilant watch on the bridge. Clearly, the guards were put on high alert. Concrete barriers had been positioned just before the patrol booth and floodlights were sweeping the bridge and river.

"There's no way we're getting over that bridge without Chipo. Where *is* she?" Marley whined. "It's been like two hours! I'm freezing."

"Cool out, dawg. If you haven't noticed, there's some crazy stuff happening," Jeylan reasoned. "Maybe she wasn't expecting a war in Kipaji. She's probably rounding up extra troops in case something kicks off on the Nanjier side."

Kazim piped, "Or maybe she had to do her nails."

"Man, why you gotta be all sexist!" Marley chided.

"Really?" Kazim retorted. "That's your biggest concern right now? Whether I'm politically correct?"

"Hey, shh." Jeylan tugged them down. A floodlight lingered over them. "We can't stay here forever," he said, angst tinging his voice.

"Well, we don't exactly have anywhere else to go," Kazim pointed out. "Do you want to head back over the mountain and get your butt ripped off by one of those explosions?"

"Where's D'Melo and Zara?" Marley fretted through chattering teeth. "They should have been here a long time ago."

"I don't know, man," Jeylan sighed. "But I'm sure they're okay."

"Chipo ain't coming," Kazim grumbled. "She left us for dead. I knew this plan wasn't gonna work!"

"Quit your groanin', dawg," Jeylan said. "She'll be here."

"Hey!" Marley's quivering finger pointed toward Nanjier. "What's that?" Tiny sparks were followed by popping sounds.

"That's gotta be Chipo!" Jeylan said. The boyz craned their necks for a better view. "There's the signal, the waving light! I told y'all she'd come. Let's go."

They hurriedly crossed the bridge. The patrol booth was pocked with bullet strikes. As they stepped around the lifeless border guards, Chipo appeared under a bridge light.

"Ah man," Kazim said. "I told these guys you'd be here. I knew you'd never leave us." Jeylan and Marley glanced incredulously at each other.

"We should get you out of this rain," Chipo said. "Your flight isn't until six, so we still have some time."

Jeylan surveyed the area. "Where are all the rebels who smoked these guards?"

"Ahhh," Chipo said. "They did their job. I sent them back to the command post."

Chipo headed toward the paltry border security office. The boyz stretched their hoods over their faces to block the stinging rain. They shook off as they entered the meagerly decorated building—four flimsy plastic chairs, a fake plant in the corner, and a framed photo of President Okoye hanging crookedly on the drab gray wall. Chipo gestured for them to have a seat.

"I'm going to warm up with tea," she said. "Would you like a cup?" The boyz crumpled their faces, *Who drinks tea?* Chipo's expression sobered before ducking into the main office in the rear of the building.

Hushed voices murmured from the office. Jeylan shushed Marley and Kazim. "Do you hear that? Who's she talking to?"

The boyz jerked from the sound of a violent thud. Chipo returned, the skin beneath her eye reddish.

"Hey," Jeylan asked, concerned. "What happened to you?"

She pointed to her muddy boots. "I slipped on the floor and knocked my head."

"But where's your tea?"

"Oh," Chipo looked at her hands. "There was none left."

Jeylan rose. "Alright, let's bounce."

"Okay. Okay," Chipo said, flustered. "But first let me use the bathroom."

A couple minutes passed. Jeylan peered down the dank hallway. "Somethin' ain't right. She's acting all strange."

A whir hummed in the distance. Jeylan scuttled to the window. "It's a helicopter! Chipo didn't say anything about a helicopter." Jeylan scooped up his backpack. "We gotta roll!"

The whirring intensified as the helicopter settled behind the building. Just then, the office door was flung open violently, slamming the wall. A burly man appeared attired in military khakis, a stretchy T-shirt that accentuated his veiny muscles, a black ski mask, and a patch over his left eye. As if that wasn't terrifying enough, he carried a serrated hunting knife on his hip, a pistol in his belt and a machine gun over his shoulder. He looked like a one-man army. The boyz let out a collective gasp.

The soldier stalked over to them. "Sit down!" he barked, glaring through his good eye. Kazim shuddered, then fell into his chair obediently. Jeylan sat defiantly. And Marley just stood frozen, like a deer in headlights.

"I said sit!" The soldier thrust Marley hard into the chair, banging him against the wall. Marley's glasses dangled, clinging to his face.

The soldier's phone buzzed. He raised it to his ear. "I can't hear you," he said, plugging his other ear with his finger. "Turn off the engine." The helicopter's rotor blades slowed to a stop. "Yeah, they're all here," he replied. "No, not yet. I'll get it now."

The soldier returned his attention to the boyz. "So let's make this snappy, shall we. I believe you have something that belongs to us." The boyz wilted. They knew exactly what this guy wanted. "Let's not make this difficult." The soldier aimed his pistol at them one by one. "Eeny, meeny, miny, moe," he threatened. "Let's see, which to shoot first. I think the chunky one." He halted the gun at Marley.

"Hey, hey. That's not chunk," Marley prattled, obviously terrified. "It's just leftover baby fat. My mom said it's a genetic thing. Apparently, we're a family of late bloomers. I think it—"

"Shut up!" the soldier growled.

"Sorry," Marley murmured, one eye now twitching. "I tend to ramble when I'm nervous. Started when—"

The soldier tightened his lips and crammed his gun into Marley's nose, crushing it flat. Marley's eyes bulged. He threw his hands in the air.

"What are you doing?" the soldier spat. "Put your hands down! You're not under arrest. I'm just gonna shoot you in the face."

"Stop!" Jeylan intervened. "Enough." He unzipped his backpack and removed the cassette. "Here." He tossed it to the soldier. "Now leave him alone."

The soldier tapped the tip of Marley's nose. "Chunky boy, you're lucky to have friends that won't let your brains get splattered all over the wall."

The soldier phoned the person in the helicopter. "I got it. I'm coming out now." He paused. "Are you sure? Ok," he said hesitantly. He put the phone on speaker and faced it toward the boyz. "Someone wants to talk to you."

A man's voice gloated, "I want to thank you guys for finding the package. I couldn't have done it without you. I've been looking for it for fifteen years," he chuckled. "And it's been right here under my nose the whole time.

"I have to admit, I caught a lucky break. My buddy here knows Chipo. They did business together a long time ago. So when I found out that D'Melo snuck into Kipaji, my gut told me that Chipo had to be involved."

The boyz exchanged looks, surprised that this guy knew D'Melo by name.

"Who else would have been able to smuggle him into Kipaji?" the man continued. "So I did some digging and discovered that Chipo and D'Melo's mom were friends in college. I put two and two together and here we are.

"But you shouldn't be upset with Chipo. She didn't cave in easily. We offered her a stack of money to give you guys up. She refused. We threatened to kill her. She still didn't cave. But then we uncovered the one thing that cracks even the most loyal and headstrong rebel. Chipo has a child. She hid him well, but not well enough. We found him way out in sticks with her parents. As soon as Chipo saw her son with my buddy, she was ready to give us anything we wanted. Children are magic!

"After my buddy took care of the border patrol guards, the only thing left was for Chipo to coax you over the bridge. And the rest, as they say, is history.

"Well guys, it looks like my job here is done. It's been a real pleasure doing business with you."

The soldier asked, "Do you want me to get rid with them?"

The boyz' eyes shot open.

"No. Let them go. They're just kids."

"But, they know too much."

"Without the package, who would ever believe them? They're nothing but ghetto hoodlums."

"I don't know about this," the soldier asserted.

"I'm not a killer. But make no mistake, if any of them decide to open their mouths, I give you permission to pay their families a visit." There was a brief pause. "Let's see here. Darren and Jocelyn Kendrick."

The boyz' terrified eyes darted to the phone.

"They must be Jeylan's parents." Jeylan's jaw clenched. "1471 Stone Street." The man then said the names and addresses for Kazim's and Marley's families.

The soldier clicked off the phone. "You're lucky he has a heart. If it were up to me—" he sneered, then sloshed out to the helicopter.

Chipo's head poked cautiously from the office. She shuffled out holding her four-year-old son, whose face was buried in her neck. She rocked him comfortingly. "It's over. We're going home now."

She turned to the boyz, her eyes filled with tears. "I'm so sorry! They had my child."

"We get it," Jeylan sympathized. "You gotta take care of yours."

"But Mujiza and Diata sacrificed their lives for the recording. And now the truth about Dimka will never be known."

"Or, maybe it will," Jeylan smirked. "Marls, please tell me you were recording what happened here with your nerd glasses."

Marley lifted his cheek and shrugged.

"Marley!" Jeylan fired, throwing his hands up exasperatedly.

Kazim glared at Marley. "You record me going to the bathroom, but you don't record this dude taking the evidence and threatening to kill us and our families!"

"Well," Marley asserted. "When you were in the bathroom, I didn't have a gun in my nose. My mind was a bit preoccupied with thoughts of my face hanging from the wall!"

"Man," Jeylan said half-jokingly. "I should have just let that dude shoot you!"

"Now that's just rude," Marley quipped. "If you did—" a triumphant smile creased his eyes, "then you wouldn't have known that I recorded the cassette when we played it in the alcove."

"Noooo," Jeylan purred, his eyes gaping.

"*Now* who's the man!" Marley gloated.

Jeylan said, "Dang, dawg. Why you gotta ruin a beautiful moment? That saying went out in the eighties . . . with Kaz's Jheri curl." They burst into uproarious laughter.

Jeylan and Kazim jumped on Marley jubilantly. His chair toppled over. They chortled, clapping Marley on the back.

Marley then played the recording. They leaned in.

"Hey, turn that up!" Jeylan said, wanting to make sure he was correct about what he was hearing.

After a few seconds, Marley shut it off. Only the lash of the rain cut the unnerved silence in the room. They realized that the man in the helicopter was the second voice on the recording.

"Oh, God," Chipo hummed, a frightful grimace overwhelming her face. "I gotta get you guys out of here!"

They ran to Chipo's pickup truck and tore for the airport.

The sizzle of lightning followed by thunderous blasts conjured dreadful thoughts in D'Melo's addled mind. Zara and the boyz were somewhere in the middle of the battle for Kipaji. *And it's all my fault.* He knew that the only way to end the war started with him getting out of the fortress prison. He gathered enough energy to prop himself against the sweating cinderblock wall, crinkling the plastic sheet behind him.

"Kavu, how can you do this to Kipaji? To our people?" He made another attempt to kindle the light he had glimpsed in Kavu's heart.

"They're not *my* people. I stopped being Kipaji the day my family abandoned me."

"You know that's not true. We didn't abandon you."

"It doesn't even matter what's true anymore," Kavu lamented. "All I know is that I was left here, while my family was off in America, never even giving me a second thought."

"Well, that's where you're wrong," D'Melo replied, unwilling to give up on him. "When things settled down after that night on the bridge, Baba came back here. He made an agreement with Dimka to exchange himself for you."

Kavu's posture shifted attentively.

"But it was a trick. Dimka was never planning to let you go. He was just going to kill Baba.

"When Baba returned to America without you, it dealt the final blow to Mama's heart. Whatever spirit she had left was crushed. She spiraled into a severe depression. A couple months later, she tried to kill herself. Does this sound like people who didn't care about you?"

"I don't believe you," Kavu said weakly, his shoulders sagging. "Anyway, it's too late now." He sighed. "What's done is done."

"You're right; what's done is done. But what happens next is up to you."

Kavu tucked his lips, clearly fighting down fresh anguish.

Kavu's phone buzzed. "That's good, sir," he muttered unconvincingly, his eyes soft. "Yes, I heard you, sir." His gaze slid away from D'Melo. "No, sir. I'm okay with it. Nothing has changed."

Kavu stared vacantly at his phone. "Well," he said in a low voice. "It seems the last bit of your luck has run out. The recording has been recovered."

D'Melo swallowed hard. "Are my friends okay?"

"You're about to have your stomach carved up, and you're asking about your *friends*?" Kavu chuckled with a mix of disbelief and admiration. "Your friends are fine."

"Can I just ask you for one thing?"

Kavu lifted his chin, indicating that he was listening.

"Please, please let Zara go. You have the recording. There's nothing she can do to hurt Dimka now."

"Wow," Kavu said, awed. "It must be really nice."

D'Melo was unsure what Kavu meant.

"To have people that you love so much that you think about their welfare when you're minutes from being killed in the most gruesome way."

Kavu headed for the door. Just before he exited the cell, D'Melo said, "Do you know the last thing Baba said to me?"

Kavu paused at the door, facing away from D'Melo.

"He said, 'You've never truly lived if you don't have anything in your life that you're willing to die for.'"

Kavu's head dipped. "The medic will be here soon," he murmured, his voice shaky. "You should prepare yourself."

"Hey," D'Melo said urgently. "What about Zara? You never answered."

At the sound of a light thud, Kavu swiveled abruptly toward the window above D'Melo. He shook his head and mumbled, "Unbelievable." He chuckled incredulously. "Well, I get the feeling you're going to find out about Zara very soon." He strolled out, the door clicking locked behind him.

Moments before, Zara had swerved and halted, skirting the flood-lights. She had made it to the prison just outside D'Melo's cell with the buckets and brick in hand. She crouched beneath the lighted window, scanning the compound to make sure she hadn't been spotted. Her heart raced as a floodlight slid along the wall. She flattened herself in the mud, the light barely passing over her.

The window was just above her eye level. She latched onto its iron bars and boosted herself up. Through the opaque plastic, she could discern a figure at the cell door. *Is that D'Melo? Kavu?* A light drifted along the wall toward her. She climbed her feet up in a panic, thumping the wall with her knee. The figure at the door swiveled searchingly toward her. She leaned back as far as her arms would allow to avoid being seen. She cringed, the wound on her shoulder ripping wider. A tear of agony joined the raindrops pelting her face. The floodlight skimmed just under her contorted frame. *That was too close.*

She strained to hear two muffled voices inside the cell, one coming from beneath the window. When the talking stopped, she lifted up cautiously. The figure by the door was exiting. Her eyes swept side to side. No one else was in the room. *This is my chance!*

She dropped down softly. Driving her wiry fingers into the muddy earth, she frantically scooped the watery soil into the buckets.

The doorknob twisted. D'Melo knew this was it. His earthly life had come to an end. He pondered how strange life could be. In the span of a few days, he had gone from basketball All-American waiting to attend the college of his dreams to a prison cell in Malunga, waiting to die.

Kavu entered first. His eyes darted between D'Melo and the window. A pair of soldiers followed, wheeling a gurney. Handcuffs clinked against its metal rails.

A deluge of gratitude flooded D'Melo's heart. His mother suffered for years, but always made sure to push a smile onto her face for him. Baba could have had the life he wanted and deserved, but instead he chose to sacrifice it, seeking justice for the Shujas who the world still believed assassinated President Amani. His friends willingly put their lives in jeopardy to help him get the recording. And Zara came back for him when she was so close to safety in Nanjier, because *she will never leave me behind.*

"Thank you all, and please forgive me," he sighed, his heart full.

Like a dark storm cloud, Nyoko stalked ominously into the cell. He greeted D'Melo with a heavy boot to the gut. D'Melo gritted his teeth, holding back a yelp. He refused to allow Nyoko the satisfaction of showing the pain radiating in his stomach.

The medic sauntered in last. Medical instruments clanked menacingly inside his shiny black bag.

"Well, D'Melo, it looks like its time," Nyoko stated the obvious. "It's a shame. All you or your father had to do was tell us where the package was. None of this would have happened. You would still be a big basketball star about to make millions in the NBA."

D'Melo glared at him.

"Yeah, that's right," Nyoko croaked. "I know everything about you and your family. Who do you think tracked you down, twice? My only regret is that I didn't have the pleasure of personally killing your traitor parents."

D'Melo seethed, feeling like his head might just blow off his shoulders.

"I would have made your father beg for his life before I put those bullets in his chest."

D'Melo smoldered, "He would *never* beg for his life, to you or to anyone else." D'Melo spat the blood that had accumulated in his mouth. "He lived with a dignity that someone like you could never understand. And he died with honor, unlike how you're gonna die."

Nyoko stomped D'Melo's face. Blood spurted from a gash under his eye. Kavu winced, then turned away.

"You talk like you're still some big warrior," Nyoko said. "You may not have noticed but you are about to die and have your lifeless body dumped in the jungle for the animals to feast on. And I, on the other hand, will die one of the richest men in the world on a beautiful beach on some island," he cackled. "Maybe I'll even buy the island."

As the general raged on, D'Melo turned his attention inward. Baba's assuring voice washed into his heart. "*Haki inakuja kwako, Justice will find you.*" Serenity cascaded through him like a warm ocean wave.

"I'm ready." D'Melo straightened against the wall. "What are we waiting for?"

"Look at this guy!" Nyoko rasped. "A hero 'til the end." He gestured to the soldiers. "Okay, you heard him. Strap him to the gurney."

Just as the soldiers moved toward D'Melo, there was huge crash. A brick blasted through the window, pushing against the plastic cover. The brick slid down and hit D'Melo on the head.

An alarm blared. Guards scrambled down from the towers. "Oh crud!" Zara latched onto the cell window bars. She hurriedly removed a shard of glass from the windowpane and used it to slice through the plastic. The soldiers in the cell hoisted their rifles and sprayed bullets through the window. Zara's ear buzzed, followed by a searing throb. She dropped to the ground, clutching her ear. The tower guards took aim at the darkness below the window. The bullets sparked against the wall around her. She dove away. The guard-controlled floodlight veered frenetically left and right, hunting her.

Zara dipped and dodged her way back to the window. She lifted a bucket overhead and dumped the watery soil into the cell. The soldiers fired through the window again, snapping the bucket from her hands. She raised the second bucket, bullets sparking the wall around her. She dumped the soil from the bucket into the cell and darted off.

Nyoko shouted at his soldiers, "Why are you still standing here! Go!" Kavu and the soldiers sprang out of the cell.

D'Melo started rubbing the watery dirt over his skin. Nyoko clamped D'Melo's foot and dragged him away from the reviving soil. D'Melo kicked Nyoko squarely, sending him sliding backward. D'Melo scrambled back to the mud and scooped it up frantically, slathering himself as fast as he could. Nyoko drew his gun and unloaded a flurry of murderous rounds. The bullets halted. D'Melo snatched them from the air and hurled the slugs across the floor.

Nyoko gasped, then ran in a panic toward the exit. D'Melo levitated to a standing position. Balls of mud swirled in his palms. They

launched, smashing Nyoko violently against the wall, knocking him
unconscious. D'Melo cupped his hands around his mouth and beckoned, like through a bullhorn, "*Viboko, tembo kupanda*! Hippos, elephants rise!" The forest awakened, quaking with exhilaration.

Zara splashed over the slick ground, chasing the shelter of darkness. Bullets thwacked into the mud as she zigzagged between
blind spots. Finally, the floodlight found her, giving the soldiers
a clear shot. But she remained determined, dipping and dashing
elusively, until her footing gave way. Her feet swung skyward and
she fell heavily into the waterlogged soil. Now a stationary target,
the guards took sure aim.

"Hold your fire!" A voice pierced through the chaos.

Zara looked up, mud dribbling from her face. Kavu hustled toward her, waving his arms. "We need her alive!" he shouted. "D'Melo
won't do anything if we have her."

Kavu snatched Zara harshly to her feet. But then he leaned in and
whispered, "Are you okay?" Zara, confounded by his concern, nodded
tentatively. He zipped plastic handcuffs on her wrists.

Just as he was about to drag her away, the jungle crackled with
furious life. The earth rattled. Shattered branches flung against the
compound fence. Out of the darkness, six elephants materialized.
They stormed through the metal links, as if they were nothing more
than a spider web. Twelve hippos rumbled thunderously behind
them.

The soldiers leveled their rifles. They asked their ancestors for
forgiveness before opening fire. Orange sparks flashed. An elephant
stumbled, then collapsed with a monumental splash. The other elephants, some pocked red from bullets, gathered around their fallen
comrade. They trumpeted a screeching cry, then charged ferociously.

The soldiers jostled for cover. Many didn't make it and were tram-
pled as they floundered in the mud. The hippos rammed the legs of

the towers, where some guards had taken refuge. The towers teetered, then plunged down to the earth.

A retreating soldier turned desperately and fired at a charging elephant, clipping her gray fleshy ear. She rose on her hind legs and blasted a bone-chilling roar. Her forelegs splashed down mightily. The soldier stood petrified as she towered over him. She snatched him up in her enormous trunk and flung him into the air. On his way down, she slashed him with her sharp tusk.

Trying to take advantage of the bedlam, Zara struggled to wrest herself free. But Kavu gripped her like a vise. He drew his knife and guided it to her stomach. She squeezed her eyes shut. Images of the pigs being slaughtered at her mother's factory flashed in her mind. Kavu brought the knife against her quivering belly. With a quick jerk, he sliced off the handcuffs.

"Go! Get as far away from here as you can," he urged.

Zara released the breath trapped in her terrified lungs. "Thank you, but I'm not going anywhere without D'Melo."

The hippos stampeded toward them. Kavu pivoted to run. Zara clamped his arm. "If you run, they'll kill you for sure. Just be still." She pulled him close. Kavu seemed to take solace in her calming eyes. The hippos were now thundering just thirty feet away and closing quickly. The power of their weight slamming into the earth pounded fear into their chests.

As the hippos were upon them, mud splattered their faces. Their breath shuddered in chorus. Then, with a massive *whoosh*, the hippos stampeded past. Wet strands of Zara's hair were plastered to her face by the tailwind.

"They're gone," she said. Kavu cracked his eyes open gratefully. Before he could get his wits about him, Zara dashed toward a fallen soldier. She slid on her knees to his side and placed a healing hand over his heart. Kavu rubbed his forehead, clearly baffled by Zara helping a soldier who was, only minutes before, trying to kill her.

Zara focused deeply, tapping into "reality—the oneness of all things." She informed the soldier, "You have three cracked ribs, but no internal bleeding."

He squinted at her suspiciously, rain filling his eyes.

"You're going to be okay," she said. She then lifted a large rock. "Sorry that I have to do this, but you might try to kill us." She crumpled her face and covered her eyes. She drove the rock down, clocking the soldier unconscious. She scampered from one soldier to the next, healing then clocking.

The hippos rumbled straight for D'Melo's prison cell. They rammed the outer wall. Cinder blocks crumbled, but the wall still stood. They backed up and tried again. This time the wall toppled to the ground, sending a plume of dust into the wet air.

When the cloud settled, Kavu eyed the cell. D'Melo wasn't there, and Nyoko was stirring to consciousness. Kavu rushed to Zara. "The general's coming! You have to go right now!"

Zara grinned, unfazed. She pointed beyond Kavu. D'Melo sat atop a hippo, his eyes pulsing with light.

"*Nenda,*" D'Melo bellowed with power and authority. The hippo pounded the earth with haste toward Zara and Kavu. As it passed, D'Melo scooped Zara. They stormed off behind the other animals toward the gate.

Bullets ripped through the rain. One tore into the flesh of the hippo's hind leg. It stumbled momentarily, but then hit full stride again. D'Melo reached back and grabbed Zara. He swung her in front of him to shield her body from the volley of bullets.

Nyoko snatched the tranquilizer gun from his belt. He shot desperately as D'Melo and Zara vanished into the forest.

Nyoko glared at Kavu. "Why are you still here? Get your guys!" He fired his gun angrily into the air. Kavu flinched, jarred by the ear-splitting bang. "And bring me a horse!" The general, Kavu, and six of his elite fighters galloped into the jungle in pursuit.

As D'Melo and Zara reached the foot of Choma Mountain, the forest became too thick and steep for the hippo to continue. They dismounted. D'Melo's feet landed heavily in the soggy undergrowth, his knees wobbly.

Zara steadied him. "D'Melo, what's going on?"

"Must be from when you busted me on the head with that brick," he smiled, his eyes glassy.

"Jokes? Right now? Really?" Zara swept his body, running her hands over his chest and back. Nothing. D'Melo lifted an arm. His skin was slit from Nyoko's tranquilizer dart.

"Oh no," she said, unable to hide her dismay. "Are you okay to run?"

"I think so." He stumbled sluggishly through the forest behind her. At that pace, they knew there was no chance they would reach Nanjier before the soldiers overtook them.

"This is just like the Poconos," Zara said, attempting to take their minds off the grim situation. "Remember? You were huffing and puffing as the elderly ladies passed you?"

"Now *you* got jokes!" D'Melo chuckled weakly.

As they crested Choma Mountain, they were momentarily comforted by the quiet. Only the crackle of dying fires interrupted the silence. Not even the animals gave voice to the forest. Movement was limited to the thick smoke churning upward, its bitterness scorching their throats.

Surveying the expanse that remained to be traversed left them disheartened. In their weakened condition, Amanzi Mountain towered dauntingly between them and Nanjier. But at least they wouldn't have to navigate the raging battle, which had moved away from the Tree and across the valley. Upepo Mountain seemed to now be its epicenter, as the once lush woodland was an inferno.

"We're lucky the dart only grazed you," Zara said, stopping at a pond. "Get in," she suggested.

"What? That water must be freezing!" D'Melo said. As proof, he puffed a white cloud from his mouth.

"You're such a punk." Zara mocked. "Just get in. I want to see something."

D'Melo squatted, reluctantly. He dipped a hand in the water, then snapped it back. "Whoa! I ain't goin' in there!"

"Okay, you big baby. Just splash some on your face."

He relented. "Ooh, this is nice." His energy stirred. He dipped an arm. "Ahh, yes. This is the ticket." He shook water beads from his face. "You know, I've been meaning to ask you," he smirked. "Why are you almost naked again?"

Zara bit her lip. "Dude, I'm not almost naked. But if you must know, let me tell you. You have no idea what I've been through saving your butt. First, I had to—" She halted abruptly, listening. "That's a horse!"

D'Melo sprung to his feet. Zara shot off at a brisk clip. He hustled to match her pace. They got a few hundred feet before Zara slowed and hunched over. Her breathing shallowed. D'Melo had seen this behavior enough times to know that she was fine. He stood by waiting for what she was sensing.

Zara stumbled off the path into the thicket. "Oh, please no!" She knelt next to a small body. "Jonju!" She rubbed his face. The smell of burnt flesh was pungent. She reached into the satchel for the nectar. *Oh, God. Don't let me be too late.*

"Hey, Jonju," she comforted. "You're going to be fine in a few minutes. Just hang in there, okay?" Jonju attempted to nod, then fell unconscious.

Zara pried his mouth open. She prayed under her breath. "I beg of you, Great Spirit. Please allow the power of Haya to bring this beautiful child back to health."

They waited, Jonju still motionless. "Jonju. Please wake up. Please." Zara turned to D'Melo, her eyes misty. "I'm too late." She buried her head in his chest, sobbing. "I promised him that I'd play with him again."

"Madam Zara? Why must you cry? If we play the bubbles game, would that make you happy?"

"JONJU!" Zara lifted him to a sitting position, then nearly squeezed the life out of him. She blew bubbles on his neck. He giggled. She covered his mouth, her eyes canvassing the forest.

"Listen carefully, Jonju. We must go now. But where we're going is much too dangerous for you. There are bad people after us. I need you to be courageous and stay right here, hidden." Jonju clung onto Zara. "Jonju, I promise, I'll come back for you. Have I ever broken a promise?" His eyes smiled, while his lips quivered in fear.

Zara's heart sank, knowing that her promise hinged on the improbable—getting D'Melo over the mountain before Nyoko and his soldiers caught up. But, if by some miracle, she could deliver D'Melo to safety, he would have time to regain his full conjuring strength.

D'Melo and Zara reached the summit of Amanzi Mountain. The storm clouds ebbed, revealing a violet-hued predawn sky. Just as the path to the bridge was within view, hooves battered the underbrush behind them.

"Stop!" a voice commanded. They made a mad dash. "I said, stop!" A pistol blasted a warning shot.

Kavu trotted toward them on his golden horse. He dismounted and marched directly toward D'Melo. D'Melo clenched his fists. Kavu walked straight into D'Melo and wrapped his arms lovingly around him. Caught off-guard, D'Melo stiffened. He so desired to return the hug, but he resisted, unsure whether this was another one of Kavu's clever deceptions.

"I'm sorry, brother," Kavu said quietly. "Please forgive me."

D'Melo's eyes shifted to Zara to gauge Kavu's sincerity. Her emerald green eyes met his heartwarmingly, signaling that Kavu was genuine. D'Melo clutched Kavu's face in his generous hands. "You don't need to be forgiven. You were given a raw deal in life."

Kavu basked for a moment in the warmth of D'Melo's grace. His moist eyes glimmered with absolution.

"My brother," he urged with dread. "You must go. The general's coming with my fighters. I was able to go ahead of them because they stopped to collect some Choma and Joto warriors to help."

Again, D'Melo pleaded for Kavu to join them.

"This is my home," Kavu said. "You know I can never leave here." He drew a resolute breath. "Please go. I'll hold them off as long as I can to give you time to cross the bridge."

"No, I can't let you die like this. You're coming with us!" D'Melo demanded. He clenched Kavu's arm.

Kavu laid a tender hand over D'Melo's. "You know," he mused, "a wise man once said, 'You've never truly lived if you don't have anything in your life that you're willing to die for.' I've finally found what I'm willing to die for, my family . . . my *real* family. I've done enough damage in this world. I want my final act to be something worthy." The tranquility of freedom washed over his face. "I'm going where I belong, back with Baba and Mama."

D'Melo's heart was filled with pride and sadness. They clasped hands and pulled into a bittersweet embrace.

Suddenly, orange fury flickered in the woods. The pop of guns rang out from the forest. Kavu's body jolted. Warm liquid splashed D'Melo's face. As the gleam in Kavu's eyes drained, his body slumped heavily through D'Melo's struggling arms into the wet earth. D'Melo was paralyzed with grief. He couldn't bear to lose another person he loved.

Bullets buzzed around them like angry bees. Then to his horror, D'Melo heard Zara screech. He turned to her. Blood was oozing down her rib cage and soaking into her soiled white leggings.

Zara grabbed D'Melo by the shirt and hauled him toward the summit river. A steam blast threw them from their feet, hurling them to the steep riverbank. Instinctively, D'Melo lifted his weary body to protect Zara. She yanked him back down, as bullets thudded into the soil around them. She crawled on her hands and knees down the bank, dragging him. She slid D'Melo to the river's edge and dunked his head into the lucid water, willing the spirits within. His blood percolated supernatural energy, sending electric charges firing through his veins. He rose, then glided up the riverbank.

"There he is!" Nyoko shouted. "Fire!" Choma conjurers launched fireballs. D'Melo moved his hands circularly. A swirling waterwall materialized before him. The fireballs slammed the wall, bursting into steam. D'Melo's arms quavered. The waterwall thinned.

"D'Melo," Zara cried. "What's wrong?"

"The effect of the seeds is wearing off. I can't protect you, Zar," he lamented. "Run for the bridge!"

"I'm not leaving you again!"

A Joto conjurer pushed a blistering gust in the shape of a spear into the waterwall. Steam penetrated, singeing D'Melo's face. He staggered backward along the bank. Zara gasped. He regained his balance just as a fireball blazed at him. It smashed into his chest, casting him into the river. Zara screamed in anguish, as D'Melo's lifeless body was swept away by the torrent over the mountain ledge.

Zara laid her face on the sodden soil. Her heart was broken.

General Nyoko slithered over to her. He drew his pistol and took aim. "Finally, we end this," he croaked.

Just as his finger tensed on the trigger, his legs wobbled beneath him. The mountain convulsed and the forest trembled in ecstasy from the surge of power emanating from the Ukuqala Pool. A brilliant golden streak sizzled upward into the dawning sky. The enemies of Kipaji squinted into its brilliance, unable to avert their gaze from the spectacle. The silhouette of a figure attired in a golden fleece rose aloft a tower of churning water.

The conjurers dropped to their knees, prostrating themselves. Nyoko ordered his soldiers to fire their tranquilizers at the figure. They hoisted their guns in tentative hands and fired the darts. D'Melo motioned upward. The water beneath him rose and coiled into a protective cocoon. The darts sliced into the water and got lost in its spiraling current. Waterballs formed on D'Melo's palms. He launched them. They each divided into six as they flew. The water missiles thrust the soldiers forcefully into the ground. D'Melo then lifted a commanding finger. Mud climbed up the soldiers' bodies, pinning them to the earth.

Nyoko yanked Zara to her feet and pressed his blade against her throat. She struggled, but Nyoko's terrified grip was unshakable. D'Melo floated atop the pillar of water toward them, his palms readied with more deadly liquid weapons.

"Back up, or she dies," Nyoko trembled. He lifted the razor-sharp steel under Zara's chin. The pressure sliced her delicate skin, leaving a thin crimson line. He dragged Zara toward the forest edge.

"If you leave, I assure you she'll live a long and happy life in Malunga. But if you try anything, I'll slice her head clean off her neck!" Nyoko spat. "Your father, mother, and brother are all dead. Are you prepared to lose your little girlfriend, as well?"

Zara heard D'Melo's voice in her heart. *She's not my girlfriend.*

She wrinkled miffed brows. Her heart responded, *That's all you have to say right now? Jerk! It's true, I'm not your girlfriend, but do you have to say it like that? You spit those words out like a bug just flew in your mouth!*

D'Melo chuckled.

Just as Nyoko was about to vanish into the thicket with Zara, she heard, *I got this.* She smiled and readied herself.

Then, surprisingly, another voice entered her heart. It was Kavu. *I got this, too!*

Duck! D'Melo warned, then launched a powerful ball of water.

Simultaneously, Kavu mustered enough strength to fling his knife into Nyoko's leg. Zara broke free and dove to the ground. The water-ball blasted Nyoko thunderously into a tree. The general leaned motionless against the splintered trunk, his heart speared with his own knife.

Zara hustled to Kavu. She laid healing hands on his chest.

In the space between life and death, Kavu had a vision of his ancestors. Baba and Mama extended welcoming arms, grinning lovingly.

Kavu gazed soulfully at Zara. "It's okay," he said. "I'm ready."

"But I can save you!" Zara reached into her satchel.

D'Melo descended from the tower. "Let him go, Zar."

Heartache dripped down Zara's cheeks, as the satchel slipped from her reluctant fingers.

Kavu's smiling eyes found D'Melo. He raised four fingers, balled his hand, then settled it over his heart. With his final breath, bursting with pride, he said, "*Taji Anaru!* The Crown Returns!"

A formless light dawned from Kavu's chest. D'Melo took in a sharp breath, as the luminescence poured like a healing balm into his heart. He felt whole for the first time since his brother was torn away from him that fateful night on the bridge.

Safiri, Kavu's horse, pranced over to D'Melo. He and Zara mounted her. With the slightest flick of a finger, D'Melo released the soldiers from the mud. His former enemies followed him into the valley, where he would unite the Wapendwa once again, as promised by the Spirit King.

CHAPTER EIGHTEEN

A New Dawn

The bitter smell of smoke sharpened as D'Melo and Zara descended into the clearing. The forest crackled from the heat of withering fires. Thousands of trees had been reduced to charcoal. Most of the buildings burned to the ashy ground. D'Melo's eyes shot anxiously toward the library, which housed centuries of art, ancient relics, and the most precious treasure in Kipaji—the notes Leda penned on the Legend. He waited with unease as wisps of black untangled and migrated lazily across the Moyo. He let out a relieved sigh. The library had been spared.

At least twenty conjurers lay strewn on the valley floor. Some bodies were charred beyond recognition, others drenched and bloated, and still others mangled into violent contortions. D'Melo clasped tormented hands, sickened by the carnage. Only the day before, the wasteland which now lay before him was the most pristine spot on earth, bursting with the energy of life and the giggles of carefree children.

Zara dismounted to tend to the fallen conjurers. Perhaps there was one with a flicker of life left to be kindled. Finding none, she walked forlornly to Haya. Nauseous with apprehension, she gripped a leafy branch obscuring her view. Before peeling it back, she drew a prayerful breath. She knew the future of the world depended on the vitality of this natural healing portal of the Great Spirit. When her eyes fell upon the Tree, a deluge of tears spilled. But this time, the tears carried liquid joy. A pair of Amanzi warriors were, wearily but faithfully, still keeping guard.

D'Melo whirled a commanding hand. Wet twisting gales materialized and swept through the forests, extinguishing lingering blazes. He motioned to an eagle soaring overhead. With a series of shrill screeches, it trumpeted the arrival of a new day. The Wapendwa, hiding in the protective cover of the forest, began trickling into the Moyo.

Zara scanned through the smoky air. Her heart dropped. There was no sign of Jonju. Suddenly, she was pummeled from behind and toppled to the ground.

"Madam Zara!"

She slung her arms around Jonju. They rolled jubilantly in the waterlogged soil.

D'Melo approached the Tabernacle. The silence of hopeful hearts blanketed the community. His long frame became momentarily obscured as he transcended the sacred threshold. An elderly woman's ululation pierced the sooty air, initiating a chorus, "*Shangwe! Shangwe! Falme Roho Anaru!* Rejoice! Rejoice! The Spirit King Returns!" The Wapendwa prostrated themselves before their king.

D'Melo implored, "We are all the children of the Great Spirit. No man or woman is more important than any other. Please lift yourselves and claim your rightful place in this world. Your station is one of honor and dignity."

D'Melo reminded the Wapendwa of the covenant their ancestors made with the original king over two millennia ago. "We once again invited the greatest of evils—our *selves*—to grow within the womb of Kipaji. As a natural consequence, it gave birth to its poisonous offspring, disunity. And what you see around you is the only possible result of its destructive influence. But, by the will of the Great Spirit, the sons and daughters of Kipaji have been graced with a new dawn."

D'Melo exited the Tabernacle and began clearing debris. The Wapendwa promptly organized into cleaning teams. Some of the Wapendwa began to fell the scorched trees. But D'Melo requested that the trees remain untouched. "As long as these trees stand, they will act as a reminder of the consuming fire of discord. And, when they eventually disintegrate and feed their minerals back into the earth, they will remind us that out of death comes new life."

The Wapendwa worked feverishly to prepare the Moyo for the Festival of the *Golide Kanzu* that evening. The festival would celebrate the anniversary of the original king's rise from the Ukuqala Pool. But now, with the Return of the Crown, the festival had something else to celebrate—the rebirth of Kipaji.

Excitement buzzed at Pharma's headquarters in San Francisco. There was standing room only for the nearly one thousand company share-holders packed into the conference hall. They eagerly anticipated the announcement of the new CEO. The chairwoman of the board of directors addressed the crowd.

"Much of our recent unprecedented success is due to the person I'm about to introduce. He has been an inspiration to me, and to many others. He's the poster child for the American dream. He lifted himself from the dregs of Detroit to now heading one of the biggest companies in the country.

"His exploits in Africa have continuously breathed new life into Pharma. He's delivered eight highly profitable drugs into our pipeline, making many in this room very rich, including me," she chuckled. The crowd cheered boisterously.

"So, with no further ado, it gives me the utmost pleasure to present to you the new CEO of Pharma Pharmaceuticals. Wilem VanLuten!" Wild applause erupted.

An orchestra began playing as Wilem strolled onto the stage, gleaming. He threw triumphant arms over his head and waved them to the music. As he reached the podium, he swept the full breadth of the crowd with clapping hands. *I wish Helen was here to see this,* he thought. *She'd realize she made a huge mistake leaving me.* The moment was only made sweeter by it happening on the anniversary of their divorce.

Wilem waited for the ovation to fade. "Well, that was quite some introduction and welcome." He nodded appreciatively at the chairwoman. "I've been dreaming about this moment for many years. I can hardly believe that I'm about to head the best and most innovative drug company in the world." The crowd hooted and hollered.

Suddenly, light filtered in from the rear of the otherwise dark hall. Wilem shaded his eyes from the bright glare of the stage lights. Several silhouetted figures loomed in the doorways.

"Umm," he continued. "I promise that Pharma is in good hands." He lifted his hands for the audience to see. "Just in case you didn't know whose hands I was referring to," he said to a smattering of laughter. "These hands will lead Pharma to a prosperity far beyond what we've already achieved." The crowd roared for the promise of greater riches.

"Before moving on, let me formalize the reason why we're all here today. I'm greatly honored to be offered the position of CEO. And I hereby officially—"

The mic went dead. Wilem tapped it, flummoxed. No sound. A hum of confusion emanated from the audience. Wilem turned to the sound crew. They shrugged.

Static then issued from the speakers, followed by two voices.

Voice 1: "He's destroying this country. If he goes through with the peace agreement and gives them sovereignty, it's going to ruin us. This country will spiral into an economic collapse. And *our* business opportunities will be closed forever."

Wilem's heart raced, beads of sweat dotting his forehead. He gripped the podium to steady his weakening legs.

> **Voice 2:** "Well, there's a solution to this problem. Get rid of him."

> **Voice 1:** "You say that so nonchalantly. I can't just get rid of him."

> **Voice 2:** "Why not? There are always ways. You just have to be creative."

Recognizing a familiar voice, the Pharma audience went stone silent.

> **Voice 1:** "Are you suggesting to assassinate him?"

> **Voice 2:** "Well, I'm not telling you what to do, but that's an option."

The crowd let out a collective gasp. Rustles of alarm filled the hall. All eyes were on Wilem. He backed away from the podium.

> **Voice 1:** "He's the president! He's the most protected person in the country."

> **Voice 2:** "Everyone can be touched. How about his motorcade on the way to the airport? He's vulnerable then. Surely, you'll know which car he'll be in."

Voice 1: "Then what?"

Voice 2: "Do I have to think of everything! What about a shoulder missile launcher?"

Voice 1: "That would implicate our military. This country would be in chaos if the people knew that our military killed the president."

Voice 2: "Well, how about you make it look like the Shuja rebels did it. This would kill two birds with one stone. The peace agreement won't go through *and* it would be the best excuse to finally put the Shujas in their place."

The betrayed shareholders stirred with indignation. Most understood that what was being discussed led to the assassination of President Amani and the genocide of the Shuja people.

Voice 1: "That's a good plan, but how can I frame the rebels?"

Voice 2: "What if I told you that I could get my hands on the type of missile launcher that the rebels use?"

The recording stopped. The silhouetted figures from the doorways streamed down the aisles of the hall. Wilem bolted for the backstage. But FBI agents were there waiting for him.

"Wilem VanLuten, you're under arrest for conspiracy to commit the murder of President Jaru Amani." An agent snapped handcuffs onto Wilem's wrists.

"I have the best lawyers in the country," Wilem threatened. "When they get a hold of you, you won't even be able to work as a mall security guard!"

The agents forcibly marched Wilem past the chairwoman.

"Don't worry, Johanna," Wilem assured her. "This is just a misunderstanding. I'll be out before our board meeting tomorrow morning." The chairwoman's face contorted with disgust.

As the agents paraded Wilem through the lobby, a voice quipped, "Who would ever believe these ghetto hoodlums?" Wilem swiveled to see Jeylan, Kazim and Marley guffawing and clapping each other's backs. "Well, Mr. VanLuten, it looks like our job here is done. It's been a pleasure doing business with you," Jeylan gloated, mocking what Wilem had said to them in Nanjier.

Just before Wilem was escorted from the building, Marley shouted, "*Now* who's the man!"

"Dawg," Jeylan gibed. "I really wish you'd stop saying that."

Kazim mimicked Marley in a squeaky voice, "*Now* who's the man!"

"Y'all just jealous you didn't think of it first," Marley retorted weakly.

Jeylan and Kazim chortled and nudged Marley gleefully.

For the first time in their relationship, Zara found herself on edge with D'Melo. After all, he *was* the King of Kipaji and possessed extraordinary abilities. So, instead of bouncing into his rondeval as she normally would have, she sounded the woodpecker doorbell. She tried to waggle the nervousness from her body. It didn't work. After only a few seconds, she thought, *Well, I guess he's busy.* Almost relieved that he didn't answer, she turned to leave.

The door swung open. Her heart jumped. D'Melo stood tall and glorious in the doorway. A majestic outfit of purple and gold draped his athletic physique. Even the tassel dangling from his kufi rang noble.

"Greetings, Zara," he addressed her formally. Statuesque, he extended a hand adorned with his father's Ibada ring.

Zara raised a brow, *What's he doing?* D'Melo gave his hand an impatient shake. She scrunched her face. *Does he expect me to kiss his ring?* She peered at him out of the corner of her squinting eye. She bowed hesitantly and puckered her lips on the ring.

"Ahem," he cleared his throat, *What are you supposed to say?*

"Uhh," she paused to think. "Ohhh . . . great . . . King of Kipaji?" She shrugged, wondering whether that met royal protocol.

D'Melo glared at her, unimpressed. He then gestured downward.

Zara goggled dubiously. "You want me to prostrate myself at your feet?"

D'Melo could no longer maintain the charade. A dimply smile broke on his delightedly satisfied face.

"Oh, my God!" She slapped his arm. "You're the biggest jerk-king in the world!" D'Melo burst into laughter. He mocked her, "Ohhh, great, King of Kipaji? I guess? Maybe?"

She grumbled, waving fists at him. "You just don't know. If you weren't a king, I'd clobber you right now."

Still in hysterics, D'Melo wrapped her up in his arms and swung her cheerfully in the air.

"Oww, oww," she winced.

"Oh sorry, I forgot about the shoulder. How is it?"

"It'll be alright. Got it stitched at the clinic."

"And the ear?"

Zara padded her bandage. "Just a scratch."

"And the ribs?"

"Can we not talk about all of my issues? There isn't enough time in the day to go through everything."

"Yeah, I hear that. Sorry." D'Melo stepped back for a better view of her. "Wow! Look at you," he said, noticing Zara in her traditional dress.

She spun around. "You like?"

"Amazing!"

"Thanks, dud—" Zara caught herself. "Umm, am I still able to call you 'dude'?"

"Please," D'Melo lifted prayerful hands. "Don't ever stop being yourself with me. Nothing's changed."

"Good to know. How about, '*punk*?"

"Don't push it. I could have a hundred wildebeests stampede you in like one minute!"

Zara chuckled, her eyes crescentic. "But seriously, nothing's changed? You're a king, dude! And you can take down a whole army by yourself."

D'Melo's eyes glinted. "I meant, nothing's changed with us." He locked eyes with her. "I will never let *anything* or *anyone* come between us again."

"Awww." She flitted her eyelashes. "Now you're the biggest sweet-king in the world . . . but soon to be jerk-king again, I'm sure."

D'Melo's face beamed. He darted to the bathroom and returned with the seeds from the Heart. He offered them to Zara.

"Ewww, yuck! I'm not touching those!"

"What do you mean? You're gonna be anointed the Milpisi. So you'll need to return the seeds to the Tree.

"Nuh-uhh, dude," she grimaced. "Those came out of your—" She pointed behind him. "How'd you get them out anyway?"

"Senna tea. Drank like four cups. Dawg, I've been nonstop on the toilet all morning!"

"Aw, man," she said squeamishly, "That's *way* too much information."

D'Melo dropped the seeds into his pocket. "Do you think I have to wear the golden fleece for the festival?"

"What! Dude, the festival is called *Golide Kanzu*." Zara rolled her wrist, gesturing for D'Melo to say what *Golide Kanzu* means.

He shrugged.

"Please tell me you're kidding? And you call yourself the King of Kipaji?" she gibed. "It means, the festival of the *Golden Fleece*. So I'm pretty sure the Wapendwa will be expecting you to wear it," she concluded sarcastically.

"Ahhh, man. But it's itchy," he whined, gyrating his shoulders.

"Oh, my God. You're such a big baby."

Zara abruptly shot off to the boyz bedroom. She returned with her hand behind her back.

"What are you hiding back there?"

"Oh, you mean this?" Zara presented D'Melo with a lit candle. "Happy birthday. Did you think I'd forget?"

"No," D'Melo smirked. "But it seems that you forgot the cake and gift that are supposed to come with the candle."

"Wow. It appears *someone's* been bitten by the greedy bug," Zara said. "But seriously, what do you get a guy who has everything, literally?"

D'Melo smiled. "I guess you did save my life. That's a pretty good birthday present."

"That's true!" Zara perked. "So actually, you owe me, big time! For my next birthday, a hike ain't gonna cut it, dude." They chuckled.

The doorbell clacked. It was Jua. She came to escort them to the festival. With lowered gaze, she bowed before D'Melo.

D'Melo pursed his lips at Zara, *You see, is that so difficult?*

D'Melo and Zara rode Safiri into the Moyo. The tail of D'Melo's fleece flipped behind him with each trot. The anticipatory hum of the Wapendwa halted. A drumbeat resounded through the valley. The pounding rhythm penetrated D'Melo, sending vibrations shivering up his spine.

With each beat, D'Melo's heart pumped with rising vigor. Blood surged through his veins, awakening tremendous energy. With un-imaginable clarity, he tapped into previously inaccessible areas of his mind. As he passed the Wapendwa, all the good deeds they had done in their lives were presented to him. The images zipped like flashes of lightening, but D'Melo's elevated mind was unchallenged.

Suddenly, the original king appeared before D'Melo's eyes. He sat majestically astride a hippo, nearly close enough for D'Melo to touch. As if it was happening at this moment, D'Melo listened to the original king give the address to the Wapendwa that gave birth to Kipaji. He relished every word.

Zara dismounted and took her place along the innermost circle of light. Chants of "*Falme Roho*" morphed into a jubilant frenzy. As D'Melo entered the Tabernacle, the Wapendwa offered the Kipaji salute.

"On this day, over two thousand years ago, we stood on this very spot," D'Melo elucidated with great poise, his eyes mighty and piercing. "We made a covenant. You promised to follow the way of the Great Spirit. In return, we promised that if you ever strayed from the path of unity, we would return unto you. We stand before you today as the embodiment of that promise. To ensure lasting harmony and the advancement of this hallowed land, we must now recommit to the Covenant of Kipaji." Clicks of approval rippled out from the innermost circle until the whole community clicked in unison.

Zara heard D'Melo in her heart. *Did you hear when I said, 'hallowed'?*

Ahhh, yeah, she responded curiously.

It was a good word, he asserted with hopeful excitement. *You need to clunk it into the good word jar!*

Dude, you're already a king. Do you really need to win the 'good word' game too?"

D'Melo, while continuing his speech to the Wapendwa, peered at Zara and nodded vigorously.

Oh, my God. She shook her head. *Okay, I'll think about it.*

The chairperson of the Council approached D'Melo, stopping just outside the Tabernacle. She addressed the Wapendwa.

"The first order of business is to officially recognize the monarchy, a calling from the Great Spirit. The Council hereby acknowledges Yabo Jakanda, son of Mujiza and Diata Jakanda, brother of Kavu Jakanda, a descendant of the people of Amanzi, and the son of Kipaji, as the *Falme wa Kipaji!* The King of Kipaji! A deafening ovation shook the valley. Zara tried to ululate. An elderly woman beside her giggled.

Zara rumpled an eye. "That bad, huh?" The woman gave a pitying nod.

"Now," the chairperson's lips stretched into a gleaming smile. "We are immensely excited and privileged to present a very special guest. The Council realizes that this is highly unusual, but we think you will want to hear what this gentleman has to say."

She signaled toward the Choma forest. The crowd vied to glimpse the visitor. "Please give a warm Kipaji reception for Taj Amani, President of Malunga." Hoots of stunned adulation resounded. President Amani thanked the chairperson and bowed before D'Melo.

"I'm truly humbled to be the only president of Malunga to ever lay feet on this sacred land. When I was a boy, my father, President Jaru Amani, would tell me stories about the Legend of the Spirit King. To most Malungans, they were just far-fetched tales that the government created to explain away its terribly unsuccessful invasion of Kipaji. But I always wanted to believe that they were true. It brought me comfort to trust that there was some supernatural force for good in the world. So I allowed my imagination to run wild. When my schoolmates and I would play-fight, I'd fancy myself a Kipaji warrior. My friends had no idea what I was I doing, but of course, I'd always win the fights." The Wapendwa chortled. "I would even imagine myself with the King of Kipaji, solving all of the world's problems together. And here I am today, standing alongside his majesty."

"I've never doubted that this land is the Great Spirit's most favored spot. Among all the regions of the world, he chose *you*—the people of Kipaji—to deliver his healing to the world, a most pressing challenge. I vow to do everything in my power to assist you with this formidable endeavor. As a start, my first official act as president of Malunga is to grant Kipaji independence. So, as of this moment, you are your own country, the determiners of your own fate." A gasp of delight erupted into booming cheers and ululation.

D'Melo thanked President Amani, then set out his plan to offer Kipaji's gift to the world. A few seeds from the Heart would be entrusted to the Global Health Organization, the institution that Ameka headed. In consultation with D'Melo and Zara, the GHO would determine the optimal regions to plant the seeds. Each Tree would be protected by conjurers trained by D'Melo.

"With the Wapendwa's blessing," D'Melo requested, "Zara and I will travel to America briefly to begin this process." Clicks of approval followed.

"Now, there is one final order of business before we commune with our ancestors. Our most venerable and beloved soul, Upendo Akachi, Milpisi, has made his ascension to the eternal realm. He departed this world the way he lived in it—a selfless servant of Kipaji." Low ululation rose from the crowd, indicating sadness. "He left very large shoes to fill. But the Great Spirit has blessed us with a worthy soul."

Chants rang out immediately: "Zar-ra! Zar-ra! Zar-ra!" Zara's face flushed red, as she joined D'Melo in the Tabernacle.

"Zara, Kipaji will be forever in your debt. Without your courage in the face of grave danger, I would not be standing here and Kipaji would now be in the hands of treacherous men. We humbly request that you accept this most lofty and weighty position as the Milpisi."

Zara covered her face and whispered, "I'll accept as long as you don't make me touch the poopie seeds."

D'Melo guffawed. The Wapendwa murmured, not understanding what just happened. "You see what you made me do?" D'Melo chided, trying to compose himself. "Now they're not gonna respect me."

"Just cause an earthquake or something. Trust me, the respect will come right back."

Zara uncovered her face and addressed the Wapendwa. "I couldn't be more honored to serve the country of Kipaji as the Milpisi."

The assembly ululated in ecstasy at hearing, "the *country* of Kipaji" for the first time.

"If I can be half the healer that Milpisi was, I will be overjoyed. Now, let me not waste one more moment. It's time to hasten the Kinfuna."

Zara pivoted to D'Melo and gibed, "*Kinfuna* means, 'Reunion.' It's when the ancestors—

"I know what it means," D'Melo said, pressing his lips together. "You're hilarious."

"Well, we know your Kipaji is a tad on the nonexistent side," she laughed, as she hustled off to do the Unveiling.

CHAPTER NINETEEN

Destiny

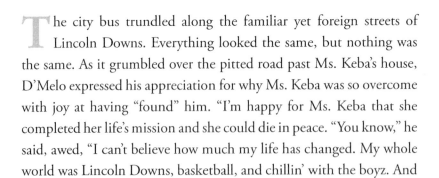

The city bus trundled along the familiar yet foreign streets of Lincoln Downs. Everything looked the same, but nothing was the same. As it grumbled over the pitted road past Ms. Keba's house, D'Melo expressed his appreciation for why Ms. Keba was so overcome with joy at having "found" him. "I'm happy for Ms. Keba that she completed her life's mission and she could die in peace. "You know," he said, awed, "I can't believe how much my life has changed. My whole world was Lincoln Downs, basketball, and chillin' with the boyz. And now…" he shook his head. "Who would have ever thought?"

Zara barely acknowledged D'Melo's incredulity. Her mind was elsewhere. She gazed out the mega-sized bus window, briefly glimpsing the tree she scaled to Ms. Keba's bedroom. Her thoughts shifted to the fragility of life. *What if something happens to me? Who will administer the nectar? What if I'm not humble enough for Haya, and people die?* The responsibility of being the Milpisi nudged anxiously against her ribs. *I'm just eighteen.* She applied relieving pressure between her eyebrows and took centering breaths. A tender hand slid into hers.

"Are you okay?" D'Melo enquired.

"Yeah, I'm good," she said without conviction.

The bus squealed to a halt in front of the drug store.

"Tell your grandparents I'll stop by tomorrow and teach them my Nečzian dance moves."

Images of D'Melo's, let's just say, *unique*, traditional Nečzian dancing tickled her. She flung her backpack over her shoulder and descended the narrow bus stairs. She lingered on the sunbaked sidewalk, her eyes fixed on D'Melo, a clenched fist over her heart. After the bus rounded the corner, she swung the shop door open. *Ding-Ding! Ding-Ding!* The bells chimed sweet welcome.

Tomáš called, "Babička, a crazy redhead just walked in the door!" A pot slammed in the kitchen sink. Babička's sixty-five-year-old legs carried her as swiftly as they could down the stairs. She wrapped Zara in her flabby grandmother arms.

"Ohhh, Zara." Her hands, wet from washing dishes, pressed Zara's face into an involuntary pucker. "We missed you so much!"

"Babička," Zara warbled, pleasantly surprised by the display of affection. "It's only been two weeks!" She rubbed her cheeks dry with the knobs of her shoulders.

"How long are you here for?" Babička asked, hopeful.

"Do you really want to talk about that already?"

Babička's eyes signaled an emphatic, *Yes.*

"Well," Zara said gently. "I go back in a few days."

The energy in the store deflated momentarily. "Well, we'll just have to make the most of each moment we have you."

Tomáš chimed, "How about my homey?"

"Ahhh . . ." Zara lifted a brow. "I assume you mean D'Melo?"

"Fo shizzle my nizzle." Tomáš explained his wildly inappropriate response. "For you street-illiterate folks, that simply means, 'For sure my n—'"

"Hey! No!" Zara shut him down, swaying a chastising finger. "You *cannot* say that word . . . *EVER!* I don't care how many street gangs you've joined since I left.

"As for D'Melo, he's going back with me." She lifted a sympathetic cheek. "Sorry, I know how much you like hanging out with him."

"Ahh, it's okay," Tomáš acquiesced. "I still got my other homies."

"Who?" Zara narrowed her eyes questioningly. "Your bingo crew?"

"No. Jey, Kaz, and Marley-Mar."

"Oh, my God." Zara shot gaping eyes at her grandmother. "Who *is* this dude?"

Babička shrugged and giggled.

The mouthwatering aroma of *jollof* rice and *githeri* filled Baba's house. Attired in traditional African garb (and Zara's chef's hats), the boyz helped D'Melo put the finishing touches on their favorite Kipaji dishes.

As Zara waltzed into the kitchen, D'Melo leered at her. "Mmmm-um!" he cooed," his eyes browsing her lasciviously.

"Quit it, dude. You don't have X-ray vision," she snipped. "I can feel your heart, remember? And trust me, if you could see through my clothes," she maneuvered her hands provocatively over her body, "your heart would be beating a *lot* faster."

"Ohhh, snap!" the boyz chorused.

"Keep him real, Zara." Jeylan chuckled at her uncharacteristic sauciness.

"Now who's the jerk!" D'Melo said, trying to bridle the smile spreading his cheeks.

While D'Melo, Zara and the boyz were in Kipaji, Zara's grandparents and Ameka had rallied the community to restore Baba's home. No hint of the horrifying tragedy remained. But still, none of them dared to acknowledge the transformation. They rather chose to reminisce about happier times—their days in Kipaji. But they found words inadequate to describe their experience. It seemed surreal, like a shared conscious dream. After a wordless moment, they simply conceded that they had experienced something extraordinary, something that had bonded them in the deepest of ways. The world of Lincoln Downs suddenly felt very small.

D'Melo expressed his lament at not having been able to be at Pharma when Wilem heard the recording on stage.

"You should've seen that fool's face," Jeylan chirped. "I think he had an accident in his underwear!" They all doubled over in laughter, as the boyz each had a go at mimicking Wilem.

They settled into their usual seats around the dinner table. Baba's chair remained his. They even arranged a place setting for him. An impromptu moment of silence was observed for Baba before D'Melo offered the Sunday dinner toast.

"Baba always had something enlightening to say. His toasts gave me the strength and belief in myself to make it through another week." They all *clicked,* like the Wapendwa. "So I think it would be fitting to offer something straight from Baba's lips. When I was hatin' on Africa, he told me something that I didn't appreciate at the time. Now it dwells deep in my heart. He said, 'Africa isn't something you can understand sitting on a couch in Lincoln Downs. To know Africa, you have to touch it, you have to breathe it, taste it, smell it. It's a place of spirit. So to understand it, you have to lead with your soul. Once you do, you'll realize that Africa is pure magic.'"

"Truth," Zara whimpered, dabbing her eyes. "Take 'em to church Baba."

They raised their glasses. "*Kwa uzima.*"

As they dug into the meal, they began discussing their futures. Kazim had received a scholarship to play basketball at a small college in Western Pennsylvania.

"That's awesome, Kaz," D'Melo said. "I'm so happy for you!"

D'Melo turned to Marley. "What about you, Marls?"

Marley flapped a letter in front of him. It was a scholarship to MIT. Apparently, someone at the university saw his interview on the news after the Pharma shareholder meeting. "When they realized that I took down Dimka and saved Kipaji, they were like—" Marley cupped his mouth for effect, "'Yo! This Marley is a boss! We gotta give him his chedda!'"

D'Melo jested about being glad that they were all there to assist Marbleman in his liberation of Kipaji. Marley paid no heed to D'Melo's sarcasm, as he crumbled the letter exaggeratedly.

"I'm a hero, so now all of a sudden they want me," Marley scoffed. "They need to recognize; I was a hero before Kipaji. I just hadn't done anything yet." He shot the balled-up letter toward the trashcan and missed terribly. "I've decided to join Kaz at his school. Y'all know this fool can't do anything without me." Marley gave Kazim a playful tap on the arm.

As for Jeylan, there was something he needed to do before he could even think about what was next for his life. He explained that upon returning from Kipaji, he went straight to the drugstore. He confessed to Tomáš that he was the one who vandalized the store. He apologized profusely and genuinely conveyed that he would understand if Tomáš called the police.

Jeylan turned to Zara. "Did your grandfather tell you what he did? He offered me a job! He said that he sees potential in me. When I thanked him," Jeylan grinned, "he gave me a fist bump and said, 'Fo shizzle my nizzle.'"

"Oh, my God!" Zara threw mortified hands over her face.

"Nah, it's cool. I like him. He's good people."

All eyes shifted to D'Melo. Now that he was no longer in jeopardy, he was free to settle back into his lifelong plan—UPenn, then the NBA. But D'Melo didn't surprise anyone when he said proudly, "Kipaji's my home. I owe it to my people to rebuild it."

The boyz smiled and sighed. "Yeah, that's what we figured."

To D'Melo's chagrin, Marley provided a less-then-merry community update. Chubby's restaurant had closed. The moment Chubby got wind that Dimka was removed from power, he packed up and moved back to Malunga. Also, after Baba was killed, Wilson's Billiards Hall relocated to the less colorful neighborhood of Leighland, seeking more peaceful surrounds.

Sensing a dispirited mood, D'Melo took it upon himself to be the bearer of glad tidings. Just before the boyz arrived, the director of the health clinic had paid him a visit. She informed him that the clinic changed its name to honor Baba. It was now called the Dr. Imari Bantu Health Clinic.

"That's real chill," Jeylan said. "Baba will never be forgotten around here."

"Yeah," D'Melo hummed, "but only if we can keep the clinic open." The clinic had been running on fumes for months. Barring a small miracle, its financial coffers would be empty before the end of the year.

"I hit up the ballers on the All-American team," D'Melo said. "They agreed to play a charity game at the Citadel to raise money for the clinic."

"Yo! That's lit," Kazim said. "You think they'll let me ball with them?" Seeing no affirmative response on the horizon, he toned it down. "Just for a couple minutes?"

D'Melo grinned. "I'll see what I can do."

Jeylan tossed a dampening dose of Lincoln Downs reality over the excitement. "You know T-Bo's gonna have his greedy hands in this. There ain't no way that fool's gonna have all that looch pour into this community without taking the lion's share."

"You don't have worry about T-Bo," D'Melo assured him. "Do you know that that dude was waiting for me outside my house when I got back from Kipaji? He tried again to persuade me to go to a better basketball college. When I told him that I was moving to Kipaji, he lost it. He pulled out his gun and pointed it at my face. If I'm not headed to the NBA, my life is worth nothing to him."

Zara gasped.

"The neighbors noticed what was happening and crowded around us. A few folks took out their phones and started videoing, I guess to dissuade T-Bo from pulling the trigger."

"What happened next?" Marley asked, anxious.

"Well, amazingly, the muzzle of the gun melted shut. It was a miracle." D'Melo smirked. "Then, T-Bo's belt buckle came loose. He grabbed his sagging pants just before they fell to his knees."

"Ah man, dawg," Jeylan said, chortling. "I would have given anything to see T-Bo's undies."

"T-Bo's belt seemed to have a mind of its own," D'Melo continued. "It slipped out of the belt loops and started whipping back and forth, with T-Bo holding on to the buckle. The people in the crowd were stunned at first, but then broke out laughing when T-Bo starting to spank his own behind with the belt."

"That's awesome!" Kazim said. "That fool finally got what he deserves."

"But that's not even the best part," D'Melo chuckled. "He took off running down the street, trying to keep his pants up with one hand and spanking himself with the other."

Zara and the boyz were now in a full guffaw. Marley laughed so hard that he fell out of his chair.

"So," D'Melo said, gratified. "As soon as the videos are uploaded to the Internet, T-Bo's street cred will be dust. He's finished in Philly… maybe everywhere."

"Well, that was quite a well-timed 'miracle,'" Zara said dubiously.

"I guess I'm just lucky," D'Melo said with a wink, as he motioned upward with his finger. A spoon lifted from the table and stood on edge. It whittled into a tiny metal person then pirouetted into a shuffle dance.

Zara shook her head. "Show off."

D'Melo began clearing the table, anticipating the usual amusing excuses from the boyz. He wondered wistfully whether their harrowing experience in Kipaji had heightened their level of responsibility and maturity, half-hoping that it didn't. Marley clinked dishes clumsily atop each other and hauled them to the kitchen, teetering all the way. D'Melo sighed disappointedly.

"All right, y'all," Jeylan muttered contentedly, rubbing his belly. "That was a slammin' meal."

Ahhh yeah! Here it comes. D'Melo clanked a bowl back onto the dining table, not wanting to miss a moment of the evening's main entertainment.

"I wish I could stay and help y'all, but I gotta bounce. My diabetic neighbor needs me to clip her toenails," Jeylan said deadpan. "Y'all got the dishes this time?"

"*This* time?" Marley snorted. "Don't you mean, *every* time!"

"Word, Jey," Kazim piled on. "You never help. You always got some excuse."

"So you gonna stay?" Jeylan said, skeptically.

"I wish I could, yo." They all shook their heads. "But I got a date early in the morning. So I gotta catch some Z's."

"You? A date?" Jeylan countered. "Man, please. At least I gave a somewhat believable excuse."

"For real, dawg," Kazim said. "I'm Skyping Jua. She can only use the library computer during her lunch break. That's 5 a.m. here!"

"Good for you, Kazim." Zara gave him a fist bump. "Tell Jua I said hello."

"What about you Marls?" D'Melo prodded. "What's your excuse?"

"Well, I didn't have a good one. But now I do. I gotta help this fool figure out how to make a Skype call."

"Tru dat!" Kazim chirped, tossing his bony arm over Marley's shoulders. "You alright, dawg."

Jeylan paused at the door. "Man, we gonna miss y'all. But we'll come to Kipaji before the end of the summer. D, you know I'm always here for you. If anyone over there is punkin' you, just holler. I mean, I know you got those superpowers and all, but you might need some muscle to deliver an old-fashioned beat down," Jeylan flexed. "Naw mean?"

"Thanks, Jey. That's comforting," D'Melo said sarcastically. "So when the flesh-burning steam and fifty-pound fireballs start raining down on us, I'll be sure to call you."

"Well . . . now that you put it that way," Jeylan waffled. "I might be like—" He pretended to hold a phone to his ear. "Huh? D'Melo? Whatcha say? I can't hear you. *Click.*" He gestured hanging up the call. The boyz chuckled, as they hopped down the stoop.

Marley spun back. "Oh, I almost forgot to tell you. Remember you had all those questions about Gemini? Well, guess what?" he beamed nerdily. "Astronomers just discovered a new star in the constellation." D'Melo and Zara together blew a satisfied breath, *It's Kavu, he's immortal now, like Castor.*

The boyz raised four fingers, clenched a fist, and tapped their hearts. "*Falme Roho!*" They bounced off into the night, cracking jokes and causing enough of a ruckus to disturb the neighbors.

"I'm gonna miss those guys," D'Melo said.

"Yeah, me too." Zara slipped her arm under D'Melo's and settled her head on his shoulder.

D'Melo started for the kitchen, where a mountain of dinnerware awaited.

"All right then," Zara jested. "I gotta go feed my plants and water my goldfish." She shuffled toward the door.

D'Melo snagged the back of her shirt. "You better get back here."

Zara chuckled. "I wash, you dry."

D'Melo was trying to embrace his new life and let go of the one he had always envisioned for himself. Returning to Kipaji meant leaving his friends, who loved him unconditionally; Lincoln Downs, the community that had warmly embraced Baba and him from the moment they arrived on that blustery winter day; and basketball, the game that he loved and that had given him so much. But his heart hollowed when he pondered his greatest sacrifice. As the King of Kipaji he could never get married or have children.

His eyes shifted to Zara. She was a whirlwind at the sink, water splashing and suds flying everywhere. Her hair was disheveled, with several unruly strands escaping the hairband, tickling her cheek. She took a swipe at them, smearing a clump of bubbly lather onto her forehead.

D'Melo smiled, the ache in his heart allayed temporarily. "Here, let me get that." He herded her silky hair into a tidy tail and twisted the band around it. He then attempted to relieve her of the washing.

"Get out of here, dude. I got this." Zara nudged him away with a sprightly hip. "You're just trying to take credit for all the work I've done so far."

"*You got this*, huh? Like that time you threw soup at those lunatics and almost scalded my face off?"

"No, I got this, *like*—" she lifted a bowl from the sink. Gray, granular water teetered menacingly at the brim. She turned his way, grinning impishly.

"You wouldn't dare."

"Really?" She slung the water at him. He threw his arms out, gaping at his soaked shirt. Zara laughed until D'Melo snatched up a dingy dishcloth.

"You better not!" she said, backpedaling. She turned and dashed off in a giggle. D'Melo chased her into the living room. He wrapped her in a bear hug from behind. She squealed and twisted from side to side as he smothered her face in the sopping cloth.

Pluh-pluh, she puffed the bitter metallic detergent from her lips. "You're lucky I'm not wearing makeup, dude. You'd be in big trouble."

D'Melo spun her around, their bodies so close he could feel her quickened heartbeat thumping against his ribs. He gazed longingly into her twinkly emerald eyes. His heart throbbed achingly, fighting the urge to touch her lips with his. Words edged tentatively to his tongue.

"I—" he waffled, his heartbeat now keeping pace with hers. He blew a long steadying breath, then tried again. "I lo—"

Zara laid a finger over his lips. "Please don't." Her voice quavered. "This is hard enough already. I'm still trying to accept that we can never be together. But if I hear you say those words—" She blinked back tears, trying desperately to prevent her emotions from sweeping her to places she couldn't go. "This is our destiny."

D'Melo leaned in. His stubble brushed lightly against her moist cheek. She shuddered. His hot breath must have tingled her neck because goosebumps immediately rose on her arms. He then whispered tenderly in her welcoming ear. "Your face smells like a dirty dish rag."

"Oh, my God! You're the biggest jerk in the world!" she said, through a laughing cry.

Just then, the wall clock chimed nine times, awakening crestfallen memories. The momentary cheer on D'Melo's face drained.

"Hey punk," she said. "*The World This Week* is starting. Wanna watch with me?"

A bittersweet smile passed swiftly across D'Melo's lips. He hemmed and hawed like he always would with Baba. "There's only gonna be horrible things on there, you know."

Zara replied just how Baba would have. "You need to be informed about what's happening in the world you live in." She padded the sofa cushion next to her. D'Melo plopped himself down.

The newscaster opened with a story from Nečzia. The program cut to the reporter on the ground. The reporter pressed an earpiece tightly to her ear. "Thanks, Rob," she shouted over the clamor of the protesters behind her.

Reporter: "I'm live in Venn, the capital city of the Republic of Nečzia. Thousands of people have poured onto the streets to protest the presidential election results. A little over an hour ago, it was announced that Pavlik Drobny won by a narrow margin."

Zara's face swelled tensely. D'Melo quickly switched off the television, realizing that the program was about the man who assaulted her mother. "Turn it back on, please," Zara said, trembling. "I need to watch this." D'Melo reluctantly compiled. He scooted closer to her and laid a sympathetic arm around her.

Reporter: "I'm here with Jakub Novák, the organizer of the protest. So Jakub, tell us what's the reason for the outcry?"

Jakub Novák: "We've had a democratic society for twenty-six years. That's all changed now. Drobny used his money and influence to sway the election in his favor. He sent hundreds of people to communities that support the opposing party to threaten violence if they didn't vote for him. Also, tens of thousands of ballots have been 'lost' from opposition areas."

Reporter: "I interviewed the Director for the EU commission overseeing the elections. She said those allegations are being investigated."

Jakub Novák: "Let's be real. The Western world will never force a revote, no matter what the commission finds. It got the guy it wanted. It's common knowledge that Nečzia is the number one producer of livestock in Europe. But did you know that Drobny's livestock company is the continent's largest, making it critical to the economy. So the EU will never risk having Nečzia implode over a revote.

"Ten years ago, we were a quiet country of hard-working people enjoying a simple life. And then one man decided that Nečzia would become a world leader in livestock production. His company deforested millions of pristine acres to make room for pastureland and growing animal feed. People protested vehemently as slaughterhouses overwhelmed their communities with the stench of death and caustic pollutants. During a short period, the incidents of cancer rose over 500 percent. The community protests mushroomed and spread to major cities. Then suddenly, the movement's most prominent leaders started disappearing one by one. To this day, their families don't know what happened to them—but we do.

"Then, a few years ago, the government finally cracked down on deforestation for animal feed. Because Drobny could no longer expand his empire in Nečzia, he made a deal with Malunga for seven million acres. There have already been reports of a growing health crisis in the villages near the slaughterhouses."

> **Reporter:** "Just before the election, three women came forward and accused Drobny of assault. He brushed it off as a ploy by the opposition to defame him before the voting. Your thoughts?"

D'Melo looked at Zara, whose face had blanched. He slipped his hand into hers and gave a gentle squeeze, reminding her that she wasn't alone.

> **Jakub Novák:** "I don't know about those particular accusations. But what I can tell you is, Drobny has a very long history of such allegations from scores of women."

Reporter: "Thank you, Jakub. Back to you, Rob."

Zara remained perfectly motionless, rooted in her cushion for seemingly an eternity. D'Melo waited anxiously for which Zara would emerge from the news that her father was now the president of Nečzia. *Will she crumble into an emotional heap, like she did on the way home from the Poconos? Will she spiral inward and shut down, like she did when grappling with telling me about moving to Malunga. Or will she fly into a rage and want to burn everything to the ground, like she did when . . . well, like she usually does.*

Zara scooted to the edge of the couch. She braced herself with her hands, as if preparing to leave. She tucked her lips and took in a lengthy breath. Her eyes placid, she turned calmly to D'Melo.

Hmmm, this is new, D'Melo thought, wondering who this woman was sitting next to him. *She looks like Zara, but—*

"On our way back to Kipaji," she uttered, intensely even. "What do you say we take a detour?"

D'Melo's expression turned dimly pleased. "I was hoping you'd say that."

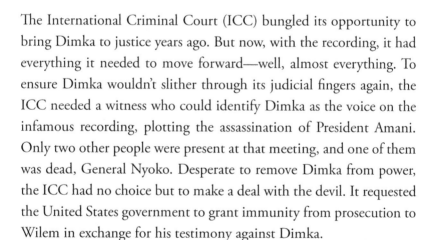

EPILOGUE

The Fire of Justice

The International Criminal Court (ICC) bungled its opportunity to bring Dimka to justice years ago. But now, with the recording, it had everything it needed to move forward—well, almost everything. To ensure Dimka wouldn't slither through its judicial fingers again, the ICC needed a witness who could identify Dimka as the voice on the infamous recording, plotting the assassination of President Amani. Only two other people were present at that meeting, and one of them was dead, General Nyoko. Desperate to remove Dimka from power, the ICC had no choice but to make a deal with the devil. It requested the United States government to grant immunity from prosecution to Wilem in exchange for his testimony against Dimka.

When Wilem was approached with the immunity deal, he rejected it outright. Immunity in the United States alone would not do. He knew he could still be prosecuted in Malunga. So Wilem demanded that the deal include that he could not be extradited to Malunga to face trial. At the urging of the ICC, the U.S. Attorney General agreed.

The immunity deal leaked to the public. Social media caught fire. Protests erupted outside Pharma headquarters. In a flash, they turned violent. Protesters hurled bricks at the building, shattering windows. Luxury cars in the Pharma parking lot were overturned and set ablaze. Police disbursed the mob with tear gas and rubber bullets. The protesters, lungs burning and throats constricting, scrambled frantically for breathable air.

Meanwhile, Wilem was released from jail. A gaggle of reporters spat questions at him like poisonous darts. At the instruction of his attorney, Wilem ignored the questions as he edged through the horde and ducked into a limousine. But unable to resist the temptation to rub his victory in everyone's face, he slid down the tinted window. The reporters bustled toward the car and readied their notepads.

"When I was wrongfully arrested," Wilem said, "I told the FBI agents that I have the best lawyers in the country and that I'd be out in no time. And what do you know," he shrugged gloatingly. "*Voila*. Here I am! That's why America is the greatest country in the world. Justice is always served!" The window slid up and the limo shot for the airport.

The following morning, Wilem was escorted to The Hague in the Netherlands. He arrived at the ICC in a black government van. United Nations security personnel scoped the streets and rooftops, assessing potential threats. Getting the all-clear signal, Wilem emerged. Security ushered him hurriedly past the jeers of a furious crowd. Upon entering the ICC, Wilem observed, "It's amazing how people can be so hateful." Disgust surfaced on the faces of the typically stoic security guards.

Wilem, dressed in his finest Armani suit, took a seat at a shiny wooden table. A panel of four dignified and no-nonsense jurists sat before him on a raised platform. Wilem avoided the stern of eye of the panelist wearing a traditional African dress—Senegalese, to be more precise. She gestured to the court stenographer to begin transcribing the hearing.

The proceeding commenced with a formal explanation of what was expected of Wilem. He was required to answer all the panel's questions, honestly and fully. Failing to do so would violate the terms of his immunity deal.

During the first hour, Wilem delved into Dimka's corrupt financial practices. Sensing that Wilem was minimizing Pharma's role in the corruption, the panel pressed him on the millions of dollars he paid to Dimka for access to the sacred land of the Shujas. Wilem defensively alleged that Dimka had similar deals with several industries—mining, oil, and animal agriculture. The companies were from all over the world, including America, China, Nečzia, "and," Wilem paused smugly, "this country we're sitting in right now, The Netherlands."

Panelist (Senegal): "Mr. VanLuten, the panel hears the point you're attempting to make. But for the purposes of this hearing, it is neither here nor there. So let us get to the objective for the day. Please tell the panel what you know about the plot to assassinate President Jaru Amani."

Wilem VanLuten: "When it was discovered that Amani was going to enter a peace agreement with the Shujas and grant sovereignty over the Nyumbani, Dimka flew into a rage. Shuja sovereignty meant no more access to valuable resources—namely oil, gold, and medicinal products.

"Dimka called me, ranting. I suggested that President Amani could be dealt with. Dimka shushed me. He said, 'Not over the phone.' That evening, I received a call. The voice on the other end told me to go to an abandoned warehouse on the outskirts of Yandun. From there, I was driven to a secret location in the countryside. I found out later that it was the family cottage of General Nyoko's wife. During the meeting, I suggested that one option was to get rid of Amani."

Panelist (Brazil): "Could you be more specific when you say, 'get rid of Amani'"?

Wilem VanLuten: "I think you know what I mean."

Panelist (Brazil): "We need you to be clear for the record."

Wilem VanLuten: Wilem sighed, irritated. "Ending his life, okay? Is that clear enough!"

Panelist (Senegal): "What was your interest in, as you so nonchalantly put it, 'ending Amani's life'"?

Wilem VanLuten: "Purely business. I had no animus toward President Amani. Amani's granting of sovereignty of the Nyumbani would have had a devastating effect on Pharma's financial interests. I didn't care one way or another how Amani was removed."

Panelist (Germany): "Exactly what suggestion did you offer?"

Wilem VanLuten: "I mentioned that President Amani would be most vulnerable on his way to the airport. General Nyoko was responsible for his security, so he was privy to which vehicle Amani would be in. With that information, it would be relatively simple to kill Amani. They could blow up his car with missiles from shoulder launchers."

Panelist (Vietnam): "I think you're neglecting another part of your involvement. The launchers were not the type that the Malungan military used. You secured those weapons for President Dimka, correct?"

Wilem VanLuten: "No, not exactly. All I did was connect Dimka with someone that could get him the launchers."

Panelist (Brazil): *"Someone?"* The interviewer leafed through documents and slid out a photo of a burly guy wearing an eye patch. "This someone?" She flipped the photo over for Wilem to see. "Isn't this Zachariah Rotman? Your friend?"

Wilem VanLuten: "Well, I guess you can say he was my friend. We were in the Marines together."

Panelist (Brazil): "Isn't he the same friend who was granted land in the Nyumbani, through your insistence with Dimka, to grow poppy for his illegal opium business?"

Wilem VanLuten: "Yes."

Panelist (Senegal): "I understand that you benefitted substantially from that opium business." The interviewer ran her finger down the page. "Here it is. You made approximately $12 million."

Wilem turned to his attorney, unsure whether he should respond to this allegation. His attorney gestured for him to answer.

Wilem VanLuten: "I don't have the exact figures, but that sounds about right."

Panelist (Vietnam): "Mr. VanLuten. You sit before this panel and try to distance yourself from the assassination of President Amani. But the truth is, it was your idea to kill him. Then you provided President Dimka the means to execute the plan. Not only that, but you also suggested to make it look as though the Shuja rebels were responsible. Is that not a fair representation of your involvement?"

Wilem VanLuten: Wilem stiffened, veins protruding on his temples.

"I want to remind this panel that I am not the one under investigation here." Wilem's attorney clutched his elbow to calm him. Wilem angrily thrust the attorney's hand off. "Even if that's a fair representation, and I'm not saying that it is, I have immunity, so why does it matter!"

Wilem's callousness riled the panelists. They vied to respond to his question, overlapping one another with scorn. The Senegalese interviewer's voice rose above the rest.

Panelist (Senegal): "Mr. VanLuten, do you not realize that your actions set in motion a genocide in Malunga? I don't think we have to remind you that over a half a million Shujas were killed. Innocent men, women, and children were butchered all because the Borutus were led to believe that the Shuja rebels assassinated President Amani, which was your suggestion!"

Wilem VanLuten: "Well, I couldn't have known that would happen!" Wilem shouted. "What kind of people would slaughter their own countrymen like that? I just wanted to do business. It's not my fault the Borutus are savages!"

Panelist (Senegal): "Mr. VanLuten, your anger isn't helping anyone. I would encourage you to take a break to get a hold of yourself before you say something that you'll regret."

Wilem VanLuten: "No. I'm fine. Let's finish this so I can get out of this godforsaken country."

Panelist (Germany): "As you wish. Please tell the panel who recorded your conversation with Dimka."

Wilem VanLuten: "General Nyoko suggested we hold the meeting at the cottage so he could set up the recording. Obviously, neither

Dimka nor I knew what he was planning. Nyoko was shrewd. He wanted something in his back pocket in case he ever needed leverage—you know, for a 'rainy day.'" Wilem shrugged, "That's how things work in Africa."

Panelist (Senegal): "Africa may work that way, but it's thanks to people like you," she simmered. The other panelists reeled her in, reminding her to stay focused on the matter at hand. "My apologies. My personal feelings have no place in this hearing. So, getting back to the recording, are you saying that President Dimka never knew it existed?"

Wilem VanLuten: "That's correct." The panelists shuffled anxiously through their documents. They searched for evidence of Dimka's involvement in the recovery of the recording, which would link him to the killing of D'Melo's parents.

  Wilem elucidated, "Nyoko only told Dimka that Dr. Bantu had some incriminating evidence against him. He couldn't say what that evidence was exactly. If Dimka discovered it was a recording of our conversation, he would have known that Nyoko betrayed him."

Panelist (Germany): "So how did the recording get into the hands of Dr. Bantu?"

Wilem VanLuten: "When this court was investigating Dimka and Nyoko back in 2004 for the assassination and the Shuja genocide, Nyoko set up an exile for himself. Kuzbejistan was going to grant him asylum, but for one million dollars. He didn't have that much money on hand, so he blackmailed me. He knew I'd pay him the money, whereas Dimka was more likely to pay him with a bullet through his skull.

  "The general called me to set up a meeting to exchange the money for the recording. I couldn't risk being seen with Nyoko because of the ICC's unsavory allegations against him. That would have reflected poorly on me and Pharma. I also couldn't send Zac because a meeting between General Nyoko and a mercenary who at one time trained Shuja rebels would have raised eyebrows. So I sent my assistant, Jasiri Tomu. But I didn't tell her the contents of exchange." Wilem's gaze briefly dropped to the table. In all that he had done, the only thing he seemed to regret was Jasiri's death. Jasiri had been with Wilem from his earliest days in Africa.

"I sent Zac with Jasiri to shadow her. The exchange went smoothly. But in the days following, I noticed that Jasiri was acting strange. She was distant and unusually fidgety. Then she said she needed to fly to England to take care of her sick father. Her father had visited her only a month earlier and seemed as healthy and spry as a person half his age.

"My gut was telling me that something was wrong. So I asked Zac whether he was with Jasiri the whole time—up to the meeting with Nyoko and until they returned. He assured me that she never left his sight. But then he remembered that after the exchange, Jasiri said she was having stomach trouble and dashed off to the bathroom.

"Zac knew that Jasiri was a trusted employee—well, I'd even call her a friend. So he didn't have a reason to doubt her. But after a couple of minutes, he got nervous. He shot to the bathroom. By the time he got there, Jasiri was already on her way out. She was only in there for a short time, but obviously long enough to copy the part of the recording that you've heard."

Panelist (Vietnam): "Pardon the interruption, but I'm confused, Mr. VanLuten. You mentioned that Ms. Tomu didn't know what was being exchanged. So why would she have been prepared to make a copy of the recording?"

Wilem VanLuten: "Well, I didn't say that Jasiri didn't know. I said that I didn't tell her. I assume that when Nyoko called to set up the meeting, Jasiri never disconnected her end when she passed the call to my phone. That's the only thing I can figure. So, unbeknownst to me, she must have overheard our conversation.

"At first, it didn't make sense why Jasiri would risk her life to copy the recording. But after she died, I discovered that her mother was Shuja. You see, in Malunga, you take on the tribe of your father. So the Tribal Records Office registered her as a Borutu. Apparently, Jasiri's mother was brutally killed in the geno-cide. So the recording was her chance to get justice for her mother and all Shujas.

"Now, to finish answering your original question, on the day Jasiri was to leave for England, she became gravely ill. She was rushed to the hospital. Dr. Bantu was the physician who treated her. Jasiri must have realized that she wasn't going to survive. So she slipped Dr. Bantu the copy of the recording before she died."

Panelist (Vietnam): "I believe you are again leaving out pertinent information. How did Ms. Tomu die?"

Wilem VanLuten: "Apparently, she ate a poisonous mushroom."

Panelist (Germany): "That particular deadly mushroom, Death Cap, isn't found in Central Africa. How did it get to Malunga?"

Wilem VanLuten: "I don't know."

Panelist (Germany): The interviewer held up a document. "At that time, you were based in South Africa, where Death Cap grows. This is quite a coincidence. Mr. VanLuten, I want to remind you that your immunity is dependent on your full cooperation and truthful testi-mony. Now, I'm going to ask you one more time, how did that poi-sonous mushroom end up in Jasiri's breakfast?"

Wilem VanLuten: Wilem sighed lamentably. "I brought it from South Africa at the request of General Nyoko. He threatened the cook at the restaurant where Jasiri ate every morning. The cook mixed the mushroom into her meal."

Panelist (Vietnam): "Before we move on, Mr. VanLuten, you should know that Ms. Tomu did not die from the mushroom. The autopsy revealed that she died by asphyxiation. Someone suffocated her."

Wilem sagged heavily in his chair, while the panel thumbed through the next set of documents.

Panelist (Brazil): "Please tell us about your involvement in the killing of Dr. Bantu and Diata Bantu."

Wilem turned to his attorney, who then addressed the panel.

Jake Swarnson (VanLuten's Attorney): "Before Mr. VanLuten answers this question, he wants the panel to confirm that his immunity deal extends to the matter of the Bantus."

Panelist (Senegal): "It does. Whatever Mr. VanLuten offers in this hearing that implicates himself in the commission of a crime, he will have full immunity from. We just want all the truth to come out so people can begin to heal from what happened."

Wilem VanLuten: "General Nyoko wanted to track down the Bantus. I recommended that he hire Zac. He paid Zac $10,000 to kill them and/or recover the recording. Nyoko instructed him to make it look like an accident. So on Christmas morning 2008, in Washington, D.C., Zac stole an SUV. He drove it into the Bantus' car and pushed them in front of a truck. He then staged the SUV to appear as if the driver was drunk. Zac was sure that no one could have survived the accident, but only the mother was killed.

"After the car wreck, Dr. Bantu and his son, D'Melo, disappeared. A few months ago, Zac found them again, this time in Philadelphia. He went to the Bantu house on a Sunday evening because Dr. Bantu and D'Melo were always at home at that time. But that night, only Dr. Bantu was there. He roughed up the doctor to get him to hand over the recording. Dr. Bantu refused. Zac shot him and fled before the police arrived. Zac planned to return to kill D'Melo once things settled down with the police. But D'Melo unexpectedly left for Kipaji."

After six hours, the investigative hearing concluded.

Panelist (Senegal): "That's all the questions we have for you, Mr. VanLuten. While we are shocked at your depravity and clear lack of remorse, we assure you that your immunity deal will be honored."

The Senegalese interviewer closed her file, disgusted. She turned to the stenographer. "This is off the record." The stenographer ceased typing.

"Mr. VanLuten, what I say now is solely from me and does not represent this panel or the ICC. You are the most vile human being I have ever come across—and trust me, sitting on this panel, I've heard things that would make most people curl up in a corner and never leave their house. You instigated one of the most horrifying tragedies this world has ever suffered, wreaking destruction upon a country and hundreds of thousands of innocent lives. One day, Mr. VanLuten, the fire of justice will find you in all the murky darkness you slither in. And when she does, I'll be there basking in her light, smiling most gratifyingly."

Wilem yawned. "Am I free to leave now?"

"Unfortunately, you are," she sighed.

Wilem rose and straightened his suit. As he exited the ICC, clamoring reporters scaled the steps. "Mr. VanLuten! Mr. VanLuten!"

Wilem halted at the top stair. "I just want to say one thing. The reason I came clean about Dimka is because the people of Malunga deserve justice. They are good, hard-working people. They deserve a better president. I innocently got caught up in Dimka's devious plots. That was my mistake. I should have blown the whistle on him long ago. If I did," Wilem sniffled, rubbing his eyes as if crying, "maybe I could have prevented the genocide. The one thing that gives me comfort is that Dimka will spent the rest of his miserable life behind bars."

Wilem descended the steps. A reporter shouted, "Mr. VanLuten, Pharma has rescinded its offer for you to be CEO. What are you going to do now?"

Wilem grinned, "I've proven myself to be a rainmaker, able to make pharmaceutical companies rich. And trust me, that's all they care about. So rest assured, before long, I'll be at the top once again." Wilem strode to the vehicle waiting to whisk him to the airport.

Just as he reached the car, D'Melo stepped in front of him. Wilem studied D'Melo's face, feeling like he knew him from something. "Excuse me, son. I have a plane to catch."

D'Melo didn't budge.

"Hey!" Wilem snarled, trying to nudge D'Melo aside. "Let me in my car!"

"Mr. VanLuten," D'Melo said evenly, "you are under arrest for conspiracy to kill Dr. Imari Bantu and Diata Bantu."

Wilem glared patronizingly at D'Melo. "I don't know who you think you are," he smirked. "But it doesn't even matter. You can't arrest me." Wilem reached inside his jacket for the immunity agreement. "See here?" he tapped the agreement agitatedly. "It says I'm immune from prosecution in the United States *and* can't be extradited to Malunga. So you can get out of my way now!"

"Mr. VanLuten, before I do that, there's someone who wants meet you." D'Melo gestured to a slender and stately African man.

Wilem didn't seem to know who he was.

"Surely you recognize this gentleman. He's the new president of

Malunga, Taj Amani. You probably knew his father better. You remember him, right? You had him killed."

Momentarily stunned, Wilem inclined his head, mortified. "Even so," he huffed. "There's nothing you can do to me." He waved the immunity document in D'Melo's face. "Malunga can't touch me!"

"That's true," D'Melo conceded. "Malunga can't prosecute you. But I guess you haven't heard." D'Melo clutched Taj's shoulder. "President Amani granted independence to Kipaji." Blood drained from Wilem's ashen face. "So Kipaji is now a sovereign nation, with the power of prosecution. And because you conspired to murder two Kipaji citizens—my mom and dad—Kipaji is fully within its rights to bring you to justice.

"Did your agreement," D'Melo pointed to the document that was now dangling at Wilem's side, "include immunity from prosecution in Kipaji?" Wilem was silent, squeezing his temples defeatedly. "Aww," D'Melo shrugged. "That's a shame. I guess the 'best lawyers in the country' missed that one when they okayed the agreement.

"But there's some good news for you," D'Melo noted. "Kipaji has never had a need for a prison, so President Amani has graciously agreed to keep you in the Malungan prison," D'Melo gloated, "you know—the prison that *you* built. You'll be very comfortable there. It's brand-new. And you'll have the honor of being its first inmate.

"It's ironic, don't you think? You spent millions of dollars to build—" D'Melo paused to recall the exact words from Wilem's interview, 'the most secure and harsh prison in Africa. It will break even the most hardened of criminals.' And, as it turns out, you built it for yourself. Well, actually, that's not true. You won't be alone. You'll have a cellmate. And lucky for you, he's your friend, Zachariah. I'm sure you'll have plenty to talk about," D'Melo said sarcastically. "I mean, being that he'll be in prison for the rest of his life because you rolled over on him in your testimony."

Wilem's breath became ragged. He wobbled on the brink of passing out.

The ICC panelist from Senegal strutted over. "Wow, the fire of justice acts quickly! Do you feel the burn yet, Mr. VanLuten?" She threw her arms to her sides and lifted her face into the sunlight. "Do you know what this is, Mr. VanLuten? This is me basking in the light of justice." She winked at D'Melo before waltzing off, victorious.

A pair of conjurers marched over to Wilem. They clasped his arms and escorted him to the airport, where a plane awaited to fly him to Malunga. Ululation rang out from a bystander in the captivated crowd. D'Melo craned his neck to see who it was. His heart swelled. It was Zara.

The weight anchoring D'Melo's heart was finally cut loose. His parents' killers had been brought to justice. He could breathe.

Zara bounced over to him. "You did it!" she cheered.

"No. We *all* did it," he said, overwhelming gratitude dripping from his eyes.

They ventured off to catch a bus bound for Nečzia. Zara nestled her head in its favorite spot—D'Melo's shoulder.

"You know," D'Melo observed. "That was *the absolute worst* ululation I've ever heard. I thought someone was stepping on a cat's tail.

"What a jerk."

ABOUT THE AUTHOR

DASHIEL DOUGLAS is an adventurer and unabashed dream chaser. His thirsty soul and love of the world's beautiful cultures and peoples led him to set sail from the shores of America to the promise of adventure across the Atlantic to Africa. The magic of Africa inspired him to write his first book, *This Is Africa: A Dream Chaser's Odyssey*. In *Spirit King*, Dashiel continues to artfully weave the allure of Africa  into his storytelling, while bringing to life the charm of Eastern Europe. He currently lives between the Czech Republic and wherever his dreams take him next.